NAUSEA
THE WALL
AND OTHER STORIES

TWO VOLUMES IN ONE

jean-paul sartre

TRANSLATED FROM THE FRENCH BY LLOYD ALEXANDER

MJF BOOKS
NEW YORK

Published by MJF Books
Fine Communications
Two Lincoln Square
60 West 66th Street
New York, NY 10023

Nausea/The Wall and Other Stories
Library of Congress Catalog Card Number 99-74094
ISBN 1-56731-334-5

This edition published by arrangement with New Directions Publishing Corporation.

Manufactured in the United States of America on acid-free paper

MJF Books and the MJF colophon are trademarks of Fine Creative Media, Inc.

10   9   8   7   6   5   4   3   2   1

JEAN-PAUL SARTRE

Nausea

Translated from the French by
LLOYD ALEXANDER

Introduction by
HAYDEN CARRUTH

TRANSLATOR'S NOTE

I wish to express my sincere thanks to Mrs. Violet Hammersley for her work in revising and correcting certain passages of this work.

INTRODUCTION

Hayden Carruth

Existentialism entered the American consciousness like an elephant entering a dark room: there was a good deal of breakage and the people inside naturally mistook the nature of the intrusion. What would it be? An engine of destruction perhaps, a tank left over from the war? After a while the lights were turned on and it was seen to be "only" an elephant; everyone laughed and said that a circus must be passing through town. But no, soon they found the elephant was here to stay; and then, looking closer, they saw that although he was indeed a newcomer, an odd-looking one at that, he was not a stranger: they had known him all along.

This was in 1946 and 1947. And in no time at all Existentialism became a common term. No question of what it meant; it meant the life re-emerging after the war in the cafés of the Left Bank—disreputable young men in paint-smeared jeans, and their companions, those black-stockinged, makeupless girls who smoked too many cigarettes and engaged in who knows what follies besides. And their leader, apparently, was this fellow Sartre, who wrote books with loathsome titles like *Nausea* and *The Flies*. What nonsense, the wiseheads concluded. Perfectly safe to dismiss it as a fad, very likely a hoax.

Meanwhile at centers of serious thought the texts of Existentialism, especially Sartre's, were being translated and studied, with a resulting profound shock to the American intellectual establishment. On one hand the Neo-Thomists and other moral philosophers were alarmed by Existentialism's disregard for traditional schemes of value; on the other the positivists and analytical philosophers were outraged by Existentialism's willingness to abandon rational categories and rely on nonmental processes of consciousness. Remarkably violent attacks issued from both these camps, set off all the more sharply by the enthusiasm, here and there, of small welcoming bands of the *avant garde*. That the welcomers were no less ill-informed about Existentialism than the attackers, didn't help matters.

Nevertheless Existentialism, gradually and then more rapidly, won adherents, people who took it seriously. Someone has said that Existentialism is a philosophy—if a philosophy at all— that has been independently invented by millions of people simply responding to the emergency of life in a modern world. Coming for the first time to the works of Sartre, Jaspers, or Camus is often like reading, on page after page, one's own intimate thoughts and feelings, expressed with new precision and concreteness. Existentialism *is* a philosophy, as a matter of fact, because it has been lengthily adumbrated by men trained in the philosophical disciplines; but it is also and more fundamentally a shift in ordinary human attitudes that has altered every aspect of life in our civilization.

The name, however, like the names we give all great movements of the human spirit—Romanticism, Transcendentalism—is misleading if we try to use it as a definition. There are so many branches of Existentialism that a number of the principal Existentialist writers have repudiated the term altogether; they deny they are Existentialists and they refuse to associate in the common ferment. Nevertheless we go on calling them Existentialists, and we are quite right to do so: as long as we use the term as a proper name, an agreed-upon semanteme, it is as good as any, or perhaps better, for signifying what unites the divergent interests.

It is nothing new. William Barrett, in his excellent book *Irrational Man* (1958), has shown that what we now call the Existentialist impulse is coeval with the myths of Abraham and Job; it is evident in the pre-Socratic philosophies of Greece, in the dramas of Aeschylus and Euripides, and in the later Greek and Byzantine culture of mystery; and it is a thread that winds, seldom dominant but always present, through the central European tradition: the Church Fathers, Augustine, the Gnostics, Abélard, Thomas, and then the extraordinary Pascal and the Romantic tradition that took up his standard a century later. And in the Orient, concurrently, the entire development of religious and philosophical attitudes, particularly in the Buddhist and Taoist writings, seems to us now to have been frequently closer to the actual existence of mankind than the rationalist discourses of the West.

Yet in spite of these precursors and analogues we would be gravely wrong to deny the modernity of Existentialism. Philosophical truth assumes many forms precisely because times change and men's needs change with them. Thus what we call Existentialism today, in all its philosophical, religious, and artistic manifestations, springs with remarkable directness from three figures of the last century. Two were philosophers, Søren Kierkegaard and Friedrich Nietzsche, who, although they lived a generation apart, worked and wrote independently. They arrived at positions that were in many respects entirely contrary, for Kierkegaard was deeply committed to the idea of the Christian God while Nietzsche was just as deeply divorced from it; but in other respects they were alike. They shared the same experience of loneliness, anguish, and doubt, and the same profound concern for the fate of the individual person. These were the driving forces too in the work of the third great originator, the novelist Dostoevski, from whose writings, especially *The Brothers Karamazov* and *Notes from Underground*, springs virtually the whole flowering of Existentialist sensibility in literature.

Our own century has devoted much labor and intelligence to the elaboration of these beginnings. It is customary to say that the principal Existentialist philosophers of our time are Martin Heidegger, Karl Jaspers, Gabriel Marcel, and of course Sartre. But many others, including thinkers as diverse as José Ortega, Martin Buber, Nikolai Berdyaev, and A. N. Whitehead, have been influenced by the main factors of Existentialist concern. In literature many, or even most, of the chief modern authors have been, consciously or not, Existentialists; certainly the tradition is very strong in the line of development represented by Kafka, Unamuno, Lawrence, Malraux, Hesse, Camus, and Faulkner. Even a writer as far removed as Robert Frost from the centers of self-conscious Existentialism joins in this alignment, as we see when we reread such poems as "The Census-Taker" and "Stopping by Woods." Then what is it, finally, that has produced such wide effects?

Nobody knows. That is, nobody can pin it down in a statement, though a number of people, including Sartre, have tried. Simply because Existentialism is not a produce of antecedent intellectual determinations, but a free transmutation of living experience, it cannot be defined. Nevertheless the important tendencies are evident enough.

In the first place, Existentialism is a recoil from rationalism. Not that Existentialists deny the role of reason; they merely insist that its limits be acknowledged. Most of them probably like to think that their speculations are eminently reasonable, yet not rational; and they emphasize the distinction between the terms. In particular, Existentialism is opposed to the entire rationalist tradition deriving from the Renaissance and culminating, a hundred-odd years ago, in the "cosmic rationalism" of Hegel. Hegel's writing is difficult and often obscure, but his purpose was to unite Final Reality with Ideal Reason in a system that sublimated all negative or oppositional tendencies. It was a magnificent work, symphonic in its harmonies and variations, and it took hold on men's imaginations so compellingly that today its effects are dominant everywhere, both in the academic and "practical" worlds. But for a few men, notably Kierkegaard, this apotheosis of the mind did not account for human experience. Pain and ecstasy, doubt and intuition, private anguish and despair—these could not be explained in terms of the rational categories. Long before Freud, Kierkegaard was aware of the hidden forces within the self, forces that, simply by existing, destroyed all rational, positivistic, and optimistic delusions.

Hegelianism was the philosophy of history and the mass. By projecting a Final Reality toward which all history flows in a process of ever-refining synthesis, Hegel submerged the individual consciousness in a grand unity of ideal mind. But for the Existentialist, who insists that reality is only what he himself knows and experiences, this is meaningless. Not only that, it is cruel and coercive. The Existentialist knows that the self is not submerged, it is present, here and now, a suffering existent, and any system of thought that overrides this suffering is tyrannical. "A crowd is untruth," Kierkegaard repeats with choric insistence. Only in the self can the drama of truth occur.

Yet when the Existentialist looks inside himself, what does he find? Nothing. Looking back beyond birth or forward beyond death, he sees the void; looking into his own center, thrusting aside all knowledge, all memory, all sensation, he sees the chasm of the ego, formless and inconceivable, like the nucleus of an electron. And he is led to ask, as philosophers throughout history have asked: why is there anything instead of nothing, why the world, the universe, rather than a void? By concentrating all attention on this nothing within himself and underlying the objective surface of reality, he gradually transforms nothing into the concept of Nothingness, one of the truly great accomplishments of human sensibility. Nothingness as a force, a ground, a reality —in a certain sense *the* reality. From this comes man's despair, but also, if he has courage, his existential integrity.

From this comes, too, the Existentialist's opposition to humanism. Not that he is inhumane; quite the contrary, his entire preoccupation is with the sanity and efficacy of the individual person. But he insists that men must confront Nothingness. In a universe grounded in Nothingness, the anthropocentric vision of reality that characterized rational humanism from the Renaissance to the nineteenth century is clearly untenable. Mankind, instead of being the central figure on the stage of reality, the rational creature for whom the nonrational world exists, is actually an accident, a late and adventitious newcomer whose life is governed by contingency; and the proof, paradoxically, comes from rationalism itself, from the Darwinian idea of evolution. Whatever may be the case with trees and stones and stars, man the thinker is a by-product, a nonessential component of reality, and he and all his works cling to existence with a hold that is tenuous and feeble.

Beyond this, generalities must cease. Each of the great Existentialist thinkers pursues his separate course toward the reestablishment of the individual person in the face of Nothingness and absurdity. Sartre is only one of them. But clearly Existentialism, the confrontation with anguish and despair, is a philosophy of our age. No wonder the time and place of its greatest flowering has been Europe in the middle decades of our century. It has deep significance for those who have lived through social chaos, uprootedness, irrational torture, and this accounts for the pessimism and nightmarish imagery that pervade much Existentialist writing. But it is worth remembering that if Existentialism flowered in the world of Graham Greene, André Malraux, and Arthur Koestler, it originated in the world of Dickens, Balzac, and Pushkin. Neither Kierkegaard nor Nietzsche lived in circumstances that outsiders would judge to be in the least uncomfortable. The aspects of the human condition that they discovered in their inner searching are far more deeply rooted than the particular catastrophes of history.

"Suffering is the origin of consciousness," Dostoevski wrote. But suffering is anywhere in the presence of thought and sensitivity. Sartre for his part has written, and with equal simplicity: "Life begins on the other side of despair."

To Existentialism Sartre has contributed a classically brilliant French mind. If he is not the leader that Americans first took him to be, he is certainly one of the leaders. And his forthrightness, his skill as a writer, his acuity and originality, have won him a wider audience than any philosopher, probably, has ever enjoyed in his own lifetime. He has brought to his work a characteristically French mentality, viz., attuned less to metaphysical than to psychological modes of reasoning. Paradoxically—for Descartes was a leader of Renaissance rationalism—Sartre is an Existentialist who operates in the Cartesian tradition; at the beginning of any investigation he poses the *cogito,* the self-that-is and the self that observes the self-that-is. From this duality, in almost endless brilliant progressions, he moves through other dualities: knowing-doing, being-becoming, nature-freedom, etc. Only the professional philosopher can follow all the way. But Sartre would undoubtedly subscribe to Nietzsche's remark: "I honor a philosopher only if he is able to be an example." He himself is an example, and has been at great pains to define and enforce his exemplitude: in journalism, in fiction, in drama, in political activity, and in teaching. The question naturally arises: who is this Sartre?

Jean-Paul Sartre was born in Paris in 1905. Brought up chiefly in his mother's family—the Schweitzers; Albert Schweitzer was his older cousin—the boy was educated by his grandfather, who had invented the Berlitz method for teaching languages. In fact Sartre spent so much time in his grandfather's library that he began writing, he said later, out of sheer boredom. Eventually he studied philosophy at French and German universities, and taught at Le Havre, which he took as the model for Bouville in *Nausea,* his first full-scale work. When it was published in 1938 it was condemned, predictably, in academic circles; but younger readers welcomed it, and it was far more successful than most first novels. Then came the war. Sartre entered the army, was captured and sent to prison camp, then released because of ill health. He returned to Paris. There, under the Occupation, he wrote several plays and his first major philosophical work, *Being and Nothingness* (1943). By the end of the war he was known as a leader of the entire war-bred generation of Parisian intellectuals.

Since then Sartre's activity has been intense. He has produced novels, short stories, plays, literary and philosophical essays, biographies, many political and journalistic works, pamphlets, manifestoes, etc. He has been called the most brilliant Frenchman of our time; and no wonder. For wit, learning, argumentative skill and polemical zeal, none can match him. Certainly *Being and Nothingness,* whatever faults its critics, including Sartre, may now find in it, was a brilliant contribution to philosophy; and *Nausea* was not only a powerful novel but a crucial event in the evolution of sensibility.

In the quarter-century since Antoine Roquentin, the "hero" of *Nausea,* made his appearance, he has become a familiar of our world, one of those men who, like Hamlet or Julien Sorel, live outside the pages of the books in which they assumed their characters. If it is not strictly correct to call him an archetype, nevertheless he is an original upon whom many copies, both fictional and actual, have been formed. This is not to say that Roquentin was the first "Existentialist man," or *Nausea* the first "Existentialist novel"; we have already spoken of the precursors. But Roquentin is a man living at an extraordinary metaphysical pitch, at least in the pages of the journal he has left us. His account of himself offers us many shrewd perceptions of life in our world that we appropriate, as parts of our cultural equipment, in defining our own attitudes. It is scarcely possible to read seriously in contemporary literature, philosophy, or psychology without encountering references to Roquentin's confrontation with the chestnut tree, for example, which is one of the sharpest pictures ever drawn of self-doubt and metaphysical anguish.

How did Roquentin arrive at his crisis of despair? It helps if the reader bears in mind a philosophical distinction that has been the source of endless debate over the centuries: the distinction between existence and essence. Take any object; a Venetian glass paperweight, for example. Its essence is everything that permits us to recognize it: its roundness, heaviness, smoothness, color, etc. Its existence is simply the fact that it *is*. This is the distinction that Roquentin discovers one day when he picks up a stone on the seashore and is suddenly overcome by an "odd feeling"; it is the feeling of being confronted by a bare existence. For him, quite unexpectedly, the essence of the stone disappears; he "sees through" it; and then as the days proceed he gradually discovers that all essences are volatile, until, in the confrontation with the chestnut tree, he finds himself in the presence of reality itself reduced to pure existence: disgusting and fearsome.

This is a point that all existential writers have repeated over and over: the detestability of existence. Jaspers has written: "The non-rational is found in the opacity of the here and now, . . . in the actual empirical existence which is just as it is and not otherwise." Why is it not otherwise? Why *is* it at all? What is this is-ness? Isn't it simply nothing, or rather Nothingness, the unknowable, indispensable Void? What could be more absurd, "non-rational," meaningless? The mind of man, which he did not ask to be given, demands a reason and a meaning—this is its self-defining cause—and yet it finds itself in the midst of a radically meaningless existence. The result: impasse. And nausea.

One by one Roquentin is offered the various traditional

means for escaping his predicament, and his examination and rejection of them provide some of the most evocative scenes in the book. Rational humanism, as offered by the *autodidacte* who is trying to read all the books in the town library, seems at first a good, almost charming possibility, until it collapses in a scene of terrible comic force. The life of the town, its commercial and pietistic affectations, clearly is unacceptable. But even more important are the parts of himself that Roquentin finds he must now reject as useless. His love of travel, of "adventures," in short, of objective experience—this has no value. "For the thinker, as for the artist," William Barrett writes, "what counts in life is not the number of rare and exciting adventures he encounters, but the inner depth in that life." Hence Roquentin must turn within himself, but when he does so, where is the "inner depth"—or rather *what* is it? Again, Nothingness. Neither the experience of the outside world nor the contemplation of the inner world can give meaning to existence. Perhaps the past has something to offer? Roquentin redoubles his efforts in connection with the research he has been engaged in for some time; but finds only that the myth of history cannot help him—it is gone, dead, crumbled to dust, its meanings are academic. Roquentin's last hope is love, human love, yet he knows now that this is a thin hope. He goes to meet his former mistress; expectantly, to be sure, but not confidently; and his defeat, when it occurs, is something that he had, in a sense, already acknowledged.

In his suffering Roquentin is reduced to nothing, to the nauseated consciousness of nothing. He is filled with meaningless, anarchic visions. Yet perhaps he is experiencing what Jaspers calls "the preparing power of chaos." At any rate suffering is the necessary prelude to the re-establishment of the self, as both philosophy and folk wisdom attest. Roquentin's way out of his predicament is not given in detail, but in his remarks about the jazz recording and about his own plans for future literary endeavors, he seems to indicate that he knows a means of survival. It is unfortunate that Sartre chose to call by the name of "jazz" a recording that, from Roquentin's description of it, most musically minded Americans will recognize as commercial pseudo-jazz; but this does not alter the validity of the point Sartre introduces through a reference to the music. What is the point? What is Roquentin's "way out"? The matter has been debated by many commentators, partly because it is not specified in the book, partly because it raises issues that extend far beyond the book. If

Roquentin's way out is to be through art, what use is it to the nonartist? What elements in the music make it suggestive of a possible mode of survival? What does "survival" mean in Roquentin's catastrophe? What is the real, ultimate relationship of Roquentin to his former mistress and to the people of Bouville? These are extremely important questions. But they cannot be decided in a few pages, nor can they be answered dogmatically by any individual reader. They are questions that Sartre—at least in this book—purposely leaves open.

Later in his philosophical development the idea of freedom became Sartre's main theme. Man, beginning in the loathsome emptiness of his existence, creates his essence—his self, his being —through the choices that he freely makes. Hence his being is never fixed. He is always becoming, and if it were not for the contingency of death he would never end. Nor would his philosophy. "Existentialists," wrote the Irish philosopher Arland Ussher, "have a notable difficulty in finishing their books: of necessity, for their philosophy—staying close to the movement of life—can have no finality." To what extent this applies to *Nausea* the individual reader must decide.

Another question, even more difficult, is the line between jest and sermon in the novel. Sartre, for all his anguished disgust, can play the clown as well, and has done so often enough; a sort of fool at the metaphysical court. How much self-mockery is detectable in Roquentin's account of the chestnut tree? Some, certainly. The rhetoric at points turns coy: the "suspicious transparency" of the glass of beer, the trees that "did not want to exist" and "quietly minded their own business." And what does Roquentin mean, at the end of the episode, by the "smile of the trees" that "meant something . . . the real secret of existence"? What is the relationship between the smile of the trees and Roquentin's description of the jazz recording: "The disc is scratched and wearing out, perhaps the singer is dead. . . . But behind the existence which falls from one present to the other, without a past, without a future, behind these sounds which decompose from day to day, peel off and slip towards death, the melody stays the same, young and firm, like a pitiless witness"?

What is the "melody"? For that matter, what is the novel, which is another kind of melody? Is it a good novel? Is it a work of art? We know that Sartre, the philosopher, is also a marvelous writer; in the techniques of realistic fiction—the construction of dialogue, the evocation of scene and mood—he is the equal of anyone. But a novel is more than technique; it is a self-consistent and dynamic whole. As if this weren't difficult enough, Sartre compounds the aesthetic problems by insisting that the novel must conform to the details of his philosophy. He is not content, like some philosophers, to write fable, allegory, or a philosophical tale in the manner of *Candide;* he is content only with a proper work of art that is at the same time a synthesis of philosophical specifications. A tall order; and the critics, although widely divergent in their interpretation of the substance of *Nausea,* seem to agree that Sartre, brilliant though his verbal gifts may be, has not quite brought it off. Germaine Brée and Margaret Guiton (in *An Age of Fiction,* 1957) have written: "When Sartre, the philosopher, informs us that we have an immediate intuition of existence in the sensations of boredom and of nausea, we tend to raise an eyebrow. But when Sartre, the novelist, describes this situation, we are almost convinced." William Barrett, a keener critic of the philosophy, has called *Nausea* Sartre's best novel "for the very reason that in it the intellectual and the creative artist come closest to being joined," but the joining is not complete: "*Nausea* is not so much a full novel as an extraordinary fragment of one." Similarly a recent anonymous critic, writing in the *London Times Literary Supplement,* has mentioned the "bite and energy . . . [of] the best pages of *La Nausée.*" And so on and so on. The tone of reluctant praise—"almost," "fragment," "the best pages"—pervades nearly all the criticism of Sartre's fiction.

Literary critics are a cheerless, canny breed, inclined always to say that a given work has its good and bad points. Perhaps the best comment on their scrupulosity is that *Nausea* was published twenty-six years ago and they are still writing about it. Something must hold their attention. If it is not Sartre's novelistic technique, then perhaps novelistic technique is not a just criterion of what is pertinent or valuable. Certainly *Nausea* gives us a few of the clearest and hence most useful images of man in our time that we possess; and this, as Allen Tate has said, is the supreme function of art.

William Blake once remarked that he had to create his own system of thought in order to avoid being enslaved by those of others, and Sartre has said that genius is what a man invents when he is looking for a way out. The power of Sartre's fiction resides in the truth of our lives as he has written it. The validity of his fiction resides not only in the genius but in the courage that he has invented as an example for the age.

Editors' Note

These notebooks were found among the papers of Antoine Roquentin. They are published without alteration.

The first sheet is undated, but there is good reason to believe it was written some weeks before the diary itself. Thus it would have been written around the beginning of January, 1932, at the latest.

At that time, Antoine Roquentin, after travelling through Central Europe, North Africa and the Far East, settled in Bouville for three years to conclude his historical research on the Marquis de Rollebon.

The Editors

UNDATED PAGES

The best thing would be to write down events from day to day. Keep a diary to see clearly—let none of the nuances or small happenings escape even though they might seem to mean nothing. And above all, classify them. I must tell how I see this table, this street, the people, my packet of tobacco, since *those* are the things which have changed. I must determine the exact extent and nature of this change.

For instance, here is a cardboard box holding my bottle of ink. I should try to tell how I saw it *before* and now how I[1] Well, it's a parallelopiped rectangle, it opens—that's stupid, there's nothing I can say about it. This is what I have to avoid, I must not put in strangeness where there is none. I think that is the big danger in keeping a diary: you exaggerate everything. You continually force the truth because you're always looking for something. On the other hand, it is certain that from one minute to the next—and precisely *à propos* of this box or any other object at

[1] Word left out.

all I can recapture this impression of day-before-yesterday. I must always be ready, otherwise it will slip through my fingers. I must never[2] but carefully note and detail all that happens.

Naturally, I can write nothing definite about this Saturday and the day-before-yesterday business. I am already too far from it; the only thing I can say is that in neither case was there anything which could ordinarily be called an event. Saturday the children were playing ducks and drakes and, like them, I wanted to throw a stone into the sea. Just at that moment I stopped, dropped the stone and left. Probably I looked somewhat foolish or absent-minded, because the children laughed behind my back.

So much for external things. What has happened inside of me has not left any clear traces. I saw something which disgusted me, but I no longer know whether it was the sea or the stone. The stone was flat and dry, especially on one side, damp and muddy on the other. I held it by the edges with my fingers wide apart so as not to get them dirty.

Day before yesterday was much more complicated. And there was also this series of coincidences, of *quid-pro-quos* that I can't explain to myself. But I'm not going to spend my time putting all that down on paper. Anyhow, it was certain that I was afraid or had some other feeling of that sort. If I had only known what I was afraid of, I would have made a great step forward.

The strangest thing is that I am not at all inclined to call myself insane, I clearly see that I am not: all these changes concern objects. At least, that is what I'd like to be sure of.

10.30[1]

Perhaps it was a passing moment of madness after all. There is no trace of it any more. My odd feelings of the other week seem to me quite ridiculous today: I can no longer enter into them. I am quite at ease this evening, quite solidly *terre-à-terre* in the world. Here is my room facing north-east. Below the Rue des Mutilés and the construction-yard of the new station. From my window I see the red and white flame of the "Railwaymen's Rendezvous" at the corner of the Boulevard Victor-Noir. The Paris train has just come in. People are coming out of the old station

[2] Word crossed out (possibly "force" or "forge"), another word added above, is illegible.

[1] Evidently in the evening. The following paragraph is much later than the preceding ones. We are inclined to believe it was written the following day at the earliest.

2

and spreading into the streets. I hear steps and voices. A lot of people are waiting for the last tramway. They must make a sad little group around the street light just under my window. Well, they have a few minutes more to wait: the tram won't pass before 10.45. I hope no commercial travellers will come to-night: I have such a desire to sleep and am so much behind in my sleep. A good night, one good night and all this nonsense will be swept away.

Ten forty-five: nothing more to fear, they would be here already. Unless it's the day for the man from Rouen. He comes every week. They reserve No. 2, on the second floor for him, the room with a bidet. He might still show up: he often drinks a beer at the "Railwaymen's Rendezvous" before going to bed. But he doesn't make too much noise. He is very small and clean with a waxed, black moustache and a wig. Here he is now.

Well, when I heard him come up the stairs, it gave me quite a thrill, it was so reassuring: what is there to fear in such a regular world? I think I am cured.

Here is tramway number seven, *Abattoirs-Grands Bassins*. It stops with a clank of iron rails. It's leaving again. Now loaded with suitcases and sleeping children, it's heading towards Grands Bassins, towards the factories in the black East. It's the next to the last tramway; the last one will go by in an hour.

I'm going to bed. I'm cured. I'll give up writing my daily impressions, like a little girl in her nice new notebook.

In one case only it might be interesting to keep a diary: it would be if . . .[1]

[1] The text of the undated pages ends here.

Monday, 29 *January,* 1932:

Something has happened to me, I can't doubt it any more. It came as an illness does, not like an ordinary certainty, not like anything evident. It came cunningly, little by little; I felt a little strange, a little put out, that's all. Once established it never moved, it stayed quiet, and I was able to persuade myself that nothing was the matter with me, that it was a false alarm. And now, it's blossoming.

I don't think the historian's trade is much given to psychological analysis. In our work we have to do only with sentiments in the whole to which we give generic titles such as Ambition and Interest. And yet if I had even a shadow of self-knowledge, I could put it to good use now.

For instance, there is something new about my hands, a certain way of picking up my pipe or fork. Or else it's the fork which now has a certain way of having itself picked up, I don't know. A little while ago, just as I was coming into my room, I stopped short because I felt in my hand a cold object which held my attention through a sort of personality. I opened my hand, looked: I was simply holding the door-knob. This morning in the library, when the Self-Taught Man[1] came to say good morning to me, it took me ten seconds to recognize him. I saw an unknown face, barely a face. Then there was his hand like a fat white worm in my own hand. I dropped it almost immediately and the arm fell back flabbily.

There are a great number of suspicious noises in the streets, too.

So a change *has* taken place during these last few weeks. But where? It is an abstract change without object. Am I the one who has changed? If not, then it is this room, this city and this nature; I must choose.

*   *   *   *   *

I think I'm the one who has changed: that's the simplest solution. Also the most unpleasant. But I must finally realize

[1] Ogier P . . . , who will be often mentioned in this journal. He was a bailiff's clerk. Roquentin met him in 1930 in the Bouville library.

that I am subject to these sudden transformations. The thing is that I rarely think; a crowd of small metamorphoses accumulate in me without my noticing it, and then, one fine day, a veritable revolution takes place. This is what has given my life such a jerky, incoherent aspect. For instance, when I left France, there were a lot of people who said I left for a whim. And when I suddenly came back after six years of travelling, they still could call it a whim. I see myself with Mercier again in the office of that French functionary who resigned after the Petrou business last year. Mercier was going to Bengal on an archeological mission. I always wanted to go to Bengal and he pressed me to go with him. Now I wonder why. I don't think he was too sure of Portal and was counting on me to keep an eye on him. I saw no reason to refuse. And even if I had suspected that little deal with Portal, it would have been one more reason to accept with enthusiasm. Well, I was paralysed, I couldn't say a word. I was staring at a little Khmer statuette on a green carpet, next to a telephone. I seemed to be full of lymph or warm milk. With angelic patience veiling a slight irritation, Mercier told me:

"Now look, I have to be officially fixed up. I know you'll end up by saying yes, so you might as well accept right away."

He had a reddish-black beard, heavily scented. I got a waft of perfume at each movement of his head. And then, suddenly, I woke from a six-year slumber.

The statue seemed to me unpleasant and stupid and I felt terribly, deeply bored. I couldn't understand why I was in Indo-China. What was I doing there? Why was I talking to these people? Why was I dressed so oddly? My passion was dead. For years it had rolled over and submerged me; now I felt empty. But that wasn't the worst: before me, posed with a sort of indolence, was a voluminous, insipid idea. I did not see clearly what it was, but it sickened me so much I couldn't look at it. All that was confused with the perfume of Mercier's beard.

I pulled myself together, convulsed with anger, and answered dryly:

"Thank you, but I believe I've travelled enough, I must go back to France now." Two days later I took the boat for Marseilles.

If I am not mistaken, if all the signs which have been amassed are precursors of a new overthrow in my life, well then I am terrified. It isn't that my life is rich, or weighty or precious. But I'm afraid of what will be born and take possession of me—

and drag me—where? Shall I have to go off again, leaving my research, my book and everything else unfinished? Shall I awake in a few months, in a few years, broken, deceived, in the midst of new ruins? I would like to see the truth clearly before it is too late.

Tuesday, 30 January:

Nothing new.

I worked from nine till one in the library. I got Chapter XII started and all that concerns Rollebon's stay in Russia up to the death of Paul I. This work is finished: nothing more to do with it until the final revision.

It is one-thirty. I am eating a sandwich in the Café Mably, everything is more or less normal. Anyway, everything is always normal in cafés and especially the Café Mably, because of the manager, M. Fasquelle, who has a raffish look which is positively reassuring. It will soon be time for his nap and his eyes are pink already, but he stays quick and decisive. He strolls among the tables and speaks confidently to the customers.

"Is everything all right, Monsieur?"

I smile at seeing him thus; when his place empties his head empties too. From two to four the café is deserted, then M. Fasquelle takes a few dazed steps, the waiters turn out the lights and he slips into unconsciousness: when this man is lonely he sleeps.

There are still about twenty customers left, bachelors, small-time engineers, office employees. They eat hurriedly in boarding-houses which they call their *"popotes"* and, since they need a little luxury, they come here after their meals. They drink a cup of coffee and play poker dice; they make a little noise, an inconsistent noise which doesn't bother me. In order to exist, they also must consort with others.

I live alone, entirely alone. I never speak to anyone, never; I receive nothing, I give nothing. The Self-Taught Man doesn't count. There is Françoise, the woman who runs the "Railwaymen's Rendezvous." But do I speak to her? Sometimes after dinner, when she brings my beer, I ask her:

"Have you time this evening?"

She never says no and I follow her into one of the big rooms on the second floor she rents by the hour or by the day. I do not pay her: our need is mutual. She takes pleasure in it (she has to have a man a day and she has many more besides me) and thus I purge myself of a certain nostalgia the cause of which I know too well. But we hardly speak. What good is it? Every man for himself: besides, as far as she's concerned, I am pre-eminently a customer in her café. Taking off her dress, she tells me:

"Say, have you ever heard of that apéritif, *Bricot?* Because there are two customers who asked for some this week. The girl didn't know and she came to ask me. They were commercial travellers, they must have drunk that in Paris. But I don't like to buy without knowing. I'll keep my stockings on if you don't mind."

In the past—even a long while after she left me—I thought about Anny. Now I think of no one any more. I don't even bother looking for words. It flows in me, more or less quickly. I fix nothing, I let it go. Through the lack of attaching myself to words, my thoughts remain nebulous most of the time. They sketch vague, pleasant shapes and then are swallowed up: I forget them almost immediately.

I marvel at these young people: drinking their coffee, they tell clear, plausible stories. If they are asked what they did yesterday, they aren't embarrassed: they bring you up to date in a few words. If I were in their place, I'd fall over myself. It's true that no one has bothered about how I spend my time for a long while. When you live alone you no longer know what it is to tell something: the plausible disappears at the same time as the friends.

You let events flow past; suddenly you see people pop up who speak and who go away, you plunge into stories without beginning or end: you'd make a terrible witness. But in compensation, one misses nothing, no improbability or story too tall to be believed in cafés. For example, Saturday, about four in the afternoon, on the end of the timbered sidewalk of the new station yard, a little woman in sky blue was running backwards, laughing, waving a handkerchief. At the same time, a Negro in a cream-coloured raincoat, yellow shoes and a green hat, turned the corner of the street and whistled. Still going backwards, the woman bumped into him, underneath a lantern which hangs on a paling and which is lit at night. All at once there was the paling smelling strongly of wet wood, this lantern and this little blonde woman in the Negro's arms under a sky the colour of fire. If there had been four or five of us, I suppose we would have noticed the jolt, the soft colours, the beautiful blue coat that looked like an eiderdown quilt, the light raincoat, the red panes of the lantern; we would have laughed at the stupefaction which appeared on those two childish faces.

A man rarely feels like laughing alone: the whole thing was animated enough for me, but it was a strong, even a fierce, yet pure sensation. Then everything came asunder, there was nothing left but the lantern, the palisade and the sky; it was still rather beautiful. An hour later the lantern was lit, the wind blew, the sky was black; nothing at all was left.

All that is nothing new; I have never resisted these harmless emotions; far from it. You must be just a little bit lonely in order to feel them, just lonely enough to get rid of plausibility at the proper time. But I remained close to people, on the surface of solitude, quite resolved to take refuge in their midst in case of emergency. Up to now I was an amateur at heart.

Everywhere, now, there are objects like this glass of beer on the table there. When I see it, I feel like saying: "Enough." I realize quite well that I have gone too far. I don't suppose you can "take sides" with solitude. That doesn't mean that I look under my bed before going to sleep, or think I see the door of my room open suddenly in the middle of the night. Still, somehow I am not at peace: I have been *avoiding* looking at this glass of beer for half an hour. I look above, below, right and left; but I don't want to see *it*. And I know very well that all these bachelors around me can be of no help: it is too late, I can no longer take refuge among them. They could come and tap me on the shoulder and say, "Well, what's the matter with that glass of beer?" It's just like all the others. It's bevelled on the edges, has a handle, a little coat of arms with a spade on it and on the coat of arms is written "Spartenbrau," I know all that, but I know there is something else. Almost nothing. But I can't explain what I see. To anyone. There: I am quietly slipping into the water's depths, towards fear.

I am alone in the midst of these happy, reasonable voices. All these creatures spend their time explaining, realizing happily that they agree with each other. In Heaven's name, why is it so important to think the same things all together. It's enough to see the face they make when one of these fishy-eyed men with an inward look and with whom no agreement is possible, passes them. When I was eight years old and used to play in the Luxembourg gardens there was a man who came and sat in a sentry-box, against the iron fence which runs along the Rue Auguste-Comte. He did not speak but from time to time stretched out his leg and looked at his foot fearfully. The foot was encased in a boot, but the other one was in a slipper. The guard told my uncle that the man was a former proctor. They retired him because he used to come, dressed up as an academician, to read the school term marks. We had a horrible fear of him because we sensed he was alone. One day he smiled at Robert, holding out his arms to him from a distance: Robert almost fainted. It wasn't this creature's poverty-stricken look which frightened us, nor the tumour he had on his neck that rubbed against the edge of his collar: but we felt that he was shaping thoughts of crab or lobster in his head. And that terrified us, the fact that one could conjure thoughts of lobsters on the sentry-box, on our hoops, on the bushes.

Is that what awaits me then? For the first time I am disturbed at being alone. I would like to tell someone what is happening to me before it is too late and before I start frightening little boys. I wish Anny were here.

This is odd: I have just filled up ten pages and I haven't told the truth—at least, not the whole truth. I was writing "Nothing new" with a bad conscience: as a matter of fact I boggled at bringing out a quite harmless little incident. "Nothing new." I admire the way we can lie, putting reason on our side. Evidently, nothing new has happened, if you care to put it that way: this morning at eight-fifteen, just as I was leaving the Hotel Printania to go to the library, I wanted to and could not pick up a paper lying on the ground. This is all and it is not even an event. Yes —but, to tell the whole truth, I was deeply impressed by it: I felt I was no longer free. I tried unsuccessfully to get rid of this idea at the library. I wanted to escape from it at the Café Mably. I hoped it would disappear in the bright light. But it stayed there, like a dead weight inside me. It is responsible for the preceding pages.

Why didn't I mention it? It must be out of pride, and then, too, a little out of awkwardness. I am not in the habit of telling myself what happens to me, so I cannot quite recapture the succession of events, I cannot distinguish what is important. But now it is finished: I have re-read what I wrote in the Café Mably and I am ashamed; I want no secrets or soul-states, nothing ineffable; I am neither virgin nor priest enough to play with the inner life.

There is nothing much to say: I could not pick up the paper, that's all.

I very much like to pick up chestnuts, old rags and especially papers. It is pleasant to me to pick them up, to close my hand on them; with a little encouragement I would carry them to my mouth the way children do. Anny went into a white rage when I picked up the corners of heavy, sumptuous papers, probably soiled by excrement. In summer or the beginning of autumn, you can find remnants of sun-baked newspapers in gardens, dry and fragile as dead leaves, so yellow you might think they had been washed with picric acid. In winter, some pages are pounded to pulp; crushed, stained, they return to the earth. Others quite new when covered with ice, all white, all throbbing, are like swans about to fly, but the earth has already caught them from below. They twist and tear themselves from the mud, only to be finally flattened out a little further on. It is good to pick up all that. Sometimes I simply feel them, looking at them closely; other times I tear them to hear their drawn-out crackling, or, if they are damp, I light them, not without difficulty; then I wipe my muddy hands on a wall or tree trunk.

So, today, I was watching the riding boots of a cavalry officer who was leaving his barracks. As I followed them with my eyes, I saw a piece of paper lying beside a puddle. I thought the officer was going to crush the paper into the mud with his heel, but no: he straddled paper and puddle in a single step. I went up to it: it was a lined page, undoubtedly torn from a school notebook. The rain had drenched and twisted it, it was covered with blisters and swellings like a burned hand. The red line of the margin was smeared into a pink splotch; ink had run in places. The bottom of the page disappeared beneath a crust of mud. I bent down, already rejoicing at the touch of this pulp, fresh and tender, which I should roll in my fingers into greyish balls

I was unable.

I stayed bent down for a second, I read "Dictation: The White Owl," then I straightened up, empty-handed. I am no longer free, I can no longer do what I will.

Objects should not *touch* because they are not alive. You use them, put them back in place, you live among them: they are useful, nothing more. But they touch me, it is unbearable. I am afraid of being in contact with them as though they were living beasts.

Now I see: I recall better what I felt the other day at the seashore when I held the pebble. It was a sort of sweetish sickness. How unpleasant it was! It came from the stone, I'm sure of it, it passed from the stone to my hand. Yes, that's it, that's just it—a sort of nausea in the hands.

Thursday morning in the library:

A little while ago, going down the hotel stairs, I heard Lucie, who, for the hundredth time, was complaining to the landlady, while polishing the steps. The proprietress spoke with difficulty, using short sentences, because she had not put in her false teeth; she was almost naked, in a pink dressing-gown and Turkish slippers. Lucie was dirty, as usual; from time to time she stopped rubbing and straightened up on her knees to look at the proprietress. She spoke without pausing, reasonably:

"I'd like it a hundred times better if he went with other women," she said, "it wouldn't make the slightest difference to me, so long as it didn't do him any harm."

She was talking about her husband: at forty this swarthy little woman had offered herself and her savings to a handsome young man, a fitter in the Usines Lecointe. She has an unhappy home life. Her husband does not beat her, is not unfaithful to her, but he drinks, he comes home drunk every evening. He's burning his candle at both ends; in three months I have seen him turn yellow and melt away. Lucie thinks it is drink. I believe he is tubercular.

"You have to take the upper hand," Lucie said.

It gnaws at her, I'm sure of it, but slowly, patiently: she takes the upper hand, she is able neither to console herself nor abandon herself to her suffering. She thinks about it a little bit, a very little bit, now and again she passes it on. Especially when she is with people, because they console her and also because it comforts her a little to talk about it with poise, with an air of giving advice. When she is alone in the rooms I hear her humming to keep herself from thinking. But she is morose all day, suddenly weary and sullen.

"It's there," she says, touching her throat, "it won't go down."

She suffers as a miser. She must be miserly with her pleasures, as well. I wonder if sometimes she doesn't wish she were free of this monotonous sorrow, of these mutterings which start as soon as she stops singing, if she doesn't wish to suffer once and for all, to drown herself in despair. In any case, it would be impossible for her: she is bound.

Thursday afternoon:

"M. de Rollebon was quite ugly. Queen Marie Antoinette called him her 'dear ape.' Yet he had all the ladies of the court, but not by clowning like Voisenon the baboon: but by a magnetism which carried his lovely victims to the worst excesses of passion. He intrigues, plays a fairly suspect role in the affair of the Queen's necklace and disappears in 1790, after having dealings with Mirabeau-Tonneau and Nerciat. He turns up again in Russia where he attempts to assassinate Paul I, and from there, he travels to the farthest countries; the Indies, China, Turkestan. He smuggles, plots, spies. In 1813 he returns to Paris. By 1816, he has become all-powerful: he is the sole confidant of the Duchess d'Angoulême. This capricious old woman, obsessed by horrible childhood memories, grows calm and smiles when she sees him. Through her, he works his will at court. In March 1820, he marries Mlle de Roquelaure, a very beautiful girl of eighteen. M. de Rollebon is seventy; he is at the height of distinction, at the apogee of his life. Seven months later, accused of treason, he is arrested, thrown into a cell, where he dies after five years of imprisonment, without ever being brought to trial."

I re-read with melancholy this note of Germain Berger.[1]

It was by those few lines that I first knew M. de Rollebon. How attractive he seemed and how I loved him after these few words! It is for him, for this mannikin that I am here. When I came back from my trip I could just as well have settled down in Paris or Marseilles. But most of the documents concerning the Marquis' long stays in France are in the municipal library of Bouville. Rollebon was the *Lord of the Manor of Marmommes*. Before the war, you could still find one of his descendants in this little town, an architect named Rollebon-Campouyre', who, at his death in 1912, left an important legacy to the Bouville library: letters of the Marquis, the fragment of a journal, and all sorts of papers. I have not yet gone through it all.

I am glad to have found these notes. I had not read them for ten years. My handwriting has changed, or so it seems to me; I used to write in a smaller hand. How I loved M. de Rollebon that year! I remember one evening—a Tuesday evening: I had worked all day in the Mazarine; I had just gathered, from his correspondence, of 1789–90, in what a magisterial way he duped

[1] Editor's Footnote: Germain Berger: Mirabeau-Tonneau et ses amis, page 406, note 2. Champion 1906.

Nerciat. It was dark, I was going down the Avenue du Maine and I bought some chestnuts at the corner of the Rue de la Gaîté. Was I happy! I laughed all by myself thinking of the face Nerciat must have made when he came back from Germany. The face of the Marquis is like this ink: it has paled considerably since I have worked over it.

In the first place, starting from 1801, I understand nothing more about his conduct. It is not the lack of documents: letters, fragments of memoirs, secret reports, police records. On the contrary I have almost too many of them. What is lacking in all this testimony is firmness and consistency. They do not contradict each other, neither do they agree with each other; they do not seem to be about the same person. And yet other historians work from the same sources of information. How do they do it? Am I more scrupulous or less intelligent? In any case, the question leaves me completely cold. In truth, what am I looking for? I don't know. For a long time, Rollebon the man has interested me more than the book to be written. But now, the man . . . the man begins to bore me. It is the book which attracts me. I feel more and more need to write—in the same proportion as I grow old, you might say.

Evidently it must be admitted that Rollebon took an active part in the assassination of Paul I, that he then accepted an extremely important espionage mission to the Orient from the Czar and constantly betrayed Alexander to the advantage of Napoleon. At the same time he was able to carry on an active correspondence with the Comte d'Artois and send him unimportant information in order to convince him of his fidelity: none of all that is improbable; Fouché, at the same time, was playing a comedy much more dangerous and complex. Perhaps the Marquis also carried on a rifle-supplying business with the Asiatic principalities for his own profit.

Well, yes: he could have done all that, but it is not proved: I am beginning to believe that nothing can ever be proved. These are honest hypotheses which take the facts into account: but I sense so definitely that they come from me, and that they are simply a way of unifying my own knowledge. Not a glimmer comes from Rollebon's side. Slow, lazy, sulky, the facts adapt themselves to the rigour of the order I wish to give them; but it remains outside of them. I have the feeling of doing a work of pure imagination. And I am certain that the characters in a novel would have a more genuine appearance, or, in any case, would be more agreeable.

Friday:

Three o'clock. Three o'clock is always too late or too early for anything you want to do. An odd moment in the afternoon. Today it is intolerable.

A cold sun whitens the dust on the window-panes. Pale sky clouded with white. The gutters were frozen this morning.

I ruminate heavily near the gas stove; I know in advance the day is lost. I shall do nothing good, except, perhaps, after nightfall. It is because of the sun; it ephemerally touches the dirty white wisps of fog, which float in the air above the construction-yards, it flows into my room, all gold, all pale, it spreads four dull, false reflections on my table.

My pipe is daubed with a golden varnish which first catches the eye by its bright appearance; you look at it and the varnish melts, nothing is left but a great dull streak on a piece of wood. Everything is like that, everything, even my hands. When the sun begins shining like that the best thing to do is go to bed. Only I slept like a log last night, and I am not sleepy.

I liked yesterday's sky so much, a narrow sky, black with rain, pushing against the windows like a ridiculous, touching face. This sun is not ridiculous, quite the contrary. On everything I like, on the rust of the construction girders, on the rotten boards of the fence, a miserly, uncertain light falls, like the look you give, after a sleepless night, on decisions made with enthusiasm the day before, on pages you have written in one spurt without crossing out a word. The four cafés on the Boulevard Victor-Noir, shining in the night, side by side, and which are much more than cafés—aquariums, ships, stars or great white eyes—have lost their ambiguous charm.

A perfect day to turn back to one's self: these cold clarities which the sun projects like a judgment shorn of pity, over all creatures—enter through my eyes; I am illuminated within by a diminishing light. I am sure that fifteen minutes would be enough to reach supreme self-contempt. No thank you, I want none of that. Neither shall I re-read what I wrote yesterday on Rollebon's stay in St. Petersburg. I stay seated, my arms hanging, or write a few words, without courage: I yawn, I wait for night to come. When it is dark, the objects and I will come out of limbo.

Did Rollebon, or did he not, participate in the assassination of Paul I? That is the question for today: I am that far and can't go on without deciding.

According to Tcherkoff, he was paid by Count Pahlen. Most of the other conspirators, Tcherkoff says, were content with deposing and imprisoning the Czar. In fact, Alexander seems to have been a partisan of that solution. But Pahlen, it was alleged, wanted to do away with Paul completely, and M. de Rollebon was charged with persuading the individual conspirators to the assassination.

"He visited each one of them and, with an incomparable power, mimed the scene which was to take place. Thus he caused to be born or developed in them a madness for murder."

But I suspect Tcherkoff. He is not a reasonable witness, he is a half-mad, sadistic magician: he turns everything into the demoniacal. I cannot see M. de Rollebon in this melodramatic role or as mimic of the assassination scene! Never on your life! He is cold, not carried away: he exposes nothing, he insinuates, and his method, pale and colourless, can succeed only with men of his own level, intriguers accessible to reason, politicians.

"Adhèmar de Rollebon," writes Mme de Charrières, "painted nothing with words, made no gestures, never altered the tone of his voice. He kept his eyes half-closed and one could barely make out, between his lashes, the lowest rim of his grey iris. It has only been within the past few years that I dare confess he bored me beyond all possible limits. He spoke a little in the way Abbé Mably used to write."

And this is the man who, by his talent for mimicry? . . . But then how was he able to charm women? Then there is this curious story Ségur reports and which seems true to me.

"In 1787, at an inn near Moulins, an old man was dying, a friend of Diderot, trained by the philosophers. The priests of the neighbourhood were nonplussed: they had tried everything in vain; the good man would have no last rites, he was a pantheist. M. de Rollebon, who was passing by and who believed in nothing, bet the Curé of Moulins that he would need less than two hours to bring the sick man back to Christian sentiments. The Curé took the bet and lost: Rollebon began at three in the morning, the sick man confessed at five and died at seven. "Are you so forceful in argument?" asked the Curé, "You outdo even us." "I did not argue," answered M. de Rollebon, "I made him fear Hell.""

How did he take an effective part in the assassination? That evening, one of his officer friends conducted him to his door. If he had gone out again, how could he have crossed St. Petersburg without trouble? Paul, half-insane, had given the order that after nine o'clock at night, all passers except midwives and doctors were to be arrested. Can we believe the absurd legend that Rollebon disguised himself as a midwife to get as far as the palace? After all, he was quite capable of it. In any case, he was not at home on the night of the assassination, that seems proved. Alexander must have suspected him strongly, since one of his official acts was to send the Marquis away on the vague pretext of a mission to the Far East.

M. de Rollebon bores me to tears. I get up. I move through this pale light; I see it change beneath my hands and on the sleeves of my coat: I cannot describe how much it disgusts me. I yawn. I light the lamp on the table: perhaps its light will be able to combat the light of day. But no: the lamp makes nothing more than a pitiful pond around its base. I turn it out; I get up. There is a white hole in the wall, a mirror. It is a trap. I know I am going to let myself be caught in it. I have. The grey thing appears in the mirror. I go over and look at it, I can no longer get away.

It is the reflection of my face. Often in these lost days I study it. I can understand nothing of this face. The faces of others have some sense, some direction. Not mine. I cannot even decide whether it is handsome or ugly. I think it is ugly because I have been told so. But it doesn't strike me. At heart, I am even shocked that anyone can attribute qualities of this kind to it, as if you called a clod of earth or a block of stone beautiful or ugly.

Still, there is one thing which is pleasing to see, above the flabby cheeks, above the forehead; it is the beautiful red flame which crowns my head, it is my hair. That is pleasant to see. Anyhow, it is a definite colour: I am glad I have red hair. There it is in the mirror, it makes itself seen, it shines. I am still lucky: if my forehead was surmounted by one of those neutral heads of hair which are neither chestnut nor blond, my face would be lost in vagueness, it would make me dizzy.

My glance slowly and wearily travels over my forehead, my cheeks: it finds nothing firm, it is stranded. Obviously there are a nose, two eyes and a mouth, but none of it makes sense, there is not even a human expression. Yet Anny and Vélines thought I looked so alive: perhaps I am too used to my face. When I was little, my Aunt Bigeois told me "If you look at yourself too long in the mirror, you'll see a monkey." I must have looked at myself even longer than that: what I see is well below the monkey, on the fringe of the vegetable world, at the level of jellyfish. It is alive, I can't say it isn't; but this was not the life that Anny contemplated: I see a slight tremor, I see the insipid flesh blossoming and palpitating with abandon. The eyes especially are horrible seen so close. They are glassy, soft, blind, red-rimmed, they look like fish scales.

I lean all my weight on the porcelain ledge, I draw my face closer until it touches the mirror. The eyes, nose and mouth disappear: nothing human is left. Brown wrinkles show on each side of the feverish swelled lips, crevices, mole holes. A silky white down covers the great slopes of the cheeks, two hairs protrude from the nostrils: it is a geological embossed map. And, in spite of everything, this lunar world is familiar to me. I cannot say I *recognize* the details. But the whole thing gives me an impression of something seen before which stupefies me: I slip quietly off to sleep.

I would like to take hold of myself: an acute, vivid sensation would deliver me. I plaster my left hand against my cheek, I pull the skin; I grimace at myself. An entire half of my face yields, the left half of the mouth twists and swells, uncovering a tooth, the eye opens on a white globe, on pink, bleeding flesh. That is not what I was looking for: nothing strong, nothing new; soft, flaccid, stale! I go to sleep with my eyes open, already the face is growing larger, growing in the mirror, an immense, light halo gliding in the light. . . .

I lose my balance and that wakes me. I find myself straddling a chair, still dazed. Do other men have as much difficulty in appraising their face? It seems that I see my own as I feel my body, through a dumb, organic sense. But the others? Rollebon, for example, was he also put to sleep by looking in the mirror at what Mme de Genlis calls "his small, wrinkled countenance, clean and sharp, all pitted with smallpox, in which there was a strange malice which caught the eye, no matter what effort he made to dissemble it? He took," she adds, "great care with his coiffure and I never saw him without his wig. But his cheeks were blue, verging on black, owing to his heavy beard which he shaved himself, not being at all expert. It was his custom to wash his face with white lead, in the manner of

Grimm. M. de Dangeville said that with all this white and all this blue he looked like a Roquefort cheese".

It seems to me he must have been quite pleasing. But, after all, this is not the way he appeared to Mme de Charrières. I believe she found him rather worn. Perhaps it is impossible to understand one's own face. Or perhaps it is because I am a single man? People who live in society have learned how to see themselves in mirrors as they appear to their friends. I have no friends. Is that why my flesh is so naked? You might say—yes you might say, nature without humanity.

I have no taste for work any longer, I can do nothing more except wait for night.

5.30:

Things are bad! Things are very bad: I have it, the filth, the Nausea. And this time it is new: it caught me in a café. Until now cafés were my only refuge because they were full of people and well lighted: now there won't even be that any more; when I am run to earth in my room, I shan't know where to go.

I was coming to make love but no sooner had I opened the door than Madeleine, the waitress, called to me:

"The patronne isn't here, she's in town shopping."

I felt a sharp disappointment in the sexual parts, a long, disagreeable tickling. At the same time I felt my shirt rubbing against my breasts and I was surrounded, seized by a slow, coloured mist, and a whirlpool of lights in the smoke, in the mirrors, in the booths glowing at the back of the café, and I couldn't see why it was there or why it was like that. I was on the doorstep, I hesitated to go in and then there was a whirlpool, an eddy, a shadow passed across the ceiling and I felt myself pushed forward. I floated, dazed by luminous fogs dragging me in all directions at once. Madeleine came floating over to take off my overcoat and I noticed she had drawn her hair back and put on earrings: I did not recognize her. I looked at her large cheeks which never stopped rushing towards the ears. In the hollow of the cheeks, beneath the cheekbones, there were two pink stains which seemed weary on this poor flesh. The cheeks ran, ran towards the ears and Madeleine smiled:

"What will you have, Monsieur Antoine?"

Then the Nausea seized me, I dropped to a seat, I no longer knew where I was; I saw the colours spin slowly around me,

I wanted to vomit. And since that time, the Nausea has not left me, it holds me.

I paid, Madeleine took away my saucer. My glass crushes a puddle of yellow beer against the marble table top, a bubble floating in it. The bottom of my seat is broken and in order not to slide, I am compelled to press my heels firmly against the ground; it is cold. On the right, they are playing cards on a woollen cloth. I did not see them when I came in: I simply felt there was a warm packet, half on the seat, half on the table in the back, with pairs of waving arms. Afterwards, Madeleine brought them cards, the cloth and chips in a wooden bowl. There are three or five of them, I don't know, I haven't the courage to look at them. I have a broken spring: I can move my eyes but not my head. The head is all pliable and elastic, as though it had been simply set on my neck; if I turn it, it will fall off. All the same, I hear a short breath and from time to time, out of the corner of my eye I see a reddish flash covered with hair. It is a hand.

When the patronne goes shopping her cousin replaces her at the bar. His name is Adolphe. I began looking at him as I sat down and I have kept on because I cannot turn my head. He is in shirtsleeves, with purple suspenders; he has rolled the sleeves of his shirt above the elbows. The suspenders can hardly be seen against the blue shirt, they are all obliterated, buried in the blue, but it is false humility; in fact, they will not let themselves be forgotten, they annoy me by their sheep-like stubbornness, as if, starting to become purple, they stopped somewhere along the way without giving up their pretentions. You feel like saying, "All right, *become* purple and let's hear no more about it." But now, they stay in suspense, stubborn in their defeat. Sometimes the blue which surrounds them slips over and covers them completely: I stay an instant without seeing them. But it is merely a passing wave, soon the blue pales in places and I see the small island of hesitant purple reappear, grow larger, rejoin and reconstitute the suspenders. Cousin Adolphe has no eyes: his swollen, retracted eyelids open only on a little of the whites. He smiles sleepily; from time to time he snorts, yelps and writhes feebly, like a dreaming dog.

His blue cotton shirt stands out joyfully against a chocolate-coloured wall. That too brings on the Nausea. The Nausea is not inside me: I feel it *out there* in the wall, in the suspenders, everywhere around me. It makes itself one with the café, I am the one who is within *it*.

On my right, the warm packet begins to rustle, it waves its pair of arms.

"Here, there's your trump—what are trumps?" Black neck bent over the game: "Hahaha! What? He's just played trumps." "I don't know, I didn't see . . ." "Yes I played trumps just now." "Ah, good, hearts are trumps then." He intones: "Hearts are trumps, hearts are trumps, hea-arts are trumps." Spoken: "What is it, Sir? What is it, Sir? I take it!"

Again, silence—the taste of sugar in the air at the back of my throat. The smells. The suspenders.

The cousin has got up, and taken a few steps, put his hands behind his back, smiling, raising his head and leaning back on his heels. He goes to sleep in this position. He is there, oscillating, always smiling: his cheeks tremble. He is going to fall. He bends backwards, bends, bends, the face turned completely up to the ceiling, then just as he is about to fall, he catches himself adroitly on the ledge of the bar and regains his balance. After which, he starts again. I have enough, I call the waitress:

"Madeleine, if you please, play something on the phonograph. The one I like, you know: *Some of these days.*"

"Yes, but maybe that'll bother these gentlemen; these gentlemen don't like music when they're playing. But I'll ask them."

I make a great effort and turn my head. There are four of them. She bends over a congested old man who wears black-rimmed eyeglasses on the end of his nose. He hides his cards against his chest and glances at me from under the glasses.

"Go ahead, Monsieur."

Smiles. His teeth are rotten. The red hand does not belong to him, it is his neighbour's, a fellow with a black moustache. This fellow with the moustache has enormous nostrils that could pump air for a whole family and that eat up half his face, but in spite of that, he breathes through his mouth, gasping a little. With them there is also a young man with a face like a dog. I cannot make out the fourth player.

The cards fall on the woollen cloth, spinning. The hands with ringed fingers come and pick them up, scratching the cloth with their nails. The hands make white splotches on the cloth, they look puffed up and dusty. Other cards fall, the hands go and come. What an odd occupation: it doesn't look like a game or a rite, or a habit. I think they do it to pass the time, nothing more. But time is too large, it can't be filled up. Everything you plunge into it is stretched and disintegrates. That gesture, for instance, the red hand picking up the cards and fumbling: it is all flabby. It would have to be ripped apart and tailored inside.

Madeleine turns the crank on the phonograph. I only hope she has not made a mistake; that she hasn't put on *Cavalleria Rusticana,* as she did the other day. But no, this is it, I recognize the melody from the very first bars. It is an old rag-time with a vocal refrain. I heard American soldiers whistle it in 1917 in the streets of LaRochelle. It must date from before the War. But the recording is much more recent. Still, it is the oldest record in the collection, a Pathé record for sapphire needle.

The vocal chorus will be along shortly: I like that part especially and the abrupt manner in which it throws itself forward, like a cliff against the sea. For the moment, the jazz is playing; there is no melody, only notes, a myriad of tiny jolts. They know no rest, an inflexible order gives birth to them and destroys them without even giving them time to recuperate and exist for themselves. They race, they press forward, they strike me a sharp blow in passing and are obliterated. I would like to hold them back, but I know if I succeeded in stopping one it would remain between my fingers only as a raffish languishing sound. I must accept their death; I must even *will* it. I know few impressions stronger or more harsh.

I grow warm, I begin to feel happy. There is nothing extraordinary in this, it is a small happiness of Nausea: it spreads at the bottom of the viscous puddle, at the bottom of *our* time—the time of purple suspenders and broken chair seats; it is made of wide, soft instants, spreading at the edge, like an oil stain. No sooner than born, it is already old, it seems as though I have known it for twenty years.

There is another happiness: outside there is this band of steel, the narrow duration of the music which traverses our time through and through, rejecting it, tearing at it with its dry little points; there is another time.

"Monsieur Randu plays hearts . . . and you play an ace."

The voice dies away and disappears. Nothing bites on the ribbon of steel, neither the opening door, nor the breath of cold air flowing over my knees, nor the arrival of the veterinary surgeon and his little girl: the music transpierces these vague figures and passes through them. Barely seated, the girl has been seized by it: she holds herself stiffly, her eyes wide open; she listens, rubbing the table with her fist.

A few seconds more and the Negress will sing. It seems inevitable, so strong is the necessity of this music: nothing can interrupt it, nothing which comes from this time in which the world has fallen; it will stop of itself, as if by order. If I love this beautiful voice it is especially because of that: it is neither for its fulness nor its sadness, rather because it is the event for which so many notes have been preparing, from so far away, dying that it might be born. And yet I am troubled; it would take so little to make the record stop: a broken spring, the whim of Cousin Adolphe. How strange it is, how moving, that this hardness should be so fragile. Nothing can interrupt it yet all can break it.

The last chord has died away. In the brief silence which follows I feel strongly that there it is, that *something has happened*.

Silence.

> *Some of these days*
> *You'll miss me honey*

What has just happened is that the Nausea has disappeared. When the voice was heard in the silence, I felt my body harden and the Nausea vanish. Suddenly: it was almost unbearable to become so hard, so brilliant. At the same time the music was drawn out, dilated, swelled like a waterspout. It filled the room with its metallic transparency, crushing our miserable time against the walls. I am *in* the music. Globes of fire turn in the mirrors; encircled by rings of smoke, veiling and unveiling the hard smile of light. My glass of beer has shrunk, it seems heaped up on the table, it looks dense and indispensable. I want to pick it up and feel the weight of it, I stretch out my hand . . . God! That is what has changed, my gestures. This movement of my arm has developed like a majestic theme, it has glided along the song of the Negress; I seemed to be dancing.

Adolphe's face is there, set against the chocolate-coloured wall; he seems quite close. Just at the moment when my hand closed, I saw his face; it witnessed to the necessity of a conclusion. I press my fingers against the glass, I look at Adolphe: I am happy.

"*Voilà!*"

A voice rises from the tumult. My neighbour is speaking, the old man burns. His cheeks make a violet stain on the brown leather of the bench. He slaps a card down on the table. Diamonds.

But the dog-faced young man smiles. The flushed opponent, bent over the table, watches him like a cat ready to spring.

"*Et voilà!*"

The hand of the young man rises from the shadow, glides an instant, white, indolent, then suddenly drops like a hawk and presses a card against the cloth. The great red-faced man leaps up:

"Hell! He's trumped."

The outline of the king of hearts appears between his curled fingers, then it is turned on its face and the game goes on. Mighty king, come from so far, prepared by so many combinations, by so many vanished gestures. He disappears in turn so that other combinations can be born, other gestures, attacks, counterattacks, turns of luck, a crowd of small adventures.

I am touched, I feel my body at rest like a precision machine. I have had real adventures. I can recapture no detail but I perceive the rigorous succession of circumstances. I have crossed seas, left cities behind me, followed the course of rivers or plunged into forests, always making my way towards other cities. I have had women, I have fought with men; and never was I able to turn back, any more than a record can be reversed. And all that led me—*where?*

At this very instant, on this bench, in this translucent bubble all humming with music.

And when you leave me

Yes, I who loved so much to sit on the banks of the Tiber at Rome, or in the evening, in Barcelona, ascend and descend the Ramblas a hundred times, I, who near Angkor, on the island of Baray Prah-Kan, saw a banyan tree knot its roots about a Naga chapel, I am here, living in the same second as these card players, I listen to a Negress sing while outside roves the feeble night.

The record stops.

Night has entered, sweetish, hesitant. No one sees it, but it is there, veiling the lamps; I breathe something opaque in the air: it is night. It is cold. One of the players pushes a disordered pack of cards towards another man who picks them up. One card has stayed behind. Don't they see it? It's the nine of hearts. Someone takes it at last, gives it to the dog-faced young man.

"Ah. The nine of hearts."

Enough, I'm going to leave. The purple-faced man bends over a sheet of paper and sucks his pencil. Madeleine watches him with clear, empty eyes. The young man turns and turns the nine of hearts between his fingers. God! . . .

I get up with difficulty; I see an inhuman face glide in the mirror above the veterinary's head.

In a little while I'll go to the cinema.

The air does me good: it doesn't taste like sugar, it doesn't have the winey odour of vermouth. But good God, how cold it is.

It is seven-thirty, I'm not hungry and the cinema doesn't start until nine o'clock; what am I going to do? I have to walk quickly to keep warm. I pause: behind me the boulevard leads to the heart of the city, to the great fiery jewels of central streets, to the Palais Paramount, the Imperial, the Grands Magasins Jahan. It doesn't tempt me at all: it is apéritif time. For the time being I have seen enough of living things, of dogs, of men, of all flabby masses which move spontaneously.

I turn left, I'm going to crawl into that hole down there, at the end of the row of gaslights: I am going to follow the Boulevard Noir as far as the Avenue Galvani. An icy wind blows from the hole: down there is nothing but stones and earth. Stones are hard and do not move.

There is a tedious little stretch of street: on the pavement at the right a gaseous mass, grey with streams of smoke, makes a noise like rattling shells: the old railway station. Its presence has fertilized the first hundred yards of the Boulevard Noir—from the Boulevard de la Redoute to the Rue Paradis—has given birth there to a dozen streetlights and, side by side, four cafés, the "Railwaymen's Rendezvous" and three others which languish all through the day but which light up in the evening and cast luminous rectangles on the street.

I take three more baths of yellow light, see an old woman come out of the *épicerie-mercerie* Rabache, drawing her shawl over her head and starting to run: now it's finished. I am on the kerb of the Rue Paradis, beside the last lamp-post. The asphalt ribbon breaks off sharply. Darkness and mud are on the other side of the street. I cross the Rue Paradis. I put my right foot in a puddle of water, my sock is soaked through; my walk begins.

No one lives in this section of the Boulevard Noir. The climate is too harsh there, the soil too barren for life to be established there and grow. The three *Scieries des Frères Soleil* (the

Frères Soleil furnished the panelled arch of the Eglise Saint-Cécile de la Mer, which cost a hundred thousand francs) open on the West with all their doors and windows, on the quiet Rue Jeanne-Berthe-Coeuroy which they fill with purring sounds. They turn their backs of triple adjoining walls on the Boulevard Victor-Noir. These buildings border the left-hand pavement for 400 yards: without the smallest window, not even a skylight.

This time I walked with both feet in the gutter. I cross the street: on the opposite sidewalk, a single gaslight, like a beacon at the extreme end of the earth, lights up a dilapidated fence, broken down in places.

Bits of old posters still clung to the boards. A fine face full of hatred, grimacing against a green background torn into the shape of a star; just below the nose someone had pencilled in a curling moustache. On another strip I could still decipher the word "purâtre" from which red drops fall, drops of blood perhaps. The face and the word might have been part of the same poster. Now the poster is lacerated, the simple, necessary lines which united them have disappeared, but another unity has established itself between the twisted mouth, the drops of blood, the white letters, and the termination "âtre": as though a restless and criminal passion were seeking to express itself by these mysterious signs. I can see the lights from the railroad shining between the boards. A long wall follows the fence. A wall without opening, without doors, without windows, a well which stops 200 yards further on, against a house. I have passed out of range of the lamp-post; I enter the black hole. Seeing the shadow at my feet lose itself in the darkness, I have the impression of plunging into icy water. Before me, at the very end, through the layers of black, I can make out a pinkish pallor: it is the Avenue Galvani. I turn back; behind the gaslamp, very far, there is a hint of light: that is the station with the four cafés. Behind me, in front of me, are people drinking and playing cards in pubs. Here there is nothing but blackness. Intermittently, the wind carries a solitary, faraway ringing to my ears. Familiar sounds, the rumble of motor cars, shouts, and the barking of dogs which hardly venture from the lighted streets, they stay within the warmth. But the ringing pierces the shadows and comes thus far: it is harder, less human than the other noises.

I stop to listen. I am cold, my ears hurt; they must be all red. But I no longer feel myself; I am won over by the purity surrounding me; nothing is alive, the wind whistles, the straight

25

lines flee in the night. The Boulevard Noir does not have the indecent look of bourgeois streets, offering their regrets to the passers-by. No one has bothered to adorn it: it is simply the reverse side. The reverse side of the Rue Jeanne-Berthe Coeuroy, of the Avenue Galvani. Around the station, the people of Bouville still look after it a little; they clean it from time to time because of the travellers. But, immediately after that, they abandon it and it rushes straight ahead, blindly, bumping finally into the Avenue Galvani. The town has forgotten it. Sometimes a great mud-coloured truck thunders across it at top speed. No one even commits any murders there; want of assassins and victims. The Boulevard Noir is inhuman. Like a mineral. Like a triangle. It's lucky there's a boulevard like that in Bouville. Ordinarily you find them only in capitals, in Berlin, near Neuköln or Friedrichshain—in London, behind Greenwich. Straight, dirty corridors, full of drafts, with wide, treeless sidewalk. They are almost always outside the town in these strange sections where cities are manufactured near freight stations, car-barns, abattoirs, gas tanks. Two days after a rainstorm, when the whole city is moist beneath the sun and radiates damp heat, they are still cold, they keep their mud and puddles. They even have puddles which never dry up—except one month out of the year, August.

The Nausea has stayed down there, in the yellow light. I am happy: this cold is so pure, this night so pure: am I myself not a wave of icy air? With neither blood, nor lymph, nor flesh. Flowing down this long canal towards the pallor down there. To be nothing but coldness.

Here are some people. Two shadows. What did they need to come here for?

It is a short woman pulling a man by his sleeve. She speaks in a thin, rapid voice. Because of the wind I understand nothing of what she says.

"You're going to shut your trap now, aren't you?" the man says.

She still speaks. He pushes her roughly. They look at each other, uncertain, then the man thrusts his hands in his pockets and leaves without looking back.

The man has disappeared. A scant three yards separate me from this woman now. Suddenly, deep, hoarse sounds come from her, tear at her and fill the whole street with extraordinary violence.

"Charles, I beg you, you know what I told you? Charles, come back, I've had enough, I'm too miserable!"

I pass so close to her that I could touch her. It's . . . but how can I believe that this burning flesh, this face shining with sorrow? . . . and yet I recognize the scarf, the coat and the large wine-coloured birthmark on the right hand; it is Lucie, the charwoman. I dare not offer her my support, but she must be able to call for it if need be: I pass before her slowly, looking at her. Her eyes stare at me but she seems not to see me; she looks as though she were lost in her suffering. I take a few steps, turn back. . . .

Yes, it's Lucie. But transfigured, beside herself, suffering with a frenzied generosity. I envy her. There she is, standing straight, holding out her arms as if awaiting the stigmata; she opens her mouth, she is suffocating. I feel as though the walls have grown higher, on each side of the street, that they have come closer together, that she is at the bottom of a well. I wait a few moments: I am afraid she will fall: she is too sickly to stand this unwonted sorrow. But she does not move, she seems turned to stone, like everything around her. One moment I wonder if I have not been mistaken about her, if this is not her true nature which has suddenly been revealed to me.

Lucie gives a little groan. Her hand goes to her throat and she opens wide, astonished eyes. No, it is not from herself that she draws strength to suffer. It comes to her from the outside . . . from the boulevard. She should be taken by the arm, led back to the lights, in the midst of people, into quiet, pink streets: down there one cannot suffer so acutely; she would be mollified, she would find her positive look again and the usual level of her sufferings.

I turn my back on her. After all, she is lucky. I have been much too calm these past three years. I can receive nothing more from these tragic solitudes than a little empty purity. I leave.

Thursday, 11.30

I have worked two hours in the reading-room. I went down to the Cour des Hypothèques to smoke a pipe. A square paved with pinkish bricks. The people of Bouville are proud of it because it dates from the eighteenth century. At the entrance to the Rue Chamade and the Rue Suspedard, old chains bar the way to vehicles. Women in black who come to exercise their dogs glide beneath the arcades, along the walls. They rarely come out into the full light, but they cast ingénue glances from the corner of their eyes, on the statue of Gustave Impétraz. They don't know the name of this bronze giant but they see clearly from his frock coat and top hat that he was someone from the beau-monde. He holds his hat in his left hand, placing his right on a stack of papers: it is a little as though their grandfather were there on the pedestal, cast in bronze. They do not need to look at him very long to understand that he thought as they do, exactly as they do, on all subjects. At the service of their obstinately narrow, small ideas he has placed the authority and immense erudition drawn from the papers crushed in his hand. The women in black feel soothed, they can go peacefully minding their own business, running their households, walking their dogs out: they no longer have the responsibility of standing up, for their Christian ideals the high ideals which they get from their fathers; a man of bronze has made himself their guardian.

The encyclopedia devotes a few lines to this personage; I read them last year. I had set the volume on the window ledge; I could see Impétraz' green skull through the pane. I discovered that he flourished around 1890. He was a school inspector. He painted and drew charming sketches and wrote three books: *Popularity and the Ancient Greeks* (1887), *Rollin's Pedagogy* (1891) and a poetic Testament in 1899. He died in 1902, to the deep regret of his dependents and people of good taste.

I lean against the front of the library. I suck out my pipe which threatens to go out. I see an old lady fearfully leaving the gallery of arcades, looking slyly and obstinately at Impétraz. She suddenly grows bolder, she crosses the courtyard as fast as her legs can carry her, stops for a moment in front of the statue, her jaws trembling. Then she leaves, black against the pink pavement, and disappears into a chink in the wall.

This place might have been gay, around 1800, with its pink bricks and houses. Now there is something dry and evil about it, a delicate touch of horror. It comes from that fellow up there on his pedestal. When they cast this scholar in bronze they also turned out a sorcerer.

I look at Impétraz full in the face. He has no eyes, hardly any nose, and beard eaten away by that strange leprosy which sometimes descends, like an epidemic, on all the statues in one neighbourhood. He bows; on the left hand side near his heart his waistcoat is soiled with a light green stain. He looks. He does not live, but neither is he inanimate. A mute power emanates from him: like a wind driving me backwards: Impétraz would like to chase me out of the Cour des Hypothèques. But I shall not leave before I finish this pipe.

A great, gaunt shadow suddenly springs up behind me. I jump.

"Excuse me, Monsieur, I didn't mean to disturb you. I saw your lips moving. You were undoubtedly repeating passages from your book." He laughs. "You were hunting Alexandrines."

I look at the Self-Taught Man with stupor. But he seems surprised at my surprise:

"Should we not, Monsieur, carefully avoid Alexandrines in prose?"

I have been slightly lowered in his estimation. I ask him what he's doing here at this hour. He explains that his boss has given him the day off and he came straight to the library; that he is not going to eat lunch, that he is going to read till closing time. I am not listening to him any more, but he must have strayed from his original subject because I suddenly hear:

". . . to have, as you, the good fortune of writing a book."

I have to say something.

"Good fortune," I say, dubiously.

He mistakes the sense of my answer and rapidly corrects himself:

"Monsieur, I should have said: 'merit.'"

We go up the steps. I don't feel like working. Someone has left *Eugénie Grandet* on the table, the book is open at page 27. I pick it up, mechanically, and begin to read page 27, then page 28: I haven't the courage to begin at the beginning. The Self-Taught Man has gone quickly to the shelves along the wall; he brings back two books which he places on the table, looking like a dog who has found a bone.

"What are you reading?"

He seems reluctant to tell me: he hesitates, rolls his great, roving eyes, then stiffly holds out the books. *Peat-Mosses and Where to Find Them* by Larbalétrier, and *Hitopadesa, or, Useful Instruction* by Lastex. So? I don't know what's bothering him: the books are definitely decent. Out of conscience I thumb through *Hitopadesa* and see nothing but the highest types of sentiment.

3.00 *p.m.*

I have given up *Eugénie Grandet* and begun work without any heart in it. The Self-Taught Man, seeing that I am writing,

29

observes me with respectful lust. From time to time I raise my head a little and see the immense, stiff collar and the chicken-like neck coming out of it. His clothes are shabby but his shirt is dazzling white. He has just taken another book from the same shelf, I can make out the title upside-down: *The Arrow of Caudebec, A Norman Chronicle* by Mlle Julie Lavergne. The Self-Taught Man's choice of reading always disconcerts me.

Suddenly the names of the authors he last read come back to my mind: Lambert, Langlois, Larbalétrier, Lastex, Lavergne. It is a revelation; I have understood the Self-Taught Man's method; he teaches himself alphabetically.

I study him with a sort of admiration. What will-power he must have to carry through, slowly, obstinately, a plan on such a vast scale. One day, seven years ago (he told me he had been a student for seven years) he came pompously into this reading-room. He scanned the innumerable books which lined the walls and he must have said, something like Rastignac, "Science! It is up to us." Then he went and took the first book from the first shelf on the far right; he opened to the first page, with a feeling of respect and fear mixed with an unshakable decision. Today he has reached "L"—"K" after "J," "L" after "K." He has passed brutally from the study of coleopterae to the quantum theory, from a work on Tamerlaine to a Catholic pamphlet against Darwinism, he has never been disconcerted for an instant. He has read everything; he has stored up in his head most of what anyone knows about parthenogenesis, and half the arguments against vivisection. There is a universe behind and before him. And the day is approaching when closing the last book on the last shelf on the far left: he will say to himself, "Now what?"

This is his lunch time; innocently he eats a slice of bread and a bar of Gala Peter. His eyes are lowered and I can study at leisure his fine, curved lashes, like a woman's. When he breathes he gives off an aroma of old tobacco mixed with the sweet scent of chocolate.

Friday, 3.00 p.m.

A little more and I would have fallen into the lure of the mirror. I avoid it only to fall into that of the window: indolent, arms dangling, I go to the window. The Building Yard, the Fence, the Old Station—the Old Station, the Fence, the Building Yard. I give such a big yawn that tears come into my eyes. I hold my pipe in my right hand and my tobacco in my left. I should fill this pipe. But I don't have the heart to do it. My arms hang loosely, I lean my forehead against the windowpane. That old woman annoys me. She trots along obstinately, with unseeing eyes. Sometimes she stops, frightened, as if an invisible fear had brushed against her. There she is under my window, the wind blows her skirts against her knees. She stops, straightens her kerchief. Her hands tremble. She is off again: now I can see her from the back. Old wood louse! I suppose she's going to turn right, into the Boulevard Victor-Noir. That gives her a hundred yards to go: it will take her ten minutes at the rate she's going, ten minutes during which time I shall stay like this, watching her, my forehead glued against the window. She is going to stop twenty times, start again, stop again . . .

I *see* the future. It is there, poised over the street, hardly more dim than the present. What advantage will accrue from its realisation? The old woman stumps further and further away, she stops, pulls at a grey lock of hair which escapes from her kerchief. She walks, she was there, now she is here . . . I don't know where I am any more: do I *see* her motions, or do I *foresee* them? I can no longer distinguish present from future and yet it lasts, it happens little by little; the old woman advances in the deserted street, shuffling her heavy, mannish brogues. This is time, time laid bare, coming slowly into existence, keeping us waiting, and when it does come making us sick because we realise it's been there for a long time. The old woman reaches the corner of the street, no more than a bundle of black clothes. All right then, it's new, she wasn't there a little while ago. But it's a tarnished deflowered newness, which can never surprise. She is going to turn the corner, she turns—during an eternity.

I tear myself from the window and stumble across the room; I glue myself against the looking glass. I stare at myself, I disgust myself: one more eternity. Finally I flee from my image and fall on the bed. I watch the ceiling, I'd like to sleep.

Calm. Calm. In can no longer feel the slipping, the rustling of time. I see pictures on the ceiling. First rings of light, then crosses. They flutter. And now another picture is forming, at the bottom of my eyes this time. It is a great, kneeling animal. I see its front paws and pack saddle. The rest is in fog. But I recognize it: it is a camel I saw at Marrakesh, tethered to a stone. He knelt and stood up six times running; the urchins laughed and shouted at him.

It was wonderful two years ago: all I had to do was close to my eyes and my head would start buzzing like a bee-hive: I could conjure faces, trees, houses, a Japanese girl in Kamaishiki washing herself naked in a wooden tub, a dead Russian, emptied of blood by a great, gaping wound, all his blood in a pool beside him. I could recapture the taste of kouskouss, the smell of olive oil which fills the streets of Burgos at noon, the scent of fennel floating through the Tetuan streets, the piping of Greek shepherds; I was touched. This joy was used up a long time ago. Will it be reborn today?

A torrid sun moves stiffly in my head like a magic lantern slide. A fragment of blue sky follows; after a few jolts it becomes motionless. I am all golden within. From what Moroccan (or Algerian or Syrian) day did this flash suddenly detach itself? I let myself flow into the past.

Meknes. What was that man from the hills like—the one who frightened us in the narrow street between the Berdaine mosque and that charming square shaded by a mulberry tree? He came towards us, Anny was on my right. Or on my left?

This sun and blue sky were only a snare. This is the hundredth time I've let myself be caught. My memories are like coins in the devil's purse: when you open it you find only dead leaves.

Now I can only see the great, empty eye socket of the hill tribesman. Is this eye really his? The doctor at Baku who explained the principle of state abortions to me was also blind of one eye, and the white empty socket appears every time I want to remember his face. Like the Norns these two men have only one eye between them with which they take turns.

As for the square at Meknes, where I used to go every day, it's even simpler: I do not see it at all any more. All that remains is the vague feeling that it was charming, and these five words are indivisibly bound together: a charming square at Meknes. Undoubtedly, if I close my eyes or stare vaguely at the ceiling I can re-create the scene: a tree in the distance, a short dingy figure run towards me. But I am inventing all this to make out a case. That Moroccan was big and weather-beaten, besides, I only saw him after he had touched me. So I *still* know he was big and weather-beaten: certain details, somewhat curtailed, live in my memory. But I don't *see* anything any more: I can search the past in vain, I can only find these scraps of images and I am not sure what they represent, whether they are memories or just fiction.

There are many cases where even these scraps have disappeared: nothing is left but words: I could still tell stories, tell them too well (as far as anecdotes are concerned, I can stand up to anyone except ship's officers and professional people) but these are only the skeletons. There's the story of a person who does this, does that, but it isn't I, I have nothing in common with him. He travels through countries I know no more about than if I had never been there. Sometimes, in my story, it happens that I pronounce these fine names you read in atlases, Aranjuez or Canterbury. New images are born in me, images such as people create from books who have never travelled. My words are dreams, that is all.

For a hundred dead stories there still remain one or two living ones. I evoke these with caution, occasionally, not too often, for fear of wearing them out, I fish one out, again I see the scenery, the characters, the attitudes. I stop suddenly: there is a flaw, I have seen a word pierce through the web of sensations. I suppose that this word will soon take the place of several images I love. I must stop quickly and think of something else; I don't want to tire my memories. In vain; the next time I evoke them a good part will be congealed.

I make a pretence of getting up, going to look for my photos of Meknes in the chest I pushed under my table. What good would it do? These aphrodisiacs scarcely affect my memory any more. I found a faded little photo under my blotter the other day. A woman was smiling, near a tank. I studied this person for a moment without recognizing her. Then on the other side I read, "Anny, Portsmouth, April 7, '27."

I have never before had such a strong feeling that I was devoid of secret dimensions, confined within the limits of my body, from which airy thoughts float up like bubbles. I build memories with my present self. I am cast out, forsaken in the present: I vainly try to rejoin the past: I cannot escape.

Someone knocks. It's the Self-Taught Man: I had forgotten him. I had promised to show him the photographs of my travels. He can go to Hell.

He sits down on a chair; his extended buttocks touch the back of it and his stiff torso leans forward. I jump from the end of my bed and turn on the light.

"Oh, do we really need that? We were quite comfortable."

"Not for looking at pictures. . . ."

I relieve him of his hat.

"True, Monsieur? Do you really want to show me your pictures?"

"Of course."

This is a plot: I hope he will keep quiet while he looks at them. I dive under the table and push the chest against his patent leather shoes, I put an armload of post cards and photos on his lap: Spain and Spanish Morocco.

But I see by his laughing, open look that I have been singularly mistaken in hoping to reduce him to silence. He glances over a view of San Sebastian from Monte Igueldo, sets it cautiously on the table and remains silent for an instant. Then he sighs:

"Ah, Monsieur, you're lucky . . . if what they say is true—travel is the best school. Is that your opinion, Monsieur?"

I make a vague gesture. Luckily he has not finished.

"It must be such an upheaval. If I were ever to go on a trip, I think I should make written notes of the slightest traits of my character before leaving, so that when I returned I would be able to compare what I was and what I had become. I've read that there are travellers who have changed physically and morally to such an extent that even their closest relatives did not recognize them when they came back."

He handles a thick packet of photographs, abstractedly. He takes one and puts it on the table without looking at it; then he stares intently at the next picture showing Saint Jerome sculptured on a pulpit in the Burgos cathedral.

"Have you seen the Christ made of animal skins at Burgos? There is a very strange book, Monsieur, on these statues made of animal skin and even human skin. And the Black Virgin? She isn't at Burgos but at Saragossa, I think? Yet there may possibly be one at Burgos. The Pilgrims kiss her, don't they?—the one at Saragossa, I mean. And isn't there the print of her foot on a stone?—in a hole—where the mothers push their children?"

Stiffly he pushes an imaginary child with his hands. You'd think he was refusing the gifts of Artaxerxes.

"Ah, manners and customs, Monsieur, they are . . . they are curious."

A little breathless, he points his great ass's jawbone at me. He smells of tobacco and stagnant water. His fine, roving eyes shine like globes of fire and his sparse hair forms a steaming halo on his skull. Under this skull, Samoyeds, Nyam-Nyams,

Malgaches and Fuegians celebrate their strangest solemnities, eat their old fathers, their children, spin to the sound of tom-toms until they faint, run amok, burn their dead, exhibit them on the roofs, leave them to the river current in a boat, lighted by a torch, copulate at random, mother with son, father with daughter, brother with sister, mutilate themselves, castrate themselves, distend their lips with plates, have monstrous animals sculptured on their backs.

"Can one say, with Pascal, that custom is second nature?"

He has fixed his black eyes on mine, he begs for an answer.

"That depends," I say.

He draws a deep breath.

"That's just what I was saying to myself, Monsieur. But I distrust myself so much; one should have read everything."

He almost goes mad over the next photo and shouts joyfully:

"Segovia! Segovia! I've read a book about Segovia!"

Then he adds with a certain nobility:

"Monsieur, I don't remember the name any more. I sometimes have spells of absent-mindedness . . . Na . . . No . . . Nod . . ."

"Impossible," I tell him quickly, "you were only up to Lavergne."

I regret my words immediately: after all, he had never told me about his reading methods, it must have been a precious secret. And in fact, his face falls and his thick lips jut out as if he were going to cry. Then he bows his head and looks at a dozen more post cards without a word.

But after thirty seconds I can see that a powerful enthusiasm is mounting in him and that he will burst if he doesn't speak:

"When I've finished my instruction (I allow six more years for that) I shall join, if I am permitted, the group of students and professors who take an annual cruise to the Near East. I should like to make some new acquaintances," he says unctuously. "To speak frankly, I would also like something unexpected to happen to me, something new, adventures."

He has lowered his voice and his face has taken on a roguish look.

"What sort of adventures?" I ask him, astonished.

"All sorts, Monsieur. Getting on the wrong train. Stopping in an unknown city. Losing your briefcase, being arrested by mistake, spending the night in prison. Monsieur, I believed the word adventure could be defined: an event out of the ordinary without being necessarily extraordinary. People speak of the magic of adventures. Does this expression seem correct to you? I would like to ask you a question, Monsieur."

"What is it?"

He blushes and smiles.

"Possibly it is indiscreet!"

"Ask me, anyway."

He leans towards me, his eyes half-closed, and asks:

"Have you had many adventures, Monsieur?"

"A few," I answer mechanically, throwing myself back to avoid his tainted breath. Yes. I said that mechanically, without thinking. In fact, I am generally proud of having had so many adventures. But today, I had barely pronounced the words than I was seized with contrition; it seems as though I am lying, that I have never had the slightest adventure in my life, or rather, that I don't even know what the word means any more. At the same time, I am weighed down by the same discouragement I had in Hanoi—four years ago when Mercier pressed me to join him and I stared at a Khmer statuette without answering. And the IDEA is there, this great white mass which so disgusted me then: I hadn't seen it for four years.

"Could I ask you . . ." the Self-Taught Man begins . . .

By Jove! To tell him one of those famous tales. But I won't say another word on the subject.

"There," I say, bending down over his narrow shoulders, putting my finger on a photograph, "there, that's Santillana, the prettiest town in Spain."

"The Santillana of Gil Blas? I didn't believe it existed. Ah, Monsieur, how profitable your conversation is. One can tell you've travelled."

I put out the Self-Taught Man after filling his pockets with post cards, prints and photos. He left enchanted and I switched off the light. I am alone now. Not quite alone. Hovering in front of me is still this idea. It has rolled itself into a ball, it stays there like a large cat; it explains nothing, it does not move, and contents itself with saying no. No, I haven't had any adventures.

I fill my pipe, light it and stretch out on the bed, throwing a coat over my legs. What astonishes me is to feel so sad and exhausted. Even if it were true—that I never had any adventures —what difference would that make to me? First, it seems to be a pure question of words. This business at Meknes, for example, I was thinking about a little while ago: a Moroccan jumped on me and wanted to stab me with an enormous knife. But I hit him just below the temple . . . then he began shouting in Arabic and a swarm of lousy beggars came up and chased us all the way to Souk Attarin. Well, you can call that by any name you like, in any case, it was an event which *happened to* ME.

It is completely dark and I can't tell whether my pipe is lit. A trolley passes: red light on the ceiling. Then a heavy truck which makes the house tremble. It must be six o'clock.

I have never had adventures. Things have happened to me, events, incidents, anything you like. But no adventures. It isn't a question of words; I am beginning to understand. There is something to which I clung more than all the rest—without completely realizing it. It wasn't love. Heaven forbid, not glory, not money. It was . . . I had imagined that at certain times my life could take on a rare and precious quality. There was no need for extraordinary circumstances: all I asked for was a little precision. There is nothing brilliant about my life now: but from time to time, for example, when they play music in the cafés, I look back and tell myself: in old days, in London, Meknes, Tokyo, I have known great moments, I have had adventures. Now I am deprived of this. I have suddenly learned, without any apparent reason, that I have been lying to myself for ten years. And naturally, everything they tell about in books can happen in real life, but not in the same way. It is to this way of happening that I clung so tightly.

The beginnings would have had to be real beginnings. Alas! Now I see so clearly what I wanted. Real beginnings are like a fanfare of trumpets, like the first notes of a jazz tune, cutting short tedium, making for continuity: then you say about these evenings within evenings: "I was out for a walk, it was an evening in May." You walk, the moon has just risen, you feel lazy, vacant, a little empty. And then suddenly you think: "Something has happened." No matter what: a slight rustling in the shadow, a thin silhouette crossing the street. But this paltry event is not like the others: suddenly you see that it is the beginning of a great shape whose outlines are lost in mist and you tell yourself, "Something is beginning."

Something is beginning in order to end: adventure does not let itself be drawn out; it only makes sense when dead. I am drawn, irrevocably, towards this death which is perhaps mine as well. Each instant appears only as part of a sequence. I cling to each instant with all my heart: I know that it is unique, irreplaceable—and yet I would not raise a finger to stop it from being annihilated. This last moment I am spending—in Berlin, in London—in the arms of a woman casually met two days ago—moment I love passionately, woman I may adore—all is going to end, I know it. Soon I shall leave for another country. I shall never rediscover either this woman or this night. I grasp at each second, trying to suck it dry: nothing happens which I do not seize, which I do not fix forever in myself, nothing, neither the fugitive tenderness of those lovely eyes, nor the noises of the street, nor the false dawn of early morning: and even so the minute passes and I do not hold it back, I like to see it pass.

All of a sudden something breaks off sharply. The adventure is over, time resumes its daily routine. I turn; behind me, this beautiful melodious form sinks entirely into the past. It grows smaller, contracts as it declines, and now the end makes one with the beginning. Following this gold spot with my eyes I think I would accept—even if I had to risk death, lose a fortune, a friend—to live it all over again, in the same circumstances, from end to end. But an adventure never returns nor is prolonged.

Yes, it's what I wanted—what I still want. I am so happy when a Negress sings: what summits would I not reach if *my own life* made the subject of the melody.

The idea is still there, unnameable. It waits, peacefully. Now it seems to say:

"Yes? Is *that* what you wanted? Well, that's exactly what you've never had (remember you fooled yourself with words, you called the glitter of travel, the love of women, quarrels, and trinkets adventure) and this is what you'll never have—and no one other than yourself."

But Why? why?

Saturday noon:

The Self-Taught Man did not see me come into the reading-room. He was sitting at the end of a table in the back; he had set his book down in front of him but he was not reading. He was smiling at a seedy-looking student who often comes to the library. The student allowed himself to be looked at for a moment, then suddenly stuck his tongue out and made a horrible face. The Self-Taught Man blushed, hurriedly plunged his nose into his book and became absorbed by his reading.

I have reconsidered my thoughts of yesterday. I was completely dry: it made no difference to me whether there had been no adventures. I was only curious to know whether there could *never be any*.

This is what I thought: for the most banal even to become an adventure, you must (and this is enough) begin to recount it. This is what fools people: a man is always a teller of tales, he lives surrounded by his stories and the stories of others, he sees everything that happens to him through them; and he tries to live his own life as if he were telling a story.

But you have to choose: live or tell. For example, when I was in Hamburg, with that Erna girl I didn't trust and who was afraid of me, I led a funny sort of life. But I was in the middle of it, I didn't think about it. And then one evening, in a little café in San Pauli, she left me to go to the ladies' room. I stayed alone, there was a phonograph playing "Blue Skies." I began to tell myself what had happened since I landed. I told myself, "The third evening, as I was going into a dance hall called *La Grotte Bleue,* I noticed a large woman, half seas over. And that woman is the one I am waiting for now, listening to 'Blue Skies,' the woman who is going to come back and sit down at my right and put her arms around my neck." Then I felt violently that I was having an adventure. But Erna came back and sat down beside me, she wound her arms around my neck and I hated her without knowing why. I understand now: one had to begin living again and the adventure was fading out.

Nothing happens while you live. The scenery changes, people come in and go out, that's all. There are no beginnings. Days are tacked on to days without rhyme or reason, an interminable, monotonous addition. From time to time you make a semi-total: you say: I've been travelling for three years, I've been in Bouville for three years. Neither is there any end: you never leave a woman, a friend, a city in one go. And then everything looks alike: Shanghai, Moscow, Algiers, everything is the same after two weeks. There are moments—rarely—when you make a landmark, you realize that you're going with a woman, in some messy business. The time of a flash. After that, the procession starts again, you begin to add up hours and days: Monday, Tuesday, Wednesday. April, May, June. 1924, 1925, 1926.

That's living. But everything changes when you tell about life; it's a change no one notices: the proof is that people talk about true stories. As if there could possibly be true stories; things happen one way and we tell about them in the opposite sense. You seem to start at the beginning: "It was a fine autumn evening in 1922. I was a notary's clerk in Marommes." And in reality you have started at the end. It was there, invisible and present, it is the one which gives to words the pomp and value of a beginning. "I was out walking, I had left the town without realizing it, I was thinking about my money troubles." This sentence, taken simply for what it is, means that the man was absorbed, morose, a hundred leagues from an adventure, exactly in the mood to let things happen without noticing them. But the end is there, transforming everything. For us, the man is already the hero of the story. His moroseness, his money troubles are much more precious than ours, they are all gilded by the light of future passions. And the story goes on in the reverse: instants have stopped piling themselves in a lighthearted way one on top of the other, they are snapped up by the end of the story which draws them and each one of them in turn, draws out the preceding instant: "It was night, the street was deserted." The phrase is cast out negligently, it seems superfluous; but we do not let ourselves be caught and we put it aside: this is a piece of information whose value we shall subsequently appreciate. And we feel that the hero has lived all the details of this night like annunciations, promises, or even that he lived only those that were promises, blind and deaf to all that did not herald adventure. We forget that the future was not yet there; the man was walking in a night without forethought, a night which offered him a choice of dull rich prizes, and he did not make his choice.

I wanted the moments of my life to follow and order themselves like those of a life remembered. You might as well try and catch time by the tail.

Sunday:

I had forgotten that this morning was Sunday. I went out and walked along the streets as usual. I had taken along *Eugénie Grandet*. Then, suddenly, when opening the gate of the public park I got the impression that something was signalling to me. The park was bare and deserted. But . . . how can I explain?

It didn't have its usual look, it smiled at me. I leaned against the railing for a moment then suddenly realized it was Sunday. It was there—on the trees, on the grass, like a faint smile. It couldn't be described, you would have had to repeat very quickly: "This is a public park, this is winter, this is Sunday morning."

I let go of the railing, turned back towards the houses and streets of the town and half-aloud I murmured, "It's Sunday."

It's Sunday: behind the docks, along the seacoast, near the freight station, all around the city there are empty warehouses and motionless machines in the darkness. In all the houses, men are shaving behind their windows; their heads are thrown back, sometimes they stare at the looking glass, sometimes at the sky to see whether it's going to be a fine day. The brothels are opening to their first customers, rustics and soldiers. In the churches, in the light of candles, a man is drinking wine in the sight of kneeling women. In all the suburbs, between the interminable walls of factories, long black processions have started walking, they are slowly advancing towards the centre of the town. To receive them, the streets have taken on the look they have when disturbance is expected, all the stores, except the ones on the Rue Tournebride, have lowered their iron shutters. Soon, silently, these black columns are going to invade the death-shamming streets: first the railroad workers from Tourville and their wives who work in the Saint-Symphorin soap factories, then the little bourgeois from Jouxtebouville, then the workers from the Pinot weaving mills, then all the odd jobbers from the Saint-Maxence quarter; the men from Thierache will arrive last on the eleven o'clock trolley. Soon the Sunday crowd will be born, between bolted shops and closed doors.

A clock strikes half-past ten and I start on my way: Sundays, at this hour, you can see a fine show in Bouville, but you must not come too late after High Mass.

The little Rue Joséphin-Soulary is dead, it smells of a cellar. But, as on every Sunday, it is filled with a sumptuous noise, a noise like a tide. I turn into the Rue de Président-Chamart where the houses have four storeys with long white venetian blinds. This street of notaries is entirely filled by the voluminous clamour of Sunday. The noise increases in the Passage Gillet and I recognize it: it is a noise which men make. Then suddenly, on the left, comes an explosion, of light and sound: here is the Rue Tournebride, all I have to do is take my place among my fellows and watch them raising their hats to each other.

Sixty years ago no one could have forseen the miraculous destiny of the Rue Tournebride, which the inhabitants of Bouville today call the Little Prado. I saw a map dated 1847 on which the street was not even mentioned. At that time it must have been a dark, stinking bowel, with a trench between the paving stones in which fishes' heads and entrails were stacked. But, at the end of 1873, the Assemblée Nationale declared the construction of a

41

church on the slope of Montmartre to be of public utility. A few months later, the mayor's wife had a vision: Sainte Cécile, her patron saint, came to remonstrate with her. Was it tolerable for the élite to soil themselves every Sunday going to Saint-René or Saint-Claudien to hear mass with shopkeepers? Hadn't the Assemblée Nationale set an example? Bouville now had, thanks to the protection of Heaven, a first-class financial position; wouldn't it be fitting to build a church wherein to give thanks to the Lord?

These visions were accepted: the city council held a historic meeting and the bishop agreed to organize a subscription. All that was left was the choice of locality. The old families of businessmen and shipowners were of the opinion that the building should be constructed on the summit of the Coteau Vert where they lived, "so that Saint Cécile could watch over Bouville as the Sacré-Coeur-de-Jésus over Paris." The *nouveau-riche* gentlemen of the Boulevard Maritime, of which there were only a few, shook their heads: they would give all that was needed but the church would have to be built on the Place Marignan; if they were going to pay for a church they expected to be able to use it; they were not reluctant to make their power felt by the higher bourgeoisie who considered them parvenus. The bishop suggested a compromise: the church was built halfway between the Coteau Vert and the Boulevard Maritime, on the Place de la Halle-aux-Morues which was baptised Place Sainte-Cécile-de-la-Mer. This monstrous edifice, completed in 1887, cost no less than fourteen million francs.

The Rue Tournebride, wide but dirty and of ill-repute, had to be entirely rebuilt and its inhabitants firmly pushed back behind the Place Saint-Cécile; the Little Prado became—especially on Sunday mornings—the meeting place of elegant and distinguished people. Fine shops opened one by one on the passage of the élite. They stayed open Easter Monday, all Christmas Night, and every Sunday until noon. Next to Julien, the pork butcher, renowned for his *pâtés chauds,* Foulon, the pastry cook exhibits his famous specialties, conical petits-fours made of mauve butter, topped by a sugar violet. In the window of Dupaty's library you can see the latest books published by Plon, a few technical works such as a theory of navigation or a treatise on sails and sailing, an enormous illustrated history of Bouville and elegantly appointed editions de luxe: *Koenigsmark* bound in blue leather, the *Livre de mes Fils* by Paul Doumer, bound in tan leather with purple flowers. Ghislaine (Haute Couture, Parisian Models) separates Piégeois the florist from Paquin, the antique dealer. Gustave, the hair dresser, who employs four manicurists, occupies the second floor of an entirely new yellow painted building.

Two years ago, at the corner of the Impasse des Moulins-Gémeaux and the Rue Tournebride, an impudent little shop still advertised for the Tu-Pu-Nez insecticide. It had flourished in the time when codfish were hawked in the Place Sainte-Cécile; it was a hundred years old. The windows were rarely washed: it required a great effort to distinguish, through dust and mist, a crowd of tiny wax figures decked out in orange doublets, representing rats and mice. These animals were disembarking from a high-decked ship, leaning on sticks; barely had they touched the ground when a peasant girl, attractively dressed but filthy and black with dirt, put them all to flight by sprinkling them with Tu-Pu-Nez. I liked this shop very much, it had a cynical and obstinate look, it insolently recalled the rights of dirt and vermin, only two paces from the most costly church in France.

The old herborist died last year and her nephew sold the house. It was enough to tear down a few walls: it is now a small lecture hall, "La Bonbonnière." Last year Henry Bordeaux gave a talk on Alpinism there.

You must not be in a hurry in the Rue Tournebride: the families walk slowly. Sometimes you move up a step because one family has turned into Foulon's or Piégeois'. But, at other times, you must stop and mark time because two families, one going up the street, the other coming down, have met and have solidly clasped hands. I go forward slowly. I stand a whole head above both columns and I see hats, a sea of hats. Most of them are black and hard. From time to time you see one fly off at the end of an arm and you catch the soft glint of a skull; then, after a few instants of heavy flight, it returns. At 16 Rue Tournebride, Urbain, the hatter, specializing in forage caps, has hung up as a symbol, an immense, red archbishop's hat whose gold tassels hang six feet from the ground.

A halt: a group has collected just under the tassels. My neighbour waits impatiently, his arms dangling: this little old man, pale and fragile as porcelain—I think he must be Coffier—president of the Chamber of Commerce. It seems he is intimidating because he never speaks. He lives on the summit of the Coteau Vert, in a great brick house whose windows are always wide open. It's over: the group has broken up. Another group

43

starts forming but it takes up less space: barely formed, it is pushed against Ghislaine's window front. The column does not even stop: it hardly makes a move to step aside; we are walking in front of six people who hold hands: "Bonjour, Monsieur, bonjour cher Monsieur, comment allez-vous? Do put your hat on again, you'll catch cold; Thank you, Madame, it isn't very warm out, is it? My dear, let me present Doctor Lefrançois; Doctor, I am very glad to make your acquaintance, my husband always speaks of Doctor Lefrançois who took such care of him, but do put your hat on, Doctor, you'll catch cold. But a doctor would get well quickly; Alas! Madame, doctors are the least well looked after; the Doctor is a remarkable musician. Really, Doctor? But I never knew, you play the violin? The Doctor is very gifted."

The little old man next to me is surely Coffier; one of the women of the group, the brunette, is devouring him with her eyes, all the while smiling at the Doctor. She seems to be thinking, "There's Monsieur Coffier, president of the Chamber of Commerce; how intimidating he looks, they say he's so frigid." But M. Coffier deigns to see nothing: these people are from the Boulevard Maritime, they do not belong to his world. Since I have been coming to this street to see the Sunday hat-raising, I have learned to distinguish people from the Boulevard and people from the Coteau. When a man wears a new overcoat, a soft felt hat, a dazzling shirt, when he creates a vacuum in passing, there's no mistaking it: he is someone from the Boulevard Maritime. You know people from the Coteau Vert by some kind of shabby, sunken look. They have narrow shoulders and an air of insolence on their worn faces. This fat gentleman holding a child by the hand—I'd swear he comes from the Coteau: his face is all grey and his tie knotted like a string.

The fat man comes near us: he stares at M. Coffier. But, just before he crosses his path, he turns his head away and begins joking in a fatherly way with his little boy. He takes a few more steps, bent over his son, his eyes gazing in the child's eyes, nothing but a father; then suddenly he turns quickly towards us, throws a quick glance at the little old man and makes an ample, quick salute with a sweep of his arm. Disconcerted, the little boy has not taken off his hat: this is an affair between grown-ups.

At the corner of the Rue Basse-de-Vieille our column abuts into a column of the faithful coming out of Mass: a dozen persons rush forward, shaking each other's hand and whirling round, but the hat-raising is over too quickly for me to catch the details; the Eglise Sainte-Cécile stands a monstrous mass above the fat, pale crowd: chalk white against a sombre sky; its sides hold a little of the night's darkness behind these shining walls. We are off again in a slightly modified order. M. Coffier has been pushed behind me. A lady dressed in navy blue is glued to my left side. She has come from Mass. She blinks her eyes, a little dazzled at coming into the light of morning. The gentleman walking in front of her, who has such a thin neck, is her husband.

On the other side of the street a gentleman, holding his wife by the arm, has just whispered a few words in her ear and has started to smile. She immediately wipes all expression from her chalky, cream coloured face and blindly takes a few steps. There is no mistaking these signs: they are going to greet somebody. Indeed, after a moment, the gentleman throws his hands up. When his fingers reach his felt hat, they hesitate a second before coming down delicately on the crown. While he slowly raises his hat, bowing his head a little to help its removal, his wife gives a little start and forces a young smile on her face. A bowing shadow passes them: but their twin smiles do not disappear immediately: they stay on their lips a few instants by a sort of magnetism. The lady and gentleman have regained their impassibility by the time they pass me, but a certain air of gaiety still lingers around their mouths.

It's finished: the crowd is less congested, the hat-raisings less frequent, the shop windows have something less exquisite about them: I am at the end of the Rue Tournebride. Shall I cross and go up the street on the other side? I think I have had enough: I have seen enough pink skulls, thin, distinguished and faded countenances. I am going to cross the Place Marignan. As I cautiously extricate myself from the column, the face of a real gentleman in a black hat springs up near me. The husband of the lady in navy blue. Ah, the fine, long dolichocephalic skull planted with short, wiry hair, the handsome American moustache sown with silver threads. And the smile, above all, the admirable, cultivated smile. There is also an eyeglass, somewhere on a nose.

Turning to his wife he says:

"He's a new factory designer. I wonder what he can be doing here. He's a good boy, he's timid and he amuses me."

Standing against the window of Julien, the pork butcher's shop, the young designer who has just done his hair, still pink,

45

his eyes lowered, an obstinate look on his face, has all the appearance of a voluptuary. This is undoubtedly the first Sunday he has dared cross the Rue Tournebride. He looks like a lad who has been to his First Communion. He has crossed his hands behind his back and turned his face towards the window with an air of exciting modesty; without appearing to see, he looks at four small sausages shining in gelatine, spread out on a bed of parsley.

A woman comes out of the shop and takes his arm. His wife. She is quite young, despite her pocked skin. She can stroll along the Rue Tournebride as much as she likes, no one will mistake her for a lady; she is betrayed by the cynical sparkle of her eyes, by her sophisticated look. Real ladies do not know the price of things, they like adorable follies; their eyes are like beautiful, hothouse flowers.

I reach the Brasserie Vézelise on the stroke of one. The old men are there as usual. Two of them have already started to eat. Four are playing cards and drinking apéritifs. The others are standing, watching them play while their table is being laid. The biggest, the one with a flowing beard, is a stockbroker. Another is a retired commissioner from the Inscription Maritime. They eat and drink like men of twenty. They eat sauerkraut on Sunday. The late arrivals question the others who are already eating:

"The usual Sunday sauerkraut?"

They sit down and breathe sighs of relaxation:

"Mariette, dear, a beer without a head and a sauerkraut."

This Mariette is a buxom wench. As I sit down at a table in the back a red-faced old man begins coughing furiously while being served with a vermouth.

"Come on, pour me out a little more," he says, coughing. But she grows angry herself: she hadn't finished pouring:

"Well, let me pour, will you? Who said anything to you? You holler before you're hurt."

The others begin to laugh.

"*Touché!*"

The stockbroker, going to his seat, takes Mariette by the shoulders:

"It's Sunday, Mariette. I guess we have our boyfriend to take us to the movies?"

"Oh sure! This is Antoinette's day off. I've got a date in here all day."

The stockbroker has taken a chair opposite the clean-shaven, lugubrious-looking old man. The clean-shaven old man immediately begins an animated story. The stockbroker does not listen to him: he makes faces and pulls at his beard. They never listen to each other.

I recognize my neighbours: small businessmen in the neighbourhood. Sunday is their maids' day off. So they come here, always sitting at the same table. The husband eats a fine rib of underdone beef. He looks at it closely and smells it from time to time. The wife picks at her plate. A heavy blonde woman of forty with red, downy cheeks. She has fine, hard breasts under her satin blouse. Like a man, she polishes off a bottle of Bordeaux at every meal.

I am going to read *Eugénie Grandet*. It isn't that I get any great pleasure out of it: but I have to do something. I open the book at random: the mother and daughter are speaking of Eugénie's growing love:

Eugénie kissed her hand saying:

"How good you are, dear Mama!"

At these words, the maternal old face, worn with long suffering, lights up.

"Don't you think he's nice?" Eugénie asked.

Mme Grandet answered only by a smile; then, after a moment of silence, she lowered her voice and said:

"Could you love him already? It would be wrong."

"Wrong?" Eugénie repeated. "Why? You like him, Nanon likes him, why shouldn't I like him? Now, Mama, let's set the table for his luncheon."

She dropped her work, her mother did likewise, saying:

"You are mad."

But she wanted to justify her daughter's madness by sharing it.

Eugénie called Nanon:

"What do you want, Mam'selle?"

"You'll have cream for noon, Nanon?"

"Ah, for noon—yes," the old servant answered.

"Well, give him his coffee very strong. I heard M. des Grassins say that they make coffee very strong in Paris. Put in a lot."

"Where do you want me to get it?"

"Buy some."

"And if Monsieur sees me?"

"He's out in the fields."

My neighbours had been silent ever since I had come, but, suddenly, the husband's voice distracted me from my reading.

The husband, amused and mysterious:

"Say, did you see that?"

The woman gives a start and looks, coming out of a dream. He eats and drinks, then starts again, with the same malicious air:

"Ha ha!"

A moment of silence, the woman has fallen back into her dream.

Suddenly she shudders and asks:

"What did you say?"

"Suzanne, yesterday."

"Ah, yes," the woman says, "she went to see Victor."

"What did I tell you?"

The woman pushes her plate aside impatiently.

"It's no good."

The side of her plate is adorned with lumps of gristle she spits out. The husband follows his idea.

"That little woman there . . ."

He stops and smiles vaguely. Across from us, the old stock-broker is stroking Mariette's arm and breathing heavily. After a moment:

"I told you so, the other day."

"What did you tell me?"

"Victor—that she'd go and see him. What's the matter?" he asks brusquely with a frightened look, "don't you like that?"

"It's no good."

"It isn't the same any more," he says with importance, "it isn't the way it was in Hécart's time. Do you know where he is, Hécart?"

"Domremy, isn't he?"

"Yes, who told you?"

"You did. You told me Sunday."

She eats a morsel of crumb which is scattered on the paper tablecloth. Then, her hand smoothing the paper on the edge of the table, with hesitation:

"You know, you're mistaken, Suzanne is more . . ."

"That may well be, my dear, that may well be," he answers, distractedly. He tries to catch Mariette's eyes, makes a sign to her.

"It's hot."

Mariette leans familiarly on the edge of the table.

"Yes, it is hot," the woman says, sighing deeply, "it's stifling here and besides the beef's no good, I'm going to tell the manager, it's not the way it used to be, do open the window a little, Mariette."

Amused, the husband continues:

"Say, didn't you see her eyes?"

"When, darling?"

He apes her impatiently:

"When, darling! That's you all over: in summer, when it snows."

"Ah! you mean yesterday?"

He laughs, looks into the distance, and recites quickly, with a certain application:

"The eyes of a cat on live coals."

He is so pleased that he seems to have forgotten what he wanted to say.

She laughs in her turn, without malice:

"Ha ha, old devil!"

She taps on his shoulder.

"Old devil, old devil!"

He repeats, with assurance:

"The eyes of a cat on live coals!"

But she stops laughing:

"No, seriously, you know, she's really respectable."

He leans over, whispers a long story in her ear. Her mouth hangs open for a moment, the face a little drawn like someone who is going to burst out laughing, then suddenly she throws herself back and claws at his hands.

"It isn't true, it isn't true."

He says, in a considered way:

"Listen to me, my pet, will you; since he said so himself. If it weren't true why should he have said it?"

"No, no."

"But he said so: listen, suppose . . ."

She began to laugh:

"I'm laughing because I'm thinking about René."

"Yes."

He laughs too. She goes on in a low, earnest voice:

"So he noticed it Tuesday."

"Thursday."

"No, Tuesday, you know because of the . . ."

She sketches a sort of ellipsis in the air.

A long silence. The husband dips his bread in the gravy, Mariette changes the plates and brings them tart. I too shall

49

want a tart. Suddenly the woman, a little dreamy, with a proud and somewhat shocked smile on her lips, says in a slow, dragging voice:

"Oh no, now come."

There is so much sensuality in her voice that it stirs him: he strokes the back of her neck with his fat hand.

"Charles, stop, you're getting me excited, darling," she murmurs, smiling, her mouth full.

I try to go back to my reading:

"Where do you want me to get it?"

"Buy some."

"And if Monsieur sees me?"

But I still hear the woman, she says:

"Say, I'm going to make Marthe laugh, I'm going to tell her . . ."

My neighbours are silent. After the tart, Mariette serves them prunes and the woman is busy, gracefully laying stones in her spoon. The husband staring at the ceiling, taps out a rhythm on the table. You might think that silence was their normal state and speech a fever that sometimes takes them.

"Where do you want me to get it?"

"Buy some."

I close the book. I'm going out for a walk.

It was almost three o'clock when I came out of the Brasserie vézelise; I felt the afternoon all through my heavy body. Not my afternoon, but theirs, the one a hundred thousand Bouvillois were going to live in common. At this same time, after the long and copious Sunday meal, they were getting up from the table, for them something had died. Sunday had spent its fleeting youth. You had to digest the chicken and the tart, get dressed to go out.

The bell of the Ciné-Eldorado resounded in the clear air. This is a familiar Sunday noise, this ringing in broad daylight. More than a hundred people were lined up along the green wall. They were greedily awaiting the hour of soft shadows, of relaxation, abandon, the hour when the screen, glowing like a white stone under water, would speak and dream for them. Vain desire: something would stay, taut in them: they were too afraid someone would spoil their lovely Sunday. Soon, as every Sunday, they would be disappointed: the film would be ridiculous, their neighbour would be smoking a pipe and spitting between his knees or else Lucien would be disagreeable, he wouldn't have a decent word to say, or else, as if on purpose, just for today, for the one time they went to the movies their intercostal neural-gia would start up again. Soon, as on every Sunday, small, mute rages would grow in the darkened hall.

I followed the calm Rue Bressan. The sun had broken through the clouds, it was a fine day. A family had just come out of a villa called "The Wave." The daughter was buttoning her gloves, standing on the pavement. She could have been about thirty. The mother, planted on the first step, was looking straight ahead with an assured air, breathing heavily. I could only see the enormous back of the father. Bent over the keyhole, he was closing the door and locking it. The house would remain black and empty till they got back. In the neighbouring houses, already bolted and deserted, the floor and furniture creaked gently. Before going out they had put out the fire in the dining-room fire-place. The father rejoins the two women, and the family walks away without a word. Where were they going? On Sunday you go to the memorial cemetery or you visit your parents, or, if you're completely free, you go for a walk along the jetty. I was free: I followed the Rue Bressan which leads to the Jetty Promenade.

The sky was pale blue: a few wisps of smoke, and from time to time, a fleeting cloud passed in front of the sun. In the distance I could see the white cement balustrade which runs along the Jetty Promenade; the sea glittered through the inter-stices. The family turns right on the Rue de l'Aumônier-Hilaire which climbs up the Coteau Vert. I saw them mount slowly, making three black stains against the sparkling asphalt. I turned left and joined the crowd streaming towards the sea.

There was more of a mixture than in the morning. It seemed as though all these men no longer had strength to sustain this fine social hierarchy they were so proud of before luncheon. Businessmen and officials walked side by side; they let them-selves be elbowed, even jostled out of the way by shabby em-ployees. Aristocrats, élite, and professional groups had melted into the warm crowd. Only scattered men were left who were not representative.

A puddle of light in the distance—the sea at low tide. Only a few reefs broke the clear surface. Fishing smacks lay on the sand not far from sticky blocks of stone which had been thrown pell-mell at the foot of the jetty to protect it from the waves, and through the interstices the sea rumbled. At the entrance to the outer harbour, against the sun-bleached sky, a dredge defined its shadow. Every evening until midnight it howls and groans and makes the devil of a noise. But on Sunday the workers are strolling over the land, there is only a watchman on board: there is silence.

The sun was clear and diaphanous like white wine. Its light barely touched the moving figures, gave them no shadow, no relief: faces and hands made spots of pale gold. All these men in topcoats seemed to float idly a few inches above the ground. From time to time the wind cast shadows against us which trembled like water; faces were blotted out for an instant, chalky white.

It was Sunday; massed between the balustrade and the gates of residents' chalets, the crowd dispersed slowly, forming itself into a thousand rivulets behind the "Grand Hôtel de la Compagnie Transatlantique." And children! Children in carriages, children in arms, held by the hand, or walking by twos and threes, in front of their parents, with a stiff and formal look. I had seen all these faces a little while before, almost triumphant in the youth of a Sunday morning. Now, dripping with sunlight, they expressed nothing more than calm, relaxation and a sort of obstinacy.

Little movement: there was still a little hat-raising here and there, but without the expansiveness, the nervous gaiety of the morning. The people all let themselves lean back a little, head high, looking into the distance, abandoned to the wind which swept them and swelled out their coats. From time to time, a short laugh, quickly stifled, the call of a mother, *Jeannot, Jeannot, come here.* And then silence. A faint aroma of pale tobacco: the commercial travellers are smoking it. Salammbô, Aicha; Sunday cigarettes. I thought I could detect sadness on some of the more relaxed faces: but no, these people were neither sad nor gay: they were at rest. Their wide-open, staring eyes passively reflected sea and sky. They would soon go back, drink a cup of family tea together round the dining-room table. For the moment they wanted to live with the least expenditure, economize words, gestures, thoughts, float: they had only one day in which to smooth out their wrinkles, their crow's feet, the bitter lines made by a hard week's work. One day only. They felt the minutes flowing between their fingers; would they have time to store up enough youth to start anew on Monday morning? They filled their lungs because sea air vivifies: only their breathing, deep and regular as that of sleepers, still testified that they were alive. I walked stealthily, I didn't know what to do with my hard, vigorous body in the midst of this tragic, relaxed crowd.

The sea was now the colour of slate; it was rising slowly. By night it would be high; tonight the Jetty Promenade would be more deserted than the Boulevard Victor-Noir. In front and on the left, a red fire would burn in the channel.

The sun went down slowly over the sea. In passing, it lit up the window a Norman chalet. A woman, dazzled by it, wearily brought her hand to her eyes, and shook her head.

"Gaston, it's blinding me," she says with a little laugh.

"Hey, that sun's all right," her husband says, "it doesn't keep you warm but it's a pleasure to watch it."

Turning to the sea, she spoke again:

"I thought we might have seen it."

"Not a chance," the man says, "it's in the sun."

They must have been talking about the Ile Caillebotte whose southern tip could sometimes be seen between the dredge and the quay of the outer-harbour.

The light grows softer. At this uncertain hour one felt evening drawing in. Sunday was already past. The villas and grey balustrade seemed only yesterday. One by one the faces lost their leisured look, several became almost tender.

A pregnant woman leaned against a fair, brutal-looking young man.

"There, there . . . there, look," she said.

"What?"

"There . . . there . . . the seagulls."

He shrugged: there were no seagulls. The sky had become almost pure, a little blush on the horizon.

"I heard them. Listen, they're crying. . . ."

He answered:

"Something's creaking, that's all."

A gas lamp glowed. I thought the lamplighter had already passed. The children watch for him because he gives the signal for them to go home. But it was only a last ray of the setting sun. The sky was still clear, but the earth was bathed in shadow. The crowd was dispersing, you could distinctly hear the death rattle of the sea. A young woman, leaning with both hands on the balustrade, raised her blue face towards the sky, barred in black by lip-stick. For a moment I wondered if I were not going to love humanity. But, after all, it was their Sunday, not mine.

The first light to go on was that of the lighthouse on the Ile

53

Caillebotte; a little boy stopped near me and murmured in ecstasy, "Oh, the lighthouse!"

Then I felt my heart swell with a great feeling of adventure.

*   *   *   *   *

I turn left and, through the Rue des Voiliers, rejoin the Little Prado. The iron shutters have been lowered on all the shop windows. The Rue Tournebride is light but deserted, it has lost its brief glory of the morning; nothing distinguishes it any longer from the neighbouring streets. A fairly strong wind has come up. I hear the archbishop's metal hat creaking.

I am alone, most of the people have gone back home, they are reading the evening paper, listening to the radio. Sunday has left them with a taste of ashes and their thoughts are already turning towards Monday. But for me there is neither Monday nor Sunday: there are days which pass in disorder, and then, sudden lightning like this one.

Nothing has changed and yet everything is different. I can't describe it; it's like the Nausea and yet it's just the opposite: at last an adventure happens to me and when I question myself I see that it happens *that I am myself and that I am here;* I am the one who splits the night, I am as happy as the hero of a novel.

Something is going to happen: something is waiting for me in the shadow of the Rue Basse-de-Vieille, it is over there, just at the corner of this calm street that my life is going to begin. I see myself advancing with a sense of fatality. There is a sort of white milestone at the corner of the street. From far away, it seemed black and, at each stride, it takes on a whiter colour. This dark body which grows lighter little by little makes an extraordinary impression on me: when it becomes entirely clear, entirely white, I shall stop just beside it and the adventure will begin. It is so close now, this white beacon which comes out of the shadows, that I am almost afraid: for a moment I think of turning back. But it is impossible to break the spell. I advance, I stretch out my hand and touch the stone.

Here is the Rue Basse-de-Vieille and the enormous mass of Sainte-Cécile crouching in the shadow, its windows glowing. The metal hat creaks. I do not know whether the whole world has suddenly shrunk or whether I am the one who unifies all sounds and shapes: I cannot even conceive of anything around me being other than what it is.

I stop for a moment, I wait, I feel my heart beating; my

eyes search the empty square. I see nothing. A fairly strong wind has risen. I am mistaken. The Rue Basse-de-Vieille was only a stage: the *thing* is waiting for me at the end of the Place Ducoton.

I am in no hurry to start walking again. It seems as if I had touched the goal of my happiness. In Marseilles, in Shanghai, Meknes, what wouldn't I have done to achieve such satisfaction? I expect nothing more today, I'm going home at the end of an empty Sunday: it is there.

I leave again. The wail of a siren comes to me on the wind. I am all alone, but I march like a regiment descending on a city. At this very moment there are ships on the sea resounding with music; lights are turned on in all the cities of Europe; Communists and Nazis shooting it out in the streets of Berlin, unemployed pounding the pavements of New York, women at their dressing-tables in a warm room putting mascara on their eyelashes. And I am here, in this deserted street and each shot from a window in Neukölln, each hiccough of the wounded being carried away, each precise gesture of women at their toilet answers to my every step, my every heartbeat.

I don't know what to do in front of the Passage Gillet. Isn't anyone waiting for me at the end of the passage? But there is also at the Place Ducoton at the end of the Rue Tournebride something which needs me in order to come to life. I am full of anguish: the slightest movement irks me. I can't imagine what they want with me. Yet I must choose: I surrender the Passage Gillet, I shall never know what had been reserved for me.

The Place Ducoton is empty. Am I mistaken? I don't think I could stand it. Will nothing really happen? I go towards the lights of the Café Mably. I am lost, I don't know whether I'm going in: I glance through the large, steamed windows.

The place is full. The air is blue with cigarette smoke and steam rising from damp clothing. The cashier is at her counter. I know her well: she's red haired, as I am; she has some sort of stomach trouble. She is rotting quietly under her skirts with a melancholy smile, like the odour of violets given off by a decomposing body. A shudder goes through me: she . . . she is the one who was waiting for me. She was there, standing erect above the counter, smiling. From the far end of the café something returns which helps to link the scattered moments of that Sunday and solder them together and which gives them a meaning. I have spent the whole day only to end there, with my nose glued against the window, to gaze at this delicate face blossoming against the red curtain. All has stopped; my life has stopped: this wide window, this heavy air, blue as water, this fleshy white plant at the bottom of the water, and I myself, we form a complete and static whole: I am happy.

When I found myself on the Boulevard de la Redoute again nothing was left but bitter regret. I said to myself: Perhaps there is nothing in the world I cling to as much as this feeling of adventure; but it comes when it pleases; it is gone so quickly and how empty I am once it has left. Does it, ironically, pay me these short visits in order to show me that I have wasted my life?

Behind me, in the town, along the great, straight streets lit up by the cold reflection from the lamp posts, a formidable social event was dissolving. Sunday was at an end.

Monday:

How could I have written that pompous, absurd sentence yesterday:

"I was alone but I marched like a regiment descending on a city."

I do not need to make phrases. I write to bring certain circumstances to light. Beware of literature. I must follow the pen, without looking for words.

At heart, what disgusts me is having been so sublime last evening. When I was twenty I used to get drunk and then explain that I was a fellow in the style of Descartes. I knew I was inflating myself with heroism, but I let myself go, it pleased me. After that, the next morning I felt as sick as if I had awakened in a bed full of vomit. I never vomit when I'm drunk but that would really be better. Yesterday I didn't even have the excuse of drunkenness. I got excited like an imbecile. I must wash myself clean with abstract thoughts, transparent as water.

This feeling of adventure definitely does not come from events: I have proved it. It's rather the way in which the moments are linked together. I think this is what happens: you suddenly feel that time is passing, that each instant leads to another, this one to another one, and so on; that each instant is annihilated, and that it isn't worth while to hold it back, etc., etc. And then you attribute this property to events which appear to you *in* the instants; what belongs to the form you carry over to the content. You talk a lot about this amazing flow of time but you hardly see it. You see a woman, you think that one day she'll be

56

old, only you don't see her grow old. But there are moments when you think you *see* her grow old and feel yourself growing old with her: this is the feeling of adventure.

If I remember correctly, they call that the irreversibility of time. The feeling of adventure would simply be that of the irreversibility of time. But why don't we always have it? Is it that time is not always irreversible? There are moments when you have the impression that you can do what you want, go forward or backward, that it has no importance; and then other times when you might say that the links have been tightened and, in that case, it's not a question of missing your turn because you could never start again.

Anny made the most of time. When she was in Djibouti and I was in Aden, and I used to go and see her for twenty-four hours, she managed to multiply the misunderstandings between us until there were only exactly sixty minutes before I had to leave; sixty minutes, just long enough to make you feel the seconds passing one by one. I remember one of those terrible evenings. I was supposed to leave at midnight. We went to an open-air movie; we were desperate, she as much as I. Only she led the game. At eleven o'clock, at the beginning of the main picture, she took my hand and held it in hers without a word. I was flooded with a bitter joy and I understood, without having to look at my watch, that it was eleven o'clock. From that time on we began to feel the minutes passing. That time we were leaving each other for three months. At one moment they threw a completely blank image on the screen, the darkness lifted, and I saw Anny was crying. Then, at midnight, she let go of my hand, after pressing it violently; I got up and left without saying a word to her. That was a good job.

7.00 *p.m.*

Work today. It didn't go too badly; I wrote six pages with a certain amount of pleasure. The more so since it was a question of abstract considerations on the reign of Paul I. After last evening's orgy I stayed tightly buttoned up all day. It would not do to appeal to my heart! But I felt quite at ease unwinding the mainsprings of the Russian autocracy.

But this Rollebon annoys me. He is mysterious in the smallest things. What could he have been doing in the Ukraine in 1804? He tells of his trip in veiled words:

"Posterity will judge whether my efforts, which no success

could recompense, did not merit something better than a brutal denial and all the humiliations which had to be borne in silence, when I had locked in my breast the wherewithal to silence the scoffers once and for all."

I let myself be caught once: he showed himself full of pompous reticence on the subject of a short trip he took to Bouville in 1790. I lost a month verifying his assertions. Finally, it came out that he had made the daughter of one of his tenant farmers pregnant. Can it be that he is nothing more than a low comedian?

I feel full of ill-will towards this lying little fop; perhaps it is spite: I was quite pleased that he lied to others but I would have liked him to make an exception of me; I thought we were thick as thieves and that he would finally tell me the truth. He told me nothing, nothing at all; nothing more than he told Alexander or Louis XVIII whom he duped. It matters a lot to me that Rollebon should have been a good fellow. Undoubtedly a rascal: who isn't? But a big or little rascal? I don't have a high enough opinion of historical research to lose my time over a dead man whose hand, if he were alive, I would not deign to touch. What do I know about him? You couldn't dream of a better life than his: but did he live it? If only his letters weren't so formal. . . . Ah, I wish I had known his look, perhaps he had a charming way of leaning his head on his shoulder or mischievously placing his long index on his nose, or sometimes, between two polished lies, having a sudden fit of violence which he stifled immediately. But he is dead: all that is left of him is "A Treatise on Strategy" and "Reflexions on Virtue."

I could imagine him so well if I let myself go: beneath his brilliant irony which made so many victims, he was simple, almost naïve. He thinks little, but at all times, by a profound intuition, he does exactly what should be done. His rascality is candid, spontaneous, generous, as sincere as his love of virtue. And when he betrays his benefactors and friends, he turns back gravely to the events, and draws a moral from them. He never thought he had the slightest right over others, any more than others over him: he considered as unjustified and gratuitous the gifts life gave him. He attached himself strongly to everything but detaches himself easily. He never wrote his own letters or his works himself: but had them composed by the public scribe.

But if this is where it all leads me, I'd be better off writing a novel on the Marquis de Rollebon.

11.00 *p.m.*

I dined at the *Rendezvous des Cheminots*. The patronne was there and I had to kiss her, but it was mainly out of politeness. She disgusts me a little, she is too white and besides, she smells like a newborn child. She pressed my head against her breast in a burst of passion: she thinks it is the right thing. I played distractedly with her sex under the cover; then my arm went to sleep. I thought about de Rollebon: after all, why shouldn't I write a novel on his life? I let my arm run along the woman's thigh and suddenly saw a small garden with low, wide trees on which immense hairy leaves were hanging. Ants were running everywhere, centipedes and ringworm. There were even more horrible animals: their bodies were made from a slice of toast, the kind you put under roast pigeons; they walked sideways with legs like a crab. The larger leaves were black with beasts. Behind the cactus and the Barbary fig trees, the Velleda of the public park pointed a finger at her sex. "This park smells of vomit," I shouted.

"I didn't want to wake you up," the woman said, "but the sheet got folded under my back and besides I have to go down and look after the customers from the Paris train."

Shrove Tuesday:

I gave Maurice Barrès a spanking. We were three soldiers and one of us had a hole in the middle of his face. Maurice Barrès came up to us and said, "That's fine!" and he gave each of us a small bouquet of violets. "I don't know where to put them," said the soldier with the hole in his head. Then Maurice Barrès said, "Put them in the hole you have in your head." The soldier answered, "I'm going to stick them up your ass." And we turned over Maurice Barrès and took his pants off. He had a cardinal's red robe on under his trousers. We lifted up the robe and Maurice Barrès began to shout: "Look out! I've got on trousers with foot-straps." But we spanked him until he bled and then we took the petals of violets and drew the face of Déroulède on his backside.

For some time now I have been remembering my dreams much too often. Moreover, I must toss quite a bit because every morning I find the blankets on the floor. Today is Shrove Tuesday but that means very little in Bouville; in the whole town there are hardly a hundred people to dress up.

As I was going down the stairs the landlady called me:

"There's a letter for you."

A letter: the last one I got was from the curator of the Rouen public library, last May. The landlady leads me to her office and holds out a long thick yellow envelope: Anny had written to me. I hadn't heard from her for five years. The letter had been sent to my old Paris address, it was postmarked the first of February.

I go out; I hold the envelope between my fingers, I dare not open it: Anny hasn't changed her letter paper, I wonder if she still buys it at the little stationer's in Piccadilly. I think that she has also kept her coiffure, her heavy blonde locks she didn't want to cut. She must struggle patiently in front of mirrors to save her face: it isn't vanity or fear of growing old; she wants to stay as she is, just as she is. Perhaps this is what I liked best in her, this austere loyalty to her most insignificant features.

The firm letters of the address, written in violet ink (she hasn't changed her ink, either) still shine a little:

"Monsieur Antoine Roquentin"

How I love to read my name on envelopes. In a mist I have recaptured one of her smiles, I can see her eyes, her inclined head: whenever I sat down she would come and plant herself in front of me, smiling. She stood half a head higher than I, she grasped my shoulders and shook me with outstretched arms.

The envelope is heavy, it must have at least six pages in it. My old concierge has scrawled hieroglyphics over this lovely writing:

"Hotel Printania—Bouville"

These small letters do not shine.

When I open the letter my disillusion makes me six years younger:

I don't know how Anny manages to fill up her envelopes: there's never anything inside.

That sentence—I said it a hundred times during the spring of 1924, struggling, as today, to extract a piece of paper, folded in four, from its lining. The lining is a splendour: dark green with gold stars; you'd think it was a heavy piece of starched cloth. It alone makes three-quarters of the envelope's weight.

Anny had written in pencil:

"I am passing through Paris in a few days. Come and see me at the Hotel d'Espagne, on February 20. Please! (she had

60

added 'I beg you' above the line and joined it to 'to see me' in a curious spiral). I *must* see you. Anny."

In Meknes, in Tangiers, when I went back, in the evening, I sometimes used to find a note on my bed: "I want to see you right away." I used to run, Anny would open the door for me, her eyebrows raised, looking surprised. She had nothing more to tell me; she was even a little irritated that I had come. I'll go; she may refuse to see me. Or they may tell me at the desk: "No one by that name is stopping here." I don't believe she'd do that. Only she could write me, a week from now and tell me she's changed her mind and to make it some other time.

People are at work. This is a flat and stale Shrove Tuesday. The Rue des Mutilés smells strongly of damp wood, as it does every time it's going to rain. I don't like these queer days: the movies have matinées, the school children have a vacation; there is a vague feeling of holiday in the air which never ceases to attract attention but disappears as soon as you notice it.

I am undoubtedly going to see Anny but I can't say that the idea makes me exactly joyous. I have felt *désoeuvré* ever since I got her letter. Luckily it is noon; I'm not hungry but I'm going to eat to pass the time. I go to Camille's, in the Rue des Horlogers.

It's a quiet place; they serve sauerkraut or cassoulet all night. People go there for supper after the theatre; policemen send travellers there who arrive late at night and are hungry. Eight marble tables. A leather bench runs along the walls. Two mirrors eaten away by rust spots. The panes of the two windows and the door are frosted glass. The counter is in a recess in the back. There is also a room on the side. But I have never been in it; it is reserved for couples.

"Give me a ham omelet."

The waitress, an enormous girl with red cheeks, can never keep herself from giggling when she speaks to a man.

"I'm afraid I can't. Do you want a potato omelet? The ham's locked up: the patron is the only one who cuts it."

I order a cassoulet. The patron's name is Camille, a hard man.

The waitress goes off. I am alone in this dark old room. There is a letter from Anny in my despatch case. A false shame keeps me from reading it again. I try to remember the phrases one by one.

"My Dear Antoine——"

I smile: certainly not, Anny certainly did not write "My Dear Antoine."

Six years ago—we had just separated by mutual agreement—I decided to leave for Tokyo. I wrote her a few words. I could no longer call her "my dear love"; in all innocence I began, "My Dear Anny."

"I admire your cheek," she answered, "I have never been and am not your dear Anny. And I must ask you to believe that you are not my dear Antoine. If you don't know what to call me, don't call me anything, it's better that way."

I take her letter from my despatch case. She did not write "My Dear Antoine." Nor was there anything further at the end of the letter: "I must see you. Anny." Nothing that could give me any indication of her feelings. I can't complain: I recognize her love of perfection there. She always wanted to have "perfect moments." If the time was not convenient, she took no more interest in anything, her eyes became lifeless, she dragged along lazily like a great awkward girl. Or else she would pick a quarrel with me:

"You blow your nose solemnly like a bourgeois, and you cough very carefully in your handkerchief."

It was better not to answer, just wait: suddenly, at some signal which escapes me now, she shuddered, her fine languishing features hardened and she began her ant's work. She had an imperious and charming magic; she hummed between her teeth, looking all around, then straightened herself up smiling, came to shake me by the shoulders, and, for a few instants, seemed to give orders to the objects that surrounded her. She explained to me, in a low rapid voice, what she expected of me.

"Listen, do you want to make an effort or don't you? You were so stupid the last time. Don't you see how beautiful this moment could be? Look at the sky, look at the colour of the sun on the carpet. I've got my green dress on and my face isn't made up, I'm quite pale. Go back, go and sit in the shadow; you understand what you have to do? Come on! How stupid you are! Speak to me!"

I felt that the success of the enterprise was in my hands: the moment had an obscure meaning which had to be trimmed and perfected; certain motions had to be made, certain words spoken: I staggered under the weight of my responsibility. I stared and saw nothing, I struggled in the midst of rites which

Anny invented on the spot and tore them to shreds with my strong arms. At those times she hated me.

Certainly, I would go to see her. I still respect and love her with all my heart. I hope that someone else has had better luck and skill in the game of perfect moments.

"Your damned hair spoils everything," she said. "What can you do with a red-head?"

She smiled. First I lost the memory of her eyes, then the memory of her long body. I kept her smile as long as possible and then, finally lost that three years ago. Just now, brusquely, as I was taking the letter from the landlady's hands, it came back to me; I thought I saw Anny smiling. I try to refresh my memory: I need to feel all the tendernes that Anny inspires; it is there, this tenderness, it is near me, only asking to be born. But the smile does not return: it is finished. I remain dry and empty.

A man comes in, shivering.

"Messieurs, dames, bonjour."

He sits down without taking off his greenish overcoat. He rubs his long hands, clasping and unclasping his fingers.

"What will you have?"

He gives a start, his eyes look worried:

"Eh? give me a Byrrh and water."

The waitress does not move. In the glass her face seems to sleep. Her eyes are indeed open but they are only slits. That's the way she is, she is never in a hurry to wait on customers, she always takes a moment to dream over their orders. She must allow herself the pleasure of imagining: I believe she's thinking about the bottle she's going to take from above the counter, the white label and red letters, the thick black syrup she is going to pour out: it's a little as though she were drinking it herself.

I slip Anny's letter back into my despatch case: she has done what she could; I cannot reach the woman who took it in her hands, folded and put it in the envelope. Is it possible even to think of someone in the past? As long as we loved each other, we never allowed the meanest of our instants, the smallest grief, to be detached and forgotten, left behind. Sounds, smells, nuances of light, even the thoughts we never told each other; we carried them all away and they remained alive: even now they have the power to give us joy and pain. Not a memory: an implacable, torrid love, without shadow, without escape, without shelter. Three years rolled into one. That is why we parted: we did not have enough strength to bear this burden. And then, when Anny left me, all of a sudden, all at once, the three years crumbled into the past. I didn't even suffer, I felt emptied out. Then time began to flow again and the emptiness grew larger. Then, in Saïgon when I decided to go back to France, all that was still left—strange faces, places, quays on the banks of long rivers—all was wiped out. Now my past is nothing more than an enormous vacuum. My present: this waitress in the black blouse dreaming near the counter, this man. It seems as though I have learned all I know of life in books. The palaces of Benares, the terrace of the Leper King, the temples of Java with their great broken steps, are reflected in my eyes for an instant, but they have remained there, on the spot. The tramway that passes in front of the Hotel Printania in the evening does not catch the reflection of the neon sign-board; it flames up for an instant, then goes on with black windows.

This little man has not stopped looking at me: he bothers me. He tries to give himself importance. The waitress has finally decided to serve him. She raises her great black arm lazily, reaches the bottle, and brings it to him with a glass.

"Here you are, Monsieur."

"Monsieur Achille," he says with urbanity.

She pours without answering; all of a sudden he takes his finger from his nose, places both hands flat on the table. He throws his head back and his eyes shine. He says in a cold voice:

"Poor girl."

The waitress gives a start and I start too: he has an indefinable expression, perhaps one of amazement, as if it were someone else who had spoken. All three of us are uncomfortable.

The fat waitress recovers first: she has no imagination. She measures M. Achille with dignity: she knows quite well that one hand alone would be enough to tear him from his seat and throw him out.

"And what makes you think I'm a poor girl?"

He hesitates. He looks taken aback, then he laughs. His face crumples up into a thousand wrinkles, he makes vague gestures with his wrist.

"She's annoyed. It was just to say something: I didn't mean to offend."

But she turns her back on him and goes behind the counter: she is really offended. He laughs again:

"Ha ha! You know that just slipped out. Are you cross? She's cross with me," he says, addressing himself vaguely to me.

I turn my head away. He raises his glass a little but he is not thinking about drinking: he blinks his eyes, looking surprised and intimidated; he looks as if he were trying to remember something. The waitress is sitting at the counter; she picks up her sewing. Everything is silent again: but it isn't the same silence. It's raining: tapping lightly against the frosted glass windows; if there are any more masked children in the street, the rain is going to spoil their cardboard masks.

The waitress turns on the lights: it is hardly two o'clock but the sky is all black, she can't see to sew. Soft glow: people are in their houses, they have undoubtedly turned on the lights too. They read, they watch the sky from the window. For them it means something different. They have aged differently. They live in the midst of legacies, gifts, each piece of furniture holds a memory. Clocks, medallions, portraits, shells, paperweights, screens, shawls. They have closets full of bottles, stuffs, old clothes, newspapers; they have kept everything. The past is a landlord's luxury.

Where shall I keep mine? You don't put your past in your pocket; you have to have a house. I have only my body: a man entirely alone, with his lonely body, cannot indulge in memories; they pass through him. I shouldn't complain: all I wanted was to be free.

The little man stirs and sighs. He is all wrapped in his overcoat but from time to time he straightens up and puts on a haughty look. He has no past either. Looking closely, you would undoubtedly find in a cousin's house a photograph showing him at a wedding, with a wing collar, stiff shirt and a slight, young man's moustache. Of myself I don't think that even that is left.

Here he is looking at me again. This time he's going to speak to me, and I feel all taut inside. There is no sympathy between us: we are alike, that's all. He is alone, as I am, but more sunken into solitude than I. He must be waiting for his own Nausea or something of that sort. Now there are still people who *recognize* me, who see me and think: "He's one of us." So? What does he want? He must know that we can do nothing for one another. The families are in their houses, in the midst of their memories. And here we are, two wanderers, without memory. If he were suddenly to stand up and speak to me, I'd jump into the air.

The door opens with a great to-do: it is Doctor Rogé.
"Good day everybody."

He comes in, ferocious and suspicious, swaying, swaying a little on his long legs which can barely support his body. I see him often, on Sundays, at the Brasserie Vézelise, but he doesn't know me. He is built like the old monitors at Joinville, arms like thighs, a chest measurement of 110, and he can't stand up straight.

"Jeanne, my little Jeanne."

He trots over to the coat rack to hang up his wide felt hat on the peg. The waitress has put away her sewing and comes without hurrying, sleep walking, to help the doctor out of his raincoat.

"What will you have, Doctor?"

He studies her gravely. That's what I call a handsome, masculine face. Worn, furrowed by life and passions. But the doctor has understood life, mastered his passions.

"I really don't know what I want," he says in a deep voice.

He has dropped onto the bench opposite me; he wipes his forehead. He feels at ease as soon as he gets off his feet. His great eyes, black and imperious, are intimidating.

"I'll have . . . I'll have . . . Oh, calvados. . . ."

The waitress, without making a move, studies this enormous, pitted face. She is dreamy. The little man raises his head with a smile of relief. And it is true: this colossus has freed us. Something horrible was going to catch us. I breathe freely: we are among men now.

"Well, is that calvados coming?"

The waitress gives a start and leaves. He has stretched out his stout arms and grasped the table at both ends. M. Achille is joyful; he would like to catch the doctor's eye. But he swings his legs and shifts about on the bench in vain, he is so thin that he makes no noise.

The waitress brings the calvados. With a nod of her head she points out the little man to the doctor. Doctor Rogé slowly turns: he can't move his neck.

"So it's you, you old swine," he shouts, "aren't you dead yet?"

He addresses the waitress:

"You let people like that in here?"

He stares at the little man ferociously. A direct look which puts everything in place. He explains:

"He's crazy as a loon, that's that."

He doesn't even take the trouble to let on that he's joking. He knows that the loony won't be angry, that he's going to smile.

And there it is: the man smiles with humility. A crazy loon: he relaxes, he feels protected against himself: nothing will happen to him today. I am reassured too. A crazy old loon: so that was it, so that was all.

The doctor laughs, he gives me an engaging, conspiratorial glance: because of my size, undoubtedly—and besides, I have a clean shirt on—he wants to let me in on his joke.

I do not laugh, I do not respond to his advances: then, without stopping to laugh, he turns the terrible fire of his eyes on me. We look at each other in silence for several seconds: he sizes me up, looking at me with half-closed eyes, up and down he places me. In the crazy loon category? In the tramp category?

Still, he is the one who turns his face away: allows himself to deflate before one lone wretch, without social importance, it isn't worth talking about—you can forget it right away. He rolls a cigarette and lights it, then stays motionless with his eyes hard and staring like an old man's.

The fine wrinkles; he has all of them: horizontal ones running across his forehead, crow's feet, bitter lines at each corner of the mouth, without counting the yellow cords depending from his chin. There's a lucky man: as soon as you perceive him, you can tell he must have suffered, that he is someone who has lived. He deserves his face for he has never, for one instant, lost an occasion of utilizing his past to the best of his ability: he has stuffed it full, used his experience on women and children, exploited them.

M. Achille is probably happier than he has ever been. He is agape with admiration; he drinks his Byrrh in small mouthfuls and swells his cheeks out with it. The doctor knew how to take him! The doctor wasn't the one to let himself be hypnotized by an old madman on the verge of having his fit; one good blow, a few rough, lashing words, that's what they need. The doctor has experience. He is a professional in experience: doctors, priests, magistrates and army officers know men through and through as if they had made them.

I am ashamed for M. Achille. We are on the same side, we should have stood up against them. But he left me, he went over to theirs: he honestly believes in experience. Not in his, not in mine. In Doctor Rogé's. A little while ago M. Achille felt queer, he felt lonely: now he knows that there are others like him, many others: Doctor Rogé has met them, he could tell M. Achille the case history of each one of them and tell him how they ended up.

M. Achille is simply a case and lets himself be brought back easily to the accepted ideas.

How I would like to tell him he's being deceived, that he is the butt of the important. Experienced professionals? They have dragged out their life in stupor and semi-sleep, they have married hastily, out of impatience, they have made children at random. They have met other men in cafés, at weddings and funerals. Sometimes, caught in the tide, they have struggled against it without understanding what was happening to them. All that has happened around them has eluded them; long, obscure shapes, events from afar, brushed by them rapidly and when they turned to look all had vanished. And then, around forty, they christen their small obstinacies and a few proverbs with the name of experience, they begin to simulate slot machines: put a coin in the left hand slot and you get tales wrapped in silver paper, put a coin in the slot on the right and you get precious bits of advice that stick to your teeth like caramels. As far as that goes, I too could have myself invited to people's houses and they'd say among themselves that I was a *"grand voyageur devant l'Eternel."* Yes: the Mohamedans squat to pass water; instead of ergot, Hindu midwives use ground glass in cow dung; in Borneo when a woman has her period she spends three days and nights on the roof of her house. In Venice I saw burials in gondolas, Holy Week festivals in Seville, I saw the Passion Play at Oberammergau. Naturally, that's just a small sample of all I know: I could lean back in a chair and begin amusement:

"Do you know Jihlava, Madame? It's a curious little town in Moravia where I stayed in 1924."

And the judge who has seen so many cases would add at the end of my story:

"How true it is, Monsieur, how human it is. I had a case just like that at the beginning of my career. It was in 1902. I was deputy judge in Limoges . . ."

But I was bothered too much by that when I was young. Yet I didn't belong to a professional family. There are also amateurs. These are secretaries, office workers, shopkeepers, people who listen to others in cafés: around forty they feel swollen, with an experience they can't get rid of. Luckily they've made children on whom they can pass it off. They would like to make us believe that their past is not lost, that their memories are condensed, gently transformed into Wisdom. Convenient past! Past handed out of a pocket! little gilt books full of fine sayings. "Believe me,

I'm telling you from experience, all I know I've learned from life." Has life taken charge of their thoughts? They explain the new by the old—and the old they explain by the older still, like those historians who turn a Lenin into a Russian Robespierre, and a Robespierre into a French Cromwell: when all is said and done, they have never understood anything at all. . . . You can imagine a morose idleness behind their importance: they see the long parade of pretences, they yawn, they think there's nothing new under the sun. "Crazy as a loon"—and Doctor Rogé vaguely recalls other crazy loons, not remembering any one of them in particular. Now, nothing M. Achille can do will surprise us: *because* he's a crazy loon!

He is not one: he is afraid. What is he afraid of? When you want to understand something you stand in front of it, alone, without help: all the past in the world is of no use. Then it disappears and what you wanted to understand disappears with it.

General ideas are more flattering. And then professionals and even amateurs always end up by being right. Their wisdom prompts them to make the least possible noise, to live as little as possible, to let themselves be forgotten. Their best stories are about the rash and the original, who were chastised. Yes, that's how it happens and no one will say the contrary. Perhaps M. Achille's conscience is not easy. Perhaps he tells himself he wouldn't be there if he had heeded his father's advice or his elder sister's. The doctor has the right to speak: he has not wasted his life; he has known how to make himself useful. He rises calm and powerful, above this flotsam and jetsam; he is a rock.

Doctor Rogé has finished his calvados. His great body relaxes and his eyelids droop heavily. For the first time I see his face without the eyes: like a cardboard mask, the kind they're selling in the shops today. His cheeks have a horrid pink colour. . . . The truth stares me in the face: this man is going to die soon. He surely knows; he need only look in the glass: each day he looks a little more like the corpse he will become. That's what their experience leads to, that's why I tell myself so often that they smell of death: it is their last defence. The doctor would like to believe, he would like to hide out the stark reality; that he is alone, without gain, without a past, with an intelligence which is clouded, a body which is disintegrating. For this reason he has carefully built up, furnished, and padded his nightmare compensation: he says he is making progress. Has he vacuums in his thoughts, moments when everything spins round in his head?

It's because his judgment no longer has the impulse of youth. He no longer understands what he reads in books? It's because he's so far away from books now. He can't make love any more? But he has made love in the past. Having made love is much better than still making it: looking back, he compares, ponders. And this terrible corpse's face! To be able to stand the sight of it in the glass he makes himself believe that the lessons of experience are graven on it.

The doctor turns his head a little. His eyelids are half-open and he watches me with the red eyes of sleep. I smile at him. I would like this smile to reveal all that he is trying to hide from himself. That would give him a jolt if he could say to himself: "There's someone who *knows* I'm going to die!" But his eyelids droop: he sleeps. I leave, letting M. Achille watch over his slumber.

The rain has stopped, the air is mild, the sky slowly rolls up fine black images: it is more than enough to frame a perfect moment; to reflect these images, Anny would cause dark little tides to be born in our hearts. I don't know how to take advantage of the occasion: I walk at random, calm and empty, under this wasted sky.

Wednesday:

I must not be afraid.

Thursday:

Four pages written. Then a long moment of happiness. Must not think too much about the value of History. You run the risk of being disgusted with it. Must not forget that de Rollebon now represents the only justification for my existence.

A week from today I'm going to see Anny.

Friday:

The fog was so thick on the Boulevard de la Redoute that I thought it wise to stick close to the walls of the Caserne; on my right, the headlights of cars chased a misty light before them and it was impossible to see the end of the pavement. There were people around me; I sometimes heard the sound of their steps or the low hum of their voices: but I saw no one. Once, a woman's face took shape somewhere at the height of my shoulder, but the fog engulfed it immediately; another time someone brushed by me breathing very heavily. I didn't know where I was going, I was too absorbed: you had to go ahead with caution, feel the ground with the end of your foot and even stretch your hands ahead of you. I got no pleasure from this exercise. Yet I wasn't thinking about going back, I was caught. Finally, after half an hour, I noticed a bluish vapour in the distance. Using this as a guide, I soon arrived at the edge of a great glow; in the centre, piercing the fog with its lights, I recognized the Café Mably.

The Café Mably has twelve electric lights, but only two of them were on, one above the counter, the other on the ceiling. The only waiter there pushed me forcibly into a dark corner.

"This way, Monsieur, I'm cleaning up."

He had on a jacket, without vest or collar, with a white and violet striped shirt. He was yawning, looking at me sourly, running his fingers through his hair.

"Black coffee and rolls."

He rubbed his eyes without answering and went away. I was up to my eyes in shadow, an icy, dirty shadow. The radiator was surely not working.

I was not alone. A woman with a waxy complexion was sitting opposite me and her hands trembled unceasingly, sometimes smoothing her blouse, sometimes straightening her black hat. She was with a big blond man eating a brioche without saying a word. The silence weighed on me, I wanted to light my pipe but I would have felt uncomfortable attracting their attention by striking the match.

The telephone bell rings. The hands stopped: they stayed clutching at the blouse. The waiter took his time. He calmly finished sweeping before going to take off the receiver. "Hello, is that Monsieur Georges? Good morning, Monsieur Georges . . . Yes, Monsieur Georges . . . The patron isn't here . . . Yes, he should be down . . . Yes, but with a fog like this . . . He generally comes down about eight . . . Yes, Monsieur Georges, I'll tell him. Good-bye, Monsieur Georges."

Fog weighed on the windows like a heavy curtain of grey velvet. A face pressed against the pane for an instant, disappeared.

The woman said plaintively:

"Tie up my shoe for me."

"It isn't untied," the man said without looking.

She grew agitated. Her hands moved along her blouse and over her neck like large spiders.

"Yes, yes, do up my shoe."

He bent down, looking cross, and lightly touched her foot under the table.

"It's done."

She smiled with satisfaction. The man called the waiter.

"How much do I owe you?"

"How many brioches?" the waiter asked.

I had lowered my eyes so as not to seem to stare at them. After a few instants I heard a creaking and saw the hem of a skirt and two shoes stained with dry mud appear. The man's shoes followed, polished and pointed. They came towards me, stopped and turned sideways: he was putting on his coat. At that moment a hand at the end of a stiff arm moved downwards; hesitated a moment, then scratched at the skirt.

"Ready?" the man asked.

The hand opened and touched a large splash of mud on the right shoe, then disappeared.

He had picked up a suitcase near the coat rack. They went out, I saw them swallowed up in the fog.

"They're on the stage," the waiter told me as he brought me coffee.

"They play the *entr'acte* at the Ciné-Palace. The woman blindfolds herself and tells the name and age of people in the audience. They're leaving today because it's Friday and the programme changes."

He went to get a plate of rolls from the table the people had just left.

"Don't bother."

I didn't feel inclined to eat those rolls.

"I have to turn off the light. Two lights for one customer at nine in the morning: the patron would give me hell."

Shadow floods the café. A feeble illumination, spattered with grey and brown, falls on the upper windows.

"I'd like to see M. Fasquelle."

I hadn't seen the old woman come in. A gust of cold air made me shiver.

"M. Fasquelle hasn't come down yet."

"Mme Florent sent me," she went on, "she isn't well. She won't be in today."

Mme Florent is the cashier, the red-haired girl.

"This weather," the old woman said, "is bad for her stomach."

The waiter put on an important air:

"It's the fog," he answered, "M. Fasquelle has the same trouble; I'm surprised he isn't down yet. Somebody telephoned for him. Usually he's down at eight."

Mechanically the old woman looked at the ceiling.

"Is he up there?"

"Yes, that's his room."

In a dragging voice, as if she were talking to herself, the old woman said:

"Suppose he's dead. . . ."

"Well! . . ." The waiter's face showed lively indignation. "Well I never!"

Suppose he were dead. . . . This thought brushed by me. Just the kind of idea you get on foggy days.

The old woman left. I should have done the same: it was cold and dark. The fog filtered in under the door, it was going to rise slowly and penetrate everything. I could have found light and warmth at the library.

Again a face came and pressed against the window; it grimaced.

"You just wait," the waiter said angrily and ran out.

The face disappeared, I was alone. I reproached myself bitterly for leaving my room. The fog would have filled it by this time; I would be afraid to go back.

Behind the cashier's table, in the shadow, something cracked. It came from the private staircase: was the manager coming down at last? No: there was no one; the steps were cracking by themselves. M. Fasquelle was still sleeping. Or else he was dead, up there above my head. Found dead in bed one foggy morning—sub-heading: in the café, customers went on eating without suspecting.

But was he still in bed? Hadn't he fallen out, dragging the sheets with him, bumping his head against the floor?

I know M. Fasquelle very well; he sometimes asks after my health. A big, jolly fellow with a carefully combed beard: if he is dead it's from a stroke. He will be the colour of eggplant with his tongue hanging out of his mouth. The beard in the air, the neck violet under the frizzle of hair.

The private stairway is lost in darkness. I can hardly make out the newel post. This shadow would have to be crossed. The stairs would creak. Above, I would find the door of the room . . .

The body is there over my head. I would turn the switch: I would touch his warm skin to see . . . I can't stand any more,

73

I get up. If the waiter catches me on the stairs I'll tell him I heard a noise.

The waiter came in suddenly, breathless.

"*Oui*, Monsieur!" he shouted.

Imbecile! He advanced towards me.

"That's two francs."

"I heard a noise up there," I told him.

"It's about time!"

"Yes, but I think something's wrong: it sounded like choking, and then there was a thud."

It sounded quite natural in the dark café with the fog behind the windows. I shall never forget his eyes.

"You ought to go up and see," I added slyly.

"Oh, no!" he said; then: "I'm afraid he'd give me hell. What time is it?"

"Ten."

"If he isn't down here by ten-thirty I'll go up."

I took a step towards the door.

"You're going? You aren't going to stay?"

"No."

"Did it sound like a death rattle?"

"I don't know," I told him as I walked out, "maybe just because I was thinking about it."

The fog had lifted a little. I hurried towards the Rue Tournebride: I longed for its lights. It was a disappointment: there was light, certainly, dripping down the store windows. But it wasn't a gay light: it was all white because of the fog and rained down on your shoulders.

A lot of people about, especially women, maids, charwomen, ladies as well, the kind who say, "I do my own buying, it's safer." They sniffed at the window displays and finally went in.

I stopped in front of Julien's pork-butcher shop. Through the glass, from time to time, I could see a hand designing the truffled pigs' feet and the sausages. Then a fat blonde girl bent over, her bosom showing, and picked up a piece of dead flesh between her fingers. In his room five minutes from there, M. Fasquelle was dead.

I looked around me for support, a refuge from my thoughts. There was none: little by little the fog lifted, but some disquieting thing stayed behind in the streets. Perhaps not a real menace: it was pale, transparent. But it was that which finally frightened me. I leaned my forehead against the window. I noticed a dark red drop on the mayonnaise of a stuffed egg: it was blood. This red on the yellow made me sick at my stomach.

Suddenly I had a vision: someone had fallen face down and was bleeding in the dishes. The egg had rolled in blood; the slice of tomato which crowned it had come off and fallen flat, red on red. The mayonnaise had run a little: a pool of yellow cream which divided the trickle of blood into two arms.

"This is really too silly, I must pull myself together. I'm going to work in the library."

Work? I knew perfectly well I shouldn't write a line. Another day wasted. Crossing the park, I saw a great blue cape, motionless on the bench where I usually sit. There's someone at least who isn't cold.

When I entered the reading-room, the Self-Taught Man was just coming out. He threw himself on me:

"I have to thank you, Monsieur. Your photographs have allowed me to spend many unforgettable hours."

I had a ray of hope when I saw him; it might be easier to get through this day together. But, with the Self-Taught Man, you only appear to be two.

He rapped on an in-quarto volume. It was a History of Religion.

"Monsieur, no one was better qualified than Nouçapié to attempt this vast synthesis. Isn't that true?"

He seemed weary and his hands were trembling.

"You look ill," I said.

"Ah, Monsieur, I should think so! Something abominable has happened to me."

The guardian came towards us: a peevish little Corsican with moustaches like a drum major. He walks for whole hours among the tables, clacking his heels. In winter he spits in his handkerchiefs then dries them on the stove.

The Self-Taught Man came close enough to breathe in my face.

"I won't tell you anything in front of this man," he said in confidence. "If you would, Monsieur . . ."

"Would what?"

He blushed and his lips swayed gracefully.

"Monsieur, ah, Monsieur: all right, I'll lay my cards on the table. Will you do me the honour of lunching with me on Wednesday?"

"With pleasure."

I had as much desire to eat with him as I had to hang myself.

"I'm so glad," the Self-Taught Man said. He added rapidly, "I'll pick you up at your hotel, if you like," then disappeared, afraid, undoubtedly, that I would change my mind if he gave me time.

It was eleven-thirty. I worked until quarter of two. Poor work: I had a book in my hands but my thoughts returned incessantly to the Café Mably. Had M. Fasquelle come down by now? At heart, I didn't believe he was dead and this was precisely what irritated me: it was a floating idea which I could neither persuade myself to believe or disbelieve. The Corsican's shoes creaked on the floor. Several times he came and stood in front of me as though he wanted to talk to me. But he changed his mind and went away.

The last readers left around one o'clock. I wasn't hungry; above all I didn't want to leave. I worked a moment more then started up; I felt shrouded in silence.

I raised my head: I was alone. The Corsican must have gone down to his wife who is the concierge of the library; I wanted to hear the sound of his footsteps. Just then I heard a piece of coal fall in the stove. Fog had filled the room: not the real fog, that had gone a long time ago—but the other, the one the streets were still full of, which came out of the walls and pavements. The inconsistency of inanimate objects! The books were still there, arranged in alphabetical order on the shelves with their brown and black backs and their labels *up 1f* 7.996 (For Public Use–French Literature–) or *up sn* (For Public Use–Natural Science). But . . . how can I explain it? Usually, powerful and squat, along with the stove, the green lamps, the wide windows, the ladders, they dam up the future. As long as you stay between these walls, whatever happens must happen on the right or the left of the stove. Saint Denis himself could come in carrying his head in his hands and he would still have to enter on the right, walk between the shelves devoted to French Literature and the table reserved for women readers. And if he doesn't touch the ground, if he floats ten inches above the floor, his bleeding neck will be just at the level of the third shelf of books. Thus these objects serve at least to fix the limits of probability.

Today they fixed nothing at all: it seemed that their very existence was subject to doubt, that they had the greatest difficulty in passing from one instant to the next. I held the book I was reading tightly in my hands: but the most violent sensations went dead. Nothing seemed true; I felt surrounded by cardboard scenery which could quickly be removed. The world was waiting, holding its breath, making itself small—it was waiting for its convulsion, its Nausea, just like M. Achille the other day.

I got up. I could no longer keep my place in the midst of these unnatural objects. I went to the window and glanced out at the skull of Impétraz. I murmured: *Anything* can happen, *anything*. But evidently, it would be nothing horrible, such as humans might invent. Impétraz was not going to start dancing on his pedestal: it would be something else entirely.

Frightened, I looked at these unstable beings which, in an hour, in a minute, were perhaps going to crumble: yes, I was there, living in the midst of these books full of knowledge describing the immutable forms of the animal species, explaining that the right quantity of energy is kept integral in the universe; I was there, standing in front of a window whose panes had a definite refraction index. But what feeble barriers! I suppose it is out of laziness that the world is the same day after day. Today it seemed to want to change. And then, *anything, anything* could happen.

I had no time to lose: the Café Mably affair was at the root of this uneasiness. I must go back there, see M. Fasquelle alive, touch his beard or his hands if need be. Then, perhaps, I would be free.

I seized my overcoat and threw it round my shoulders; I fled. Crossing the Public Gardens I saw once more the man in the blue cape. He had the same ghastly white face with two scarlet ears sticking out on either side.

The Café Mably sparkled in the distance: this time the twelve lights must have been lit. I hurried: I had to get it over. First I glanced in through the big window, the place was deserted. The cashier was not there, nor the waiter—nor M. Fasquelle.

I had to make a great effort to go in; I did not sit down. I shouted "Waiter!" No one answered. An empty cup on a table. A lump of sugar on the saucer.

"Anyone here?"

An overcoat hung from a peg. Magazines were piled up in black cardboard boxes on a low table. I was on the alert for the slightest sound, holding my breath. The private stairway creaked slightly. I heard a foghorn outside. I walked out backwards, my eyes never leaving the stairway.

I know: customers are rare at two in the afternoon. M. Fasquelle had influenza; he must have sent the waiter out on an errand—maybe to get a doctor. Yes, but I needed to see M. Fasquelle. At the Rue Tournebride I turned back, I studied the garish, deserted café with disgust. The blinds on the second floor were drawn.

A real panic took hold of me. I didn't know where I was going. I ran along the docks, turned into the deserted streets in the Beauvoisis district; the houses watched my flight with their mournful eyes. I repeated with anguish: Where shall I go? where shall I go? *Anything* can happen. Sometimes, my heart pounding, I made a sudden right-about-turn: what was happening behind my back? Maybe it would start behind me and when I would turn around, suddenly, it would be too late. As long as I could stare at things nothing would happen: I looked at them as much as I could, pavements, houses, gaslights; my eyes went rapidly from one to the other, to catch them unawares, stop them in the midst of their metamorphosis. They didn't look too natural, but I told myself forcibly: this is a gaslight, this is a drinking fountain, and I tried to reduce them to their everyday aspect by the power of my gaze. Several times I came across barriers in my path: the Café des Bretons, the Bar de la Marine. I stopped, hesitated in front of their pink net curtains: perhaps these snug places had been spared, perhaps they still held a bit of yesterday's world, isolated, forgotten. But I would have to push the door open and enter. I didn't dare; I went on. Doors of houses frightened me especially. I was afraid they would open of themselves. I ended by walking in the middle of the street.

I suddenly came out on the Quai des Bassins du Nord. Fishing smacks and small yachts. I put my foot on a ring set in the stone. Here, far from houses, far from doors, I would have a moment of respite. A cork was floating on the calm, black-speckled water.

"And *under* the water? You haven't thought what could be *under* the water."

A monster? A giant carapace? sunk in the mud? A dozen pairs of claws or fins labouring slowly in the slime. The monster rises. At the bottom of the water. I went nearer, watching every eddy and undulation. The cork stayed immobile among the black spots.

Then I heard voices. It was time. I turned and began my race again.

I caught up with two men who were talking in the Rue Castiglione. At the sound of footsteps they started violently and both turned round. I saw their worried eyes upon me, then behind me to see if something else was coming. Were they like me? were they, too, afraid? We looked at each other in passing: a little more and we would have spoken. But the looks suddenly expressed defiance: on a day like this you don't speak to just anyone.

I found myself breathless on the Rue Boulibet. The die was cast: I was going back to the library, take a novel and try to read. Going along the park railing I noticed the man in the cape. He was still there in the deserted park; his nose had grown as red as his ears.

I was going to push open the gate but the expression on his face stopped me: he wrinkled his eyes and half-grinned, stupidly and affectedly. But at the same time he stared straight ahead at something I could not see with a look so hard and with such intensity that I suddenly turned back.

Opposite to him, one foot raised, her mouth half-opened, a little girl of about ten, fascinated, was watching him, pulling nervously at her scarf, her pointed face thrusting forward.

The man was smiling to himself, like someone about to play a good joke. Suddenly he stood up, his hands in the pockets of his cloak which fell to his feet. He took two steps forward, his eyes rolling. I thought he was going to fall. But he kept on smiling sleepily.

I suddenly understood: the cloak! I wanted to stop it. It would have been enough to cough or open the gate. But in my turn I was fascinated by the little girl's face. Her features were drawn with fear and her heart must have been beating horribly: yet I could also read something powerful and wicked on that rat-like face. It was not curiosity but rather a sort of assured expectation. I felt impotent: I was outside, on the edge of the park, on the edge of their little drama: but they were riveted one to the other by the obscure power of their desires, they made a pair together. I held my breath, I wanted to see what expression would come on that elfish face when the man, behind my back, would spread out the folds of his cloak.

But suddenly freed, the little girl shook her head and began to run. The man in the cloak had seen me: that was what stopped him. For a second he stayed motionless in the middle of the path, then went off, his back hunched. The cloak flapped against his calves.

I pushed open the gate and was next to him in one bound. "Hey!" I shouted.

He began to tremble.

"A great menace weighs over the city," I said politely, and went on.

I went into the reading-room and took the *Chartreuse de Parme* from a table. I tried to absorb myself in reading, to find a refuge in the lucid Italy of Stendhal. Sometimes I succeeded, in spurts, in short hallucinations, then fell back again into this day of menace; opposite an old man who was clearing his throat, a young man, dreaming, leaning back in his chair.

Hours passed, the windows had turned black. There were four of us, not counting the Corsican who was in the office, stamping the latest acquisitions of the library. There was the little old man, the blond young man, a girl working for her degree—and I. From time to time one of us would look up, glance rapidly and scornfully at the other three as if he were afraid of them. Once the old man started to laugh: I saw the girl tremble from head to foot. But I had deciphered from upside down the title of the book she was reading: it was a light novel.

Ten minutes to seven. I suddenly realized that the library closed at seven. Once again I was going to be cast out into the town. Where would I go? What would I do?

The old man had finished his book. But he did not leave. He tapped his finger on the table with sharp, regular beats.

"Closing time soon," the Corsican said.

The young man gave a start and shot me a quick glance. The girl turned towards the Corsican, then picked up her book again and seemed to dive into it.

"Closing time," said the Corsican five minutes later.

The old man shook his head undecidedly. The girl pushed her book away without getting up.

The Corsican looked baffled. He took a few hesitating steps, then turned out the switch. The lamps went out at the reading tables. Only the centre bulb stayed lighted.

"Do we have to leave?" the old man asked quietly.

The young man got up slowly and regretfully. It was a question of who was going to take the longer time putting on his coat. When I left the girl was still seated, one hand flat on her book.

Below, the door gaped into the night. The young man, who was walking ahead, turned, slowly went down the stairs, and crossed the vestibule; he stopped for an instant on the threshold, then threw himself into the night and disappeared.

At the bottom of the stairs I looked up. After a moment the old man left the reading-room, buttoning his overcoat. By the time he had gone down three steps I took strength, closed my eyes and dived out.

I felt a cool little caress on my face. Someone was whistling in the distance. I raised my eyes: it was raining. A soft, calm rain. The square was lighted peacefully by four lamp-posts. A provincial square in the rain. The young man was going further away, taking great strides, and whistling. I wanted to shout to the others who did not yet know that they could leave without fear, that the menace had passed.

The old man appeared at the door. He scratched his cheek, embarrassed, then smiled broadly and opened his umbrella.

Saturday morning:

A charming sun with a light mist which promises a clear day. I had breakfast at the Café Mably.

Mme Florent, the cashier, smiled graciously at me. I called to her from my table:

"Is M. Fasquelle sick?"

"Yes; a bad go of flu: he'll have to stay in bed a few days. His daughter came from Dunkirk this morning. She's going to stay here and take care of him."

For the first time since I got her letter I am definitely happy at the idea of seeing Anny again. What has she been doing for six years? Shall we feel strange when we see each other? Anny doesn't know what it is to feel awkward. She'll greet me as if I had left her yesterday. I hope I shan't make a fool of myself, and put her off at the beginning. I must remember not to offer her my hand when I get there: she hates that.

How many days shall we stay together? Perhaps I could bring her back to Bouville. It would be enough if she would live here only for a few hours; if she would sleep at the Hotel Printania for one night. It would never be the same after that; I shouldn't be afraid any more.

Afternoon:

When I paid my first visit to the Bouville museum last year I was struck by the portrait of Olivier Blévigne. Faulty proportion? Perspective? I couldn't tell, but something bothered me: this deputy didn't seem plumb on his canvas.

I have gone back several times since then. But my worry persisted. I didn't want to admit that Bordurin, Prix de Rome, had made a mistake in his drawing.

But this afternoon, turning the pages of an old collection of the *Satirique Bouvillois,* a blackmail-sheet whose owner was accused of high treason during the war, I caught a glimpse of the truth. I went to the museum as soon as I left the library.

I crossed the shadow of the vestibule quickly. My steps made no sound on the black and white tiles. A whole race of plaster folk twisted their arms. In passing I glanced, through two great openings, and saw cracked vases, plates, and a blue and yellow satyr on a pedestal. It was the Bernard Palissy Room, devoted to ceramics and minor arts. But ceramics do not amuse me. A lady and gentleman in mourning were respectfully contemplating the baked objects.

Above the entrance to the main hall—the Salon Bordurin-Renaudas—someone had hung, undoubtedly only a little while ago, a large canvas which I did not recognize. It was signed by Richard Séverand and entitled "The Bachelor's Death." It was a gift of the State.

Naked to the waist, his body a little green, like that of a dead man, the bachelor was lying on an unmade bed. The disorder of sheets and blankets attested to a long death agony. I smiled, thinking about M. Fasquelle. But he wasn't alone: his daughter was taking care of him. On the canvas, the maid, his mistress, her features marked by vice, had already opened a bureau drawer and was counting the money. An open door disclosed a man in a cap, a cigarette stuck to his lower lip, waiting in the shadows. Near the wall a cat lapped milk indifferently.

This man had lived only for himself. By a harsh and well-deserved punishment, no one had come to his bedside to close his eyes. This painting gave me a last warning: there was still time, I could retrace my steps. But if I were to turn a deaf ear, I had been forewarned: more than a hundred and fifty portraits were hanging on the wall of the room I was about to enter;

with the exception of a few young people, prematurely taken from their families, and the mother superior of a boarding school, none of those painted had died a bachelor, none of them had died childless or intestate, none without the last rites. Their souls at peace that day as on other days, with God and the world, these men had slipped quietly into death, to claim their share of eternal life to which they had a right.

For they had a right to everything: to life, to work, to wealth, to command, to respect, and, finally, to immortality.

I took a moment to compose myself and entered. A guardian was sleeping near the window. A pale light, falling from the windows, made flecks on the paintings. Nothing alive in this great rectangular room, except a cat who was frightened at my approach and fled. But I felt the looks of a hundred and fifty pairs of eyes on me.

All who belonged to the Bouville élite between 1875 and 1910 were there, men and women, scrupulously painted by Renaudas and Bordurin.

The men had built Sainte-Cécile-de-la-Mer. In 1882, they founded the Federation of Shipowners and Merchants of Bou-ville "to group in one powerful entity all men of good will, to co-operate in national recovery and to hold in check the parties of disorder. . . ." They made Bouville the best equipped port in France for unloading coal and wood. The lengthening and widening of the quays were their work. They extended the Marine Terminal and, by constant dredging, brought the low-tide depth of anchorage to 10.7 meters. In twenty years, the catch of the fishing fleet which was 5,000 barrels in 1869, rose, thanks to them, to 18,000 barrels. Stopping at no sacrifice to assist the im-provement of the best elements in the working-class, they cre-ated, on their own initiative, various centres for technical and professional study which prospered under their lofty protection. They broke the famous shipping strike in 1898 and gave their sons to their country in 1914.

The women, worthy helpmates of these strugglers, founded most of the town's charitable and philanthropic organizations. But above all, they were wives and mothers. They raised fine children, taught them rights and duties, religion, and a respect for the traditions which made France great.

The general complexion of these portraits bordered on dark brown. Lively colours had been banished, out of decency. How-ever, in the portraits of Renaudas, who showed a partiality towards old men, the snowy hair and sidewhiskers showed up well against deep black backgrounds; he excelled in painting hands. Bordurin, who was a little weak on theory, sacrificed the hands somewhat but the collars shone like white marble.

It was very hot; the guardian was snoring gently. I glanced around the walls: I saw hands and eyes; here and there a spot of light obliterated a face. As I began walking towards the portrait of Olivier Blévigne, something held me back: from the moulding, Pacôme, the merchant, cast a bright look down on me.

He was standing there, his head thrown slightly back; in one hand he held a top hat and gloves against his pearl-grey trousers. I could not keep myself from a certain admiration: I saw nothing mediocre in him, nothing which allowed of criticism: small feet, slender hands, wide wrestler's shoulders, a hint of whimsy. He courteously offered visitors the unwrinkled purity of his face; the shadow of a smile played on the lips. But his grey eyes were not smiling. He must have been about fifty: but he was as young and fresh as a man of thirty. He was beautiful.

I gave up finding fault with him. But he did not let go of me. I read a calm and implacable judgment in his eyes.

Then I realized what separated us: what I thought about him could not reach him; it was psychology, the kind they write about in books. But his judgment went through me like a sword and questioned my very right to exist. And it was true, I had always realized it; I hadn't the right to exist. I had appeared by chance, I existed like a stone, a plant or a microbe. My life put out feelers towards small pleasures in every direction. Sometimes it sent out vague signals; at other times I felt nothing more than a harmless buzzing.

But for this handsome, faultless man, now dead, for Jean Pacôme, son of the Pacôme of the Défence Nationale, it had been an entirely different matter: the beating of his heart and the mute rumblings of his organs, in his case, assumed the form of rights to be instantly obeyed. For sixty years, without a halt, he had used his right to live. The slightest doubt had never crossed those magnificent grey eyes. Pacôme had never made a mistake. He had always done his duty, all his duty, his duty as son, husband, father, leader. He had never weakened in his demands for his due: as a child, the right to be well brought up, in a united family, the right to inherit a spotless name, a prosperous business; as a husband, the right to be cared for, surrounded with tender affection; as a father, the right to be venerated; as a leader, the right to be obeyed without a murmur. For a right is nothing more than the other aspect of duty. His extraordinary success (today the Pacômes are the richest family in Bouville) could never have surprised him. He never told himself he was happy, and while he was enjoying himself he must have done so with moderation, saying: "This is my refreshment." Thus pleasure itself, also becoming a right, lost its aggressive futility. On the left, a little above his bluish-grey hair, I noticed a shelf of books. The bindings were handsome; they were surely classics. Every evening before going to sleep, Pacôme undoubtedly read over a few pages of "his old Montaigne" or one of Horace's odes in the Latin text. Sometimes, too, he must have read a contemporary work to keep up to date. Thus he knew Barrès and Bourget. He would put his book down after a moment. He would smile. His look, losing its admirable circumspection, became almost dreamy. He would say: "How easy and how difficult it is to do one's duty."

He had never looked any further into himself: he was a leader.

There were other leaders on the walls: nothing but leaders. He was a leader—this tall, *ver-de-gris* man in his armchair. His white waistcoat was a happy reminder of his silver hair. (Attention to artistry was not excluded from these portraits, which were above all painted for moral edification, and exactitude was pushed to the furthest limit of scruple.) His long, slender hand was placed on the head of a small boy. An open book rested on his knees which were covered by a rug. But his look had strayed into the distance. He was seeing all those things which are invisible to young people. His name was written on a plaque of gilded wood below his portrait: his name must have been Pacôme or Parrottin, or Chaigneau. I had not thought of looking: for his close relatives, for this child, for himself, he was simply the grandfather; soon, if he deemed the time fitting to instruct his grandson about the scope of his future duties, he would speak of himself in the third person:

"You're going to promise your grandfather to be good, my boy, to work hard next year. Perhaps Grandfather won't be here any more next year."

In the evening of his life, he scattered his indulgent goodness over everyone. Even if he were to see me—though to him I was transparent—I would find grace in his eyes: he would think that I, too, had grandparents once. He demanded nothing: one has no more desires at that age. Nothing except for people to lower their voices slightly when he entered, nothing except a touch of tenderness and smiling respect when he passed, nothing except for his daughter-in-law to say sometimes: "Father is amazing; he's younger than all of us"; nothing except to be the only one able to calm the temper of his grandson by putting his hands on the boy's head and saying: "Grandfather knows how to take care of all those troubles"; nothing except for his son, several times a year, to come asking his advice on delicate matters; finally, nothing more than to feel himself serene, appeased, and infinitely wise. The old gentleman's hand barely weighed on his grandson's curls: it was almost a benediction. What could he be thinking of? Of his honourable past which conferred on him the right to speak on everything and to have the last word on everything. I had not gone far enough the other day: experience was much more than a defence against death; it was a right; the right of old men.

General Aubry, hanging against the moulding, with his great sabre, was a leader. Another leader: President Hébert, well read, friend of Impétraz. His face was long and symmetrical with an interminable chin, punctuated, just under the lip, by a goatee: he thrust out his jaw slightly, with the amused air of being distinguished, of rolling out an objection on principles like a faint belch. He dreamed, he held a quill pen: he was taking his relaxation too, by Heaven, and it was writing verses. But he had the eagle eye of a leader.

And soldiers? I was in the centre of the room, the cynosure of all these grave eyes. I was neither father nor grandfather, not even a husband. I did not have a vote, I hardly paid any taxes: I could not boast of being a taxpayer, an elector, nor even of having the humble right to honour which twenty years of obedience confers on an employee. My existence began to worry me seriously. Was I not a simple spectre? "Hey!" I suddenly told myself, "I am the soldier!" It really made me laugh.

A portly quinquagenarian politely returned a handsome smile. Renaudas had painted him with loving care, no touch was too tender for those fleshy, finely-chiselled little ears, especially for the hands, long, nervous, with loose fingers: the hands of a real savant or artist. His face was unknown to me: I must have passed before the canvas often without noticing it. I went up to it and read: *Rémy Parrottin, born in Bouville in* 1849, *Professor at the Ecole de Médecine, Paris.*

Parrottin: Doctor Wakefield had spoken to me of him: "Once in my life I met a great man, Rémy Parrottin. I took courses under him during the winter of 1904 (you know I spent two years in Paris studying obstetrics). He made me realize what it was to be a leader. He had it in him, I swear he did. He electrified us, he could have led us to the ends of the earth. And with all that he was a gentleman: he had an immense fortune—gave a good part of it to help poor students."

This is how this prince of science, the first time I heard him spoken of, inspired strong feelings in me. Now I stood before him and he was smiling at me. What intelligence and affability in his smile! His plump body rested leisurely in the hollow of a great leather armchair. This unpretentious wise man put people at their ease immediately. If it hadn't been for the spirit in his look you would have taken him for just anybody.

It did not take long to guess the reason for his prestige: he was loved because he understood everything; you could tell him anything. He looked a little like Renan, all in all, with more distinction. He was one of those who say:

"Socialists? Well, I go further than they do!" When you followed him down this perilous road you were soon to leave behind, not without a shiver, family, country, private property rights, and the most sacred values. You even doubted for a second the right of the bourgeois élite to command. Another step and suddenly everything was re-established, miraculously founded on solid reason, good old reasons. You turned around and saw the Socialists, already far behind you, all tiny, waving their handkerchiefs and shouting: "Wait for us!"

Through Wakefield I knew that the Master liked, as he himself said with a smile, "to deliver souls." To prolong his own, he surrounded himself with youth: he often received young men of good family who were studying medicine. Wakefield had often been to his house for luncheon. After the meal they retired to the smoking-room. The Master treated these students who were at their first cigarettes like men: he offered them cigars. He stretched out on a divan and discoursed at great length, his eyes half-closed, surrounded by an eager crowd of disciples. He evoked memories, told stories, drawing a sharp and profound moral from each. And if there were among those well-bred young men one who seemed especially headstrong, Parrottin would take a special interest in him. He made him speak, listened to him attentively, gave him ideas and subjects for meditation. It usually happened that one day the young man, full of generous ideas, excited by the hostility of his parents, weary of thinking alone, his hand against every man, asked to visit the Master privately, and, stammering with shyness, confided in him his most intimate thoughts, his indignations, his hopes. Parrottin embraced him. He said: "I understand you. I understood you from the first day." They talked on. Parrottin went far, still farther, so far that the young man followed him with great difficulty. After a few conversations of this sort one could detect a favourable change in the young rebel. He saw clearly within himself, he learned to know the deep bonds which attached him to his family, to his environment; at last he understood the admirable role of the élite. And finally, as if by magic, found himself once again, enlightened, repentant. "He cured more souls," concluded Wakefield, "than I've cured bodies."

Rémy Parrottin smiled affably at me. He hesitated, tried to understand my position, to turn gently and lead me back to the fold. But I wasn't afraid of him: I was no lamb. I looked at his fine forehead, calm and unwrinkled, his small belly, his hand set flat against his knee. I returned his smile and left.

Jean Parrottin, his brother, president of the S.A.B., leaned both hands on the edge of a table loaded with papers; his whole attitude signified to the visitor that the audience was over. His look was extraordinary; although abstracted yet shining with high endeavour. His dazzling eyes devoured his whole face. Behind this glow I noticed the thin, tight lips of a mystic. "It's odd," I said, "he looks like Rémy Parrottin." I turned to the Great Master: examining him in the light of this resemblance, a sense of aridity and desolation, a family resemblance took possession of his face. I went back to Jean Parrottin.

This man was one-ideaed. Nothing more was left in him but bones, dead flesh and Pure Right. A real case of possession, I thought. Once Right has taken hold of a man exorcism cannot drive it out; Jean Parrottin had consecrated his whole life to thinking about his Right: nothing else. Instead of the slight headache I feel coming on each time I visit a museum, he would have felt the painful right of having his temples cared for. It never did to make him think too much, or attract his attention to unpleasant realities, to his possible death, to the sufferings of others. Undoubtedly, on his death bed, at that moment when, ever since Socrates, it has been proper to pronounce certain elevated words, he told his wife, as one of my uncles told his, who had watched beside him for twelve nights, "I do not thank you, Thérèse; you have only done your duty." When a man gets that far, you have to take your hat off to him.

His eyes, which I stared at in wonderment, indicated that I must leave. I did not leave. I was resolutely indiscreet. I knew, as a result of studying at great length a certain portrait of Philip II in the library of the Escurial, that when one is confronted with a face sparkling with righteousness, after a moment this sparkle dies away, and only an ashy residue remains: this residue interested me.

Parrottin put up a good fight. But suddenly his look burned out, the picture grew dim. What was left? Blind eyes, the thin mouth of a dead snake, and cheeks. The pale, round cheeks of a child: they spread over the canvas. The employees of the S.A.B. never suspected it: they never stayed in Parrottin's office long enough. When they went in, they came up against that terrible look like a wall. From behind it, the cheeks were in shelter, white and flabby. How long did it take his wife to notice them? Two years? Five years? One day, I imagine, as her husband was sleeping, on his side with a ray of light caressing his nose, or else on a hot day, while he was having trouble with his digestion, sunk into an armchair, his eyes half-closed, with a splash of sunlight on his chin, she dared to look him in the face: all this flesh appeared to her defenceless, bloated, slobbering, vaguely obscene. From that day on, Mme Parrottin undoubtedly took command.

I took a few steps backward and in one glance covered all these great personages: Pacôme, President Hébert, both Parrottins, and General Aubry. They had worn top hats; every Sunday on the Rue Tournebride they met Mme Gratien, the mayor's wife, who saw Sainte Cécile in a dream. They greeted her with great ceremonious salutes, the secret of which is now lost.

They had been painted very minutely; yet, under the brush, their countenances had been stripped of the mysterious weakness of men's faces. Their faces, even the last powerful, were clear as porcelain: in vain I looked for some relation they could bear to trees and animals, to thoughts of earth or water. In life they evidently did not require it. But, at the moment of passing on to posterity, they had confided themselves to a renowned painter in order that he should discreetly carry out on their faces the system of dredgings, drillings, and irrigations by which, all around Bouville, they had transformed the sea and the land.

Thus, with the help of Renaudas and Bordurin, they had enslaved Nature: without themselves and within themselves. What these sombre canvases offered to me was man reconsidered by man, with, as sole adornment, the finest conquest of man: a bouquet of the Rights of Man and Citizen. Without mental reservation, I admired the reign of man.

A woman and a man came in. They were dressed in black and tried to make themselves inconspicuous. They stopped, enchanted, on the doorstep and the man automatically took off his hat.

"Ah!" the lady said, deeply touched.

The gentleman quickly regained his sang-froid. He said respectfully:

"It's a whole era!"

"Yes," the lady said, "this is in the time of my grandmother."

They took a few steps and met the look of Jean Parrottin. The woman stood gaping, but the man was not proud: he looked humble, he must have known intimidating looks and brief interviews well. He tugged gently at the woman's arm.

"Look at that one," he said.

Rémy Parrottin's smile had always put the humble at ease. The woman went forward and read studiously:

"Portrait of Rémy Parrottin, born in Bouville in 1849. Professor of the Ecole de Médecine, Paris, by Renaudas."

"Parrottin, of the Academy of Science," her husband said, "by Renaudas of the Institute. That's History!"

The lady nodded, then looked at the Great Master.

"How handsome he is," she said, "how intelligent he looks!"

The husband made an expansive gesture.

"They're the ones who made Bouville what it is," he said with simplicity.

"It's right to have had them put here, all together," the woman said tenderly.

We were three soldiers manœuvring in this immense hall. The husband who laughed with respect, silently, shot me a troubled glance and suddenly stopped laughing. A sweet joy flooded over me: well, I was right! It was really too funny.

The woman came near me.

"Gaston," she said, suddenly bold, "come here!"

The husband came towards us.

"Look," she went on, "he has a street named after him:

Olivier Blévigne. You know, the little street that goes up the Coteau Vert just before you get to Jouxtebouville."

After an instant, she added:

"He doesn't look exactly easy."

"No. Some people must have found him a pretty awkward customer."

These words were addressed to me. The man, watching me out of the corner of his eye, began to laugh softly, this time with a conceited air, a busy-body, as if he were Olivier Blévigne himself.

Olivier Blévigne did not laugh. He thrust his compact jaw towards us and his Adam's apple jutted out.

There was a moment of ecstatic silence.

"You'd think he was going to move," the lady said.

The husband explained obligingly:

"He was a great cotton merchant. Then he went into politics; he was a deputy."

I knew it. Two years ago I had looked him up in the *Petit Dictionnaire des Grands Hommes de Bouville* by Abbé Morellet. I copied the article.

"*Blévigne, Olivier-Martial, son of the late Olivier-Martial Blévigne, born and died in Bouville (1849–1908), studied law in Paris, passed Bar examinations in 1872. Deeply impressed by the Commune insurrection, which forced him, as it did so many other Parisians, to take refuge in Versailles under the protection of the National Assembly, he swore, at an age when young men think only of pleasure, 'to consecrate his life to the re-establishment of order.' He kept his word: immediately after his return to our city, he founded the famous Club de l'Ordre which every evening for many years united the principal businessmen and shipowners of Bouville. This aristocratic circle, which one might jokingly describe as being more restricted than the Jockey Club, exerted, until 1908, a salutary influence on the destiny of our great commercial port. In 1880, Olivier Blévigne married Marie-Louise Pacôme, younger daughter of Charles Pacôme, businessman (see Pacôme), and at the death of the latter, founded the company of Pacôme-Blévigne & Son. Shortly thereafter he entered actively into politics and placed his candidature before the deputation.*

"*'The country,'* he said in a celebrated speech, *'is suffering from a most serious malady: the ruling class no longer wants to rule. And who then shall rule, gentlemen, if those who, by their* heredity, their education, their experience, have been rendered most fit for the exercising of power, turn from it in resignation or weariness? I have often said: to rule is not a right of the élite; it is a primary duty of the élite. Gentlemen, I beg of you: let us restore the principle of authority!'

"Elected first on October 4, 1885, he was constantly reelected thereafter. Of an energetic and virile eloquence, he delivered many brilliant speeches. He was in Paris in 1898 when the terrible strike broke out. He returned to Bouville immediately and became the guiding spirit of the resistance. He took the initiative of negotiating with the strikers. These negotiations, inspired by an open-minded attempt at conciliation, were interrupted by the small uprising in Jouxtebouville. We know that the timely intervention of the military restored calm to our minds.

"The premature death of his son Octave, who had entered the Ecole Polytechnique at a very early age and of whom he wanted to 'make a leader' was a terrible blow to Olivier Blévigne. He was never to recover from it and died two years later, in February, 1908.

"Collected speeches: Moral Forces (1894: out of print), The Duty to Punish (1900: all speeches in this collection were given à propos of the Dreyfus Case: out of print), Will-power (1902: out of print). After his death, his last speeches and a few letters to intimate friends were collected under the title Labour Improbus (Plon, 1910). Iconography: there is an excellent portrait of him, by Bordurin, at the Bouville museum."

An excellent portrait, granted. Olivier Blévigne had a small black moustache, and his olive-tinted face somewhat resembled Maurice Barrès. The two men had surely met each other: they used to sit on the same benches. But the deputy from Bouville did not have the nonchalance of the President of the League of Patriots. He was stiff as a poker and sprang at you from his canvas like a jack-in-the-box. His eyes sparkled: the pupil was black, the cornea reddish. He pursed up his fleshy little mouth and held his right hand against his breast.

How this portrait annoyed me! Sometimes Blévigne seemed too large or too small to me. But today I knew what to look for.

I had learned the truth turning over the pages of the *Satirique Bouvillois*. The issue of 6 November, 1905 was devoted entirely to Blévigne. He was pictured on the cover, tiny, hanging on to the mane of old Combes, and the caption read: *"The*

Lion's Louse." Everything was explained from the first page on: Olivier Blévigne was only five feet tall. They mocked his small stature and squeaking voice which more than once threw the whole Chamber into hysterics. They accused him of putting rubber lifts in his shoes. On the other hand, Mme Blévigne, née Pacôme, was a horse. "Here we can well say," the paper added, "that his other half is his double."

Five feet tall! Yes, Bordurin, with jealous care, had surrounded him with objects which ran no risk of diminishing him; a hassock, a low armchair, a shelf with a few little books, a small Persian table. Only he had given him the same stature as his neighbour Jean Parrottin and both canvases had the same dimensions. The result was that the small table, in one picture, was almost as large as the immense table in the other, and that the hassock would have almost reached Parrottin's shoulder. The eye instinctively made a comparison between the two: my discomfort had come from that.

Now I wanted to laugh. Five feet tall! If I had wanted to talk to Blévigne I would have had to lean over or bend my knees. I was no longer surprised that he held up his nose so impetuously: the destiny of these small men is always working itself out a few inches above their head.

Admirable power of art. From this shrill-voiced mannikin, nothing would pass on to posterity save a threatening face, a superb gesture and the bloodshot eyes of a bull. The student terrorised by the Commune, the deputy, a bad-tempered midget; that was what death had taken. But, thanks to Bordurin, the President of the Club de l'Ordre, the orator of "Moral Forces," was immortal.

"Oh, poor little Pipo!"

The woman gave a stifled cry: under the portrait of Octave Blévigne "son of the late . . ." a pious hand had traced these words:

"Died at the Ecole Polytechnique in 1904."

"He's dead! Just like the Arondel boy. He looked intelligent. How hard it must have been for his poor mother! They make them work too hard in those big schools. The brain works, while you're asleep. I like those two-cornered hats, it looks so stylish. Is that what you call a 'cassowary?'"

"No. They have cassowaries at Saint-Cyr."

In my turn I studied the prematurely dead polytechnician. His wax complexion and well-groomed moustache would have been enough to turn one's idea to approaching death. He had foreseen his fate as well: a certain resignation could be read in his clear, far-seeing eyes. But at the same time he carried his head high; in this uniform he represented the French Army.

Tu Marcellus eris! Manibus date lilia plenis . . .

A cut rose, a dead polytechnician: what could be sadder?

I quietly followed the long gallery, greeting in passing, without stopping, the distinguished faces which peered from the shadows: M. Bossoire, President of the Board of Trade; M. Faby, President of the Board of Directors of the Autonomous Port of Bouville; M. Boulange, businessman, with his family; M. Rannequin, Mayor of Bouville; M. de Lucien, born in Bouville, French Ambassador to the United States and a poet as well; an unknown dressed like a prefect; Mother Sainte-Marie-Louise, Mother Superior of the Orphan Asylum; M. and Mme Théréson; M. Thiboust-Gouron, General President of the Trades Council; M. Bobot, principle administrator of the Inscription Maritime; Messrs. Brion, Minette, Grelot, Lefèbvre, Dr. and Mme Pain, Bordurin himself, painted by his son, Pierre Bordurin. Clear, cold looks, fine features, thin lips, M. Boulange was economical and patient, Mother Sainte-Marie-Louise of an industrious piety, M. Thiboust-Gouron was as hard on himself as on others. Mme Théréson struggled without weakening against deep illness. Her infinitely weary mouth told unceasingly of her suffering. But this pious woman had never said: "It hurts." She took the upper hand: she made up bills of fare and presided over welfare societies. Sometimes, she would slowly close her eyes in the middle of a sentence and all traces of life would leave her face. This fainting spell lasted hardly more than a second; shortly afterward, Mme Théréson would re-open her eyes and finish her sentence. And in the work room they whispered: "Poor Mme Théréson! She never complains."

I had crossed the whole length of the salon Bordurin-Renaudas. I turned back. Farewell, beautiful lilies, elegant in your painted little sanctuaries, good-bye, lovely lilies, our pride and reason for existing, good-bye you bastards!

Monday:

I'm not writing my book on Rollebon any more; it's finished, I *can't* write any more of it. What am I going to do with my life?

It was three o'clock. I was sitting at my table; I had set beside me the file of letters I stole in Moscow; I was writing:

"Care had been taken to spread the most sinister rumours. M. de Rollebon must have let himself be taken in by this manœuvre since he wrote to his nephew on the 13th of September that he had just made his will."

The Marquis was there: waiting for the moment when I should have definitively installed him in a niche in history, I had loaned him my life. I felt him like a glow in the pit of my stomach.

I studdenly realized an objection someone might raise: Rollebon was far from being frank with his nephew, whom he wanted to use, if the plot failed, as his defence witness with Paul I. It was only too possible that he had made up the story of the will to make himself appear completely innocent.

This was a minor objection; it wouldn't hold water. But it was enough to plunge me into a brown study. Suddenly I saw the fat waitress at "Camille's" again, the haggard face of M. Achille, the room in which I had so clearly felt I was forgotten, forsaken in the present. Wearily I told myself:

How can I, who have not the strength to hold to my own past, hope to save the past of someone else?

I picked up my pen and tried to get back to work; I was up to my neck in these reflections on the past, the present, the world. I asked only one thing: to be allowed to finish my book in peace.

But as my eyes fell on the pad of white sheets, I was struck by its look and I stayed, pen raised, studying this dazzling paper: so hard and far seeing, so present. The letters I had just inscribed on it were not even dry yet and already they belonged to the past.

"Care had been taken to spread the most sinister rumours . . ."

I had thought out this sentence, at first it had been a small part of myself. Now it was inscribed on the paper, it took sides against me. I didn't recognize it any more. I couldn't conceive it again. It was there, in front of me; in vain for me to trace some sign of its origin. Anyone could have written it. But I . . . I wasn't sure I wrote it. The letters glistened no longer, they were dry. That had disappeared too; nothing was left but their ephemeral spark.

I looked anxiously around me: the present, nothing but the present. Furniture light and solid, rooted in its present, a table, a bed, a closet with a mirror—and me. The true nature of the present revealed itself: it was what exists, and all that was not present did not exist. The past did not exist. Not at all. Not in things, not even in my thoughts. It is true that I had realized a long time ago that mine had escaped me. But until then I believed that it had simply gone out of my range. For me the past was only a pensioning off: it was another way of existing, a state of vacation and inaction; each event, when it had played its part, put itself politely into a box and became an honorary event: we have so much difficulty imagining nothingness. Now I knew: things are entirely what they appear to be—and behind them . . . there is nothing.

This thought absorbed me a few minutes longer. Then I violently moved my shoulders to free myself and pulled the pad of paper towards me.

". . . that he had just made his will."

An immense sickness flooded over me suddenly and the pen fell from my hand, spluttering ink. What happened? Did I have the Nausea? No, it wasn't that, the room had its paternal, every-day look. The table hardly seemed heavier and more solid to me, nor my pen more compact. Only M. de Rollebon had just died for the second time.

He was still there inside me a little while ago, quiet and warm, and I could feel him stir from time to time. He was quite alive, more alive to me than the Self-Taught Man or the woman at the "Railwaymen's Rendezvous." He undoubtedly had his whims, he could stay several days without showing himself; but often, on a mysteriously fine day, like a weather prophet, he put his nose out and I could see his pale face and bluish cheeks. And even when he didn't show himself, he was a weight on my heart and I felt full up.

Nothing more was left now. No more than, on these traces of dry ink, is left the memory of their freshness. It was my fault: I had spoken the only words I should not have said: I had said that the past did not exist. And suddenly, noiseless, M. de Rollebon had returned to his nothingness.

I held his letters in my hands, felt them with a kind of despair:

He is the one, I said, he is the one who made these marks, one by one. He leaned on this paper, he put his hand against the sheets to prevent them from turning under his pen.

Too late: these words had no more sense. Nothing existed but a bundle of yellow pages which I clasped in my hands. It is true there was that complicated affair. Rollebon's nephew assassinated by the Czar's police in 1810, his papers confiscated and taken to the Secret Archives, then, a hundred and ten years later, deposited by the Soviets who acted for him, in the State Library where I stole them in 1923. But that didn't seem true, and I had no real memory of a theft I had committed myself. It would not have been difficult to find a hundred more credible stories to explain the presence of these papers in my room: all would seem hollow and ephemeral in face of these scored sheets. Rather than count on them to put me in communication with Rollebon, I would do better to take up spirit rapping. Rollebon was no more. No more at all. If there were still a few bones left of him, they existed for themselves, independently, they were nothing more than a little phosphate and calcium carbonate with salts and water.

I made one last attempt; I repeated the words of Mme de Genlis by which I usually evoked the Marquis: "His small, wrinkled countenance, clean and sharp, all pitted with smallpox, in which there was a singular malice which struck the eye, no matter what effort he made to dissemble it."

His face appeared to me with docility, his pointed nose, his bluish cheeks, his smile. I could shape his features at will, perhaps with even greater ease than before. Only it was nothing more than an image in me, a fiction. I sighed, let myself lean back against the chair, with an intolerable sense of loss.

Four o'clock strikes. I'v been sitting here an hour, my arms hanging. It's beginning to get dark. Apart from that, nothing in this room has changed: the white paper is still on the table, next to the pen and inkwell. But I shall never write again on this page already started. Never again, following the Rue des Mutilés and the Boulevard de la Redoute, shall I turn into the library to look through their archives.

I want to get up and go out, do anything—no matter what—to stupefy myself. But if I move one finger, if I don't stay absolutely still, I know what will happen. I don't *want* that to happen to me yet. It will happen too soon as it is. I don't move; mechanically I read the paragraph I left unfinished on the pad of paper:

"Care had been taken to spread the most sinister rumours. M. de Rollebon must have let himself be caught by this manœuvre since he wrote to his nephew on the 13th of September that he had just made his will."

The great Rollebon affair was over, like a great passion. I must find something else. A few years ago, in Shanghai, in

97

Mercier's office, I suddenly woke from a dream. Then I had another dream, I lived in the Czar's court, in old palaces so cold that the icicles formed above the doors in winter. Today I wake up in front of a pad of white paper. The torches, the ice carnivals, the uniforms, the lovely cool shoulders have disappeared. *Something* has stayed behind in this warm room, something I don't want to see.

M. de Rollebon was my partner; he needed me in order to exist and I needed him so as not to feel my existence. I furnished the raw material, the material I had to re-sell, which I didn't know what to do with: existence, *my* existence. His part was to have an imposing appearance. He stood in front of me, took up my life to *lay bare* his own to me. I did not notice that I existed any more, I no longer existed in myself, but in him; I ate for him, breathed for him, each of my movements had its sense outside, there, just in front of me, in him; I no longer saw my hand writing letters on the paper, not even the sentence I had written—but behind, beyond the paper, I saw the Marquis who had claimed the gesture as his own, the gesture which prolonged, consolidated his existence. I was only a means of making him live, he was my reason for living, he had delivered me from myself. What shall I do now?

Above all, not move, *not move* . . . Ah!

I could not prevent this movement of the shoulders . . .

The thing which was waiting was on the alert, it has pounced on me, it flows through me, I am filled with it. It's nothing: I am the Thing. Existence, liberated, detached, floods over me. I exist.

I exist. It's sweet, so sweet, so slow. And light: you'd think it floated all by itself. It stirs. It brushes by me, melts and vanishes. Gently, gently. There is bubbling water in my mouth. I swallow. It slides down my throat, it caresses me—and now it comes up again into my mouth. For ever I shall have a little pool of whitish water in my mouth—lying low—grazing my tongue. And this pool is still me. And the tongue. And the throat is me.

I see my hand spread out on the table. It lives—it is me. It opens, the fingers open and point. It is lying on its back. It shows me its fat belly. It looks like an animal turned upside down. The fingers are the paws. I amuse myself by moving them very rapidly, like the claws of a crab which has fallen on its back.

The crab is dead: the claws draw up and close over the belly of my hand. I see the nails—the only part of me that doesn't live. And once more. My hand turns over, spreads out flat on its stomach, offers me the sight of its back. A silvery back, shining a little—like a fish except for the red hairs on the knuckles. I feel my hand. I am these two beasts struggling at the end of my arms. My hand scratches one of its paws with the nail of the other paw; I feel its weight on the table which is not me. It's long, long, this impression of weight, it doesn't pass. There is no reason for it to pass. It becomes intolerable . . . I draw back my hand and put it in my pocket; but immediately I feel the warmth of my thigh through the stuff. I pull my hand out of my pocket and let it hang against the back of the chair. Now I feel a weight at the end of my arm. It pulls a little, softly, insinuatingly it exists. I don't insist: no matter where I put it it will go on existing; I can't suppress it, nor can I suppress the rest of my body, the sweaty warmth which soils my shirt, nor all this warm obesity which turns lazily, as if someone were stirring it with a spoon, nor all the sensations going on inside, going, coming, mounting from my side to my armpit or quietly vegetating from morning to night, in their usual corner.

I jump up: it would be much better if I could only stop thinking. Thoughts are the dullest things. Duller than flesh. They stretch out and there's no end to them and they leave a funny taste in the mouth. Then there are words, inside the thoughts, unfinished words, a sketchy sentence which constantly returns: "I have to fi. . . I ex. . . Dead . . . M. de Roll is dead . . . I am not . . . I ex. . ." It goes, it goes . . . and there's no end to it. It's worse than the rest because I feel responsible and have complicity in it. For example, this sort of painful rumination: *I exist,* I am the one who keeps it up. I. The body lives by itself once it has begun. But thought—I am the one who continues it, unrolls it. I exist. How serpentine is this feeling of existing—I unwind it, slowly. . . . If I could keep myself from thinking! I try, and succeed: my head seems to fill with smoke . . . and then it starts again: "Smoke . . . not to think . . . don't want to think . . . I think I don't want to think. I mustn't think that I don't want to think. Because that's still a thought." Will there never be an end to it?

My thought is *me*: that's why I can't stop. I exist because I think . . . and I can't stop myself from thinking. At this very moment—it's frightful—if I exist, it is because I am horrified at existing. *I am the one* who pulls myself from the nothingness to which I aspire: the hatred, the disgust of existing, there are as many ways to *make* myself exist, to thrust myself into existence. Thoughts are born at the back of me, like sudden giddiness, I feel them being born behind my head . . . if I yield, they're going to come round in front of me, between my eyes—and I always yield, the thought grows and grows and there it is, immense, filling me completely and renewing my existence.

My saliva is sugary, my body warm: I feel neutral. My knife is on the table. I open it. Why not? It would be a change in any case. I put my left hand on the pad and stab the knife into the palm. The movement was too nervous; the blade slipped, the wound is superficial. It bleeds. Then what? What has changed? Still, I watch with satisfaction, on the white paper, across the lines I wrote a little while ago, this tiny pool of blood which has at last stopped being me. Four lines on a white paper, a spot of blood, that makes a beautiful memory. I must write beneath it: "Today I gave up writing my book on the Marquis de Rollebon."

Am I going to take care of my hand? I wonder. I watch the small, monotonous trickle of blood. Now it is coagulating. It's over. My skin looks rusty around the cut. Under the skin, the only thing left is a small sensation exactly like the others, perhaps even more insipid.

Half-past five strikes. I get up, my cold shirt sticks to my flesh. I go out. Why? Well, because I have no reason not to. Even if I stay, even if I crouch silently in a corner, I shall not forget myself. I will be there, my weight on the floor. I am.

I buy a newspaper along my way. Sensational news. Little Lucienne's body has been found! Smell of ink, the paper crumples between my fingers. The criminal has fled. The child was raped. They found her body, the fingers clawing at the mud. I roll the paper into a ball, my fingers clutching at the paper; smell of ink; my God how strongly things exist today. Little Lucienne was raped. Strangled. Her body still exists, her flesh bleeding. *She* no longer exists. Her hands. She no longer exists. The houses. I walk between the houses, I am between the houses, on the pavement; the pavement under my feet exists, the houses close around me, as the water closes over me, on the paper the shape of a swan. I am. I am, I exist, I think, therefore I am; I am because I think, why do I think? I don't want to think any more, I am because I think that I don't want to be, I think that

I . . . because . . . ugh! I flee. The criminal has fled, the violated body. She felt this other flesh pushing into her own. I . . . there I . . . Raped. A soft, criminal desire to rape catches me from behind, gently behind the ears, the ears race behind me, the red hair, it is red on my head, the wet grass, red grass, is it still I? Hold the paper, existence against existence, things exist one against the other, I drop the paper. The house springs up, it exists; in front of me, along the wall I am passing, along the wall I exist, in front of the wall, one step, the wall exists in front of me, one, two, behind me, a finger scratching at my pants, scratches, scratches and pulls at the little finger soiled with mud, mud on my finger which came from the muddy gutter and falls back slowly, softly, softening, scratching less strongly than the fingers of the little girl the criminal strangled, scratching the mud, the earth less strong, the finger slides slowly, the head falls first and rolling embraces my thigh; existence is soft, and rolls and tosses, I toss between the houses, I am, I exist, I think therefore I toss, I am, existence is a fallen chute, will not fall, will fall, the finger scratches at the window, existence is an imperfection. The gentleman. The handsome gentleman exists. The gentleman feels that he exists. No, the handsome gentleman who passes, proud and gentle as a convolvulus, does not feel that he exists. To expand; my cut hand hurts, exist, exist, exist. The handsome gentleman exists, the Legion of Honour, the moustache exists, it is all; how happy one must be to be nothing more than a Legion of Honour and a moustache and no one sees the rest, he sees the two pointed ends of his moustache on both sides of the nose; I do not think, therefore I am a moustache. He sees neither his gaunt body nor his big feet, if you looked in the crotch of the trousers you would surely discover a pair of little balls. He has the Legion of Honour, the bastards have the right to exist: "I exist because it is my right," I have the right to exist, therefore I have the right not to think: the finger is raised. Am I going to . . . caress in the opening of white sheets the white ecstatic flesh which falls back gently, touch the blossoming moisture of armpits, the elixis and cordials and florescence of flesh, enter into the existence of another, into the red mucus with the heavy, sweet, sweet odour of existence, feel myself exist between these soft, wet lips, the lips red with pale blood, throbbing lips yawning, all wet with existence, all wet with clear pus, between the wet sugary lips weeping like eyes? My body of living flesh which murmurs and turns gently, liquors which turn to cream, the flesh which turns, turns, the sweet sugary water of my flesh, the blood on my hand. I suffer in my wounded flesh which turns, walks, I walk, I flee, I am a criminal with bleeding flesh, bleeding with existence to these walls. I am cold, I take a step, I am cold, a step, I turn left, he turns left, he thinks he turns left, mad, am I mad? He says he is afraid of going mad, existence, do you see into existence, he stops, the body stops, he thinks he stops, where does he come from? What is he doing? He starts off, he is afraid, terribly afraid, the criminal, desire like a fog, desire, disgust, he says he is disgusted with existence, is he disgusted, weary of being disgusted with existence? He runs. What does he hope for? He runs to flee to throw himself into the lake? He runs, the heart, the heart beats, it's a holiday, the heart exists, the legs exist, the breath exists, they exist running, breathing, beating, all soft, all gently breathless, leaving me breathless, he says he's breathless; existence takes my thoughts from behind and gently expands them *from behind*; someone takes me from behind, they force me to think from behind, therefore to be something, behind me, breathing in light bubbles of existence, he is a bubble of fog and desire, he is pale as death in the glass, Rollebon is dead, Antoine Roquentin is not dead, I'm fainting: he says he would like to faint, he runs, he runs like a ferret, "from behind" from behind *from behind*, little Lucienne assaulted from behind, violated by existence from behind, he begs for mercy, he is ashamed of begging for mercy, pity, help, help therefore I exist, he goes into the Bar de la Marine, the little mirrors of the little brothel, he is pale in the little mirrors of the little brothel the big redhead who drops onto a bench, the gramophone plays, exists, all spins, the gramophone exists, the heart beats: spin, spin, liquors of life, spin, jellies, sweet sirups of my flesh, sweetness, the gramophone:

> *When that yellow moon begins to beam*
> *Every night I dream my little dream.*

The voice, deep and hoarse, suddenly appears and the world vanishes, the world of existence. A woman in the flesh had this voice, she sang in front of a record, in her finest get up, and they recorded her voice. The woman: bah! she existed like me, like Rollebon, I don't want to know her. But there it is. You can't say it exists. The turning record exists, the air struck by the voice which vibrates, exists, the voice which made an impression the record existed. I who listen, I exist. All is full, existence everywhere, dense, heavy and sweet. But, beyond all this sweetness, inaccessible, near and so far, young, merciless and serene, there is this . . . this rigour.

Tuesday:

Nothing. Existed.

Wednesday:

There is a sunbeam on the paper napkin. In the sunbeam there is a fly, dragging himself along, stupefied, sunning himself and rubbing his antennæ one against the other. I am going to do him the favour of squashing him. He does not see this giant finger advancing with the gold hairs shining in the sun.

"Don't kill it, Monsieur!" the Self-Taught Man shouted.

"I did it a favour."

Why am I here?—and why shouldn't I be here? It is noon, I am waiting for it to be time to sleep. (Fortunately sleep has not fled from me.) In four days I shall see Anny again: for the moment, my sole reason for living. And afterwards? When Anny leaves me? I know what I surreptitiously hope for: I hope she will never leave me. Yet I should know that Anny would never agree to grow old in front of me. I am weak and lonely, I need her. I would have liked to see her again in my strength: Anny is without pity for strayed sheep.

"Are you well, Monsieur? Do you feel all right?"

The Self-Taught Man looks at me out of the corner of his eyes, laughing. He pants a little, his mouth open, like a dog. I admit: this morning I was almost glad to see him, I needed to talk.

"How glad I am to have you at my table," he says. "If you're cold, we could go and sit next to the stove. These gentlemen are leaving soon, they've asked for the bill."

Someone is taking care of me, asking if I am cold: I am speaking to another man: that hasn't happened to me for years.

"They're leaving, do you want to change places?"

The two men have lighted cigarettes. They leave, there they are in the pure air, in the sunlight. They pass along the wide windows, holding their hats in both hands. They laugh; the wind bellies out their overcoats. No, I don't want to change places. What for? And then, through the windows, between the white roofs of the bathing-cabins I see the sea, green, compact.

The Self-Taught Man has taken two rectangles of purple cardboard from his wallet. He will soon hand them over the counter. I decipher on the back of one of them:

Maison Bottanet, cuisine bourgeoise
Le déjeuner à prix fixe: 8 francs
Hors d'œuvre au choix
Viande garnie
Fromage ou dessert
140 francs les 20 cachets

The man eating at the round table near the door—I recognize him now: he often stops at the Hotel Printania, he's a commercial traveller. From time to time he looks at me, attentive and smiling; but he doesn't see me; he is too absorbed in his food. On the other side of the counter, two squat, red-faced men are eating mussels and drinking white wine. The smaller, who has a thin yellow moustache is telling a story which makes him laugh. He pauses, laughs, showing sparkling teeth. The other does not laugh; his eyes are hard. But he often nods his head affirmatively. Near the window, a slight, dark-complexioned man with distinguished features and fine white hair, brushed back, reads his paper thoughtfully. A leather despatch case is on the bench beside him. He drinks Vichy water. In a moment all these people are going to leave; weighted down by food, caressed by the breeze, coat wide open, face a little flushed, their heads muzzy, they will walk along by the balustrade, watching the children on the beach and the ships on the sea; they will go to work. I will go nowhere, I have no work.

The Self-Taught Man laughs innocently and the sun plays through his sparse hair:

"Would you like to order?"

He hands me the menu: I am allowed one hors d'œuvre: either five slices of sausage or radishes or shrimps, or a dish of stuffed celery. Snails are extra.

"I'll have sausage," I tell the waitress.

He tears the menu from my hands:

"Isn't there anything better? Here are Bourgogne snails."

"I don't care to much for snails."

"Ah! What about oysters?"

"They're four francs more," the waitress says.

"All right, oysters, Mademoiselle—and radishes for me."

Blushing, he explains to me:

"I like radishes very much."

So do I.

I glance over the list of meats. Spiced beef tempts me. But I know in advance that I shall have chicken, the only extra meat.

"This gentleman will have," he says, "the chicken. Spiced beef for me."

He turns the card. The wine list is on the back:

"We shall have some wine," he says solemnly.

"Well!" the waitress says, "times have changed. You never drank any before."

"I can stand a glass of wine now and then. Will you bring us a carafe of pink Anjou?"

The Self-Taught Man puts down the menu, breaks his bread into small bits and rubs his knife and fork with his napkin. He glances at the white-haired man reading the paper, then smiles at me:

"I usually come here with a book, even though it's against doctor's orders: one eats too quickly and doesn't chew. But I have a stomach like an ostrich, I can swallow anything. During the winter of 1917, when I was a prisoner, the food was so bad that everyone got ill. Naturally, I went on the sick list like everybody else: but nothing was the matter."

He had been a prisoner of war. . . . This is the first time he mentioned it to me; I can't get over it: I can't picture him as anything other than the Self-Taught Man.

"Where were you a prisoner?"

He doesn't answer. He puts down his fork and looks at me with prodigious intensity. He is going to tell me his troubles: now I remember he said something was wrong, in the library. I am all ears: I am only too glad to feel pity for other people's troubles, that will make a change. I have no troubles, I have money like a capitalist, no boss, no wife, no children; I exist, that's all. And that trouble is so vague, so metaphysical that I am ashamed of it.

The Self-Taught Man doesn't seem to want to talk. What a curious look he gives me. It isn't a casual glance, but heart searching. The soul of the Self-Taught Man is in his eyes, his magnificent, blindman's eyes, where it blooms. Let mine do the same, let it come and stick its nose against the windows: they could exchange greetings.

I don't want any communion of souls, I haven't fallen so low. I draw back. But the Self-Taught Man throws his chest

105

out above the table, his eyes never leaving mine. Fortunately the waitress brings him his radishes. He drops back in his chair, his soul leaves his eyes, and he docilely begins to eat.

"Have you straightened out your troubles?"

He gives a start.

"What troubles, Monsieur?" he asks, nervously.

"You know, the other day you told me . . ."

He blushes violently.

"Ha!" he says in a dry voice. "Ha! Yes, the other day. Well, it's that Corsican, Monsieur, that Corsican in the library."

He hesitates a second time, with the obstinate look of a sheep.

"It's really nothing worth bothering you about, Monsieur."

I don't insist. Without seeming to, he eats, with extraordinary speed. He has already finished his radishes when the girl brings me the oysters. Nothing is left on his plate but a heap of radish stalks and a little damp salt.

Outside, a young couple has stopped in front of the menu which a cook in cardboard holds out to them in his left hand (he has a frying pan in his right). They hesitate. The woman is cold, she tucks her chin into her fur collar. The man makes up his mind first, he opens the door and steps inside to let the woman pass.

She enters. She looks around her amiably and shivers a little:

"It's hot," she says gravely.

The young man closes the door.

"Messieurs, dames," he says.

The Self-Taught Man turns round with a pleasant: "Messieurs, dames."

The other customers do not answer, but the distinguished-looking gentleman lowers his paper slightly and scrutinizes the new arrivals with a profound look.

"Don't bother, thank you."

Before the waitress, who had run up to help him, could make a move, the young man had slipped out of his raincoat. In place of a morning coat he wears a leather blouse with a zip. The waitress, a little disappointed, turns to the young woman. But once more he is ahead of her and helps the girl out of her coat with gentle, precise movements. They sit near us, one against the other. They don't look as if they'd known each other very long. The young woman has a weary face, pure and a little sullen. She suddenly takes off her hat, shakes her black hair and smiles.

The Self-Taught Man studies them at great length, with a kindly eye; then he turns to me and winks tenderly as if to say: "How wonderful they are!"

They are not ugly. They are quiet, happy at being together, happy at being seen together. Sometimes when Anny and I went into a restaurant in Piccadilly we felt ourselves the objects of admiring attention. It annoyed Anny, but I must confess that I was somewhat proud. Above all, amazed; I never had the clean-cut look that goes so well with that young man and no one could even say that my ugliness was touching. Only we were young: now, I am at the age to be touched by the youth of others. But I am not touched. The woman has dark, gentle eyes; the young man's skin has an orange hue, a little leathery, and a charming, small, obstinate chin. They are touching, but they also make me a little sick. I feel them so far from me: the warmth makes them languid, they pursue the same dream in their hearts, so low, so feeble. They are comfortable, they look with assurance at the yellow walls, the people, and they find the world pleasant as it is just as it is, and each one of them, temporarily, draws life from the life of the other. Soon the two of them will make a single life, a slow, tepid life which will have no sense at all—but they won't notice it.

They look as though they frighten each other. Finally, the young man, awkward and resolute, takes the girl's hand with the tips of his fingers. She breathes heavily and together they lean over the menu. Yes, they're happy. So what.

The Self-Taught Man puts on an amused, mysterious air: "I saw you the day before yesterday."

"Where?"

"Ha, ha!" he says, respectfully teasing.

He makes me wait for a second, then:

"You were coming out of the museum."

"Oh, yes," I say, "not the day before yesterday: Saturday."

The day before yesterday I certainly had no heart for running around museums.

"Have you seen that famous reproduction in carved wood—Orsini's attempted assassination?"

"I don't recall it."

"Is it possible? It's in a little room on the right, as you go in. It's the work of an insurgent of the Commune who lived in

107

Bouville until the amnesty, hiding in an attic. He wanted to go to America but the harbour police there were too quick for him. An admirable man. He spent his spare time carving a great oak panel. The only tools he had were a penknife and a nail file. He did the delicate parts with the file: the hands and eyes. The panel is five feet long by three feet wide; there are seventy figures, each one no larger than a hand, without counting the two horses pulling the emperor's carriage. And the faces, Monsieur, the faces made by the file, they have a distinct physiognomy, a human look. Monsieur, if I may allow myself to say so, it is a work worth seeing."

I don't want to be involved:

"I had simply wanted to see Bordurin's paintings again."

The Self-Taught Man suddenly grows sad:

"Those portraits in the main hall, Monsieur?" he asks, with a trembling smile, "I understand nothing about painting. Of course, I realize that Bordurin is a great painter, I can see he has a certain touch, a certain knack as they say. But pleasure, Monsieur, aesthetic pleasure is foreign to me."

I tell him sympathetically:

"I feel the same way about sculpture."

"Ah, Monsieur, I too, alas! And about music and about dancing. Yet I am not without a certain knowledge. Well, it is inconceivable: I have seen young people who don't know half what I know who, standing in front of a painting, seem to take pleasure in it."

"They must be pretending," I said to encourage him.

"Perhaps. . . ."

The Self-Taught Man dreams for a moment:

"What I regret is not so much being deprived of a certain taste, but rather that a whole branch of human activity is foreign to me. . . . Yet I am a man and *men* have painted those pictures. . . ."

Suddenly his tone changes:

"Monsieur, at one time I ventured to think that the beautiful was only a question of taste. Are there not different rules for each epoch? Allow me, Monsieur. . . ."

With surprise I see him draw a black leather notebook from his pocket. He goes through it for an instant: a lot of blank pages, and further on, a few lines written in red ink. He has turned pale. He has set the notebook flat on the tablecloth and spread his huge hand on the open page. He coughs with embarrassment:

"Sometimes things come to my mind—I dare not call them thoughts. It is very curious, I am there, I'm reading when suddenly, I don't know where it comes from, I feel illuminated. First I paid no attention and then I resolved to buy a notebook."

He stops and looks at me: he is waiting.

"Ah," I say.

"Monsieur, these maxims are naturally unpolished: my instruction is not yet completed."

He picks up the notebook with trembling hands, he is deeply moved:

"And there just happens to be something here about painting. I should be very happy if you would allow me to read . . ."

"With pleasure," I say.

He reads:

"No longer do people believe what the eighteenth century held to be true. Why should we still take pleasure in works because they thought them beautiful?"

He looks at me pleadingly.

"What must one think, Monsieur? Perhaps it is a paradox? I thought to endow my idea with the quality of a caprice."

"Well, I . . . I find that very interesting."

"Have you read it anywhere before?"

"No, of course not."

"Really, nowhere? Then, Monsieur," he says, his face growing sad, "it is because it is not true. If it were true, someone would already have thought of it."

"Wait a minute," I tell him, "now that I think about it, I believe I have read something like that."

His eyes are shining; he takes out his pencil.

"Which author?" he asks me, his voice precise.

"Oh . . . Renan."

He is in Paradise.

"Would you be kind enough to quote the exact passage for me?" he asks, sucking the point of his pencil.

"Oh, as a matter of fact, I read that quite a while ago."

"Oh, it doesn't matter, it doesn't matter."

He writes *Renan* in his notebook, just below his maxim.

"I have come upon Renan! I wrote the name in pencil," he explains, delighted, "but this evening I'll go over it in red ink."

He looks ecstatically at his notebook for a moment, and I

109

expect him to read me other maxims. But he closes it cautiously and stuffs it back in his pocket. He undoubtedly has decided that this is enough happiness for one time.

"How pleasant it is," he says intimately, "to be able to talk sometimes, as now, with abandon."

This, as might be supposed, puts an end to our languishing conversation. A long silence follows.

The atmosphere of the restaurant has changed since the arrival of the young couple. The two red-faced men are silent; they are nonchalantly detailing the young lady's charms. The distinguished-looking gentleman has put down his paper and is watching the couple with kindness, almost complicity. He thinks that old age is wise and youth is beautiful, he nods his head with a certain coquetry: he knows quite well that he is still handsome, well preserved, that with his dark complexion and his slender figure he is still attractive. He plays at feeling paternal. The waitress' feelings appear simpler: she is standing in front of the young people staring at them open-mouthed.

They are speaking quietly. They have been served their hors d'œuvres but they don't touch them. Listening carefully I can make out snatches of their conversation. I understand better what the woman says, her voice is rich and veiled.

"No, Jean, no."

"Why not?" the young man murmurs with passionate vivacity.

"I told you why."

"That's not a reason."

A few words escape me then the young woman makes a charming, lax gesture:

"I've tried too often. I'm past the age when you can start your life again. I'm old, you know."

The young man laughs ironically. She goes on:

"I couldn't stand being deceived."

"You must have confidence in life," the young man says; "the way you are this moment isn't living."

She sighs:

"I know!"

"Look at Jeannette."

"Yes," she says, making a little grimace.

"Well, I think what she did was splendid. She had courage."

"You know," the young woman says, "she rather jumped at

the opportunity. You must know that if I'd wanted, I could have had a hundred opportunities likes that. I preferred to wait."

"You were right," he says, tenderly, "you were right in waiting for me."

She laughs in turn:

"Great stupid! I didn't say that."

I don't listen to them any more: they annoy me. They're going to sleep together. They know it. Each one knows that the other knows it. But since they are young, chaste and decent, since each one wants to keep his self-respect and that of the other, since love is a great poetic thing which you must not frighten away, several times a week they go to dances and restaurants, offering the spectacle of their ritual, mechanical dances. . . .

After all, you have to kill time. They are young and well built, they have enough to last them another thirty years. So they're in no hurry, they delay and they are not wrong. Once they have slept together they will have to find something else to veil the enormous absurdity of their existence. Still . . . is it absolutely necessary to lie?

I glance around the room. What a comedy! All these people sitting there, looking serious, eating. No, they aren't eating: they are recuperating in order to successfully finish their tasks. Each one of them has his little personal difficulty which keeps him from noticing that he exists; there isn't one of them who doesn't believe himself indispensable to something or someone. Didn't the Self Taught Man tell me the other day: "No one better qualified than Nouçapié to undertake this vast synthesis?" Each one of them does one small thing and no one is better qualified than he to do it. No one is better qualified than the commercial traveller over there to sell Swan Toothpaste. No one is better qualified than that interesting young man to put his hand under his girl friend's skirts. And I am among them and if they look at me they must think that no one is better qualified than I to do what I'm doing. But *I know.* I don't look like much, but I know I exist and that they exist. And if I knew how to convince people I'd go and sit down next to that handsome white-haired gentleman and explain to him just what existence means. I burst out laughing at the thought of the face he would make. The Self-Taught Man looks at me with surprise. I'd like to stop but I can't; I laugh until I cry.

"You are gay, Monsieur," the Self-Taught Man says to me circumspectly.

"I was just thinking," I tell him, laughing, "that here we sit, all of us, eating and drinking to preserve our precious existence and really there is nothing, nothing, absolutely no reason for existing."

The Self-Taught Man becomes serious, he makes an effort to understand me. I laughed too loud: I saw several faces turn towards me. Then I regretted having said so much. After all, that's nobody's business.

He repeats slowly:

"No reason for existing . . . you undoubtedly mean, Monsieur, that life is without a goal? Isn't that what one might call pessimism?"

He thinks for an instant, then says gently:

"A few years ago I read a book by an American author. It was called *Is Life Worth Living*? Isn't that the question you are asking yourself?"

Certainly not, that is not the question I am asking myself. But I have no desire to explain.

"His conclusion," the Self-Taught Man says, consolingly, "is in favour of voluntary optimism. Life has a meaning if we choose to give it one. One must first act, throw one's self into some enterprise. Then, if one reflects, the die is already cast, one is pledged. I don't know what you think about that, Monsieur?"

"Nothing," I say.

Rather I think that that is precisely the sort of lie that the commercial traveller, the two young people and the man with white hair tell themselves.

The Self-Taught Man smiles with a little malice and much solemnity.

"Neither is it my opinion. I do not think we need look so far to know the direction our life should take."

"Ah?"

"There is a goal, Monsieur, there is a goal . . . there is humanity."

That's right: I forgot he was a humanist. He remains silent for a moment, long enough to make most of his spiced beef and a whole slice of bread disappear cleanly and inexorably. "There are people . . ." He has just painted a whole picture of himself, this philanthropist. Yes, but he doesn't know how to express himself. His soul is in his eyes, unquestionably, but soul is not enough. Before, when I used to hang around some Parisian humanists, I would hear them say a hundred times: "there are

112

people," and it was quite another thing. Virgan was without equal. He would take off his spectacles, as if to show himself naked in his man's flesh, and stare at me with eloquent eyes, with a weary, insistent look which seemed to undress me, and drag out my human essence, then he would murmur melodiously: "There are people, old man, there are people," giving the "there are" a sort of awkward power, as if his love of people, perpetually new and astonished, was caught up in its giant wings.

The Self-Taught Man's mimicry had not acquired this smoothness; his love for people is naïve and barbaric: a provincial humanist.

"People," I told him, "people . . . in any case, you don't seem to worry about them very much: you're always alone, always with your nose in a book."

The Self-Taught Man clapped his hands and began to laugh maliciously:

"You're wrong. Ah, Monsieur, allow me to tell you so: what an error!"

He pulls himself together for an instant, and finishes a discreet gulp. His face is radiant as dawn. Behind him, the young woman breaks out in a light laugh. Her friend bends over her, whispering in her ear.

"Your error is only too natural," the Self-Taught Man says, "I should have told you a long time ago. . . . But I am so timid, Monsieur: I was waiting for the opportunity."

"Here it is," I told him politely.

"I think so too. I think so too! Monsieur, what I am about to tell you . . ." He stops, blushing: "But perhaps I am imposing on you?"

I assure him that he isn't. He breathes a sigh of happiness.

"One does not find men like you every day, Monsieur, men whose breadth of vision is joined to so much penetration. I have been wanting to speak to you for months, explain to you what I have been, what I have become. . . ."

His plate is as empty and clean as if it had just been brought to him. I suddenly discover, next to my plate, a small tin dish where a drum-stick swims in a brown gravy. It has to be eaten.

"A little while ago I spoke of my captivity in Germany. It all started there. Before the War I was lonely and didn't realize it; I lived with my parents, good people, but I didn't get on with them. When I think of those years . . . how could I have lived

113

that way? I was dead, Monsieur, and I didn't know it; I had a collection of postage stamps."

He looks at me and interrupts himself:

"Monsieur, you are pale, you look fatigued. I hope I'm not disturbing you?"

"You interest me greatly."

"Then the War came and I enlisted without knowing why. I spent two years without understanding, because life at the front left little time for thoughts and besides, the soldiers were too common. I was taken prisoner at the end of 1917. Since then I have been told that many soldiers recovered their childhood faith while they were prisoners. Monsieur," the Self-Taught Man says, lowering his eyelids over bloodshot eyes, "I do not believe in God; His existence is belied by science. But, in the internment camp, I learned to believe in men."

"They bore their fate with courage?"

"Yes," he says vaguely, "there was that, too. Besides, we were well treated. But I wanted to speak of something else; the last months of the War, they hardly gave us any work to do. When it rained they made us go into a big wooden shed, about two hundred of us altogether, jammed in tightly. They closed the door and left us there, pressed one against the other, in almost total darkness."

He hesitated an instant.

"I don't know how to explain it, Monsieur. All those men were there, you could hardly see them but you could feel them against you, you could hear the sound of their breathing. . . . One of the first times they locked us in the shed, the crush was so great that at first I thought I was going suffocate, then, suddenly, an overwhelming joy came over me, I almost fainted: then I felt that I loved these men like brothers, I wanted to embrace all of them. Each time I went back there I felt the same joy."

I have to eat my chicken which by now must be cold. The Self-Taught Man has been silent for a long time and the waitress is waiting to change the plates.

"That shed took on a sacred character in my eyes. Sometimes I managed to escape the watchfulness of my guards, I slipped into it all alone and there, in the shadow, the memory of the joys I had known, filled me with a sort of ecstasy. Hours passed and I did not notice them. Sometimes I wept."

I must be sick: there is no other way of explaining this terrible rage which suddenly overwhelms me. Yes, the rage of a sick man: my hands were shaking, the blood had rushed to my face, and finally my lips began to tremble. All this simply because the chicken was cold. I was cold too and that was the worst: I mean that inside me I was cold, freezing, and had been like that for thirty-six hours. Anger passed through me like a whirlwind, my conscience, effort to react, to fight against this lowered temperature caused something like a tremor to pass through me. Vain effort: undoubtedly, for nothing. I would have rained down blows and curses on the Self-Taught Man or the waitress. But I should not have been in the spirit of it. My rage and fury struggled to the surface and, for a moment, I had the terrible impression of being turned into a block of ice enveloped in fire, a kind of "omelette surprise." This momentary agitation vanished and I heard the Self-Taught Man say:

"Every Sunday I used to go to Mass. Monsieur, I have never been a believer. But couldn't one say that the real mystery of the Mass is the communion of souls? A French chaplain, who had only one arm, celebrated the Mass. We had a harmonium. We listened, standing, our heads bare, and as the sounds of the harmonium carried me away, I felt myself at one with all the men surrounding me. Ah, Monsieur, how I loved those Masses. Even now, in memory of them, I sometimes go to church on Sunday morning. We have a remarkable organist at Sainte-Cécile."

"You must have often missed that life?"

"Yes, Monsieur, in 1919, the year of my liberation, I spent many miserable months. I didn't know what to do with myself, I was wasting away. Whenever I saw men together I would insert myself into their group. It has happened to me," he added, smiling, "to follow the funeral procession of a stranger. One day, in despair, I threw my stamp collection in the fire. . . . But I found my vocation."

"Really?"

"Someone advised me . . . Monsieur, I know that I can count on your discretion. I am—perhaps these are not your ideas, but you are so broad-minded—I am a Socialist."

He lowered his eyes and his long lashes trembled:

"I have been a registered member of the Socialist Party, S.F.I.O., since the month of September 1921. That is what I wanted to tell you."

He is radiant with pride. He gazes at me, his head thrown back, his eyes half-closed, mouth open, looking like a martyr.

"That's very fine," I say, "that's very fine."

"Monsieur, I knew that you would commend me. And how could you blame someone who comes and tells you: I have spent my life in such and such a way, I am perfectly happy?"

He spreads his arms and presents his open palms to me, the fingers pointing to the ground, as if he were about to receive the stigmata. His eyes are glassy, I see a dark pink mass rolling in his mouth.

"Ah," I say, "as long as you're happy. . . ."

"Happy?" His look is disconcerting, he has raised his eyelids and stares harshly at me. "You will be able to judge, Monsieur. Before taking this decision I felt myself in a solitude so frightful that I contemplated suicide. What held me back was the idea that no one, absolutely no one, would be moved by my death, that I would be even more alone in death than in life."

He straightens himself, his cheeks swell.

"I am no longer lonely, Monsieur. I shall never be so."

"Ah, you know a lot of people?" I ask.

He smiles and I immediately realize my mistake.

"I mean that I no longer *feel* alone. But naturally, Monsieur, it is not necessary for me to be with anyone."

"But," I say, "what about the Socialist section. . . ."

"Ah! I know everybody there. But most of them only by name. Monsieur," he says mischievously, "is one obliged to choose his friends so narrowly? All men are my friends. When I go to the office in the morning, in front of me, behind me, there are other men going to work. I see them, if I dared I would smile at them, I think that I am a Socialist, that all of them are my life's goal, the goal of my efforts and that they don't know it yet. It's a holiday for me, Monsieur."

His eyes question me; I nod approval, but I feel he is a little disappointed, that he would like more enthusiasm. What can I do? Is it my fault if, in all he tells me, I recognize the lack of the genuine article? Is it my fault if, as he speaks, I see all the humanists I have known rise up? I've known so many of them! The radical humanist is the particular friend of officials. The so-called "left" humanist's main worry is keeping human values; he belongs to no party because he does not want to betray the human, but his sympathies go towards the humble; he consecrates his beautiful classic culture to the humble. He is generally a widower with a fine eye always clouded with tears: he weeps at anniversaries. He also loves cats, dogs, and all the higher mammals. The Communist writer has been loving men since the second Five-Year Plan; he punishes because he loves. Modest as all strong men, he knows how to hide his feelings, but he also knows, by a look, an inflection of his voice, how to recognize, behind his rough and ready justicial utterances, his passion for his brethren. The Catholic humanist, the late-comer, the Benjamin, speaks of men with a marvellous air. What a beautiful fairy tale, says he, is the humble life of a London dockhand, the girl in the shoe factory! He has chosen the humanism of the angels; he writes, for their edification, long, sad and beautiful novels which frequently win the Prix Femina.

Those are the principal rôles. But there are others, a swarm of others: the humanist philosopher who bends over his brothers like a wise elder brother who has a sense of his responsibilities; the humanist who loves men as they are, the humanist who loves men as they ought to be, the one who wants to save them with their consent and the one who will save them in spite of themselves, the one who wants to create new myths, and the one who is satisfied with the old ones, the one who loves death in man, the one who loves life in man, the happy humanist who always has the right word to make people laugh, the sober humanist whom you meet especially at funerals or wakes. They all hate each other: as individuals, naturally not as men. But the Self-Taught Man doesn't know it: he has locked them up inside himself like cats in a bag and they are tearing each other in pieces without his noticing it.

He is already looking at me with less confidence.

"Don't you feel as I do, Monsieur?"

"Gracious . . ."

Under his troubled, somewhat spiteful glance, I regret disappointing him for a second. But he continues amiably:

"I know: you have your research, your books, you serve the same cause in your own way."

My books, *my* research: the imbecile. He couldn't have made a worse howler.

"That's not why I'm writing."

At that instant the face of the Self-Taught Man is transformed: as if he had scented the enemy. I had never seen that expression on his face before. Something has died between us.

Feigning surprise, he asks:

"But . . . if I'm not being indiscreet, why do you write, Monsieur?"

"I don't know: just to write."

He smiles, he thinks he has put me out:

"Would you write on a desert island? Doesn't one always write to be read?"

He gave this sentence his usual interrogative turn. In reality, he is affirming. His veneer of gentleness and timidity has peeled off; I don't recognize him any more. His features assume an air of heavy obstinacy; a wall of sufficiency. I still haven't got over my astonishment when I hear him say:

"If someone tells me: I write for a certain social class, for a group of friends. Good luck to them. Perhaps you write for posterity. . . . But, Monsieur, in spite of yourself, you write for someone."

He waits for an answer. When it doesn't come, he smiles feebly.

"Perhaps you are a misanthrope?"

I know what this fallacious effort at conciliation hides. He asks little from me: simply to accept a label. But it is a trap: if I consent, the Self-Taught Man wins, I am immediately turned round, reconstituted, overtaken, for humanism takes possession and melts all human attitudes into one. If you oppose him head on, you play his game; he lives off his opponents. There is a race of beings, limited and headstrong, who lose to him every time: he digests all their violences and worst excesses; he makes a white, frothy lymph of them. He has digested anti-intellectualism, Manicheism, mysticism, pessimism, anarchy and egotism: they are nothing more than stages, unfinished thoughts which find their justification only in him. Misanthropy also has its place in the concert: it is only a dissonance necessary to the harmony of the whole. The misanthrope is a man: therefore the humanist must be misanthropic to a certain extent. But he must be a scientist as well to have learned how to water down his hatred, and hate men only to love them better afterwards.

I don't want to be integrated, I don't want my good red blood to go and fatten this lymphatic beast: I will not be fool enough to call myself "anti-humanist." I *am not* a humanist, that's all there is to it.

"I believe," I tell the Self-Taught Man, "that one cannot hate a man more than one can love him."

The Self-Taught Man looks at me pityingly and aloof. He murmurs, as though he were paying no attention to his words:

"You must love them, you must love them. . . ."

"Whom must you love? The people here?"

"They too. All."

He turns towards the radiant young couple: that's what you must love. For a moment he contemplates the man with white hair. Then his look returns to me: I read a mute question on his face. I shake my head: "No." He seems to pity me.

"You don't either," I tell him, annoyed, "you don't love them."

"Really, Monsieur? Would you allow me to differ?"

He has become respectful again, respectful to the tip of his toes, but in his eyes he has the ironic look of someone who is amusing himself enormously. He hates me. I should have been wrong to have any feeling for this maniac. I question him in my turn.

"So, those two young people behind you—you love them?"

He looks at them again, ponders:

"You want to make me say," he begins, suspiciously, "that I love them without knowing them. Well, Monsieur, I confess, I don't know them. . . . Unless love is knowing," he adds with a foolish laugh.

"But what do you love?"

"I see they are young and I love the youth in them. Among other things, Monsieur."

He interrupts himself and listens:

"Do you understand what they're saying?"

Do I understand? The young man, emboldened by the sympathy which surrounds him, tells, in a loud voice, about a football game his team won against a club from Le Havre last year.

"He's telling a story," I say to the Self-Taught Man.

"Ah! I can't hear them very well. But I hear the voices, the soft voice, the grave voice: they alternate. It's . . . it's so sympathetic."

"Only I also hear what they're saying, unfortunately."

"Well?"

"They're playing a comedy."

"Really? The comedy of youth, perhaps?" he asks ironically. "Allow me, Monsieur, to find that quite profitable. Is playing it enough to make one young again?"

I stay deaf to his irony; I continue:

"You turn your back on them, what they say escapes you. . . . What colour is the woman's hair?"

He is worried:

119

"Well, I . . ." He glances quickly at the young couple and regains his assurance. "Black!"

"So you see!"

"See what?"

"You see that you don't love them. You wouldn't recognize them in the street. They're only symbols in your eyes. You are not at all touched by them: you're touched by the Youth of the Man, the Love of Man and Woman, the Human Voice."

"Well? Doesn't that exist?"

"Certainly not, it doesn't exist! Neither Youth nor Maturity nor Old Age nor Death. . . ."

The face of the Self-Taught Man, hard and yellow as a quince, has stiffened into a reproachful lockjaw. Nevertheless, I keep on:

"Just like that old man drinking Vichy water there behind you. I suppose you love the Mature Man in him: Mature Man going courageously towards his decline and who takes care of himself because he doesn't want to let himself go?"

"Exactly," he says definitely.

"And you don't think he's a bastard?"

He laughs, he finds me frivolous, he glances quickly at the handsome face framed in white hair:

"But Monsieur, admitting that he seems to be what you say, how can you judge a man by his face? A face, Monsieur, tells nothing when it is at rest."

Blind humanists! This face is so outspoken, so frank—but their tender, abstract soul will never let itself be touched by the sense of a face.

"How can you," the Self-Taught Man says, "*stop* a man, say he *is* this or that? Who can empty a man! Who can know the resources of a man?"

Empty a man! I salute, in passing, the Catholic humanism from which the Self-Taught Man borrowed this formula without realizing it.

"I know," I tell him, "I know that all men are admirable. You are admirable. I am admirable. In as far as we are creations of God, naturally."

He looks at me without understanding, then with a thin smile:

"You are undoubtedly joking, Monsieur, but it is true that all men deserve our admiration. It is difficult, Monsieur, very difficult to be a man."

Without realizing it, he has abandoned the love of men in Christ; he nods his head, and by a curious phenomenon of mimicry, he resembles this poor man of Gehenna.

"Excuse me," I say, "but I am not quite sure of being a man: I never found it very difficult. It seemed to me that you had only to let yourself alone."

The Self-Taught Man laughs candidly, but his eyes stay wicked:

"You are too modest, Monsieur. In order to tolerate your condition, the human condition, you, as everybody else, need much courage. Monsieur, the next instant may be the moment of your death, you know it and you can smile: isn't that admirable? In your most insignificant actions," he adds sharply, "there is an enormous amount of heroism."

"What will you gentlemen have for dessert?" the waitress says.

The Self-Taught Man is quite white, his eyelids are half-shut over his stony eyes. He makes a feeble motion with his hand, as if inviting me to choose.

"Cheese," I say heroically.

"And you?"

He jumps.

"Eh? Oh, yes: well . . . I don't want anything. I've finished."

"Louise!"

The two stout men pay and leave. One of them limps. The patron shows them to the door: they are important customers, they were served a bottle of wine in a bucket of ice.

I study the Self-Taught Man with a little remorse: he has been happy all the week imagining this luncheon, where he could share his love of men with another man. He has so rarely the opportunity to speak. And now I have spoiled his pleasure. At heart he is as lonely as I am: no one cares about him. Only he doesn't realize his solitude. Well, yes: but it wasn't up to me to open his eyes. I feel very ill at ease: I'm furious, but not against him, against Virgan and the others, all the ones who have poisoned this poor brain. If I could have them here in front of me I would have much to say to them. I shall say nothing to the Self-Taught Man, I have only sympathy for him: he is someone like M. Achille, someone on my side, but who has been betrayed by ignorance and good will!

A burst of laughter from the Self-Taught Man pulls me out of my sad reflections.

"You will excuse me, but when I think of the depth of my love for people, of the force which impels me towards them and when I see us here, reasoning, arguing . . . it makes me want to laugh."

I keep quiet, I smile constrainedly. The waitress puts a plate of chalky Camembert in front of me. I glance around the room and a violent disgust floods me. What am I doing here? Why did I have to get mixed up in a discussion on humanism? Why are these people here? Why are they eating? It's true they don't know they exist. I want to leave, go to some place where I will be really in my own niche, where I will fit in. . . . But my place is nowhere; I am unwanted, *de trop.*

The Self-Taught Man grows softer. He expected more resistance on my part. He is ready to pass a sponge over all I have said. He leans towards me confidentially:

"You love them at heart, Monsieur, you love them as I do: we are separated by words."

I can't speak any more, I bow my head. The Self-Taught Man's face is close to mine. He smiles foolishly, all the while close to my face, like a nightmare. With difficulty I chew a piece of bread which I can't make up my mind to swallow. People. You must love people. Men are admirable. I want to vomit—and suddenly, there it is: the Nausea.

A fine climax: it shakes me from top to bottom. I saw it coming more than an hour ago, only I didn't want to admit it. This taste of cheese in my mouth. . . . The Self-Taught Man is babbling and his voice buzzes gently in my ears. But I don't know what he's talking about. I nod my head mechanically. My hand is clutching the handle of the dessert knife. I *feel* this black wooden handle. My hand holds it. My hand. Personally, I would rather let this knife alone: what good is it to be always touching something? Objects are not made to be touched. It is better to slip between them, avoiding them as much as possible. Sometimes you take one of them in your hand and you have to drop it quickly. The knife falls on the plate. The white-haired man starts and looks at me. I pick up the knife again, I rest the blade against the table and bend it.

So this is Nausea: this blinding evidence? I have scratched my head over it! I've written about it. Now I know: I exist—the world exists—and I know that the world exists. That's all. It makes no difference to me. It's strange that everything makes so little difference to me: it frightens me. Ever since the day I wanted to play ducks and drakes. I was going to throw that pebble, I looked at it and then it all began: I felt that it *existed*. Then after that there were other Nauseas; from time to time objects start existing in your hand. There was the Nausea of the "Railwaymen's Rendezvous" and then another, before that, the night I was looking out the window; then another in the park, one Sunday, then others. But it had never been as strong as today.

". . . Of ancient Rome, Monsieur?"

The Self-Taught Man is asking me a question, I think. I turn towards him and smile. Well? What's the matter with him? Why is he shrinking back into his chair? Do I frighten people now? I shall end up that way. But it makes no difference to me. They aren't completely wrong to be afraid: I feel as though I could do anything. For example, stab this cheese knife into the Self-Taught Man's eye. After that, all these people would trample me and kick my teeth out. But that isn't what stops me: a taste of blood in the mouth instead of this taste of cheese makes no difference to me. Only I should make some move, introduce some superfluous event: the Self-Taught Man's cry would be too much—and the blood flowing down the cheek and all the people jumping up. There are quite enough things like that which exist already.

Everyone is watching me; the two representatives of youth have interrupted their gentle chat. The woman's mouth looks like a chicken's backside. And yet they ought to see that I am harmless.

I get up, everything spins around me. The Self-Taught Man stares at me with his great eyes which I shall not gouge out.

"Leaving already?" he murmurs.

"I'm a little tired. It was very nice of you to invite me. Good-bye."

As I am about to leave I notice that I have kept the dessert knife in my left hand. I throw it on my plate which begins to clink. I cross the room in the midst of silence. No one is eating: they are watching me, they have lost their appetite. If I were to go up to the young woman and say "Boo!" she'd begin screaming, that's certain. It isn't worth the trouble.

Still, before going out, I turn back and give them a good look at my face so they can engrave it in their memory.

"Good-bye, ladies and gentlemen."

They don't answer. I leave. Now the colour will come back to their cheeks, they'll begin to jabber.

I don't know where to go, I stay planted in front of the cardboard chef. I don't need to turn around to know they are watching me through the windows: they are watching my back with surprise and disgust; they thought I was like them, that I was a man, and I deceived them. I suddenly lost the appearance of a man and they saw a crab running backwards out of this human room. Now the unmasked intruder has fled: the show goes on. It annoys me to feel on my back this stirring of eyes and frightened thoughts. I cross the street. The other pavement runs along the beach and the bath houses.

Many people are walking along the shore, turning poetic springtime faces towards the sea; they're having a holiday because of the sun. There are lightly dressed women who have put on last spring's outfit; they pass, long and white as kid gloves; there are also big boys who go to high school and the School of Commerce, old men with medals. They don't know each other but they look at each other with an air of connivance because it's such a fine day and they are men. Strangers embrace each other when war is declared; they smile at each other every spring. A priest advances slowly, reading his breviary. Now and then he raises his head and looks at the sea approvingly:—the sea is also a breviary, it speaks of God. Delicate colours, delicate perfumes, souls of spring. "What a lovely day, the sea is green, I like this dry cold better than the damp." Poets! If I grabbed one of them by the back of the coat, if I told him: "Come, help me," he'd think, "What's this crab doing here?" and would run off, leaving his coat in my hands.

I turn back, lean both hands on the balustrade. The *true* sea is cold and black, full of animals; it crawls under this thin green film made to deceive human beings. The sylphs all round me have let themselves be taken in: they only see the thin film, which proves the existence of God. I see beneath it! The veneer melts, the shining velvety scales, the scales of God's catch explode everywhere at my look, they split and gape. Here is the Saint-Elémir tramway, I turn round and the objects turn with me, pale and green as oysters.

Useless, it was useless to get in since I don't want to go anywhere.

Bluish objects pass the windows. In jerks all stiff and brittle; people, walls; a house offers me its black heart through open windows; and the windows pale, all that is black becomes blue, blue this great yellow brick house advancing uncertainly, trembling, suddenly stopping and taking a nose dive. A man gets on and sits down opposite to me. The yellow house starts up again, it leaps against the windows, it is so close that you can only see part of it, it is obscured. The windows rattle. It rises, crushing, higher than you can see, with hundreds of windows opened on black hearts; it slides along the car brushing past it; night has come between the rattling windows. It slides interminably, yellow as mud, and the windows are sky blue. Suddenly it is no longer there, it has stayed behind, a sharp, grey illumination fills the car and spreads everywhere with inexorable justice: it is the sky; through the windows you can still see layer on layer of sky because we're going up Eliphar Hill and you can see clearly between the two slopes, on the right as far as the sea, on the left as far as the airfield. No smoking—not even a *gitane*.

I lean my hand on the seat but pull it back hurriedly: it exists. This thing I'm sitting on, leaning my hand on, is called a seat. They made it purposely for people to sit on, they took leather, springs and cloth, they went to work with the idea of making a seat and when they finished, *that* was what they had made. They carried it here, into this car and the car is now rolling and jolting with its rattling windows, carrying this red thing in its bosom. I murmur: "It's a seat," a little like an exorcism. But the word stays on my lips: it refuses to go and put itself on the thing. It stays what it is, with its red plush, thousands of little red paws in the air, all still, little dead paws. This enormous belly turned upward, bleeding, inflated—bloated with all its dead paws, this belly floating in this car, in this grey sky, is not a seat. It could just as well be a dead donkey tossed about in the water, floating with the current, belly in the air in a great grey river, a river of floods; and I could be sitting on the donkey's belly, my feet dangling in the clear water. Things are divorced from their names. They are there, grotesque, headstrong, gigantic and it seems ridiculous to call them seats or say anything at all about them: I am in the midst of things, nameless things. Alone, without words, defenceless, they surround me, are beneath me, behind me, above me. They demand nothing, they don't impose themselves: they are there. Under the cushion on the seat there is a thin line of shadow, a thin black line running along the seat, mysteriously and mischievously, almost a smile. I know very well that it isn't a smile and yet it exists, it runs under the whitish windows, under the jangle of glass, obstinately, obstinately behind the blue images which pass in a throng, like the inexact memory of a smile, like a half forgotten word of which you can only remember the first syllable and the best thing you can do is turn your eyes away and think about something else, about that man half-lying down on the seat opposite me, there. His blue-eyed, terra cotta face. The whole right side of his body has sunk, the right arm is stuck to the body, the right side barely lives, it lives with difficulty, with avarice, as if it were paralysed. But on the whole left side there is a little parasitic existence, which proliferates; a chance: the arm begins to tremble and then is raised up and the hand at the end is stiff. Then the hand begins to tremble too and when it reaches the height of the skull, a finger stretches out and begins scratching the scalp with a nail. A sort of voluptuous grimace comes to inhabit the right side of the mouth and the left side stays dead. The windows rattle, the arm shakes, the nail scratches, scratches, the mouth smiles under the staring eyes and the man tolerates, hardly noticing it, this tiny existence which swells his right side, which has borrowed his right arm and right cheek to bring itself into being. The conductor blocks my path.

"Wait until the car stops."

But I push him aside and jump out of the tramway. I couldn't stand any more. I could no longer stand things being so close. I push open a gate, go in, airy creatures are bounding and leaping and perching on the peaks. Now I recognize myself, I know where I am: I'm in the park. I drop onto a bench between great black tree-trunks, between the black, knotty hands reaching towards the sky. A tree scrapes at the earth under my feet with a black nail. I would so like to let myself go, forget myself, sleep. But I can't, I'm suffocating: existence penetrates me everywhere, through the eyes, the nose, the mouth. . . .

And suddenly, suddenly, the veil is torn away, I have understood, I have *seen*.

6.00 *p.m.*

I can't say I feel relieved or satisfied; just the opposite, I am crushed. Only my goal is reached: I know what I wanted to know; I have understood all that has happened to me since January. The Nausea has not left me and I don't believe it will leave me so soon; but I no longer have to bear it, it is no longer an illness or a passing fit: it is I.

So I was in the park just now. The roots of the chestnut tree were sunk in the ground just under my bench. I couldn't remember it was a root any more. The words had vanished and with them the significance of things, their methods of use, and the feeble points of reference which men have traced on their surface. I was sitting, stooping forward, head bowed, alone in front of this black, knotty mass, entirely beastly, which frightened me. Then I had this vision.

It left me breathless. Never, until these last few days, had I understood the meaning of "existence." I was like the others, like the ones walking along the seashore, all dressed in their spring finery. I said, like them, "The ocean *is* green; that white speck up there *is* a seagull," but I didn't feel that it existed or that the seagull was an "existing seagull"; usually existence hides itself. It is there, around us, in us, it is *us*, you can't say two words without mentioning it, but you can never touch it. When I believed I was thinking about it, I must believe that I was thinking nothing, my head was empty, or there was just one word in my head, the word "to be." Or else I was thinking . . . how can I explain it? I was thinking of *belonging*, I was telling myself that the sea belonged to the class of green objects, or that the green was a part of the quality of the sea. Even when I looked at things, I was miles from dreaming that they existed: they looked like scenery to me. I picked them up in my hands, they served me as tools, I foresaw their resistance. But that all happened on the surface. If anyone had asked me what existence was, I would have answered, in good faith, that it was nothing, simply an empty form which was added to external things without changing anything in their nature. And then all of a sudden, there it was, clear as day: existence had suddenly unveiled itself. It had lost the harmless look of an abstract category: it was the very paste of things, this root was kneaded into existence. Or rather the root, the park gates, the bench, the sparse grass, all that had vanished: the diversity of things, their individuality, were only an appearance, a veneer. This veneer had melted, leaving soft, monstrous masses, all in disorder—naked, in a frightful, obscene nakedness.

I kept myself from making the slightest movement, but I didn't need to move in order to see, behind the trees, the blue columns and the lamp posts of the bandstand and the Velleda, in the midst of a mountain of laurel. All these objects . . . how can I explain? They inconvenienced me; I would have liked them to exist less strongly, more dryly, in a more abstract way, with more reserve. The chestnut tree pressed itself against my eyes. Green rust covered it half-way up; the bark, black and swollen, looked like boiled leather. The sound of the water in the Masqueret Fountain sounded in my ears, made a nest there, filled them with signs; my nostrils overflowed with a green, putrid odour. All things, gently, tenderly, were letting themselves drift into existence like those relaxed women who burst out laughing and say: "It's good to laugh," in a wet voice; they were parading, one in front of the other, exchanging abject secrets about their existence. I realized that there was no half-way house between non-existence and this flaunting abundance. If you existed, you had to *exist all the way*, as far as mouldiness, bloatedness, obscenity were concerned. In another world, circles, bars of music keep their pure and rigid lines. But existence is a deflection. Trees, night-blue pillars, the happy bubbling of a fountain, vital smells, little heat-mists floating in the cold air, a red-haired man digesting on a bench: all this somnolence, all these meals digested together, had its comic side. . . . Comic . . . no: it didn't go as far as that, nothing that exists can be comic; it was like a floating analogy, almost entirely elusive, with certain aspects of vaudeville. We were a heap of living creatures, irritated, embarrassed at ourselves, we hadn't the slightest reason to be there, none of us, each one, confused, vaguely alarmed, felt in the way in relation to the others. *In the way*: it was the only relationship I could establish between these trees, these gates, these stones. In vain I tried to *count* the chestnut trees, to *locate* them by their relationship to the Velleda, to compare their height with the height of the plane trees: each of them escaped the relationship in which I tried to enclose it, isolated itself, and overflowed. Of these relations (which I insisted on maintaining in order to delay the crumbling of the human world, measures, quantities, and directions)—I felt myself to be the arbitrator; they no longer had their teeth into things. *In the way*, the chestnut tree there, opposite me, a little to the left. *In the way*, the Velleda. . . .

And I—soft, weak, obscene, digesting, juggling with dismal thoughts—I, too, was *In the way*. Fortunately, I didn't feel it, although I realized it, but I was uncomfortable because I was afraid of feeling it (even now I am afraid—afraid that it might catch me behind my head and lift me up like a wave). I dreamed vaguely of killing myself to wipe out at least one of these superfluous lives. But even my death would have been *In the way*. *In the way*, my corpse, my blood on these stones, between these plants, at the back of this smiling garden. And the decomposed flesh would have been *In the way* in the earth which would receive my bones, at last, cleaned, stripped, peeled, proper and clean as teeth, it would have been *In the way*: I was *In the way* for eternity.

The word absurdity is coming to life under my pen; a little while ago, in the garden, I couldn't find it, but neither was I looking for it, I didn't need it: I thought without words, *on* things, *with* things. Absurdity was not an idea in my head, or the sound of a voice, only this long serpent dead at my feet, this wooden serpent. Serpent or claw or root or vulture's talon, what difference does it make. And without formulating anything clearly, I understood that I had found the key to Existence, the key to my Nauseas, to my own life. In fact, all that I could grasp beyond that returns to this fundamental absurdity. Absurdity: another word; I struggle against words; down there I touched the thing. But I wanted to fix the absolute character of this absurdity here. A movement, an event in the tiny coloured world of men is only relatively absurd: by relation to the accompanying circumstances. A madman's ravings, for example, are absurd in relation to the situation in which he finds himself, but not in relation to his delirium. But a little while ago I made an experiment with the absolute or the absurd. This root—there was nothing in relation to which it was absurd. Oh, how can I put it in words? Absurd: in relation to the stones, the tufts of yellow grass, the dry mud, the tree, the sky, the green benches. Absurd, irreducible; nothing—not even a profound, secret upheaval of nature—could explain it. Evidently I did not know everything, I had not seen the seeds sprout, or the tree grow. But faced with this great wrinkled paw, neither ignorance nor knowledge was important: the world of explanations and reasons is not the world of existence. A circle is not absurd, it is clearly explained by the rotation of a straight segment around one of its extremities. But neither does a circle exist. This root, on the other hand, existed in such a way that I could not explain it. Knotty, inert, nameless, it fascinated me, filled my eyes, brought me back unceasingly to its own existence. In vain to repeat: "This is a root"—it didn't work any more. I saw clearly that you could not pass from its function as a root, as a breathing pump, *to that,* to this hard and compact skin of a sea lion, to this oily, callous, headstrong look. The function explained nothing: it allowed you to understand generally that it was a root, but not *that one* at all. This root, with its colour, shape, its congealed movement, was . . . below all explanation. Each of its qualities escaped it a little, flowed out

129

of it, half solidified, almost became a thing; each one was *In the way* in the root and the whole stump now gave me the impression of unwinding itself a little, denying its existence to lose itself in a frenzied excess. I scraped my heel against this black claw: I wanted to peel off some of the bark. For no reason at all, out of defiance, to make the bare pink appear absurd on the tanned leather: to *play* with the absurdity of the world. But, when I drew my heel back, I saw that the bark was still black.

Black? I felt the word deflating, emptied of meaning with extraordinary rapidity. Black? The root *was not* black, there was no black on this piece of wood—there was . . . something else: black, like the circle, did not exist. I looked at the root: was it *more than* black or *almost* black? But I soon stopped questioning myself because I had the feeling of knowing where I was. Yes, I had already scrutinized innumerable objects, with deep uneasiness. I had already tried—vainly—to think something *about* them: and I had already felt their cold, inert qualities elude me, slip through my fingers. Adolphe's suspenders, the other evening in the "Railwaymen's Rendezvous." They *were not* purple. I saw the two inexplicable stains on the shirt. And the stone—the well-known stone, the origin of this whole business: it was not . . . I can't remember exactly just what it was that the stone refused to be. But I had not forgotten its passive resistance. And the hand of the Self-Taught Man; I held it and shook it one day in the library and then I had the feeling that it wasn't quite a hand. I had thought of a great white worm, but that wasn't it either. And the suspicious transparency of the glass of beer in the Café Mably. Suspicious: that's what they were, the sounds, the smells, the tastes. When they ran quickly under your nose like startled hares and you didn't pay too much attention, you might believe them to be simple and reassuring, you might believe that there was real blue in the world, real red, a real perfume of almonds or violets. But as soon as you held on to them for an instant, this feeling of comfort and security gave way to a deep uneasiness: colours, tastes, and smells were never real, never themselves and nothing but themselves. The simplest, most indefinable quality had too much content, in relation to itself, in its heart. That black against my foot, it didn't look like black, but rather the confused effort to imagine black by someone who had never seen black and who wouldn't know how to stop, who would have imagined an ambiguous being beyond colours. It *looked* like a colour, but also . . . like a bruise or a secretion, like an oozing—and something

130

else, an odour, for example, it melted into the odour of wet earth, warm, moist wood, into a black odour that spread like varnish over this sensitive wood, in a flavour of chewed, sweet fibre. I did not simply *see* this black: sight is an abstract invention, a simplified idea, one of man's ideas. That black, amorphous, weakly presence, far surpassed sight, smell and taste. But this richness was lost in confusion and finally was no more because it was too much.

This moment was extraordinary. I was there, motionless and icy, plunged in a horrible ecstasy. But something fresh had just appeared in the very heart of this ecstasy; I understood the Nausea, I possessed it. To tell the truth, I did not formulate my discoveries to myself. But I think it would be easy for me to put them in words now. The essential thing is contingency. I mean that one cannot define existence as necessity. To exist is simply *to be there*; those who exist let themselves be encountered, but you can never deduce anything from them. I believe there are people who have understood this. Only they tried to overcome this contingency by inventing a necessary, causal being. But no necessary being can explain existence: contingency is not a delusion, a probability which can be dissipated; it is the absolute, consequently, the perfect free gift. All is free, this park, this city and myself. When you realize that, it turns your heart upside down and everything begins to float, as the other evening at the "Railwaymen's Rendezvous": here is Nausea; here there is what those bastards—the ones on the Coteau Vert and others—try to hide from themselves with their idea of their rights. But what a poor lie: no one has any rights; they are entirely free, like other men, they cannot succeed in not feeling superfluous. And in themselves, secretly, they are *superfluous*, that is to say, amorphous, vague, and sad.

How long will this fascination last? I *was* the root of the chestnut tree. Or rather I was entirely conscious of its existence. Still detached from it—since I was conscious of it—yet lost in it, nothing but it. An uneasy conscience which, notwithstanding, let itself fall with all its weight on this piece of dead wood. Time had stopped: a small black pool at my feet; it was impossible for something to come *after* that moment. I would have liked to tear myself from that atrocious joy, but I did not even imagine it would be possible; I was inside; the black stump did *not move*, it stayed there, in my eyes, as a lump of food sticks in the windpipe. I could neither accept nor refuse it. At what a cost did I raise my eyes? Did I raise them? Rather did I not obliterate myself for an instant in order to be reborn in the following instant with my head thrown back and my eyes raised upward? In fact, I was not even conscious of the transformation. But suddenly it became impossible for me to think of the existence of the root. It was wiped out, I could repeat in vain: it exists, it is still there, under the bench, against my right foot, it no longer meant anything. Existence is not something which lets itself be thought of from a distance: it must invade you suddenly, master you, weigh heavily on your heart like a great motionless beast—or else there is nothing more at all.

There was nothing more, my eyes were empty and I was spellbound by my deliverance. Then suddenly it began to move before my eyes in light, uncertain motions: the wind was shaking the top of the tree.

It did not displease me to see a movement, it was a change from these motionless beings who watched me like staring eyes. I told myself, as I followed the swinging of the branches: movements never quite exist, they are passages, intermediaries between two existences, moments of weakness, I expected to see them come out of nothingness, progressively ripen, blossom: I was finally going to surprise beings in the process of being born.

No more than three seconds, and all my hopes were swept away. I could not attribute the passage of time to these branches groping around like blind men. This idea of passage was still an invention of man. The idea was too transparent. All these paltry agitations, drew in on themselves, isolated. They overflowed the leaves and branches everywhere. They whirled about these empty hands, enveloped them with tiny whirlwinds. Of course a movement was something different from a tree. But it was still an absolute. A thing. My eyes only encountered completion. The tips of the branches rustled with existence which unceasingly renewed itself and which was never born. The existing wind rested on the tree like a great bluebottle, and the tree shuddered. But the shudder was not a nascent quality, a passing from power to action; it was a thing; a shudder-thing flowed into the tree, took possession of it, shook it and suddenly abandoned it, going further on to spin about itself. All was fullness and all was active, there was no weakness in time, all, even the least perceptible stirring, was made of existence. And all these existents which bustled about this tree came from nowhere and were going nowhere. Suddenly they existed, then suddenly they existed no longer: existence is without memory; of the vanished it retains nothing—not even a memory. Existence everywhere, infinitely, in excess, for ever and everywhere; existence—which is limited only by existence. I sank down on the bench, stupefied, stunned by this profusion of beings without origin: everywhere blossomings, hatchings out, my ears buzzed with existence, my very flesh throbbed and opened, abandoned itself to the universal burgeoning. It was repugnant. But why, I thought, why so many existences, since they all look alike? What good are so many duplicates of trees? So many existences missed, obstinately begun again and again missed—like the awkward efforts of an insect fallen on its back? (I was one of those efforts.) That abundance did not give the effect of generosity, just the opposite. It was dismal, ailing, embarrassed at itself. Those trees, those great clumsy bodies. . . . I began to laugh because I suddenly thought of the formidable springs described in books, full of crackings, burstings, gigantic explosions. There were those idiots who came to tell you about will-power and struggle for life. Hadn't they ever seen a beast or a tree? This plane-tree with its scaling bark, this half-rotten oak, they wanted me to take them for rugged youthful endeavour surging towards the sky. And that root? I would have undoubtedly had to represent it as a voracious claw tearing at the earth, devouring its food?

Impossible to see things that way. Weaknesses, frailties, yes. The trees floated. Gushing towards the sky? Or rather a collapse; at any instant I expected to see the tree-trunks shrivel like weary wands, crumple up, fall on the ground in a soft, folded, black heap. *They did not want* to exist, only they could not help themselves. So they quietly minded their own business; the sap rose up slowly through the structure, half reluctant, and the roots sank slowly into the earth. But at each instant they seemed on the verge of leaving everything there and obliterating themselves. Tired and old, they kept on existing, against the grain, simply because they were too weak to die, because death could only come to them from the outside: strains of music alone can proudly carry their own death within themselves like an internal necessity: only they don't exist. Every existing thing is born without reason, prolongs itself out of weakness and dies by chance. I leaned back and closed my eyes. But the images, forewarned, immediately leaped up and filled my closed eyes with existences: existence is a fullness which man can never abandon.

Strange images. They represented a multitude of things. Not

real things, other things which looked like them. Wooden objects which looked like chairs, shoes, other objects which looked like plants. And then two faces: the couple who were eating opposite to me last Sunday in the Brasserie Vézelise. Fat, hot, sensual, absurd, with red ears. I could see the woman's neck and shoulders. Nude existence. Those two—it suddenly gave me a turn—those two were still existing somewhere in Bouville; somewhere—in the midst of smells?—this soft throat rubbing up luxuriously against smooth stuffs, nestling in lace; and the woman picturing her bosom under her blouse, thinking: "My titties, my lovely fruits," smiling mysteriously, attentive to the swelling of her breasts which tickled . . . then I shouted and found myself with my eyes wide open.

Had I dreamed of this enormous presence? It was there, in the garden, toppled down into the trees, all soft, sticky, soiling everything, all thick, a jelly. And I was inside, I with the garden. I was frightened, furious, I thought it was so stupid, so out of place, I hated this ignoble mess. Mounting up, mounting up as high as the sky, spilling over, filling everything with its gelatinous slither, and I could see depths upon depths of it reaching far beyond the limits of the garden, the houses, and Bouville, as far as the eye could reach. I was no longer in Bouville, I was nowhere, I was floating. I was not surprised, I knew it was the World, the naked World suddenly revealing itself, and I choked with rage at this gross, absurd being. You couldn't even wonder where all that sprang from, or how it was that a world came into existence, rather than nothingness. It didn't make sense, the World was everywhere, in front, behind. There had been nothing *before* it. Nothing. There had never been a moment in which it could not have existed. That was what worried me: of course there was no *reason* for this flowing larva to exist. *But it was impossible* for it is not to exist. It was unthinkable: to imagine nothingness you had to be there already, in the midst of the World, eyes wide open and alive; nothingness was only an idea in my head, an existing idea floating in this immensity: this nothingness had not come *before* existence, it was an existence like any other and appeared after many others. I shouted "filth! what rotten filth!" and shook myself to get rid of this sticky filth, but it held fast and there was so much, tons and tons of existence, endless: I stifled at the depths of this immense weariness. And then suddenly the park emptied as through a great hole, the World disappeared as it had come, or else I woke up—in any case, I saw no more of it; nothing was left but the yellow earth around me, out of which dead branches rose upward.

I got up and went out. Once at the gate, I turned back. Then the garden smiled at me. I leaned against the gate and watched for a long time. The smile of the trees, of the laurel, *meant* something; that was the real secret of existence. I remembered one Sunday, not more than three weeks ago, I had already detected everywhere a sort of conspiratorial air. Was it in my intention? I felt with boredom that I had no way of understanding. No way. Yet it was there, waiting, looking at one. It was there on the trunk of the chestnut tree . . . it was *the* chestnut tree. Things—you might have called them thoughts—which stopped halfway, which were forgotten, which forgot what they wanted to think and which stayed like that, hanging about with an odd little sense which was beyond them. That little sense annoyed me: I *could not* understand it, even if I could have stayed leaning against the gate for a century; I had learned all I could know about existence. I left, I went back to the hotel and I wrote.

Night:

I have made my decision: I have no more reason for staying in Bouville since I'm not writing my book any more; I'm going to live in Paris. I'll take the five o'clock train, on Saturday I'll see Anny; I think we'll spend a few days together. Then I'll come back here to settle my accounts and pack my trunks. By March 1, at the latest, I will be definitely installed in Paris.

Friday:

In the "Railwaymen's Rendezvous." My train leaves in twenty minutes. The gramophone. Strong feeling of adventure.

Saturday:

Anny opens to me in a long black dress. Naturally, she does not put out her hand, she doesn't say hello. Sullenly and quickly, to get the formalities over with, she says:

"Come in and sit down anywhere—except on the armchair near the window."

It's really she. She lets her arms hang, she has the morose face which made her look like an awkward adolescent girl. But she doesn't look like a little girl any more. She is fat, her breasts are heavy.

135

She closes the door, and says meditatively to herself:

"I don't know whether I'm going to sit on the bed. . . ."

Finally she drops on to a sort of chest covered with a carpet. Her walk is no longer the same: she moves with a majestic heaviness, not without grace: she seems embarrassed at her youthful fleshiness. But, in spite of everything, it's really Anny.

Anny bursts out laughing.

"What are you laughing at?"

As usual, she doesn't answer right away, and starts looking quarrelsome.

"Tell me why you're laughing."

"Because of that wide smile you've been wearing ever since you got here. You look like a father who's just married off his daughter. Come on, don't just stand there. Take off your coat and sit down. Yes, over there if you want."

A silence follows. Anny does not try to break it. How bare this room is! Before, Anny always used to carry an immense trunk full of shawls, turbans, mantillas, Japanese masks, pictures of Epinal. Hardly arrived at an hotel—even if it is only for one night —than her first job is to open this trunk and take out all her wealth which she hangs on the walls, on lamps, spreads over tables or on the floor, following a changeable and complicated order; in less than thirty minutes the dullest room became invested with a heavy, sensual, almost intolerable personality. Perhaps the trunk got lost—or stayed in the check room. . . . This cold room with the door half-open on the bathroom has something sinister about it. It looks like—only sadder and more luxurious— like my room in Bouville.

Anny laughs again. How will I recognize this high-pitched, nasal little laugh?

"Well, you haven't changed. What are you looking for with that bewildered look on your face?"

She smiles, but studies my face with almost hostile curiosity.

"I was only thinking this room doesn't look as if you were living in it."

"Really?" she answers vaguely.

Another silence. Now she is sitting on the bed, very pale in her black dress. She hasn't cut her hair. She is still watching me, calmly, raising her eyebrows a little. Has she got nothing to say to me? Why did she make me come here? This silence is unbearable.

Suddenly, I say pitifully:

"I'm glad to see you."

The last word sticks in my throat: I would have done better to keep quiet. She is surely going to be angry. I expected the first fifteen minutes to be difficult. In the old days, when I saw Anny again, whether after a twenty-four-hour absence or on waking in the morning, I could never find the words she expected, the words which went with her dress, with the weather, with the last words we had spoken the night before. What does she want? I can't guess.

I raise my eyes again. Anny looks at me with a sort of tenderness.

"You haven't changed at all? You're still just as much of a fool?"

Her face shows satisfaction. But how tired she looks!

"You're a milestone," she says, "a milestone beside a road. You explain imperturbably and for the rest of your life you'll go on explaining that Melun is twenty-seven kilometres and Montargis is forty-two. That's why I need you so much."

"Need me? You mean you needed me these four years I haven't seen you? You've been pretty quiet about it."

I spoke lightly: she might think I am resentful. I feel a false smile on my mouth, I'm uncomfortable.

"What a fool you are! Naturally I don't need to see you, if that's what you mean. You know you're not exactly a sight for sore eyes. I need you to exist and not to change. You're like that platinum wire they keep in Paris or somewhere in the neighbourhood. I don't think anyone's ever needed to see it."

"That's where you're mistaken."

"Not I. Anyhow, it doesn't matter. I'm glad to know that it exists, that it measures the exact ten-millionth part of a quarter of a meridian. I think about it every time they start taking measurements in an apartment or when people sell me cloth by the yard."

"Is that so?" I say coldly.

"But you know, I could very well think of you only as an abstract virtue, a sort of limit. You should be grateful to me for remembering your face each time."

Here we are back to these alexandrine discussions I had to go through before when in my heart I had the simplest, commonest desires, such as telling her I loved her, taking her in my arms. Today I have no such desire. Except perhaps a desire to be quiet and to look at her, to realize in silence all the importance of this extraordinary event: the presence of Anny opposite me. Is this day like any other day for her? Her hands are not trembling. She must have had something to tell me the day she wrote—or perhaps it was only a whim. Now there has been no question of it for a long time.

Anny suddenly smiles at me with a tenderness so apparent that tears come to my eyes.

"I've thought about you much more often than that yard of platinum. There hasn't been a day when I haven't thought of you. And I remembered exactly what you looked like—every detail."

She gets up, comes and rests her arms on my shoulders.

"You complain about me, but you daren't pretend you rememebered my face."

"That's not fair," I say, "you know I have a bad memory."

"You admit it: you'd forgotten me completely. Would you have known me in the street?"

"Naturally. It's not a question of that."

"Did you at least remember the colour of my hair?"

"Of course. Blonde."

She begins to laugh.

"You're really proud when you say that. Now that you see it. You aren't worth much."

She rumples my hair with one sweep of her hand.

"And you—your hair is red," she says, imitating me: "the first time I saw you, I'll never forget, you had a mauvish homburg hat and it swore horribly with your red hair. It was hard to look at. Where's your hat? I want to see if your taste is as bad as ever."

"I don't wear one any more."

She whistles softly, opening her eyes wide.

"You didn't think of that all by yourself! Did you? Well, congratulations. Of course! I should have realized. That hair can't stand anything, it swears with hats, chair cushions, even at a wallpaper background. Or else you have to pull your hat down over your ears like that felt you bought in London. You tucked all your hair away under the brim. You might have been bald for all anyone could see."

She adds, in the decisive tone with which you end old quarrels:

"It didn't look at all nice on you."

I don't know what hat she's talking about.

"Did I say it looked good on me?"

"I should say you did! You never talked of anything else. And you were always sneaking a look in the glass when you thought I wasn't watching you."

This knowledge of the past overwhelms me. Anny does not even seem to be evoking memories, her tone of voice does not have the touch of tender remoteness suitable to that kind of occupation. She seems to be speaking of today rather than yesterday; she has kept her opinions, her obstinacies, and her past resentments fully alive. Just the opposite for me, all is drowned in poetic impression; I am ready for all concessions.

Suddenly she says in a toneless voice:

"You see, I'm getting fat, I'm getting old. I have to take care of myself."

Yes. And how weary she looks! Just as I am about to speak, she adds:

"I was in the theatre in London."

"With Candler?"

"No, of course not with Candler. How like you! You had it in your head that I was going to act with Candler. How many times must I tell you that Candler is the orchestra leader? No, in a little theatre, in Soho Square. We played *The Emperor Jones*, some Synge and O'Casey, and *Britannicus*."

"*Britannicus?*" I say, amazed.

"Yes, *Britannicus*. I quit because of that. I was the one who gave them the idea of putting on *Britannicus* and they wanted to make me play Junie."

"Really?"

"Well, naturally I could only play Agrippine."

"And now what are you doing?"

I was wrong in asking that. Life fades entirely from her face. Still she answers at once:

"I'm not acting any more. I travel. I'm being kept."

She smiles:

"Oh, don't look at me in that solicitous way. I always told you it didn't make any difference to me, being kept. Besides, he's an old man, he isn't any trouble."

"English?"

"What does it matter to you?" she says, irritated. "We're not going to talk about him. He has no importance whatsoever for you or me. Do you want some tea?"

She goes into the bathroom. I hear her moving around, rattling cups, talking to herself; a sharp, unintelligible murmur. On the night-table by her bed, as always, there is a volume of Michelet's *History of France*. Now I can make out a single picture hung above the bed, a reproduction of a portrait of Emily Brontë, done by her brother.

Anny returns and suddenly tells me:

"Now you must talk to me about you."

Then she disappears again into the bathroom. I remember that in spite of my bad memory: that was the way she asked those direct questions which annoyed me so much, because I felt a genuine interest and a desire to get things over with at the same time. In any case, after that question, I know for certain that she wants something from me. These are only the preliminaries: you get rid of anything that might be disturbing, you definitely rule out secondary questions: "Now you must talk to me about you." Soon she will talk to me about herself. All of a sudden I no longer have the slightest desire to tell her anything. What good would it be? The Nausea, the fear, existence. . . . It is better to keep all that to myself.

"Come on, hurry up," she shouts through the partition.

She returns with a teapot.

"What are you doing? Are you living in Paris?"

"I live in Bouville."

"Bouville? Why? You aren't married, I hope."

"Married?" I say with a start.

It is very pleasant for me to have Anny think that. I tell her:

"It's absurd. That's exactly the sort of naturalistic imagination you accused me of before. You know: when I used to imagine you a widow and mother of two boys. And all the stories I used to tell about what would happen to us. You hated it."

"And you liked it," she answers, unconcernedly. "You said that to put on a big act. Besides, even though you get indignant in conversation, you're traitor enough to get married one day on the sly. You swore indignantly for a year that you wouldn't see *Violettes Impériales*. Then one day when I was sick you went and saw it alone in a cheap movie."

"I am in Bouville," I say with dignity, "because I am writing a book on the Marquis de Rollebon."

Anny looks at me with studied interest.

"Rollebon? He lived in the eighteenth century?"

"Yes."

"As a matter of fact, you did mention something about it. It's a history book, then?"

"Yes."

"Ha, ha!"

If she asks me one more question I will tell her everything. But she asks nothing more. Apparently, she has decided that she knows enough about me. Anny knows how to be a good listener, but only when she wants to be. I watch her: she has lowered her eyelids, she is thinking about what she's going to tell me, how she is going to begin. Do I have to question her now? I don't think she expects it. She will speak when she decides it will be good to do so. My heart is beating very fast.

She says suddenly:

"I've changed."

This is the beginning. But she is silent now. She pours tea into the white porcelain cups. She is waiting for me to speak: I must say something. Not just anything, it must be what she is expecting. It is torture. Has she really changed? She has gotten heavier, she looks tired: that is surely not what she means.

"I don't know, I don't think so. I've already found your laugh again, your way of getting up and putting your hands on my shoulders, your mania for talking to yourself. You're still reading Michelet's *History*. And a lot of other things. . . ."

This profound interest which she brings to my eternal essence and her total indifference to all that can happen to me in this life—and then this curious affectation, at once charming and pedantic—and this way of suppressing from the very outset all the mechanical formulas of politeness, friendship, all that makes relationships between people easier, forever obliging her partners to invent a rôle.

She shrugs:

"Yes, I have changed," she says dryly, "I have changed in every way. I'm not the same person any more. I thought you'd notice it as soon as you saw me. Instead you talk to me about Michelet's *History*."

She comes and stands in front of me.

"We'll see whether this man is as strong as he pretends. Guess: how have I changed?"

I hesitate; she taps her foot, still smiling, but sincerely annoyed.

"There was something that tormented you before. Or at

141

least you pretended it did. And now it's gone, disappeared. You should notice it. Don't you feel more comfortable?"

I dare only to answer no: I am, just as before, sitting on the edge of the chair, careful to avoid ambushes, ready to conjure away inexplicable rages.

She sits down again.

"Well," she says, nodding her head with conviction, "if you don't understand, it's because you've forgotten things. More than I thought. Come on, don't you remember your misdeeds any more? You came, you spoke, you went: all contrarily. Supposing nothing had changed: you would have come in, there'd have been masks and shawls on the wall, I'd have been sitting on the bed and I'd have said (she throws her head back, dilates her nostrils and speaks in a theatrical voice, as if in self-mockery): 'Well, what are you waiting for? Sit down.' And naturally, I'd have carefully avoided telling you: 'except on the armchair near the window.'"

"You set traps for me."

"They weren't traps. . . . So, naturally, you'd have gone straight over and sat down."

"And what would have happened to me?" I ask, turning and looking at the armchair with curiosity.

It looks ordinary, it looks paternal and comfortable.

"Only something bad," Anny answers briefly.

I leave it at that: Anny always surrounded herself with taboos.

"I think," I tell her suddenly, "that I guess something. But it would be so extraordinary. Wait, let me think: as a matter of fact, this room is completely bare. Do me the justice of admitting that I noticed it right away. All right. I would have come in, I'd have seen these masks on the wall, and the shawls and all that. The hotel always stopped at your door. Your room was something else. . . . You wouldn't have come to open the door for me. I'd have seen you crouched in a corner, maybe sitting on that piece of red carpet you always carried with you, looking at me pitilessly, waiting. . . . I would have hardly said a word, made a move, taken a breath before you'd have started frowning and I would have felt deeply guilty without knowing why. Then with every moment that passed I'd have plunged deeper into error."

"How many times has that happened?"

"A hundred times."

"At least. Are you more adept, sharper now?"

"No!"

"I like to hear you say it. Well then?"

"Well then, it's because there are no more . . ."

"Ha, ha!" she shouts theatrically, "he hardly dares believe it!"

Then she continues softly:

"Well you can believe me: there are no more."

"No more perfect moments?"

"No."

I am dumfounded. I insist.

"You mean you . . . it's all over, those . . . tragedies, those instantaneous tragedies where the masks and shawls, the furniture, and myself . . . where we each had a minor part to play—and you had the lead?"

She smiles.

"He's ungrateful. Sometimes I gave him greater rôles than my own: but he never suspected. Well, yes: it's finished. Are you really surprised?"

"Yes, I'm surprised! I thought that was a part of you, that if it were taken away from you it would have been like tearing out your heart."

"I thought so too," she says, without regret. Then she adds, with a sort of irony that affects me unpleasantly:

"But you see I can live without that."

She has laced her fingers and holds one knee in her hands. She looks with a vague smile which rejuvenates her whole face. She looks like a fat little girl, mysterious and satisfied.

"Yes, I'm glad you've stayed the same. My milestone. If you'd been moved, or repainted, or planted by the side of a different road, I would have nothing fixed to orient myself. You are indispensable to me: I change, you naturally stay motionless and I measure my changes in relation to you."

I still feel a little vexed.

"Well, that's most inaccurate," I say sharply. "On the contrary, I have been evolving all this time, and at heart I . . ."

"Oh," she says with crushing scorn, "intellectual changes! I've changed to the very whites of my eyes."

To the very whites of her eyes. . . . What startles me about her voice? Anyhow, I suddenly give a jump. I stop looking for an Anny who isn't there. This is the girl, here, this fat girl with a ruined look who touches me and whom I love.

"I have a sort of . . . physical certainty. I feel there are no more perfect moments. I feel it in my legs when I walk. I feel it all the time, even when I sleep. I can't forget it. There has never been anything like a revelation; I can't say: starting on such and such a day, at such a time, my life has been transformed. But now I always feel a bit as if I'd suddenly seen it yesterday. I'm dazzled, uncomfortable, I can't get used to it."

She says these words in a calm voice with a touch of pride at having changed. She balances herself on the chest with extraordinary grace. Not once since I came has she more strongly resembled the Anny of before, the Anny of Marseilles. She has caught me again, once more I have plunged into her strange universe, beyond ridicule, affectation, subtlety. I have even recovered the little fever that always stirred in me when I was with her, and this bitter taste in the back of my mouth.

Anny unclasps her hands and drops her knee. She is silent. A concerted silence, as when, at the Opera, the stage is empty for exactly seven measures of music. She drinks her tea. Then she puts down her cup and holds herself stiffly, leaning her clasped hands on the back of the chest.

Suddenly she puts on her superb look of Medusa, which I loved so much, all swollen with hate, twisted, venomous. Anny hardly changes expression; she changes faces; as the actors of antiquity changed masks: suddenly. And each one of the masks is destined to create atmosphere, to give tone to what follows. It appears and stays without modification as she speaks. Then it falls, detached from her.

She stares at me without seeming to see me. She is going to speak. I expect a tragic speech, heightened to the dignity of her mask, a funeral oration.

She does not say a single word.

"I outlive myself."

The tone does not correspond in any way to her face. It is not tragic, it is . . . horrible: it expresses a dry despair, without tears, without pity. Yes, something in her has irremediably dried out.

The masks falls, she smiles.

"I'm not at all sad. I am often amazed at it, but I was wrong: why should I be sad? I used to be capable of rather splendid passions. I hated my mother passionately. And you," she says defiantly, "I loved you passionately."

She waits for an answer. I say nothing.

"All that is over, of course."

"How can you tell?"

"I know. I know that I shall never again meet anything or anybody who will inspire me with passion. You know, it's quite a job starting to love somebody. You have to have energy, generosity, blindness. There is even a moment, in the very beginning, when you have to jump across a precipice: if you think about it you don't do it. I know I'll never jump again."

"Why?"

She looks at me ironically and does not answer.

"Now," she says, "I live surrounded with my dead passions. I try to recapture the fine fury that threw me off the fourth floor, when I was twelve, the day my mother whipped me."

She adds with apparent inconsequence, and a far-away look:

"It isn't good for me to stare at things too long. I look at them to find out what they are, then I have to turn my eyes away quickly."

"Why?"

"They disgust me."

It would almost seem . . . There are surely similarities, in any case. It happened once in London, we had separately thought the same things about the same subjects, almost at the same time. I'd like so much to . . . But Anny's mind takes many turnings, you can never be sure you've understood her completely. I must get to the heart of it.

"Listen, I want to tell you something: you know, I never quite knew what perfect moments were; you never explained them to me."

"Yes, I know. You made absolutely no effort. You sat beside me like a lump on a log."

"I know what it cost me."

"You deserved everything that happened to you, you were very wicked; you annoyed me with your stolid look. You seemed to say: I'm normal; and you practically breathed health, you dripped with moral well-being."

"Still, I must have asked you a hundred times at least what a . . ."

"Yes, but in what a tone of voice," she says, angrily; "you condescended to inform yourself, and that's the whole truth. You were kindly and *distrait*, like the old ladies who used to ask me what I was playing when I was little. At heart," she says dreamily, "I wonder if you weren't the one I hated most."

145

She makes a great effort to collect herself and smiles, her cheeks still flaming. She is very beautiful.

"I want to explain what they are. I'm old enough now to talk calmly to old women like you about my childhood games. Go ahead, talk, what do you want to know?"

"What they were."

"I told you about the privileged situations?"

"I don't think so."

"Yes," she says with assurance. "It was in Aix, in that square, I don't remember the name any more. We were in the courtyard of a café, in the sun, under orange parasols. You don't remember: we drank lemonade and I found a dead fly in the powdered sugar."

"Ah yes, maybe . . ."

"Well, I talked to you about that in the café. I talked to you about it à propos of the big edition of Michelet's *History,* the one I had when I was little. It was a lot bigger than this one and the pages were livid, like the inside of a mushroom. When my father died, my Uncle Joseph got his hands on it and took away all the volumes. That was the day I called him a dirty pig and my mother whipped me and I jumped out the window."

"Yes, yes . . . you must have told me about that *History of France.* . . . Didn't you read it in the attic? You see, I remember. You see, you were unjust when you accused me of forgetting everything a little while ago."

"Be quiet. Yes, as you remember so well, I carried those enormous books to the attic. There were very few pictures in them, maybe three or four in each volume. But each one had a big page all to itself, and the other side of the page was blank. That had much more effect on me than the other pages where they'd arranged the text in two columns to save space. I had an extraordinary love for those pictures; I knew them all by heart, and whenever I read one of Michelet's books, I'd wait for them fifty pages in advance; it always seemed a miracle to find them again. And then there was something better: the scene they showed never had any relation to the text on the next page, you had to go looking for the event thirty pages farther on."

"I beg you, tell me about the perfect moments."

"I'm talking about privileged situations. They were the ones the pictures told about. I called them privileged, I told myself they must have been terribly important to be made the subject of such rare pictures. They had been chosen above all the others, do you understand: and yet there were many episodes which had a greater plastic value, others with a greater historical interest. For example, there were only three pictures for the whole sixteenth century: one for the death of Henri II, one for the assassination of the Duc de Guise and one for the entry of Henri IV into Paris. Then I imagined that there was something special about these events. The pictures confirmed the idea: the drawings were bad, the arms and legs were never too well attached to the bodies. But it was full of grandeur. When the Duc de Guise was assassinated, for example, the spectators showed their amazement and indignation by stretching out their hands and turning their faces away, like a chorus. And don't think they left out any pleasant details. You could see pages falling to the ground, little dogs running away, jesters sitting on the steps of the throne. But all these details were treated with so much grandeur and so much clumsiness that they were in perfect harmony with the rest of the picture: I don't think I've ever come across pictures that had such a strict unity. Well, they came from there."

"The privileged situations?"

"The idea I had of them. They were situations which had a rare and precious quality, style, if you like. To be king, for example, when I was eight years old, seemed a privileged situation to me. Or to die. You may laugh, but there were so many people drawn at the moment of their death, and so many who spoke such sublime words at that moment that I quite genuinely thought . . . well, I thought that by dying you were transported above yourself. Besides, it was enough just to be in the room of a dying person: death being a privileged situation, something emanated from it and communicated itself to everyone there. A sort of grandeur. When my father died, they took me up to his room to see him for the last time. I was very unhappy going up the stairs, but I was also drunk with a sort of religious ecstasy; I was finally entering a privileged situation. I leaned against the wall, I tried to make the proper motions. But my aunt and mother were kneeling by the bed, and they spoiled it all by crying."

She says these last words with anger, as if the memory still scorched her. She interrupts herself; eyes staring, eyebrows raised, she takes advantage of the occasion to live the scene once more.

"I developed all that later on: first I added a new situation, love (I mean the act of love). Look, if you never understood why I refused . . . certain of your demands, here's your opportunity to understand now: for me, there was something to be saved. Then I told myself that there should be many more privileged situations than I could count, finally I admitted an infinite number of them."

"Yes, but what were they?"

"But I've told you," she says with amazement, "I've been explaining to you for fifteen minutes."

"Well, was it especially necessary for people to be impassioned, carried away by hatred or love, for example; or did the exterior aspect of the event have to be great, I mean—what you could see of it. . . ."

"Both . . . it all depended," she answers ungraciously.

"And the perfect moments? Where do they come in?"

"They came afterwards. First there are annunciatory signs. Then the privileged situation, slowly, majestically, comes into people's lives. Then the question whether you want to make a perfect moment out of it."

"Yes," I say, "I understand. In each one of these privileged situations there are certain acts which have to be done, certain attitudes to be taken, words which must be said—and other attitudes, other words are strictly prohibited. Is that it?"

"I suppose so. . . ."

"In fact, then, the situation is the material: it demands exploitation."

"That's it," she says. "First you had to be plunged into something exceptional and feel as though you were putting it in order. If all those conditions had been realized, the moment would have been perfect."

"In fact, it was a sort of work of art."

"You've already said that," she says with irritation. "No: it was . . . a duty. You *had* to transform privileged situations into perfect moments. It was a moral question. Yes, you can laugh if you like: it was moral."

I am not laughing at all.

"Listen," I say spontaneously, "I'm going to admit my shortcomings, too. I never really understood you, I never sincerely tried to help you. If I had known . . ."

"Thank you, thank you very much," she says ironically. "I hope you're not expecting recognition for your delayed regrets. Besides, I hold nothing against you; I never explained anything to you clearly, I was all in knots, I couldn't tell anyone about it, not even you—especially not you. There was always something that rang false at those moments. Then I was lost. But I still had the feeling I was doing everything I could."

"But what had to be done? What actions?"

"What a fool you are. I can't give you any examples, it all depends."

"But tell me what you were trying to do."

"No, I don't want to talk about it. But here's a story if you like, a story that made a great impression on me when I was in school. There was a king who had lost a battle and was taken prisoner. He was there, off in a corner, in the victor's camp. He saw his son and daughter pass by in chains. He didn't weep, he didn't say anything. Then he saw one of his servants pass by, in chains too. Then he began to groan and tear out his hair. You can make up your own examples. You see: there are times when you mustn't cry—or else you'll be unclean. But if you drop a log on your foot, you can do as you please, groan, cry, jump around on the other foot. It would be foolish to be stoical all the time: you'd wear yourself out for nothing."

She smiles:

"Other times you must be *more* than stoical. Naturally, you don't remember the first time I kissed you?"

"Yes, very clearly," I say triumphantly, "it was in Kew Gardens, by the banks of the Thames."

"But what you never knew was that I was sitting on a patch of nettles: my dress was up, my thighs were covered with stings, and every time I made the slightest movement I was stung again. Well, stoicism wouldn't have been enough there. You didn't bother me at all, I had no particular desire for your lips, the kiss I was going to give you was much more important, it was an engagement, a pact. So you understand that this pain was irrelevant, I wasn't allowed to think about my thighs at a time like that. It wasn't enough not to show my suffering: it was necessary not to suffer."

She looks at me proudly, still surprised at what she had done.

"For more than twenty minutes, all the time you were insisting on having the kiss I had decided to give you, all the time I had you begging me—because I had to give it to you according to form—I managed to anaesthetize myself completely. And God knows I have a sensitive skin: I felt *nothing* until we got up."

149

That's it. There are no adventures—there are no perfect moments . . . we have lost the same illusions, we have followed the same paths. I can guess the rest—I can even speak for her and tell myself all that she has left to tell:

"So you realized that there were always women in tears, or a red-headed man, or something else to spoil your effects?"

"Yes, naturally," she answers without enthusiasm.

"Isn't that it?"

"Oh, you know, I might have resigned myself in the end to the clumsiness of a red-headed man. After all, I was always interested in the way other people played their parts . . . no, it's that . . ."

"That there are no more privileged situations?"

"That's it. I used to think that hate or love or death descended on us like tongues of fire on Good Friday. I thought one could radiate hate or death. What a mistake! Yes, I really thought that 'Hate' existed, that it came over people and raised them above themselves. Naturally, I am the only one, I am the one who hates, who loves. But it's always the same thing, a piece of dough that gets longer and longer . . . everything looks so much alike that you wonder how people got the idea of inventing names, to make distinctions."

She thinks as I do. It seems as though I had never left her.

"Listen carefully," I say, "for the past moment I've been thinking of something that pleases me much more than the rôle of a milestone you generously gave me to play: it's that we've changed together and in the same way. I like that better, you know, than to see you going farther and farther away and being condemned to mark your point of departure forever. All that you've told me—I came to tell you the same thing—though with other words, of course. We meet at the arrival. I can't tell you how pleased I am."

"Yes?" she says gently, but with an obstinate look. "Well, I'd still have liked it better if you hadn't changed; it was more convenient. I'm not like you, it rather displeases me to know that someone has thought the same things I have. Besides, you must be mistaken."

I tell her my adventures, I tell her about existence—perhaps at too great length. She listens carefully, her eyes wide open and her eyebrows raised.

When I finish, she looks soothed.

"Well, you're not thinking like me at all. You complain

because things don't arrange themselves around you like a bouquet of flowers, without your taking the slightest trouble to do anything. But I have never asked as much: I wanted action. You know, when we played adventurer and adventuress: you were the one who had adventures, I was the one who made them happen. I said: I'm a man of action. Remember? Well, now I simply say: one can't be a man of action."

I couldn't have looked convinced because she became animated and began again, with more energy:

"Then there's a heap of things I haven't told you, because it would take too long to explain. For example, I had to be able to tell myself at the very moment I took action that what I was doing would have . . . fatal results. I can't explain that to you very well. . . ."

"It's quite useless," I say, somewhat pedantically," "I've thought that too."

She looks at me with scorn.

"You'd like me to believe you've thought exactly the same way I have: you really amaze me."

I can't convince her, all I do is irritate her. I keep quiet. I want to take her in my arms.

Suddenly she looks at me anxiously:

"Well, if you've thought about all that, what can you do?"

I bow my head.

"I . . . I outlive myself," she repeats heavily.

What can I tell her? Do I know any reasons for living? I'm not as desperate as she is because I didn't expect much. I'm rather . . . amazed before this life which is given to me—given for nothing. I keep my head bowed, I don't want to see Anny's face now.

"I travel," she goes on gloomily; "I'm just back from Sweden. I stopped in Berlin for a week. This man who's keeping me . . ."

Take her in my arms? What good would it do? I can do nothing for her; she is as solitary as I.

"What are you muttering about?"

I raise my eyes. She is watching me tenderly.

"Nothing. I was thinking about something."

"Oh? Mysterious person! Well, talk or be quiet, but do one or the other."

I tell her about the "Railwaymen's Rendezvous," the old rag-time I had played on the phonograph, the strange happiness it gives me.

"I was wondering if, in that direction, one couldn't find or look for . . ."

She doesn't answer, I don't think she was much interested in what I told her.

Still, after a moment, she speaks again—and I don't know whether she is following her own ideas or whether it is an answer to what I have just told her.

"Paintings, statues can't be used: they're lovely *facing* me. Music . . ."

"But the theatre . . ."

"What about the theatre? Do you want to enumerate all the fine arts?"

"Before, you used to say you wanted to act because on the stage you had to realize perfect moments!"

"Yes, I realized them: for the others. I was in the dust, in the draught, under raw lights, between cardboard sets. I usually played with Thorndyke. I think you must have seen him at Covent Garden. I was always afraid I'd burst out laughing in his face."

"But weren't you ever carried away by your part?"

"A little, sometimes: never very strongly. The essential thing, for all of us, was the black pit just in front of us, in the bottom of it there were people you didn't see; obviously you were presenting them with a perfect moment. But, you know, they didn't live in it: it unfolded in front of them. And we, the actors, do you think we lived inside it? In the end, it wasn't anywhere, not on either side of the footlights, it didn't exist; and yet everybody thought about it. So you see, little man," she says in a dragging, almost vulgar tone of voice, "I walked out on the whole business."

"I tried to write a book . . ."

She interrupts me.

"I live in the past. I take everything that has happened to me and arrange it. From a distance like that, it doesn't do any harm, you'd almost let yourself be caught in it. Our whole story is fairly beautiful. I give it a few prods and it makes a whole string of perfect moments. Then I close my eyes and try to imagine that I'm still living inside it. I have other characters, too. . . . You have to know how to concentrate. Do you know what I read? Loyola's *Spiritual Exercises*. It has been quite useful for me. There's a way of first setting up the background, then

152

making characters appear. You manage to *see*," she adds with a maniacal air.

"Well," I say, "that wouldn't satisfy me at all."

"Do you think it satisfies me?"

We stay silent for a moment. Evening is coming on; I can hardly make out the pale spot of her face. Her black dress melts with the shadow which floods the room. I pick up my cup mechanically, there's a little tea left in it and I bring it to my lips. The tea is cold. I want to smoke but I don't dare. I have the terrible feeling that we have nothing more to say to one another. Only yesterday I had so many questions to ask her: where she had been, what she had done, whom she had met. But that interested me only in so far as Anny gave her whole heart to it. Now I am without curiosity: all these countries, all these cities she has passed through, all the men who have courted her and whom she has perhaps loved—she clung to none of that, at heart she was indifferent to it all: little flashes of sun on the surface of a cold, dark sea. Anny is sitting opposite to me, we haven't seen each other for four years and we have nothing more to say.

"You'll have to leave now," Anny says suddenly, "I'm expecting someone."

"You're waiting for . . ."

"No, I'm waiting for a German, a painter."

She begins to laugh. This laugh rings strangely in the dim room.

"There's someone who isn't like us—not yet. He acts, he spends himself."

I get up reluctantly.

"When shall I see you again?"

"I don't know, I'm leaving for London tomorrow evening."

"By Dieppe?"

"Yes, and I think I'll go to Egypt after that. Maybe I'll be back in Paris next winter, I'll write you."

"I'll be free all day tomorrow," I say timidly.

"Yes, but I have a lot to do," she answers dryly. "No, I can't see you. I'll write you from Egypt. Just give me your address."

"Yes."

In the shadow I scribble my address on an envelope. I have to put down Hotel Printania so they can forward my letters when I leave Bouville. Yet I know very well that she won't write. Perhaps I shall see her again in ten years. Perhaps this is the last time I shall see her. I am not only overwhelmed at leaving her; I have a frightful fear of going back to my solitude again.

She gets up; at the door she kisses me lightly on the mouth.

"To remember your lips," she says, smiling. "I have to refresh my memories for my spiritual exercises."

I take her by the arm and draw her to me. She does not resist but she shakes her head.

"No. That doesn't interest me any more. You can't begin again. . . . And besides, for what people are worth, the first good-looking boy that comes along is worth as much as you."

"What are you going to do, then?"

"I told you, I'm going to England."

"No, I mean . . ."

"Nothing!"

I haven't let go of her arms, I tell her gently:

"Then I must leave you after finding you again."

I can see her face clearly now. Suddenly it grows pale and drawn. An old woman's face, absolutely frightful; I'm sure she didn't put that one on purposely: it is there, unknown to her, or perhaps in spite of her.

"No," she says slowly, "no. You haven't found me again."

She pulls her arms away. She opens the door. The hall is sparkling with light.

Anny begins to laugh.

"Poor boy! He never has any luck. The first time he plays his part well, he gets no thanks for it. Get out."

I hear the door close behind me.

Sunday:

This morning I consulted the Railway Guide: assuming that she hasn't lied to me, the Dieppe train will leave at 5.38. But maybe her man will be driving her. I wandered around Menilmontant all morning, then the quays in the afternoon. A few steps, a few walls separate me from her. At 5:38 our conversation of yesterday will become a memory, the opulent woman whose lips brushed against my mouth will rejoin, in the past, the slim little girl of Meknes, of London. But nothing was past yet, since she was still there, since it was still possible to see her again, to persuade her, to take her away with me forever. I did not feel alone yet.

I wanted to stop thinking about Anny, because, imagining

154

her body and her face so much, I had fallen into a state of extreme nervousness: my hands trembled and icy chills shook me. I began to look through the books on display at second-hand stalls, especially obscene ones because at least that occupies your mind.

When the Gare d'Orsay clock struck five I was looking at the pictures in a book entitled *The Doctor with the Whip*. There was little variety: in most of them, a heavy bearded man was brandishing a riding whip over monstrous naked rumps. As soon as I realized it was five o'clock, I threw the book back on the pile and jumped into a taxi which took me to the Gare Saint-Lazare.

I walked around the platform for about twenty minutes, then I saw them. She was wearing a heavy fur coat which made her look like a lady. And a short veil. The man had on a camel's-hair coat. He was tanned, still young, very big, very handsome. A foreigner, surely, but not English; possibly Egyptian. They got on the train without seeing me. They did not speak to each other. Then the man got off and bought newspapers. Anny had lowered the window of her compartment; she saw me. She looked at me for a long time, without anger, with inexpressive eyes. Then the man got back into the compartment and the train left. At that moment I clearly saw the restaurant in Piccadilly where we used to eat, before, then everything went blank. I walked. When I felt tired I came into this café and went to sleep. The waiter has just wakened me and I am writing this while half-asleep.

Tomorrow I shall take the noon train back to Bouville. Two days there will be enough to pack my bags and straighten out my accounts at the bank. I think the Hotel Printania will want me to pay two weeks extra because I didn't give them notice. Then I have to return all the books I borrowed from the library. In any case, I'll be back in Paris before the end of the week.

Will I gain anything by the change? It is still a city: this one happens to be cut in two by a river, the other one is by the sea, yet they look alike. One takes a piece of bare sterile earth and one rolls big hollow stones on to it. Odours are held captive in these stones, odours heavier than air. Sometimes people throw them out of the windows into the streets and they stay there until the wind breaks them apart. In clear weather, noises come in one end of the city and go out the other, after going through all the walls; at other times, the noises whirl around inside these sun-baked, ice-split stones.

I am afraid of cities. But you mustn't leave them. If you go too far you come up against the vegetation belt. Vegetation has crawled for miles towards the cities. It is waiting. Once the city is dead, the vegetation will cover it, will climb over the stones, grip them, search them, make them burst with its long black pincers; it will blind the holes and let its green paws hang over everything. You must stay in the cities as long as they are alive, you must never penetrate alone this great mass of hair waiting at the gates; you must let it undulate and crack all by itself. In the cities, if you know how to take care of yourself, and choose the times when all the beasts are sleeping in their holes and digesting, behind the heaps of organic debris, you rarely come across anything more than minerals, the least frightening of all existants.

I am going back to Bouville. The vegetation has only surrounded three sides of it. On the fourth side there is a great hole full of black water which moves all by itself. The wind whistles between the houses. The odours stay less time there than anywhere: chased out to sea by the wind, they race along the surface of the black water like playful mists. It rains. They let plants grow between the gratings. Castrated, domesticated, so fat that they are harmless. They have enormous, whitish leaves which hang like ears. When you touch them it feels like cartilage, everything is fat and white in Bouville because of all the water that falls from the sky. I am going back to Bouville. How horrible!

I wake up with a start. It is midnight. Anny left Paris six hours ago. The boat is already at sea. She is sleeping in a cabin and, up on deck, the handsome bronze man is smoking cigarettes.

Tuesday, in Bouville:

Is that what freedom is? Below me, the gardens go limply down towards the city, and a house rises up from each garden. I see the ocean, heavy, motionless, I see Bouville. It is a lovely day.

I am free: there is absolutely no more reason for living, all the ones I have tried have given way and I can't imagine any more of them. I am still fairly young, I still have enough strength to start again. But do I have to start again? How much, in the strongest of my terrors, my disgusts, I had counted on Anny to save me I realized only now. My past is dead. The Marquis de Rollebon is dead, Anny came back only to take all hope away.

I am alone in this white, garden-rimmed street. Alone and free. But this freedom is rather like death.

Today my life is ending. By tomorrow I will have left this town which spreads out at my feet, where I have lived so long. It will be nothing more than a name, squat, bourgeois, quite French, a name in my memory, not as rich as the names of Florence or Bagdad. A time will come when I shall wonder: whatever could I have done all day long when I was in Bouville? Nothing will be left of this sunlight, this afternoon, not even a memory.

My whole life is behind me. I see it completely, I see its shape and the slow movements which have brought me this far. There is little to say about it: a lost game, that's all. Three years ago I came solemnly to Bouville. I had lost the first round. I wanted to play the second and I lost again: I lost the whole game. At the same time, I learned that you always lose. Only the rascals think they win. Now I am going to be like Anny, I am going to outlive myself. Eat, sleep, sleep, eat. Exist slowly, softly, like these trees, like a puddle of water, like the red bench in the streetcar.

The Nausea has given me a short breathing spell. But I know it will come back again: it is my normal state. Only today my body is too exhausted to stand it. Invalids also have happy moments of weakness which take away the consciousness of their illness for a few hours. I am bored, that's all. From time to time I yawn so widely that tears roll down my cheek. It is a profound boredom, profound, the profound heart of existence, the very matter I am made of. I do not neglect myself, quite the contrary: this morning I took a bath and shaved. Only when I think back over those careful little actions, I cannot understand how I was able to make them: they are so vain. Habit, no doubt, made them for me. They aren't dead, they keep on busying themselves, gently, insidiously weaving their webs, they wash me, dry me, dress me, like nurses. Did they also lead me to this hill? I can't remember how I came any more. Probably up the Escalier Dautry: did I really climb up its hundred and ten steps one by one? What is perhaps more difficult to imagine is that I am soon going to climb down again. Yet I know I am: in a moment I shall find myself at the bottom of the Coteau Vert, if I raise my head, see in the distance the lighting windows of these houses which are so close now. In the distance. Above my head; above my head; and this instant which I cannot leave, which locks me in and

157

limits me on every side, this instant I am made of will be no more than a confused dream.

I watch the grey shimmerings of Bouville at my feet. In the sun they look like heaps of shells, scales, splinters of bone, and gravel. Lost in the midst of this debris, tiny glimmers of glass or mica intermittently throw off light flames. In an hour the ripples, trenches, and thin furrows which run between these shells will be streets, I shall walk in these streets, between these walls. These little black men I can just make out in the Rue Boulibet—in an hour I shall be one of them.

I feel so far away from them, on the top of this hill. It seems as though I belong to another species. They come out of their offices after their day of work, they look at the houses and the squares with satisfaction, they think it is *their* city, a good, solid, bourgeois city. They aren't afraid, they feel at home. All they have ever seen is trained water running from taps, light which fills bulbs when you turn on the switch, half-breed, bastard trees held up with crutches. They have proof, a hundred times a day, that everything happens mechanically, that the world obeys fixed, unchangeable laws. In a vacuum all bodies fall at the same rate of speed, the public park is closed at 4 p.m. in winter, at 6 p.m. in summer, lead melts at 335 degrees centigrade, the last streetcar leaves the Hotel de Ville at 11.05 p.m. They are peaceful, a little morose, they think about Tomorrow, that is to say, simply, a new today; cities have only one day at their disposal and every morning it comes back exactly the same. They scarcely doll it up a bit on Sundays. Idiots. It is repugnant to me to think that I am going to see their thick, self-satisfied faces. They make laws, they write popular novels, they get married, they are fools enough to have children. And all this time, great, vague nature has slipped into their city, it has infiltrated everywhere, in their house, in their office, in themselves. It doesn't move, it stays quietly and they are full of it inside, they breathe it, and they don't see it, they imagine it to be outside, twenty miles from the city. I *see* it, I *see* this nature . . . I know that its obedience is idleness, I know it has no laws: what they take for constancy is only habit and it can change tomorrow.

What if something were to happen? What if something suddenly started throbbing? Then they would notice it was there and they'd think their hearts were going to burst. Then what good would their dykes, bulwarks, power houses, furnaces and pile drivers be to them? It can happen any time, perhaps right now: the omens are present. For example, the father of a family might go out for a walk, and, across the street, he'll see something like a red rag, blown towards him by the wind. And when the rag has gotten close to him he'll see that it is a side of rotten meat, grimy with dust, dragging itself along by crawling, skipping, a piece of writhing flesh rolling in the gutter, spasmodically shooting out spurts of blood. Or a mother might look at her child's cheek and ask him: "What's that—a pimple?" and see the flesh puff out a little, split, open, and at the bottom of the split an eye, a laughing eye might appear. Or they might feel things gently brushing against their bodies, like the caresses of reeds to swimmers in a river. And they will realize that their clothing has become living things. And someone else might feel something scratching in his mouth. He goes to the mirror, opens his mouth: and his tongue is an enormous, live centipede, rubbing its legs together and scraping his palate. He'd like to spit it out, but the centipede is a part of him and he will have to tear it out with his own hands. And a crowd of things will appear for which people will have to find new names—stone-eye, great three-cornered arm, toe-crutch, spider-jaw. And someone might be sleeping in his comfortable bed, in his quiet, warm room, and wake up naked on a bluish earth, in a forest of rustling birch trees, rising red and white towards the sky like the smokestacks of Jouxtebouville, with big bumps half-way out of the ground, hairy and bulbous like onions. And birds will fly around these birch trees and pick at them with their beaks and make them bleed. Sperm will flow slowly, gently, from these wounds, sperm mixed with blood, warm and glassy with little bubbles. Or else nothing like that will happen, there will be no appreciable change, but one morning people will open their blinds and be surprised by a sort of frightful sixth sense, brooding heavily over things and seeming to pause. Nothing more than that: but for the little time it lasts, there will be hundreds of suicides. Yes! Let it change just a little, just to see, I don't ask for anything better. Then you will see other people, suddenly plunged into solitude. Men all alone, completely alone with horrible monstrosities, will run through the streets, pass heavily in front of me, their eyes staring, fleeing their ills yet carrying them with them, open-mouthed, with their insect-tongue flapping its wings. Then I'll burst out laughing even though my body may be covered with filthy, infected scabs which blossom into flowers of flesh, violets, buttercups. I'll lean against a wall and when they go by

159

I'll shout: "What's the matter with your science? What have you done with your humanism? Where is your dignity?" I will not be afraid—or at least no more than now. Will it not still be existence, variations on existence? All these eyes which will slowly devour a face—they will undoubtedly be too much, but no more so than the first two, Existence is what I am afraid of.

Evening falls, the first lamps are lit in the city. My God! How *natural* the city looks despite all its geometries, how crushed it looks in the evening. It's so . . . so evident, from here; could I be the only one to see it? Is there nowhere another Cassandra on the summit of a hill, watching a city engulfed in the depths of nature? But what difference does it make? What could I tell her?

My body slowly turns eastward, oscillates a little and begins to walk.

Wednesday: My last day in Bouville:

I have looked all over town for the Self-Taught Man. He surely hasn't gone home. He must be walking at random, filled with shame and horror—this poor humanist whom men don't want. To tell the truth, I was hardly surprised when the thing happened: for a long time I had thought that his soft, timid face would bring scandal on itself. He was so little guilty: his humble, contemplative love for young boys is hardly sensuality—rather a form of humanity. But one day he had to find himself alone. Like M. Achille, like me: he is one of my race, he has good will. Now he has entered into solitude—forever. Everything suddenly crumbled, his dreams of culture, his dreams of an understanding with mankind. First there will be fear, horror, sleepless nights, and then after that, the long succession of days of exile. In the evening he will come back to wander around the Cour des Hypothèques; from a distance he will watch the glowing windows of the library and his heart will fail him when he remembers the long rows of books, their leather bindings, the smell of their pages. I am sorry I didn't go along with him, but he didn't want me to; he begged me to let him alone: he was beginning his apprenticeship in solitude. I am writing this in the Café Mably. I went in with great ceremony, I wanted to study the manager, the cashier, and forcibly feel that I was seeing them for the last time. But I can't stop thinking about the Self-Taught Man, I still have his open face before my eyes, his face

160

full of reproach, his blood-stained collar. So I asked for some paper and I am going to tell what happened to him.

I went to the library about two o'clock this afternoon. I was thinking: "The library. I am going in here for the last time."

The room was almost deserted. It hurt me to see it because I knew I would never come back. It was light as mist, almost unreal, all reddish; the setting sun rusted the table reserved for women, the door, the back of the books. For a second I had the delightful feeling that I was going into underbrush full of golden leaves; I smiled. I thought: I haven't smiled for a long time. The Corsican was looking out of the window, his hands behind his back. What did he see? The skull of Impétraz? I shall never see that skull again, or his top hat or his morning coat. In six hours I will have left Bouville. I put the two books I borrowed last month on the assistant librarian's desk. He tore up a green slip and handed me the pieces:

"There you are, Monsieur Roquetin."

"Thank you."

I thought: now I owe them nothing more. I don't owe anything more to anybody here. Soon I'm going to say good-bye to the woman in the "Railwaymen's Rendezvous," I am free. I hesitated a few instants: would I use these last moments to take a long walk through Bouville, to see the Boulevard Victor-Noir again, the Avenue Galvani, and the Rue Tournebride. But this forest was so calm, so pure: it seemed to me as though it hardly existed and that the Nausea had spared it. I went and sat down near the stove. The *Journal de Bouville* was lying on the table. I reached out and took it.

"*Saved by His Dog.*"

"*Yesterday evening, M. Dubosc of Remiredon, was bicycling home from the Naugis Fair . . .*"

A fat woman sat down at my right. She put her felt hat beside her. Her nose was planted on her face like a knife in an apple. Under the nose, a small, obscene hole wrinkled disdainfully. She took a bound book from her bag, leaned her elbows on the table, resting her face against her fat hands. An old man was sleeping opposite me. I knew him: he was in the library the evening I was so frightened. I think he was afraid too. I thought: how far away all that is.

At four-fifteen the Self-Taught Man came in. I would have

161

liked to shake hands and say good-bye to him. But I thought our last meeting must have left him with unpleasant memories: he nodded distantly to me and, far enough away, he set down a small white package which probably contained, as usual, a slice of bread and a piece of chocolate. After a moment, he came back with an illustrated book which he placed near his package. I thought: I am seeing him for the last time. Tomorrow evening, the evening after tomorrow, and all the following evenings, he will return to read at this table, eating his bread and chocolate, he will patiently keep on with his rat's nibbling, he will read the works of Nabaud, Naudeau, Nodier, Nys, interrupting himself from time to time to jot down a maxim in his notebook. And I will be walking in Paris, in Paris streets, I will be seeing new faces. What could happen to me while he would still be here, with the lamp lighting up his heavy pondering face. I felt myself drifting back to the mirage of adventure just in time. I shrugged my shoulders and began reading again.

"Bouville and neighbouring areas:

Monistiers:

Activities of the gendarmerie for the year. The sergeant-major Gaspard, commanding the Monistiers brigade and its four gendarmes, Messrs. Lagoutte, Nizan, Pierpont, and Ghil, were hardly idle during the past year. In fact, our gendarmes have reported 7 crimes, 82 misdemeanours, 159 contraventions, 6 suicides and 15 automobile accidents, three of which resulted in death.

Jouxtebouville:

Friendly Society of Trumpet Players of Jouxtebouville. General rehearsal today; remittance of cards for the annual concert.

Compostel:

Presentation of the Legion of Honour to the Mayor.

Bouville Boy Scouts:

Monthly meeting this evening at 8.45 p.m., 10 Rue Ferdinand-Byron, Room A.
Programme: Reading of minutes. Correspondence. Annual banquet. 1932 assessment, March hiking schedule. Questions. New members.

Society for the Prevention of Cruelty to Animals:

Next Thursday, from 3 to 5 p.m., Room C, 10 Rue Ferdinand-Byron, Bouville, Public meeting. Send inquiries and
correspondence to the President, to the main office or to 154
Avenue Galvani.

*Bouville Watchdog Club . . . Bouville Association of Dis-
abled Veterans . . . Taxi-Owners' Union . . . Bouville Com-
mittee for the Friends of the Board-Schools. . . .*

Two boys with satchels come in. Students from the High-
school. The Corsican likes students from the High-school because
he can exercise a paternal supervision over them. Often, for his
own pleasure, he lets them stir around on their chairs and talk,
then suddenly tiptoes up behind them and scolds: "Is that the
way big boys behave? If you don't behave yourselves, the librarian
is going to complain to your headmaster."

And if they protest, he looks at them with terrible eyes:
"Give me your names." He also directs their reading: in the
library certain volumes are marked with a red cross; Hell: the
works of Gide, Diderot, Baudelaire and medical texts. When a
student wants to consult one of these books, the Corsican makes
a sign to him, draws him over to a corner and questions him. After
a moment he explodes and his voice fills the reading-room: "There
are a lot of more interesting books for a boy of your age. Instructive books. Have you finished your homework? What grade are
you in? And you don't have anything to do after four o'clock?
Your teacher comes in here a lot and I'm going to tell him about
you."

The two boys stay near the stove. The younger one has
brown hair, a skin almost too fine and a tiny mouth, wicked and
proud. His friend, a big heavy-set boy with the shadow of a
moustache, touched his elbow and murmured a few words. The
little brown-haired boy did not answer, but he gave an imper-
ceptible smile, full of arrogance and self-sufficiency. Then both
of them nonchalantly chose a dictionary from one of the shelves
and went over to the Self-Taught Man who was staring wearily
at them. They seemed to ignore his existence, but they sat down
right next to him, the brown-haired boy on his left and the thick-
set one on the left of the brown-haired boy. They began looking
through the dictionary. The Self-Taught Man's look wandered
over the room, then returned to his reading. Never had a library

163

offered such a reassuring spectacle: I heard no sound, except the short breathing of the fat woman, I only saw heads bent over books. Yet, at that moment, I had the feeling that something unpleasant was going to happen. All these people who lowered their eyes with such a studious look seemed to be playing a comedy: a few instants before I felt something like a breath of cruelty pass over us.

I had finished reading but hadn't decided to leave: I was waiting, pretending to read my newspaper. What increased my curiosity and annoyance was that the others were waiting too. It seemed as though my neighbour was turning the pages of her book more rapidly. A few minutes passed, then I heard whispering. I cautiously raised my head. Both boys had closed their dictionaries. The brown-haired one was not talking, his face, stamped with deference and interest, was turned to the right. Half-hidden behind his shoulder, the blond was listening and laughing silently. Who's talking? I thought.

It was the Self-Taught Man. He was bent over his young neighbour, eye to eye, smiling at him; I saw his lips move and, from time to time, his long eyelashes palpitate. I didn't recognize this look of youthfulness; he was almost charming. But, from time to time, he interrupted himself and looked anxiously behind him. The boy seemed to drink his words. There was nothing extraordinary about this little scene and I was going to go back to my reading when I saw the boy slowly slide his hand behind his back on the edge of the table. Thus hidden from the Self-Taught Man's eyes it went on its way for a moment, and began to feel around, then, finding the arm of the bigger boy, pinched it violently. The other, too absorbed in silent enjoyment of the Self-Taught Man's words, had not seen it coming. He jumped up and his mouth opened widely in surprise and admiration. The brown-haired boy had kept his look of respectful interest. One might have doubted that this mischievous hand belonged to him. What are they going to do to him? I thought. I knew that something bad was going to happen, and I saw too that there was still time to keep it from happening. But I couldn't guess what there was to prevent. For a second, I had the idea of getting up, slapping the Self-Taught Man on the shoulder and starting a conversation with him. But just at that moment he caught my look. He stopped speaking and pinched his lips together with an air of irritation. Discouraged, I quickly lowered my eyes and made a show of reading my paper. However, the fat woman had set down her book and raised her head. She seemed hypnotized. I felt sure the woman was going to burst: they all *wanted* something to burst. What could I do? I glanced at the Corsican: he wasn't looking out of the window any more, he had turned half-way towards us.

Fifteen minutes passed. The Self-Taught Man had begun his whispering again. I didn't dare look at him any more, but I could well imagine his young and tender air and those heavy looks which weighed on him without his knowing it. Once I heard his laugh, a fluted, childish little laugh. It gripped my heart: it seemed as though the two kids were going to drown a cat. Then the whispers stopped suddenly. This silence seemed tragic to me: it was the end, the deathblow. I bowed my head over my newspaper and pretended to read; but I wasn't reading: I raised my eyes as high as I could, trying to catch what was happening in this silence across from me. By turning my head slightly, I could see something out of the corner of my eye: it was a hand, the small white hand which slid along the table a little while ago. Now it was resting on its back, relaxed, soft and sensual, it had the indolent nudity of a woman sunning herself after bathing. A brown hairy object approached it, hesitant. It was a thick finger, yellowed by tobacco; inside this hand it had all the grossness of a male sex organ. It stopped for an instant, rigid, pointing at the fragile palm, then suddenly, it timidly began to stroke it. I was not surprised, I was only furious at the Self-Taught Man; couldn't he hold himself back, the fool, didn't he realize the risk he was running? He still had a chance, a small chance: if he were to put both hands on the table, on either side of the book, if he stayed absolutely still, perhaps he might be able to escape his destiny this time. But I *knew* he was going to miss his chance: the finger passed slowly, humbly, over the inert flesh, barely grazing it, without daring to put any weight on it: you might have thought it was conscious of its ugliness. I raised my head brusquely, I couldn't stand this obstinate little back-and-forth movement any more: I tried to catch the Self-Taught Man's eye and I coughed loudly to warn him. But he closed his eyes, he was smiling. His other hand had disappeared under the table. The boys were not laughing any more, they had both turned pale. The brown-haired one pinched his lips, he was afraid, he looked as though what was happening had gone beyond his control. But he did not draw his hand away,

165

he left it on the table, motionless, a little curled. His friend's mouth was open in a stupid, horrified look.

Then the Corsican began to shout. He had come up without anyone hearing him and placed himself behind the Self-Taught Man's chair. He was crimson and looked as though he were going to laugh, but his eyes were flashing. I started up from my chair, but I felt almost relieved: the waiting was too unbearable. I wanted it to be over as soon as possible. I wanted them to throw him out if they wanted, but get it over with. The two boys, white as sheets, seized their satchels and disappeared.

"I saw you," the Corsican shouted, drunk with fury, "I saw you this time, don't try and tell me it isn't true. Don't think I'm not wise to your little game, I've got eyes in my head. And this is going to cost you plenty. I know your name, I know your address, I know everything about you, I know your boss, Chuillier. And won't he be surprised tomorrow morning when he gets a letter from the librarian. What? Shut up!" he said, his eyes rolling. "And don't think it's going to stop there. We have courts in France for people like you. So you were studying, so you were getting culture! So you were always after me to get books for you. Don't think you were kidding me."

The Self-Taught Man did not look surprised. He must have been expecting this for years. He must have imagined what would happen a hundred times, the day the Corsican would slip up behind him and a furious voice would resound suddenly in his ears. Yet he came back every evening, he feverishly pursued his reading and then, from time to time, like a thief, stroked a white hand or perhaps the leg of a small boy. It was resignation that I read on his face.

"I don't know what you mean," he stammered, "I've been coming here for years. . . ."

He feigned indignation and surprise, but without conviction. He knew quite well that the event was there and that nothing could hold it back any longer, that he had to live the minutes of it one by one.

"Don't listen to him," my neighbour said, "I saw him." She got up heavily: "And that isn't the first time I've seen him; no later than last Monday I saw him and I didn't want to say anything because I couldn't believe my eyes and I'd never have thought that in a library, a serious place where people come to learn, things like that would happen; things that'd make you blush. I haven't any children, but I pity the mothers who send their own to work here thinking they're well taken care of, and all the time there are monsters with no respect for anything and who keep them from doing their homework."

The Corsican went up to the Self-Taught Man:

"You hear what the lady says?" he shouted in his face. "You don't need to try and make fools of us. We saw you, you swine!"

"Monsieur, I advise you to be polite," the Self-Taught Man said with dignity. It was his part. Perhaps he would have liked to confess and run, but he had to play his part to the end. He was not looking at the Corsican, his eyes were almost closed. His arms hung limply by his sides; he was horribly pale. And then a flush of blood rose to his face.

The Corsican was suffocating with fury:

"Polite? Filth! Maybe you think I didn't see you. I was watching you all the time. I've been watching you for months!"

The Self-Taught Man shrugged his shoulders and pretended to drop back into his reading. Scarlet, his eyes filled with tears, he had taken on a look of supreme interest and looked attentively at a reproduction of a Byzantine mosaic.

"He goes on reading. He's got a nerve," the woman said, looking at the Corsican.

The Corsican was undecided. At the same time, the assistant librarian, a timid, well-meaning young man whom the Corsican terrorised, slowly raised himself from his desk and called: "Paoli, what's the matter?" There was a moment of irresolution and I hoped the affair would end there. But the Corsican must have thought again and found himself ridiculous. Angry, not knowing what more to say to this mute victim, he drew himself up to his full stature and flung a great fist into the air. The Self-Taught Man turned around, frightened. He looked at the Corsican open-mouthed; there was a horrible fear in his eyes.

"If you strike me I shall report you," he said with difficulty, "I shall leave of my own free will."

I got up but it was too late: the Corsican gave a voluptuous little whine and suddenly crashed his fist against the Self-Taught Man's nose. For a second I could only see his eyes, his magnificent eyes, wide with shame and horror above a sleeve and swarthy fist. When the Corsican drew back his fist the Self-Taught Man's nose began pouring blood. He wanted to put his hands to his face but the Corsican struck him again on the corner of the mouth. The Self-Taught Man sank back in his chair and stared in front of him with gentle, timid eyes. The blood ran from his nose onto his coat. He groped around with his left hand, trying to find his package, while with his right he stubbornly tried to wipe his dripping nostrils.

"I'm going," he said, as if to himself.

The woman next to me was pale and her eyes were gleaming.

"Rotter," she said, "serves him right."

I shook with rage. I went round the table and grabbed the little Corsican by the neck and lifted him up, trembling: I would have liked to break him over the table. He turned blue and struggled, trying to scratch me; but his short arms didn't reach my face. I didn't say a word, but I wanted to smash in his nose and disfigure him. He understood, he raised his elbow to protect his face: I was glad because I saw he was afraid. Suddenly he began to rattle:

"Let go of me, you brute. Are you a fairy too?"

I still wonder why I let him go. Was I afraid of complications? Had these lazy years in Bouville rotted me? Before, I wouldn't have let go of him without knocking out his teeth. I turned to the Self-Taught Man who had finally got up. But he fled from my look, head bowed, and went to take his coat from the hanger. He passed his left hand constantly over his nose, as if to stop the bleeding. But the blood was still flowing and I was afraid he would be sick. Without looking at anyone, he muttered:

"I've been coming here for years. . . ."

Hardly back on his feet, the little man had become master of the situation again. . . .

"Get the hell out," he told the Self-Taught Man, "and don't ever set foot in here again or I'll have the police on you."

I caught up with the Self-Taught Man at the foot of the stairs. I was annoyed, ashamed at his shame, I didn't know what to say to him. He didn't seem to notice I was there. He had finally taken out his handkerchief and he spat continuously into it. His nose was bleeding a little less.

"Come to the drugstore with me," I told him awkwardly.

He didn't answer. A loud murmur escaped from the reading-room.

"I can never come back here," the Self-Taught Man said. He turned and looked perplexedly at the stairs, at the entrance to the reading-room. This movement made the blood run between his collar and his neck. His mouth and cheeks were smeared with blood.

"Come on," I said, taking him by the arm.

He shuddered and pulled away violently.

"Let me go!"

"But you can't stay by yourself, someone has to wash your face and fix you up."

He repeated:

"Let me go, I beg you, sir, let me go."

He was on the verge of hysterics: I let him go. The setting sun lit his bent back for a moment, then he disappeared. On the threshold there was a star-shaped splash of blood.

One hour later:

It is grey outside, the sun is setting; the train leaves in two hours. I crossed the park for the first time and I am walking down the Rue Boulibet. I *know* it's the Rue Boulibet but I don't recognize it. Usually, when I start down it I seem to cross a deep layer of good sense: squat and awkward, the Rue Boulibet, with its tarred and uneven surface, looked like a national highway when it passes through rich country towns with solid, three-storey houses for more than half a mile; I called it a country road and it enchanted me because it was so out of place, so paradoxical in a commercial port. Today the houses are there but they have lost their rural look: they are buildings and nothing more. I had the same feeling in the park a little while ago: the plants, the grass plots, the Olivier Masqueret Fountain, looked stubborn through being inexpressive. I understand: the city is the first one to abandon me. I have not left Bouville and already I am there no longer. Bouville is silent. I find it strange that I have to stay two more hours in this city which, without bothering about me any more, has straightened up its furniture and put it under dust-sheets so as to be able to uncover it in all its freshness, to new arrivals this evening, or tomorrow. I feel more forgotten than ever.

I take a few steps and stop. I savour this total oblivion into which I have fallen. I am between two cities, one knows nothing of me, the other knows me no longer. Who remembers me? Perhaps a heavy young woman in London. . . . And is it really of *me* that she thinks? Besides, there is that man, that Egyptian. Perhaps he has just gone into her room, perhaps he has taken her in his arms. I am not jealous; I know that she is outliving herself. Even if she loved him with all her heart, it would still

169

be the love of a dead woman. I had her last living love. But there is still something he can give her: pleasure. And if she is fainting and sinking into enjoyment, there is nothing more which attaches her to me. She takes her pleasure and I am no more for her than if I had never met her; she has suddenly emptied herself of me, and all other consciousness in the world has also emptied itself of me. It seems funny. Yet I know that I exist, that *I* am here.

Now when I say "I," it seems hollow to me. I can't manage to feel myself very well, I am so forgotten. The only real thing left in me is existence which feels it exists. I yawn, lengthily. No one. Antoine Roquentin exists for on one. That amuses me. And just what is Antoine Roquentin? An abstraction. A pale reflection of myself wavers in my consciousness. Antoine Roquentin . . . and suddenly the "I" pales, pales, and fades out.

Lucid, forlorn, consciousness is walled-up; it perpetuates itself. Nobody lives there any more. A little while ago someone said "me," said *my* consciousness. Who? Outside there were streets, alive with known smells and colours. Now nothing is left but anonymous walls, anonymous consciousness. That is what there is: walls, and between the walls, a small transparency, alive and impersonal. Consciousness exists as a tree, as a blade of grass. It slumbers, it grows bored. Small fugitive presences populate it like birds in the branches. Populate it and disappear. Consciousness forgotten, forsaken between these walls, under this grey sky. And here is the sense of its existence: it is conscious of being superfluous. It dilutes, scatters itself, tries to lose itself on the brown wall, along the lamp post or down there in the evening mist. But it *never* forgets itself. That is its lot. There is a stifled voice which tells it: "The train leaves in two hours," and there is the consciousness of this voice. There is also consciousness of a face. It passes slowly, full of blood, spattered, and its bulging eyes weep. It is not between the walls, it is nowhere. It vanishes; a bent body with a bleeding face replaces it, walks slowly away, seems to stop at each step, never stops. There is a consciousness of this body walking slowly in a dark street. It walks but it gets no further away. The dark street does not end, it loses itself in nothingness. It is not between the walls, it is nowhere. And there is consciousness of a stifled voice which says: "The Self-Taught Man is wandering through the city."

Not the same city, not between these toneless walls, the Self-Taught Man walks in a city where he is not forgotten. People are thinking about him; the Corsican, the fat woman; perhaps everybody in the city. He has not yet lost, he cannot lose himself, this tortured bleeding self they didn't want to kill. His lips and nostrils hurt him; he thinks: "It hurts." He walks, he must walk. If he stopped for one instant the high walls of the library would suddenly rise up around him and lock him in; the Corsican would spring from one side and the scene would begin again, exactly alike in all the details, and the woman would smirk: "They ought to be in jail, those rotters." And the scene would begin again. He thinks: "My God, if only I hadn't done that, if only that could not be true."

The troubled face passes back and forth through my consciousness: "Maybe he is going to kill himself." No: this gentle, baited soul could never dream of death.

There is knowledge of the consciousness. It sees through itself, peaceful and empty between the walls, freed from the man who inhabited it, monstrous because empty. The voice says: "The luggage is registered. The train leaves in two hours." The walls slide right and left. There is a consciousness of macadam, a consciousness of the ironmongers, the loopholes of the barracks and the voice says: "For the last time."

Consciousness of Anny, of Anny, fat old Anny in her hotel room, consciousness of suffering and the suffering is conscious between the long walls which leave and will never return: "Will there never be an end to it?" the voice sings a jazz tune between the walls "some of these days," will there never be an end to it? And the tune comes back softly, insidiously, from behind, to take back the voice and the voice sings without being able to stop and the body walks and there is consciousness of all that and consciousness of consciousness. But no one is there to suffer and wring his hands and take pity on himself. No one, it is a suffering of the crossroads, a forgotten suffering—which cannot forget itself. And the voice says: "There is the 'Railwaymen's Rendezvous'," and the *I* surges into the consciousness, it is *I*, Antoine Roquentin, I'm leaving for Paris shortly; I am going to say goodbye to the patronne.

'I'm coming to say good-bye to you."
"You're leaving, Monsieur Roquentin?"
"I'm going to Paris. I need a change."
"Lucky!"

How was I able to press my lips against this large face? Her body no longer belongs to me. Yesterday I was able to

171

imagine it under the black wool dress. Today the dress is impenetrable. This white body with veins on the surface of the skin, was it a dream?

"We'll miss you," the patronne says. "Won't you have something to drink? It's on the house."

We sit down, touch glasses. She lowers her voice a little.

"I was used to you," she says with polite regret," we got along together."

"I'll be back to see you."

"Be sure to, Monsieur Antoine. Stop in and say hello to us the next time you're in Bouville. You just tell yourself: 'I'm going to say hello to Mme Jeanne, she'll like that.' That's true, a person really likes to know what happens to others. Besides, people always come back here to see us. We have sailors, don't we, working for the Transat: sometimes I go for two years without seeing them, they're either in Brazil or New York or else working on a transport in Bordeaux. And then one fine day I see them again. 'Hello, Madame Jeanne.' And we have a drink together. You can believe it or not, but I remember what each one likes. From two years back! I tell Madeleine: Give a dry vermouth to M. Pierre, a Noilly Cinzano to M. Léon. They ask me: How can you remember that? It's my business, I tell them."

In the back of the room there is a thick-set man who has been sleeping with her recently. He calls her:

"Patronne!"

She gets up:

"Excuse me, Monsieur Antoine."

The waitress comes over to me:

"So you're leaving us just like that?"

"I'm going to Paris."

"I lived in Paris," she says proudly. "For two years. I worked in Siméon's. But I was homesick."

She hesitates a second, then realizes she has nothing more to say to me:

"Well, good-bye, Monsieur Antoine."

She wipes her hand on her apron and holds it out to me.
"Good-bye, Madeleine."

She leaves. I pull the *Journal de Bouville* over to me, then push it away again: I read it in the library a little while ago, from top to bottom.

The patronne does not come back: she abandons her fat hands to her boy friend, who kneads them with passion.

The train leaves in three-quarters of an hour.

I count my money to pass the time.

Twelve hundred francs a month isn't enormous. But if I hold myself back a little it should be enough. A room for 300 francs, 15 francs a day for food: that leaves 450 francs for petty cash, laundry, and movies. I won't need underwear or clothes for a long while. Both my suits are clean, even though they shine at the elbows a little: they'll last me three or four years if I take care of them.

Good God! Is it *I* who is going to lead this mushroom existence? What will I do all day long? I'll take walks. I'll sit on a folding chair in the Tuileries—or rather on a bench, out of economy. I'll read in the libraries. And then what? A movie once a week. And then what? Can I smoke a Voltigeur on Sunday? Shall I play croquet with the retired old men in the Luxembourg? Thirty years old! I pity myself. There are times when I wonder if it wouldn't be better to spend all my 300,000 francs in one year—and after that . . . But what good would that do me? New clothes? Women? Travel? I've had all that and now it's over, I don't feel like it any more: for what I'd get out of it! A year from now I'd find myself as empty as I am today, without even a memory, and a coward facing death.

Thirty years! And 14,400 francs in the bank. Coupons to cash every month. Yet I'm not an old man! Let them give me something to do, no matter what . . . I'd better think about something else, because I'm playing a comedy now. I know very well that I don't want to do anything: to do something is to create existence—and there's quite enough existence as it is.

The truth is that I can't put down my pen: I think I'm going to have the Nausea and I feel as though I'm delaying it while writing. So I write whatever comes into my mind.

Madeleine, who wants to please me, calls to me from the distance, holding up a record:

"Your record, Monsieur Antoine, the one you like, do you want to hear it for the last time?"

"Please."

I said that out of politeness, but I don't feel too well disposed to listen to jazz. Still, I'm going to pay attention because, as Madeleine says, I'm hearing it for the last time: it is very old, even too old for the provinces; I will look for it in vain in Paris. Madeleine goes and sets it on the gramophone, it is going to spin; in the grooves, the steel needle is going to start jumping and grinding and when the grooves will have spiralled it into the centre of the disc it will be finished and the hoarse voice singing "Some of these days" will be silent forever.

It begins.

To think that there are idiots who get consolation from the fine arts. Like my Aunt Bigeois: "Chopin's Preludes were such a help to me when your poor uncle died." And the concert halls overflow with humiliated, outraged people who close their eyes and try to turn their pale faces into receiving antennæ. They imagine that the sounds flow into them, sweet, nourishing, and that their sufferings become music, like Werther; they think that beauty is compassionate to them. Mugs.

I'd like them to tell me whether they find this music compassionate. A while ago I was certainly far from swimming in beatitudes. On the surface I was counting my money, mechanically. Underneath stagnated all those unpleasant thoughts which took the form of unformulated questions, mute astonishments and which leave me neither day nor night. Thoughts of Anny, of my wasted life. And then, still further down, Nausea, timid as dawn. But there was no music then, I was morose and calm. All the things around me were made of the same material as I, a sort of messy suffering. The world was so ugly, outside of me, these dirty glasses on the table were so ugly, and the brown stains on the mirror and Madeleine's apron and the friendly look of the gross lover of the patronne, the very existence of the world so ugly that I felt comfortable, at home.

Now there is this song on the saxophone. And I am ashamed. A glorious little suffering has just been born, an exemplary suffering. Four notes on the saxophone. They come and go, they seem to say: You must be like us, suffer in rhythm. All right! Naturally, I'd like to suffer that way, in rhythm, without complacence, without self-pity, with an arid purity. But is it my fault if the beer at the bottom of my glass is warm, if there are brown stains on the mirror, if I am not wanted, if the sincerest of my sufferings drags and weighs, with too much flesh and the skin too wide at the same time, like a sea-elephant, with bulging eyes, damp and touching and yet so ugly? No, they certainly can't tell me it's compassionate—this little jewelled pain which spins around above the record and dazzles me. Not even ironic: it spins gaily, completely self-absorbed; like a scythe it has cut through the drab intimacy of the world and now it spins and all of us, Madeleine, the thick-set man, the patronne, myself, the tables, benches, the stained mirror, the glasses, all of us abandon ourselves to existence, because we were among ourselves, only among ourselves, it has taken us unawares, in the disorder, the day to day drift: I am ashamed for myself and for what exists *in front* of it.

It does not exist. It is even an annoyance; if I were to get up and rip this record from the table which holds it, if I were to break it in two, I wouldn't reach *it*. It is beyond—always beyond something, a voice, a violin note. Through layers and layers of existence, it veils itself, thin and firm, and when you want to seize it, you find only existants, you butt against existants devoid of sense. It is behind them: I don't even hear it, I hear sounds, vibrations in the air which unveil it. It does not exist because it has nothing superfluous: it is all the rest which in relation to it is superfluous. It *is*.

And I, too, wanted to *be*. That is all I wanted; this is the last word. At the bottom of all these attempts which seemed without bonds, I find the same desire again: to drive existence out of me, to rid the passing moments of their fat, to twist them, dry them, purify myself, harden myself, to give back at last the sharp, precise sound of a saxophone note. That could even make an apologue: there was a poor man who got in the wrong world. He existed, like other people, in a world of public parks, bistros, commercial cities and he wanted to persuade himself that he was living somewhere else, behind the canvas of paintings, with the doges of Tintoretto, with Gozzoli's Florentines, behind the pages of books, with Fabrizio del Dongo and Julien Sorel, behind the phonograph records, with the long dry laments of jazz. And then, after making a complete fool of himself, he understood, he opened his eyes, he saw that it was a misdeal: he was in a bistro, just in front of a glass of warm beer. He stayed overwhelmed on the bench; he thought: I am a fool. And at that very moment, on the other side of existence, in this other world which you can see in the distance, but without ever approaching it, a little melody began to sing and dance: "You must be like me; you must suffer in rhythm."

The voice sings:

> *Some of these days*
> *You'll miss me, honey*

Someone must have scratched the record at that spot because it makes an odd noise. And there is something that clutches the heart: the melody is absolutely untouched by this tiny coughing of the needle on the record. It is so far—so far behind. I understand that too: the disc is scratched and is wearing out, perhaps the singer is dead; I'm going to leave, I'm going to take my train. But behind the existence which falls from one present to the other, without a past, without a future, behind these sounds which decompose from day to day, peel off and slip towards death, the melody stays the same, young and firm, like a pitiless witness.

The voice is silent. The disc scrapes a little, then stops. Delivered from a troublesome dream, the café ruminates, chews the cud over the pleasure of existing. The patronne's face is flushed, she slaps the fat white cheeks of her new friend, but without succeeding in colouring them. Cheeks of a corpse. I stagnate, fall half-asleep. In fifteen minutes I will be on the train, but I don't think about it. I think about a clean-shaven American with thick black eyebrows, suffocating with the heat, on the twenty-first floor of a New York skyscraper. The sky burns above New York, the blue of the sky is inflamed, enormous yellow flames come and lick the roofs; the Brooklyn children are going to put on bathing drawers and play under the water of a fire-hose. The dark room on the twenty-first floor cooks under a high pressure. The American with the black eyebrows sighs, gasps and the sweat rolls down his cheeks. He is sitting, in shirtsleeves, in front of his piano; he has a taste of smoke in his mouth and, vaguely, a ghost of a tune in his head. "Some of these days." Tom will come in an hour with his hip-flask; then both of them will lower themselves into leather armchairs and drink brimming glasses of whisky and the fire of the sky will come and inflame their throats, they will feel the weight of an immense, torrid slumber. But first the tune must be written down. "Some of these days." The moist hand seizes the pencil on the piano. "Some of these days you'll miss me, honey."

That's the way it happened. That way or another way, it makes little difference. That is how it was born. It is the worn-out body of this Jew with black eyebrows which it chose to create it. He held the pencil limply, and the drops of sweat fell from his ringed fingers on to the paper. And why not I? Why should it need precisely this fat fool full of stale beer and whisky for the miracle to be accomplished?

"Madeleine, would you put the record back? Just once, before I leave."

Madeleine starts to laugh. She turns the crank and it begins again. But I no longer think of myself. I think of the man out there who wrote this tune, one day in July, in the black heat of his room. I try to think of him *through* the melody, through the white, acidulated sounds of the saxophone. He made it. He had troubles, everything didn't work out for him the way it should have: bills to pay—and then there surely must have been a woman somewhere who wasn't thinking about him the way he would have liked her to—and then there was this terrible heat wave which turned men into pools of melting fat. There is nothing pretty or glorious in all that. But when I hear the sound and I think that that man made it, I find this suffering and sweat . . . moving. He was lucky. He couldn't have realized it. He must have thought: with a little luck, this thing will bring in fifty dollars. Well, this is the first time in years that a man has seemed moving to me. I'd like to know something about him. It would interest me to find out the type of troubles he had, if he had a woman or if he lived alone. Not at all out of humanity; on the contrary—besides, he may be dead. Just to get a little information about him and be able to think about him from time to time, listening to the record. I don't suppose it would make the slightest difference to him if he were told that in the seventh largest city of France, in the neighbourhood of a station, someone is thinking about him. But I'd be happy if I were in his place; I envy him. I have to go. I get up, but I hesitate an instant, I'd like to hear the Negress sing. For the last time.

She sings. So two of them are saved: the Jew and the Negress. Saved. Maybe they thought they were lost irrevocably, drowned in existence. Yet no one could think of me as I think of them, with such gentleness. No one, not even Anny. They are a little like dead people for me, a little like the heroes of a novel; they have washed themselves of the sin of existing. Not completely, of course, but as much as any man can. This idea suddenly knocks me over, because I was not even hoping for that any more. I feel something brush against me lightly and I dare not move because I am afraid it will go away. Something I didn't know any more: a sort of joy.

The Negress sings. Can you justify your existence then? Just a little? I feel extraordinarily intimidated. It isn't because I have much hope. But I am like a man completely frozen after a trek through the snow and who suddenly comes into a warm room. I think he would stay motionless near the door, still cold, and that slow shudders would go right through him.

Some of these days
You'll miss me, honey

Couldn't I try. . . . Naturally, it wouldn't be a question of a tune . . . but couldn't I, in another medium? . . . It would have to be a book: I don't know how to do anything else. But not a history book: history talks about what has existed—an existant can never justify the existence of another existant. My error, I wanted to resuscitate the Marquis de Rollebon. Another type of book. I don't quite know which kind—but you would have to guess, behind the printed words, behind the pages, at something which would not exist, which would be above existence. A story, for example, something that could never happen, an adventure. It would have to be beautiful and hard as steel and make people ashamed of their existence.

I must leave, I am vacillating. I dare not make a decision. If I were sure I had talent. . . . But I have never—never written anything of that sort. Historical articles, yes—lots of them. A book. A novel. And there would be people who would read this book and say: "Antoine Roquentin wrote it, a red-headed man who hung around cafés," and they would think about my life as I think about the Negress's: as something precious and almost legendary. A book. Naturally, at first it would only be a troublesome, tiring work, it wouldn't stop me from existing or feeling that I exist. But a time would come when the book would be written, when it would be behind me, and I think that a little of its clarity might fall over my past. Then, perhaps, because of it, I could remember my life without repugnance. Perhaps one day, thinking precisely of this hour, of this gloomy hour in which I wait, stooping, for it to be time to get on the train, perhaps I shall feel my heart beat faster and say to myself: "That was the day, that was the hour, when it all started." And I might succeed —in the past, nothing but the past—in accepting myself.

Night falls. On the second floor of the Hotel Printania two windows have just lighted up. The building-yard of the New Station smells strongly of damp wood: tomorrow it will rain in Bouville.

JEAN-PAUL SARTRE

The Wall

(Intimacy)

AND OTHER STORIES

Translated from the French by
LLOYD ALEXANDER

DEDICATED TO OLGA KOSZAKIEWICZ

CONTENTS

THE WALL

They pushed us into a big white room and I began to blink because the light hurt my eyes. Then I saw a table and four men behind the table, civilians, looking over the papers. They had bunched another group of prisoners in the back and we had to cross the whole room to join them. There were several I knew and some others who must have been foreigners. The two in front of me were blond with round skulls; they looked alike. I suppose they were French. The smaller one kept hitching up his pants; nerves.

It lasted about three hours; I was dizzy and my head was empty; but the room was well heated and I found that pleasant enough: for the past 24 hours we hadn't stopped shivering. The guards brought the prisoners up to the table, one after the other. The four men asked each one his name and occupation. Most of the time they didn't go any further—or they would simply ask a question here and there: "Did you have anything to do with the sabotage of munitions?" Or "Where were you the morning of the 9th and what were you doing?" They didn't listen to the answers or at least didn't seem to. They were quiet for a moment and then looking straight in front of them began to write. They asked Tom if it were true he was in the International Brigade; Tom couldn't tell them otherwise because of the papers they found in his coat. They didn't ask Juan anything but they wrote for a long time after he told them his name.

"My brother José is the anarchist," Juan said, "you know he isn't here any more. I don't belong to any party, I never had anything to do with politics."

They didn't answer. Juan went on, "I haven't done anything. I don't want to pay for somebody else."

His lips trembled. A guard shut him up and took him away. It was my turn.

"Your name is Pablo Ibbieta?"

"Yes."

The man looked at the papers and asked me, "Where's Ramon Gris?"

"I don't know."

"You hid him in your house from the 6th to the 19th."

"No."

They wrote for a minute and then the guards took me out. In the corridor Tom and Juan were waiting between two guards. We started walking. Tom asked one of the guards, "So?"

"So what?" the guard said.

"Was that the cross-examination or the sentence?"

"Sentence," the guard said.

"What are they going to do with us?"

The guard answered dryly, "Sentence will be read in your cell."

As a matter of fact, our cell was one of the hospital cellars. It was terrifically cold there because of the drafts. We shivered all night and it wasn't much better during the day. I had spent the previous five days in a cell in a monastery, a sort of hole in the wall that must have dated from the middle ages: since there were a lot of prisoners and not much room, they locked us up anywhere. I didn't miss my cell; I hadn't suffered too much from the cold but I was alone; after a long time it gets irritating. In the cellar I had company. Juan hardly ever spoke: he was afraid and he was too young to have anything to say. But Tom was a good talker and he knew Spanish well.

There was a bench in the cellar and four mats. When they took us back we sat and waited in silence. After a long moment, Tom said, "We're screwed."

"I think so too," I said, "but I don't think they'll do anything to the kid."

"They don't have a thing against him," said Tom. "He's the brother of a militiaman and that's all."

I looked at Juan: he didn't seem to hear. Tom went on, "You know what they do in Saragossa? They lay the men down on the road and run over them with trucks. A Moroccan deserter told us that. They said it was to save ammunition."

"It doesn't save gas," I said.

I was annoyed at Tom: he shouldn't have said that.

"Then there's officers walking along the road," he went on, "supervising it all. They stick their hands in their pockets and smoke cigarettes. You think they finish off the guys? Hell no.

2

They let them scream. Sometimes for an hour. The Moroccan said he damned near puked the first time."

"I don't believe they'll do that here," I said. "Unless they're really short on ammunition."

Day was coming in through four airholes and a round opening, they had made in the ceiling on the left, and you could see the sky through it. Through this hole, usually closed by a trap, they unloaded coal into the cellar. Just below the hole there was a big pile of coal dust; it had been used to heat the hospital but since the beginning of the war the patients were evacuated and the coal stayed there, unused; sometimes it even got rained on because they had forgotten to close the trap.

Tom began to shiver. "Good Jesus Christ, I'm cold," he said. "Here it goes again."

He got up and began to do exercises. At each movement his shirt opened on his chest, white and hairy. He lay on his back, raised his legs in the air and bicycled. I saw his great rump trembling. Tom was husky but he had too much fat. I thought how rifle bullets or the sharp points of bayonets would soon be sunk into this mass of tender flesh as in a lump of butter. It wouldn't have made me feel like that if he'd been thin.

I wasn't exactly cold, but I couldn't feel my arms and shoulders any more. Sometimes I had the impression I was missing something and began to look around for my coat and then suddenly remembered they hadn't given me a coat. It was rather uncomfortable. They took our clothes and gave them to their soldiers leaving us only our shirts—and those canvas pants that hospital patients wear in the middle of summer. After a while Tom got up and sat next to me, breathing heavily.

"Warmer?"

"Good Christ, no. But I'm out of wind."

Around eight o'clock in the evening a major came in with two *falangistas*. He had a sheet of paper in his hand. He asked the guard, "What are the names of those three?"

"Steinbock, Ibbieta and Mirbal," the guard said.

The major put on his eyeglasses and scanned the list: "Steinbock . . . Steinbock . . . oh yes . . . you are sentenced to death. You will be shot tomorrow morning." He went on looking. "The other two as well."

"That's not possible," Juan said. "Not me."

The major looked at him amazed. "What's your name?"

"Juan Mirbal," he said.

"Well, your name is there," said the major. "You're sentenced."

"I didn't do anything," Juan said.

The major shrugged his shoulders and turned to Tom and me.

"You're Basque?"

"Nobody is Basque."

He looked annoyed. "They told me there were three Basques. I'm not going to waste my time running after them. Then naturally you don't want a priest?"

We didn't even answer.

He said, "A Belgian doctor is coming shortly. He is authorized to spend the night with you." He made a military salute and left.

"What did I tell you," Tom said. "We get it."

"Yes," I said, "it's a rotten deal for the kid."

I said that to be decent but I didn't like the kid. His face was too thin and fear and suffering had disfigured it, twisting all his features. Three days before he was a smart sort of kid, not too bad; but now he looked like an old fairy and I thought how he'd never be young again, even if they were to let him go. It wouldn't have been too hard to have a little pity for him but pity disgusts me, or rather it horrifies me. He hadn't said anything more but he had turned grey; his face and hands were both grey. He sat down again and looked at the ground with round eyes. Tom was good hearted, he wanted to take his arm, but the kid tore himself away violently and made a face.

"Let him alone," I said in a low voice, "you can see he's going to blubber."

Tom obeyed regretfully; he would have liked to comfort the kid, it would have passed his time and he wouldn't have been tempted to think about himself. But it annoyed me: I'd never thought about death because I never had any reason to, but now the reason was here and there was nothing to do but think about it.

Tom began to talk. "So you think you've knocked guys off, do you?" he asked me. I didn't answer. He began explaining to me that he had knocked off six since the beginning of August; he didn't realize the situation and I could tell he didn't *want* to realize it. I hadn't quite realized it myself, I wondered if it hurt much, I thought of bullets, I imagined their burning hail through my body. All that was beside the real question; but I was calm: we had all night to understand. After a while Tom stopped talking

4

and I watched him out of the corner of my eye; I saw he too had turned grey and he looked rotten; I told myself "Now it starts." It was almost dark, a dim glow filtered through the airholes and the pile of coal and made a big stain beneath the spot of sky; I could already see a star through the hole in the ceiling: the night would be pure and icy.

The door opened and two guards came in, followed by a blond man in a tan uniform. He saluted us. "I am the doctor," he said. "I have authorization to help you in these trying hours."

He had an agreeable and distinguished voice. I said, "What do you want here?"

"I am at your disposal. I shall do all I can to make your last moments less difficult."

"What did you come here for? There are others, the hospital's full of them."

"I was sent here," he answered with a vague look. "Ah! Would you like to smoke?" he added hurriedly, "I have cigarettes and even cigars."

He offered us English cigarettes and *puros*, but we refused. I looked him in the eyes and he seemed irritated. I said to him, "You aren't here on an errand of mercy. Besides, I know you. I saw you with the fascists in the barracks yard the day I was arrested."

I was going to continue, but something surprising suddenly happened to me; the presence of this doctor no longer interested me. Generally when I'm on somebody I don't let go. But the desire to talk left me completely; I shrugged and turned my eyes away. A little later I raised my head; he was watching me curiously. The guards were sitting on a mat. Pedro, the tall thin one, was twiddling his thumbs, the other shook his head from time to time to keep from falling asleep.

"Do you want a light?" Pedro suddenly asked the doctor. The other nodded "Yes": I think he was about as smart as a log, but he surely wasn't bad. Looking in his cold blue eyes it seemed to me that his only sin was lack of imagination. Pedro went out and came back with an oil lamp which he set on the corner of the bench. It gave a bad light but it was better than nothing: they had left us in the dark the night before. For a long time I watched the circle of light the lamp made on the ceiling. I was fascinated. Then suddenly I woke up, the circle of light disappeared and I felt myself crushed under an enormous weight. It was not the

5

thought of death, or fear; it was nameless. My cheeks burned and my head ached.

I shook myself and looked at my two friends. Tom had hidden his face in his hands. I could only see the fat white nape of his neck. Little Juan was the worst, his mouth was open and his nostrils trembled. The doctor went to him and put his hand on his shoulder to comfort him: but his eyes stayed cold. Then I saw the Belgian's hand drop stealthily along Juan's arm, down to the wrist. Juan paid no attention. The Belgian took his wrist between three fingers, distractedly, the same time drawing back a little and turning his back to me. But I leaned backward and saw him take a watch from his pocket and look at it for a moment, never letting go of the wrist. After a minute he let the hand fall inert and went and leaned his back against the wall, then, as if he suddenly remembered something very important which had to be jotted down on the spot, he took a notebook from his pocket and wrote a few lines. "Bastard," I thought angrily, "let him come and take my pulse. I'll shove my fist in his rotten face."

He didn't come but I felt him watching me. I raised my head and returned his look. Impersonally, he said to me, "Doesn't it seem cold to you here?" He looked cold, he was blue.

"I'm not cold," I told him.

He never took his hard eyes off me. Suddenly I understood and my hands went to my face: I was drenched in sweat. In this cellar, in the midst of winter, in the midst of drafts, I was sweating. I ran my hands through my hair, gummed together with perspiration; at the same time I saw my shirt was damp and sticking to my skin: I had been dripping for an hour and hadn't felt it. But that swine of a Belgian hadn't missed a thing; he had seen the drops rolling down my cheeks and thought: this is the manifestation of an almost pathological state of terror; and he had felt normal and proud of being alive because he was cold. I wanted to stand up and smash his face but no sooner had I made the slightest gesture than my rage and shame were wiped out; I fell back on the bench with indifference.

I satisfied myself by rubbing my neck with my handkerchief because now I felt the sweat dropping from my hair onto my neck and it was unpleasant. I soon gave up rubbing, it was useless; my handkerchief was already soaked and I was still sweating. My buttocks were sweating too and my damp trousers were glued to the bench.

Suddenly Juan spoke. "You're a doctor?"

"Yes," the Belgian said.

"Does it hurt . . . very long?"

"Huh? When . . . ? Oh, no," the Belgian said paternally. "Not at all. It's over quickly." He acted as though he were calming a cash customer.

"But I . . . they told me . . . sometimes they have to fire twice."

"Sometimes," the Belgian said, nodding. "It may happen that the first volley reaches no vital organs."

"Then they have to reload their rifles and aim all over again?" He thought for a moment and then added hoarsely, "That takes time!"

He had a terrible fear of suffering, it was all he thought about: it was his age. I never thought much about it and it wasn't fear of suffering that made me sweat.

I got up and walked to the pile of coal dust. Tom jumped up and threw me a hateful look: I had annoyed him because my shoes squeaked. I wondered if my face looked as frightened as his: I saw he was sweating too. The sky was superb, no light filtered into the dark corner and I had only to raise my head to see the Big Dipper. But it wasn't like it had been: the night before I could see a great piece of sky from my monastery cell and each hour of the day brought me a different memory. Morning, when the sky was a hard, light blue, I thought of beaches on the Atlantic; at noon I saw the sun and I remembered a bar in Seville where I drank *manzanilla* and ate olives and anchovies; afternoons I was in the shade and I thought of the deep shadow which spreads over half a bull-ring leaving the other half shimmering in sunlight; it was really hard to see the whole world reflected in the sky like that. But now I could watch the sky as much as I pleased, it no longer evoked anything in me. I liked that better. I came back and sat near Tom. A long moment passed.

Tom began speaking in a low voice. He had to talk, without that he wouldn't have been able to recognize himself in his own mind. I thought he was talking to me but he wasn't looking at me. He was undoubtedly afraid to see me as I was, grey and sweating: we were alike and worse than mirrors of each other. He watched the Belgian, the living.

"Do you understand?" he said. "I don't understand."

I began to speak in a low voice too. I watched the Belgian. "Why? What's the matter?"

"Something is going to happen to us that I can't understand."

There was a strange smell about Tom. It seemed to me I was more sensitive than usual to odors. I grinned. "You'll understand in a while."

"It isn't clear," he said obstinately. "I want to be brave but first I have to know. . . . Listen, they're going to take us into the courtyard. Good. They're going to stand up in front of us. How many?"

"I don't know. Five or eight. Not more."

"All right. There'll be eight. Someone'll holler 'aim!' and I'll see eight rifles looking at me. I'll think how I'd like to get inside the wall, I'll push against it with my back . . . with every ounce of strength I have, but the wall will stay, like in a nightmare. I can imagine all that. If you only knew how well I can imagine it."

"All right, all right!" I said, "I can imagine it too."

"It must hurt like hell. You know, they aim at the eyes and mouth to disfigure you," he added mechanically. "I can feel the wounds already; I've had pains in my head and in my neck for the past hour. Not real pains. Worse. This is what I'm going to feel tomorrow morning. And then what?"

I well understood what he meant but I didn't want to act as if I did. I had pains too, pains in my body like a crowd of tiny scars. I couldn't get used to it. But I was like him, I attached no importance to it. "After," I said, "you'll be pushing up daisies."

He began to talk to himself: he never stopped watching the Belgian. The Belgian didn't seem to be listening. I knew what he had come to do; he wasn't interested in what we thought; he came to watch our bodies, bodies dying in agony while yet alive.

"It's like a nightmare," Tom was saying. "You want to think something, you always have the impression that it's all right, that you're going to understand and then it slips, it escapes you and fades away. I tell myself there will be nothing afterwards. But I don't understand what it means. Sometimes I almost can . . . and then it fades away and I start thinking about the pains again, bullets, explosions. I'm a materialist, I swear it to you; I'm not going crazy. But something's the matter. I see my corpse; that's not hard but *I'm* the one who sees it, with *my* eyes. I've got to think . . . think that I won't see anything any more and the world will go on for the others. We aren't made to think that, Pablo. Believe me: I've already stayed up a whole night waiting for something. But this isn't the same: this will creep up behind us, Pablo, and we won't be able to prepare for it."

"Shut up," I said. "Do you want me to call a priest?"

He didn't answer. I had already noticed he had the tendency to act like a prophet and call me Pablo, speaking in a toneless voice. I didn't like that: but it seems all the Irish are that way. I had the vague impression he smelled of urine. Fundamentally, I hadn't much sympathy for Tom and I didn't see why, under the pretext of dying together, I should have any more. It would have been different with some others. With Ramon Gris, for example. But I felt alone between Tom and Juan. I liked that better, anyhow: with Ramon I might have been more deeply moved. But I was terribly hard just then and I wanted to stay hard.

He kept on chewing his words, with something like distraction. He certainly talked to keep himself from thinking. He smelled of urine like an old prostate case. Naturally, I agreed with him, I could have said everything he said: it isn't *natural* to die. And since I was going to die, nothing seemed natural to me, not this pile of coal dust, or the bench, or Pedro's ugly face. Only it didn't please me to think the same things as Tom. And I knew that, all through the night, every five minutes, we would keep on thinking things at the same time. I looked at him sideways and for the first time he seemed strange to me: he wore death on his face. My pride was wounded: for the past 24 hours I had lived next to Tom, I had listened to him, I had spoken to him and I knew we had nothing in common. And now we looked as much alike as twin brothers, simply because we were going to die together. Tom took my hand without looking at me.

"Pablo, I wonder . . . I wonder if it's really true that everything ends."

I took my hand away and said, "Look between your feet, you pig."

There was a big puddle between his feet and drops fell from his pants-leg.

"What is it?" he asked, frightened.

"You're pissing in your pants," I told him.

"It isn't true," he said furiously. "I'm not pissing. I don't feel anything."

The Belgian approached us. He asked with false solicitude, "Do you feel ill?"

Tom did not answer. The Belgian looked at the puddle and said nothing.

"I don't know what it is," Tom said ferociously. "But I'm not afraid. I swear I'm not afraid."

The Belgian did not answer. Tom got up and went to piss

9

in a corner. He came back buttoning his fly, and sat down without a word. The Belgian was taking notes.

All three of us watched him because he was alive. He had the motions of a living human being, the cares of a living human being; he shivered in the cellar the way the living are supposed to shiver; he had an obedient, well-fed body. The rest of us hardly felt ours—not in the same way anyhow. I wanted to feel my pants between my legs but I didn't dare; I watched the Belgian, balancing on his legs, master of his muscles, someone who could think about tomorrow. There we were, three bloodless shadows; we watched him and we sucked his life like vampires.

Finally he went over to little Juan. Did he want to feel his neck for some professional motive or was he obeying an impulse of charity? If he was acting by charity it was the only time during the whole night.

He caressed Juan's head and neck. The kid let himself be handled, his eyes never leaving him, then suddenly, he seized the hand and looked at it strangely. He held the Belgian's hand between his own two hands and there was nothing pleasant about them, two grey pincers gripping this fat and reddish hand. I suspected what was going to happen and Tom must have suspected it too: but the Belgian didn't see a thing, he smiled paternally. After a moment the kid brought the fat red hand to his mouth and tried to bite it. The Belgian pulled away quickly and stumbled back against the wall. For a second he looked at us with horror, he must have suddenly understood that we were not men like him. I began to laugh and one of the guards jumped up. The other was asleep, his wide-open eyes were blank.

I felt relaxed and over-excited at the same time. I didn't want to think any more about what would happen at dawn, at death. It made no sense. I only found words or emptiness. But as soon as I tried to think of anything else I saw rifle barrels pointing at me. Perhaps I lived through my execution twenty times; once I even thought it was for good: I must have slept a minute. They were dragging me to the wall and I was struggling; I was asking for mercy. I woke up with a start and looked at the Belgian: I was afraid I might have cried out in my sleep. But he was stroking his moustache, he hadn't noticed anything. If I had wanted to, I think I could have slept a while; I had been awake for 48 hours. I was at the end of my rope. But I didn't want to lose two hours of life: they would come to wake me up at dawn, I would follow them, stupefied with sleep and I would have croaked without so much as an "Oof!"; I didn't want that, I didn't want to die like an animal, I wanted to understand. Then I was afraid of having nightmares. I got up, walked back and forth, and, to change my ideas, I began to think about my past life. A crowd of memories came back to me pell-mell. There were good and bad ones—or at least I called them that *before*. There were faces and incidents. I saw the face of a little *novillero* who was gored in Valencia during the *Feria*, the face of one of my uncles, the face of Ramon Gris. I remembered my whole life: how I was out of work for three months in 1926, how I almost starved to death. I remembered a night I spent on a bench in Granada: I hadn't eaten for three days. I was angry, I didn't want to die That made me smile. How madly I ran after happiness, after women, after liberty. Why? I wanted to free Spain, I admired Pi y Margall, I joined the anarchist movement, I spoke in public meetings: I took everything as seriously as if I were immortal.

At that moment I felt that I had my whole life in front of me and I thought, "It's a damned lie." It was worth nothing because it was finished. I wondered how I'd been able to walk, to laugh with the girls: I wouldn't have moved so much as my little finger if I had only imagined I would die like this. My life was in front of me, shut, closed, like a bag and yet everything inside of it was unfinished. For an instant I tried to judge it. I wanted to tell myself, this is a beautiful life. But I couldn't pass judgment on it; it was only a sketch; I had spent my time counterfeiting eternity, I had understood nothing. I missed nothing: there were so many things I could have missed, the taste of *manzanilla* or the baths I took in summer in a little creek near Cadiz; but death had disenchanted everything.

The Belgian suddenly had a bright idea. "My friends," he told us, "I will undertake—if the military administration will allow it—to send a message for you, a souvenir to those who love you. . . ."

Tom mumbled, "I don't have anybody."

I said nothing. Tom waited an instant then looked at me with curiosity. "You don't have anything to say to Concha?"

"No."

I hated this tender complicity: it was my own fault, I had talked about Concha the night before, I should have controlled myself. I was with her for a year. Last night I would have given an arm to see her again for five minutes. That was why I talked about her, it was stronger than I was. Now I had no more desire to see her, I had nothing more to say to her. I would not even have wanted to hold her in my arms: my body filled me with horror because it was grey and sweating—and I wasn't sure that her body didn't fill me with horror. Concha would cry when she found out I was dead, she would have no taste for life for months afterward. But I was still the one who was going to die. I thought of her soft, beautiful eyes. When she looked at me something passed from her to me. But I knew it was over: if she looked at me *now* the look would stay in her eyes, it wouldn't reach me. I was alone.

Tom was alone too but not in the same way. Sitting cross-legged, he had begun to stare at the bench with a sort of smile, he looked amazed. He put out his hand and touched the wood cautiously as if he were afraid of breaking something, then drew back his hand quickly and shuddered. If I had been Tom I wouldn't have amused myself by touching the bench; this was some more Irish nonsense, but I too found that objects had a funny look: they were more obliterated, less dense than usual. It was enough for me to look at the bench, the lamp, the pile of coal dust, to feel that I was going to die. Naturally I couldn't think clearly about my death but I saw it everywhere, on things, in the way things fell back and kept their distance, discreetly, as people who speak quietly at the bedside of a dying man. It was *his* death which Tom had just touched on the bench.

In the state I was in, if someone had come and told me I could go home quietly, that they would leave me my life whole, it would have left me cold: several hours or several years of waiting is all the same when you have lost the illusion of being eternal. I clung to nothing, in a way I was calm. But it was a horrible calm—because of my body; my body, I saw with its eyes, I heard with its ears, but it was no longer me; it sweated and trembled by itself and I didn't recognize it any more. I had to touch it and look at it to find out what was happening, as if it were the body of someone else. At times I could still feel it, I felt sinkings, and fallings, as when you're in a plane taking a nose dive, or I felt my heart beating. But that didn't reassure me. Everything that came from my body was all cockeyed. Most of the time it was quiet and I felt no more than a sort of weight, a filthy presence against me; I had the impression of being tied to an enormous vermin. Once I felt my pants and I felt they were damp; I didn't know whether it was sweat or urine, but I went to piss on the coal pile as a precaution.

The Belgian took out his watch, looked at it. He said, "It is three-thirty."

Bastard! He must have done it on purpose. Tom jumped; he hadn't noticed time was running out; night surrounded us like a shapeless, somber mass, I couldn't even remember that it had begun.

Little Juan began to cry. He wrung his hands, pleaded, "I don't want to die. I don't want to die."

He ran across the whole cellar waving his arms in the air then fell sobbing on one of the mats. Tom watched him with mournful eyes, without the slightest desire to console him. Because it wasn't worth the trouble: the kid made more noise than we did, but he was less touched: he was like a sick man who defends himself against illness by fever. It's much more serious when there isn't any fever.

He wept: I could clearly see he was pitying himself; he wasn't thinking about death. For one second, one single second, I wanted to weep myself, to weep with pity for myself. But the opposite happened: I glanced at the kid, I saw his thin sobbing shoulders and felt inhuman: I could pity neither the others nor myself. I said to myself, "I want to die cleanly."

Tom had gotten up, he placed himself just under the round opening and began to watch for daylight. I was determined to die cleanly and I only thought of that. But ever since the doctor told us the time, I felt time flying, flowing away drop by drop.

It was still dark when I heard Tom's voice: "Do you hear them?"

Men were marching in the courtyard.

"Yes."

"What the hell are they doing? They can't shoot in the dark."

After a while we heard no more. I said to Tom, "It's day."

Pedro got up, yawning, and came to blow out the lamp. He said to his buddy, "Cold as hell."

The cellar was all grey. We heard shots in the distance.

"It's starting," I told Tom. "They must do it in the court in the rear."

Tom asked the doctor for a cigarette. I didn't want one; I didn't want cigarettes or alcohol. From that moment on they didn't stop firing.

"Do you realize what's happening?" Tom said.

He wanted to add something but kept quiet, watching the

13

door. The door opened and a lieutenant came in with four soldiers. Tom dropped his cigarette.

"Steinbock?"

Tom didn't answer. Pedro pointed him out.

"Juan Mirbal?"

"On the mat."

"Get up," the lieutenant said.

Juan did not move. Two soldiers took him under the arms and set him on his feet. But he fell as soon as they released him. The soldiers hesitated.

"He's not the first sick one," said the lieutenant. "You two carry him; they'll fix it up down there."

He turned to Tom. "Let's go."

Tom went out between two soldiers. Two others followed, carrying the kid by the armpits. He hadn't fainted; his eyes were wide open and tears ran down his cheeks. When I wanted to go out the lieutenant stopped me.

"You Ibbieta?"

"Yes."

"You wait here; they'll come for you later."

They left. The Belgian and the two jailers left too, I was alone. I did not understand what was happening to me but I would have liked it better if they had gotten it over with right away. I heard shots at almost regular intervals; I shook with each one of them. I wanted to scream and tear out my hair. But I gritted my teeth and pushed my hands in my pockets because I wanted to stay clean.

After an hour they came to get me and led me to the first floor, to a small room that smelt of cigars and where the heat was stifling. There were two officers sitting smoking in the armchairs, papers on their knees.

"You're Ibbieta?"

"Yes."

"Where is Ramon Gris?"

"I don't know."

The one questioning me was short and fat. His eyes were hard behind his glasses. He said to me, "Come here."

I went to him. He got up and took my arms, staring at me with a look that should have pushed me into the earth. At the same time he pinched my biceps with all his might. It wasn't to hurt me, it was only a game: he wanted to dominate me. He also thought he had to blow his stinking breath square in my face. We stayed for a moment like that, and I almost felt like laughing. It takes a lot to intimidate a man who is going to die; it didn't work. He pushed me back violently and sat down again. He said, "It's his life against yours. You can have yours if you tell us where he is."

These men dolled up with their riding crops and boots were still going to die. A little later than I, but not too much. They busied themselves looking for names in their crumpled papers, they ran after other men to imprison or suppress them; they had opinions on the future of Spain and on other subjects. Their little activities seemed shocking and burlesqued to me; I couldn't put myself in their place, I though they were insane. The little man was still looking at me, whipping his boots with the riding crop. All his gestures were calculated to give him the look of a live and ferocious beast.

"So? You understand?"

"I don't know where Gris is," I answered. "I thought he was in Madrid."

The other officer raised his pale hand indolently. This indolence was also calculated. I saw through all their little schemes and I was stupefied to find there were men who amused themselves that way.

"You have a quarter of an hour to think it over," he said slowly. "Take him to the laundry, bring him back in fifteen minutes. If he still refuses he will be executed on the spot."

They knew what they were doing: I had passed the night in waiting; then they had made me wait an hour in the cellar while they shot Tom and Juan and now they were locking me up in the laundry; they must have prepared their game the night before. They told themselves that nerves eventually wear out and they hoped to get me that way.

They were badly mistaken. In the laundry I sat on a stool because I felt very weak and I began to think. But not about their proposition. Of course I knew where Gris was; he was hiding with his cousins, four kilometers from the city. I also knew that I would not reveal his hiding place unless they tortured me (but they didn't seem to be thinking about that). All that was perfectly regulated, definite and in no way interested me. Only I would have liked to understand the reasons for my conduct. I would rather die than give up Gris. Why? I didn't like Ramon Gris any more. My friendship for him had died a little while before dawn at the same time as my love for Concha, at the same time as my desire to live. Undoubtedly I thought highly of him: he was tough. But it was not for this reason that I consented to die in his place; his life had no more value than mine; no life had value. They were going to slap a man up against a wall and shoot at him till he died, whether it was I or Gris or somebody else made no difference. I knew he was more useful than I to the cause of Spain but I thought to hell with Spain and anarchy; nothing was important. Yet I was there, I could save my skin and give up Gris and I refused to do it. I found that somehow comic; it was obstinacy. I thought, "I must be stubborn!" And a droll sort of gaiety spread over me.

They came for me and brought me back to the two officers. A rat ran out from under my feet and that amused me. I turned to one of the *falangistas* and said, "Did you see the rat?"

He didn't answer. He was very sober, he took himself seriously. I wanted to laugh but I held myself back because I was afraid that once I got started I wouldn't be able to stop. The *falangista* had a moustache. I said to him again, "You ought to shave off your moustache, idiot." I thought it funny that he would let the hairs of his living being invade his face. He kicked me without great conviction and I kept quiet.

"Well," said the fat officer, "have you thought about it?"

I looked at them with curiosity, as insects of a very rare species. I told them, "I know where he is. He is hidden in the cemetery. In a vault or in the gravediggers' shack."

It was a farce. I wanted to see them stand up, buckle their belts and give orders busily.

They jumped to their feet. "Let's go. Molés, go get fifteen men from Lieutenant Lopez. You," the fat man said, "I'll let you off if you're telling the truth, but it'll cost you plenty if you're making monkeys out of us."

They left in a great clatter and I waited peacefully under the guard of *falangistas*. From time to time I smiled, thinking about the spectacle they would make. I felt stunned and malicious. I imagined them lifting up tombstones, opening the doors of the vaults one by one. I represented this situation to myself as if I had been someone else: this prisoner obstinately playing the hero, these grim *falangistas* with their moustaches and their men in uniform running among the graves; it was irresistibly funny. After half an hour the little fat man came back alone. I thought he had come to give the orders to execute me. The others must have stayed in the cemetery.

The officer looked at me. He didn't look at all sheepish. "Take him into the big courtyard with the others," he said. "After the military operations a regular court will decide what happens to him."

"Then they're not . . . not going to shoot me . . . ?"

"Not now, anyway. What happens afterwards is none of my business."

I still didn't understand. I asked, "But why . . . ?"

He shrugged his shoulders without answering and the soldiers took me away. In the big courtyard there were about a hundred prisoners, women, children and a few old men. I began walking around the central grass-plot, I was stupefied. At noon they let us eat in the mess hall. Two or three people questioned me. I must have known them, but I didn't answer: I didn't even know where I was.

Around evening they pushed about ten new prisoners into the court. I recognized Garcia, the baker. He said, "What damned luck you have! I didn't think I'd see you alive."

"They sentenced me to death," I said, "and then they changed their minds. I don't know why."

"They arrested me at two o'clock," Garcia said.

"Why?" Garcia had nothing to do with politics.

"I don't know," he said. "They arrest everybody who doesn't think the way they do. He lowered his voice. "They got Gris."

I began to tremble. "When?"

"This morning. He messed it up. He left his cousin's on Tuesday because they had an argument. There were plenty of people to hide him but he didn't want to owe anything to anybody. He said, 'I'd go and hide in Ibbieta's place, but they got him, so I'll go hide in the cemetery.'"

"In the cemetery?"

"Yes. What a fool. Of course they went by there this morning, that was sure to happen. They found him in the gravediggers' shack. He shot at them and they got him."

"In the cemetery!"

Everything began to spin and I found myself sitting on the ground: I laughed so hard I cried.

THE ROOM

Mme. Darbedat held a *rahat-loukoum* between her fingers. She brought it carefully to her lips and held her breath, afraid that the fine dust of sugar that powdered it would blow away. "Just right," she told herself. She bit quickly into its glassy flesh and a scent of stagnation filled her mouth. "Odd how illness sharpens the sensations." She began to think of mosques, of obsequious Orientals (she had been to Algeria for her honeymoon) and her pale lips started in a smile: the *rahat-loukoum* was obsequious too.

Several times she had to pass the palm of her hand over the pages of her book, for in spite of the precaution she had taken they were covered with a thin coat of white powder. Her hand made the little grains of sugar slide and roll, grating on the smooth paper: "That makes me think of Arcachon, when I used to read on the beach." She had spent the summer of 1907 at the seashore. Then she wore a big straw hat with a green ribbon; she sat close to the jetty, with a novel by Gyp or Colette Yver. The wind made swirls of sand rain down upon her knees, and from time to time she had to shake the book, holding it by the corners. It was the same sensation: only the grains of sand were dry while the small bits of sugar stuck a little to the ends of her fingers. Again she saw a band of pearl grey sky above a black sea. "Eve wasn't born yet." She felt herself all weighted down with memories and precious as a coffer of sandalwood. The name of the book she used to read suddenly came back to mind: it was called *Petite Madame*, not at all boring. But ever since an unknown illness had confined her to her room she preferred memories and historical works.

She hoped that suffering, heavy readings, a vigilant attention to her memories and the most exquisite sensations would ripen her as a lovely hothouse fruit.

She thought, with some annoyance, that her husband would soon be knocking at her door. On other days of the week he came only in the evening, kissed her brow in silence and read *Le*

Temps, sitting in the armchair across from her. But Thursday was Darbedat's *day:* he spent an hour with his daughter, generally from three to four. Before going he stopped in to see his wife and both discussed their son-in-law with bitterness. These Thursday conversations, predictable to their slightest detail, exhausted Mme. Darbedat. M. Darbedat filled the quiet room with his presence. He never sat, but walked in circles about the room. Each of his outbursts wounded Mme. Darbedat like a glass splintering. This particular Thursday was worse than usual: at the thought that it would soon be necessary to repeat Eve's confessions to her husband, and to see his great terrifying body convulse with fury, Mme. Darbedat broke out in a sweat. She picked up a *loukoum* from the saucer, studied it for a while with hesitation, then sadly set it down: she did not like her husband to see her eating *loukoums.*

She heard a knock and started up. "Come in," she said weakly.

M. Darbedat entered on tiptoe. "I'm going to see Eve," he said, as he did every Thursday. Mme. Darbedat smiled at him. "Give her a kiss for me."

M. Darbedat did not answer and his forehead wrinkled worriedly: every Thursday at the same time, a muffled irritation mingled with the load of his digestion. "I'll stop in and see Franchot after leaving her, I wish he'd talk to her seriously and try to convince her."

He made frequent visits to Dr. Franchot. But in vain. Mme. Darbedat raised her eyebrows. Before, when she was well, she shrugged her shoulders. But since sickness had weighted down her body, she replaced the gestures which would have tired her by plays of emotion in the face: she said *yes* with her eyes, *no* with the corners of her mouth: she raised her eyebrows instead of her shoulders.

"There should be some way to take him away from her by force."

"I told you already it was impossible. And besides, the law is very poorly drawn up. Only the other day Franchot was telling me that they have a tremendous amount of trouble with the families: people who can't make up their mind, who want to keep the patient at home; the doctors' hands are tied. They can give their advice, period. That's all. He would," he went on, "have to make a public scandal or else she would have to ask to have him put away herself."

19

"And that," said Mme. Darbedat, "isn't going to happen tomorrow."

"No." He turned to the mirror and began to comb his fingers through his beard. Mme. Darbedat looked at the powerful red neck of her husband without affection.

"If she keeps on," said M. Darbedat," she'll be crazier than he is. It's terribly unhealthy. She doesn't leave his side, she only goes out to see you. She has no visitors. The air in their room is simply unbreathable. She never opens the window because Pierre doesn't want it open. As if you should ask a sick man. I believe they burn incense, some rubbish in a little pan, you'd think it was a church. Really, sometimes I wonder . . . she's got a funny look in her eyes, you know."

"I haven't noticed," Mme. Darbedat said. "I find her quite normal. She looks sad, obviously."

"She has a face like an unburied corpse. Does she sleep? Does she eat? But we aren't supposed to ask her about those things. But I should think that with a fellow like Pierre next to her, she wouldn't sleep a wink all night." He shrugged his shoulders. "What I find amazing is that we, her parents, don't have the right to protect her against herself. Understand that Pierre would be much better cared for by Franchot. There's a big park. And besides, I think," he added, smiling a little, "he'd get along much better with people of his own type. People like that are children, you have to leave them alone with each other; they form a sort of freemasonry. That's where he should have been put the first day and for his own good, I'd say. Of course it's in his own best interest."

After a moment, he added, "I tell you I don't like to know she's alone with Pierre, especially at night. Suppose something happened. Pierre has a very sly way about him."

"I don't know," Mme. Darbedat said, "if there's any reason to worry. He always looked like that. He always seemed to be making fun of the world. Poor boy," she sighed, "to have had his pride and then come to that. He thought he was cleverer than all of us. He had a way of saying 'You're right' simply to end the argument. . . . It's a blessing for him that he can't see the state he's in."

She recalled with displeasure the long, ironic face, always turned a little to the side. During the first days of Eve's marriage, Mme. Darbedat asked nothing more than a little intimacy with her son-in-law. But he had discouraged her: he almost never spoke, he always agreed quickly and absent-mindedly.

M. Darbedat pursued his idea. "Franchot let me visit his place," he said. "It was magnificent. The patients have private rooms with leather armchairs, if you please, and day-beds. You know, they have a tennis court and they're going to build a swimming pool."

He was planted before the window, looking out, rocking a little on his bent legs. Suddenly he turned lithely on his heels, shoulders lowered, hands in his pockets. Mme. Darbedat felt she was going to start perspiring: it was the same thing every time: now he was pacing back and forth like a bear in a cage and his shoes squeaked at every step.

"Please, please, won't you sit down. You're tiring me." Hesitating, she added, "I have something important to tell you."

M. Darbedat sat in the armchair and put his hands on his knees; a slight chill ran up Mme. Darbedat's spine: the time had come, she had to speak.

"You know," she said with an embarrassed cough, "I saw Eve on Tuesday."

"Yes."

"We talked about a lot of things, she was very nice, she hasn't been so confiding for a long time. Then I questioned her a little, I got her to talk about Pierre. Well, I found out," she added, again embarrassed, "that she is *very* attached to him."

"I know that too damned well," said M. Darbedat.

He irritated Mme. Darbedat a little: she always had to explain things in such detail. Mme. Darbedat dreamed of living in the company of fine and sensitive people who would understand her slightest word.

"But I mean," she went on, "that she is attached to him *differently* than we imagined."

M. Darbedat rolled furious, anxious eyes, as he always did when he never completely grasped the sense of an allusion or something new.

"What does that all mean?"

"Charles," said Mme. Darbedat, "don't tire me. You should understand a mother has difficulty in telling certain things."

"I don't understand a damned word of anything you say," M. Darbedat said with irritation. "You can't mean. . . ."

"Yes," she said.

"They're still . . . now, still . . . ?"

"Yes! Yes! Yes!" she said, in three annoyed and dry little jolts.

M. Darbedat spread his arms, lowered his head and was silent.

"Charles," his wife said, worriedly, "I shouldn't have told you. But I couldn't keep it to myself."

"Our child," he said slowly. "With this madman! He doesn't even recognize her any more. He calls her Agatha. She must have lost all sense of her own dignity."

He raised his head and looked at his wife severely. "You're sure you aren't mistaken?"

"No possible doubt. Like you," she added quickly, "I couldn't believe her and I still can't. The mere idea of being touched by that wretch. . . . So . . . ," she sighed, "I suppose that's how he holds on to her."

"Do you remember what I told you," M. Darbedat said, "when he came to ask for her hand? I told you I thought he pleased Eve *too much*. You wouldn't believe me." He struck the table suddenly, blushing violently. "It's perversity! He takes her in his arms, kisses her and calls her Agatha, selling her on a lot of nonsense about flying statues and God knows what else! Without a word from her! But what in heaven's name's between those two? Let her be sorry for him, let her put him in a sanitorium and see him every day—fine. But I never thought . . . I considered her a widow. Listen, Jeannette," he said gravely, "I'm going to speak frankly to you; if she had any sense, I'd rather see her take a lover!"

"Be quiet, Charles!" Mme. Darbedat cried.

M. Darbedat wearily took his hat and the cane he had left on the stool. "After what you've just told me," he concluded, "I don't have much hope left. In any case, I'll have a talk with her because it's my duty."

Mme. Darbedat wished he would go quickly.

"You know," she said to encourage him, "I think Eve is more headstrong than . . . than anything. She knows he's incurable but she's obstinate, she doesn't want to be in the wrong."

M. Darbedat stroked his beard absently.

"Headstrong? Maybe so. If you're right, she'll finally get tired of it. He's not always pleasant and he doesn't have much to say. When I say hello to him he gives me a flabby handshake and doesn't say a word. As soon as they're alone, I think they go back to his obsessions: she tells me sometimes he screams as though his throat were being cut because of his hallucinations. He sees statues. They frighten him because they buzz. He says they fly around and make fishy eyes at him."

He put on his gloves and continued, "She'll get tired of it, I'm not saying she won't. But suppose she goes crazy before that? I wish she'd go out a little, see the world: she'd meet some nice young man—well, someone like Schroeder, an engineer with Simplon, somebody with a future, she could see him a little here and there and she'd get used to the idea of making a new life for herself."

Mme. Darbedat did not answer, afraid of starting the conversation up again. Her husband bent over her.

"So," he said, "I've got to be on my way."

"Goodbye, Papa," Mme. Darbedat said, lifting her forehead up to him. "Kiss her for me and tell her for me she's a poor dear."

Once her husband had gone, Mme. Darbedat let herself drift to the bottom of her armchair and closed her eyes, exhausted. "What vitality," she thought reproachfully. As soon as she got a little strength back, she quietly stretched out her pale hand and took a *loukoum* from the saucer, groping for it without opening her eyes.

Eve lived with her husband on the sixth floor of an old building on the Rue du Bac. M. Darbedat slowly climbed the 112 steps of the stairway. He was not even out of breath when he pushed the bell. He remembered with satisfaction the words of Mlle. Dormoy: "Charles, for your age, you're simply marvelous." Never did he feel himself stronger and healthier than on Thursday, especially after these invigorating climbs.

Eve opened the door: that's right, she doesn't have a maid. No girls *can* stay with her. I can put myself in their place. He kissed her. "Hello, poor darling."

Eve greeted him with a certain coldness.

"You look a little pale," M. Darbedat said, touching her cheek. "You don't get enough exercise."

There was a moment of silence.

"Is Mama well?" Eve asked.

"Not good, not too bad. You saw her Tuesday? Well, she's just the same. Your Aunt Louise came to see her yesterday, that pleased her. She likes to have visitors, but they can't stay too long. Aunt Louise came to Paris for that mortgage business. I think I told you about it, a very odd sort of affair. She stopped in at the office to ask my advice. I told her there was only one thing to do: sell. She found a taker, by the way: Bretonnel. You remember Bretonnel. He's retired from business now."

He stopped suddenly: Eve was hardly listening. He thought sadly that nothing interested her any more. It's like the books. Before, you had to tear them away from her. Now she doesn't even read any more.

"How is Pierre?"

"Well," Eve said. "Do you want to see him?"

"Of course," M. Darbedat said gaily. "I'd like to pay him a little call."

He was full of compassion for this poor young man, but he could not see him without repugnance. *I detest unhealthy people.* Obviously, it was not Pierre's fault: his heredity was terribly loaded down. M. Darbedat sighed: *All the precautions are taken in vain, you find out those things too late.* No, Pierre was not responsible. But still he had always carried that fault in him; it formed the base of his character; it wasn't like cancer or tuberculosis, something you could always put aside when you wanted to judge a man as he is. His nervous grace, the subtlety which pleased Eve so much when he was courting her were the flowers of madness. He was already mad when he married her only you couldn't tell.

It makes you wonder, thought M. Darbedat, *where responsibility begins, or rather, where it ends.* In any case, he was always analyzing himself too much, always turned in on himself. But was it the cause or effect of his sickness? He followed his daughter through a long, dim corridor.

"This apartment is too big for you," he said. "You ought to move out."

"You say that every time, Papa," Eve answered, "but I've already told you Pierre doesn't want to leave his room."

Eve was amazing. Enough to make you wonder if she realized her husband's state. He was insane enough to be in a strait-jacket and she respected his decisions and advice as if he still had good sense.

"What I'm saying is for your own good." M. Darbedat went on, somewhat annoyed, "It seems to me that if I were a woman I'd be afraid of these badly lighted old rooms. I'd like to see you in a bright apartment, the kind they're putting up near Auteuil, three airy little rooms. They lowered the rents because they couldn't find any tenants; this would be just the time."

Eve quietly turned the doorknob and they entered the room.

M. Darbedat's throat tightened at the heavy odor of incense. The curtains were drawn. In the shadows he made out a thin neck above the back of an armchair: Pierre's back was turning. He was eating.

"Hello, Pierre," M. Darbedat said, raising his voice. "How are we today?" He drew near him: the sick man was seated in front of a small table; he looked sly.

"I see we had soft-boiled eggs," M. Darbedat said, raising his voice higher. "That's good!"

"I'm not deaf," Pierre said quietly.

Irritated, M. Darbedat turned his eyes toward Eve as his witness. But Eve gave him a hard glance and was silent. M. Darbedat realized he had hurt her. Too bad for her. It was impossible to find just the right tone for this boy. He had less sense than a child of four and Eve wanted him treated like a man. M. Darbedat could not keep himself from waiting with impatience for the moment when all this ridiculous business would be finished. Sick people always annoyed him a little—especially madmen because they were wrong. Poor Pierre, for example, was wrong all along the line, he couldn't speak a reasonable word and yet it would be useless to expect the least humility from him, or even temporary recognition of his errors.

Eve cleared away the eggshells and the cup. She put a knife and fork in front of Pierre.

"What's he going to eat now?" M. Darbedat said jovially.

"A steak."

Pierre had taken the fork and held it in the ends of his long, pale fingers. He inspected it minutely and then gave a slight laugh.

"I can't use it this time," he murmured, setting it down, "I was warned."

Eve came in and looked at the fork with passionate interest.

"Agatha," Pierre said, "give me another one."

Eve obeyed and Pierre began to eat. She had taken the suspect fork and held it tightly in her hands, her eyes never leaving it; she seemed to make a violent effort. How suspicious all their gestures and relationships are! thought M. Darbedat.

He was uneasy.

"Be careful, Pierre, take it by the middle because of the prongs."

Eve sighed and laid the fork on the serving table. M. Darbedat felt his gall rising. He did not think it well to give in to all this poor man's whims—even from Pierre's viewpoint it was pernicious. Franchot had said: "One must never enter the delirium of a madman." Instead of giving him another fork, it would have been better to have reasoned quietly and made him understand that the first was like all the others.

He went to the serving table, took the fork ostentatiously and tested the prongs with a light finger. Then he turned to Pierre. But the latter was cutting his meat peacefully: he gave his father-in-law a gentle, inexpressive glance.

"I'd like to have a little talk with you," M. Darbedat said to Eve.

She followed him docilely into the saloon. Sitting on the couch, M. Darbedat realized he had kept the fork in his hand. He threw it on the table.

"It's much better here," he said.

"I never come here."

"All right to smoke?"

"Of course, Papa," Eve said hurriedly. "Do you want a cigar?"

M. Darbedat preferred to roll a cigarette. He thought eagerly of the discussion he was about to begin. Speaking to Pierre he felt as embarrassed about his reason as a giant about his strength when playing with a child. All his qualities of clarity, sharpness, precision, turned against him; *I must confess it's somewhat the same with my poor Jeannette.* Certainly Mme. Darbedat was not insane, but this illness had . . . stultified her. Eve, on the other hand, took after her father . . . a straight, logical nature; discussion with her was a pleasure; *that's why I don't want them to ruin her.* M. Darbedat raised his eyes. Once again he wanted to see the fine intelligent features of his daughter. He was disappointed with this face; once so reasonable and transparent, there was now something clouded and opaque in it. Eve had always been beautiful. M. Darbedat noticed she was made up with great care, almost with pomp. She had blued her eyelids and put mascara on her long lashes. This violent and perfect make-up made a painful impression on her father.

"You're green beneath your rouge," he told her. "I'm afraid you're getting sick. And the way you make yourself up now! You used to be so discreet."

Eve did not answer and for an embarrassed moment M. Darbedat considered this brilliant, worn-out face beneath the heavy mass of black hair. He thought she looked like a tragedian. *I even know who she looks like. That woman . . . that Roumanian who played* Phèdre *in French at the Mur d'Orange.* He regretted having made so disagreeable a remark: *It escaped me! Better not worry her with little things.*

"Excuse me," he said smiling, "you know I'm an old purist. I don't like all these creams and paints women stick on their face today. But I'm in the wrong. You must live in your time."

Eve smiled amiably at him. M. Darbedat lit a cigarette and drew several puffs.

"My child," he began, "I wanted to talk with you: the two of us are going to talk the way we used to. Come, sit down and listen to me nicely; you must have confidence in your old Papa."

"I'd rather stand," Eve said. "What did you want to tell me?"

"I am going to ask you a single question," M. Darbedat said a little more dryly. "Where will all this lead you?"

"All this?" Eve asked astonished.

"Yes . . . all this whole life you've made for yourself. Listen," he went on, "don't think I don't understand you" (he had a sudden illumination) "but what you want to do is beyond human strength. You want to live solely by imagination, isn't that it? You don't want to admit he's sick. You don't want to see the Pierre of today, do you? You have eyes only for the Pierre of before. My dear, my darling little girl, it's an impossible bet to win," M. Darbedat continued. "Now I'm going to tell you a story which perhaps you don't know. When we were at Sables-d'Olonne— you were three years old—your mother made the acquaintance of a charming young woman with a superb little boy. You played on the beach with this little boy, you were thick as thieves, you were engaged to marry him. A while later, in Paris, your mother wanted to see this young woman again; she was told she had had a terrible accident. That fine little boy's head was cut off by a car. They told your mother, 'Go and see her, but above all don't talk to her about the death of her child, she *will not* believe he is dead.' Your mother went, she found a half-mad creature: she lived as though her boy was still alive; she spoke to him, she set his place at the table. She lived in such a state of nervous tension that after six months they had to take her away by force to a sanitorium where she was obliged to stay three years. No, my child," M. Darbedat said, shaking his head, "these things are impossible. It would have been better if she had recognized the truth courageously. She would have suffered once, then time would have erased with its sponge. There is nothing like looking things in the face, believe me."

27

"You're wrong," Eve said with effort. "I know very well that Pierre is. . . ."

The word did not escape. She held herself very straight and put her hands on the back of the armchair: there was something dry and ugly in the lower part of her face.

"So . . . ?" asked M. Darbedat, astonished.

"So . . . ?"

"You . . . ?"

"I love him as he is," said Eve rapidly and with an irritated look.

"Not true," M. Darbedat said forcefully. "It isn't true: you don't love him, you can't love him. You can only feel that way about a healthy, normal person. You pity Pierre, I don't doubt it, and surely you have the memory of three years of happiness he gave you. But don't tell me you love him. I won't believe you."

Eve remained wordless, staring at the carpet absently.

"You could at least answer me," M. Darbedat said coldly. "Don't think this conversation has been any less painful for me than it has for you."

"More than you think."

"Well then, if you love him," he cried, exasperated, "it is a great misfortune for you, for me and for your poor mother because I'm going to tell you something I would rather have hidden from you: before three years Pierre will be sunk in complete dementia, he'll be like a beast."

He watched his daughter with hard eyes: he was angry at her for having compelled him, by stubbornness, to make this painful revelation.

Eve was motionless; she did not so much as raise her eyes. "I knew."

"Who told you?" he asked stupefied.

"Franchot. I knew six months ago."

"And I told him to be careful with you," said M. Darbedat with bitterness. "Maybe it's better. But under those circumstances you must understand that it would be unpardonable to keep Pierre with you. The struggle you have undertaken is doomed to failure, his illness won't spare him. If there were something to be done, if we could save him by care, I'd say yes. But look: you're pretty, intelligent, gay, you're destroying yourself willingly and without profit. I know you've been admirable, but now it's over . . . done, you've done your duty and more; now it would be immoral to continue. We also have duties to ourselves, child. And then you aren't thinking about us. You must," he repeated, hammering the words, "send Pierre to Franchot's clinic. Leave this apartment where you've had nothing but sorrow and come home to us. If you want to be useful and ease the sufferings of someone else, you have your mother. The poor woman is cared for by nurses, she needs someone closer to her, and *she*," he added, "can appreciate what you do for her and be grateful."

There was a long silence. M. Darbedat heard Pierre singing in the next room. It was hardly a song, rather a sort of sharp, hasty recitative. M. Darbedat raised his eyes to his daughter.

"It's no, then?"

"Pierre will stay with me," she said quietly. "I get along well with him."

"By living like an animal all day long?"

Eve smiled and shot a glance at her father, strange, mocking and almost gay. *It's true*, M. Darbedat thought furiously, *that's not all they do; they sleep together.*

"You are completely mad," he said, rising.

Eve smiled sadly and murmured, as if to herself, "Not enough so."

"Not enough? I can only tell you one thing, my child. You frighten me."

He kissed her hastily and left. Going down the stairs he thought: *we should send out two strong-arm men who'd take the poor imbecile away and stick him under a shower without asking his advice on the matter.*

It was a fine autumn day, calm and without mystery; the sunlight gilded the faces of the passers-by. M. Darbedat was struck with the simplicity of the faces; some weather-beaten, others smooth, but they reflected all the happiness and care with which he was so familiar.

I know exactly what I resent in Eve, he told himself, entering the Boulevard St. Germain. *I resent her living outside the limits of human nature. Pierre is no longer a human being: in all the care and all the love she gives him she deprives human beings of a little. We don't have the right to refuse ourselves to the world; no matter what, we live in society.*

He watched the faces of the passers-by with sympathy; he loved their clear, serious looks. In these sunlit streets, in the midst of mankind, one felt secure, as in the midst of a large family.

A woman stopped in front of an open-air display counter. She was holding a little girl by the hand.

"What's that?" the little girl asked, pointing to a radio set.
"Mustn't touch," her mother said. "It's a radio; it plays music."

They stood for a moment without speaking, in ecstacy. Touched, M. Darbedat bent down to the little girl and smiled.

II

"He's gone." The door closed with a dry snap. Eve was alone in the salon. *I wish he'd die.*

She twisted her hands around the back of the armchair: she had just remembered her father's eyes. M. Darbedat was bent over Pierre with a competent air; he had said "That's good!" the way someone says when they speak to invalids. He had looked and Pierre's face had been painted in the depths of his sharp, bulging eyes. *I hate him when he looks at him because I think he sees him.*

Eve's hands slid along the armchair and she turned to the window. She was dazzled. The room was filled with sunlight, it was everywhere, in pale splotches on the rug, in the air like a blinding dust. Eve was not accustomed to this diligent, indiscreet light which darted from everywhere, scouring all the corners, rubbing the furniture like a busy housewife and making it glisten. However, she went to the window and raised the muslin curtain which hung against the pane. Just at that moment M. Darbedat left the building; Eve suddenly caught sight of his broad shoulders. He raised his head and looked at the sky, blinking, then with the stride of a young man he walked away. *He's straining himself*, thought Eve, *soon he'll have a stitch in the side.* She hardly hated him any longer: there was so little in that head; only the tiny worry of appearing young. Yet rage took her again when she saw him turn the corner of the Boulevard St. Germain and disappear. *He's thinking about Pierre.* A little of their life had escaped from the closed room and was being dragged through the streets, in the sun, among the people. *Can they never forget about us?*

The Rue du Bac was almost deserted. An old lady crossed the street with mincing steps; three girls passed, laughing. Then men, strong, serious men carrying briefcases and talking among themselves. *Normal people*, thought Eve, astonished at finding such a powerful hatred in herself. A handsome, fleshy woman ran heavily toward an elegant gentleman. He took her in his arms and kissed her on the mouth. Eve gave a hard laugh and let the curtain fall.

Pierre sang no more but the woman on the fourth floor was playing the piano; she played a Chopin Etude. Eve felt calmer; she took a step toward Pierre's room but stopped almost immediately and leaned against the wall in anguish; each time she left the room, she was panic-stricken at the thought of going back. Yet she knew she could live nowhere else: she loved the room. She looked around it with cold curiosity as if to gain a little time: this shadowless, odorless room where she waited for her courage to return. *You'd think it was a dentist's waiting room.* Armchairs of pink silk, the divan, the tabourets were somber and discreet, a little fatherly; man's best friends. Eve imagined those grave gentlemen dressed in light suits, all like the ones she saw at the window, entering the room, continuing a conversation already begun. They did not even take time to reconnoiter, but advanced with firm step to the middle of the room; one of them, letting his hand drag behind him like a wake in passing knocked over cushions, objects on the table, and was never disturbed by their contact. And when a piece of furniture was in their way, these poised men, far from making a detour to avoid it, quietly changed its place. Finally they sat down, still plunged in their conversation, without even glancing behind them. *A living-room for normal people,* thought Eve. She stared at the knob of the closed door and anguish clutched her throat: *I must go back. I never leave him alone so long.* She would have to open the door, then stand for a moment on the threshold, trying to accustom her eyes to the shadow and the room would push her back with all its strength. Eve would have to triumph over this resistance and enter all the way into the heart of the room. Suddenly she wanted violently to see Pierre; she would have liked to make fun of M. Darbedat with him. But Pierre had no need of her; Eve could not foresee the welcome he had in store for her. Suddenly she thought with a sort of pride that she had no place anywhere. *Normal people think I belong with them. But I couldn't stay an hour among them. I need to live out there, on the other side of the wall. But they don't want me out there.*

A profound change was taking place around her. The light had grown old and greying: it was heavy, like the water in a vase of flowers that hasn't been changed since the day before. In this aged light Eve found a melancholy she had long forgotten: the melancholy of an autumn afternoon that was ending. She looked around her, hesitant, almost timid: all that was so far away: there was neither day nor night nor season nor melancholy in the room. She vaguely recalled autumns long past, autumns of her childhood, then suddenly she stiffened: she was afraid of memories.

She heard Pierre's voice. "Agatha! Where are you?"

"Coming!" she cried.

She opened the door and entered the room.

The heavy odor of incense filled her mouth and nostrils as she opened her eyes and stretched out her hands—for a long time the perfume and the gloom had meant nothing more to her than a single element, acrid and heavy, as simple, as familiar as water, air or fire—and she prudently advanced toward a pale stain which seemed to float in the fog. It was Pierre's face: Pierre's clothing (he dressed in black ever since he had been sick) melted in obscurity. Pierre had thrown back his head and closed his eyes. He was handsome. Eve looked at his long, curved lashes, then sat close to him on the low chair. *He seems to be suffering,* she thought. Little by little her eyes grew used to the darkness. The bureau emerged first, then the bed, then Pierre's personal things: scissors, the pot of glue, books, the herbarium which shed its leaves onto the rug near the armchair.

"Agatha?"

Pierre had opened his eyes. He was watching her, smiling. "You know, that fork?" he said. "I did it to frighten that fellow. There was *almost* nothing the matter with it."

Eve's apprehensions faded and she gave a light laugh. "You succeeded," she said. "You drove him completely out of his mind."

Pierre smiled. "Did you see? He played with it a long time, he held it right in his hands. The trouble is," he said, "they don't know how to take hold of things; they grab them."

"That's right," Eve said.

Pierre tapped the palm of his left hand lightly with the index of his right.

"They take with that. They reach out their fingers and when they catch hold of something they crack down on it to knock it out."

He spoke rapidly and hardly moving his lips; he looked puzzled.

"I wonder what they want," he said at last. "That fellow has already been here. Why did they send him to me? If they want to know what I'm doing all they have to do is read it on the screen, they don't even need to leave the house. They make mistakes. They have the power but they make mistakes. I never make any, that's my trump card. *Hoffka!*" he said. He shook his long hands before his forehead. "The bitch Hoffka! Paffka! Suffka! Do you want any more?"

"Is it the bell?" asked Eve.

"Yes. It's gone." He went on severely. "This fellow, he's just a subordinate. You know him, you went into the living-room with him."

Eve did not answer.

"What did he want?" asked Pierre. "He must have told you."

She hesitated an instant, then answered brutally. "He wanted you locked up."

When the truth was told quietly to Pierre he distrusted it. He had to be dealt with violently in order to daze and paralyze his suspicions. Eve preferred to brutalize him rather than lie: when she lied and he acted as if he believed it she could not avoid a very slight feeling of superiority which made her horrified at herself.

"Lock me up!" Pierre repeated ironically. "They're crazy. What can walls do to me. Maybe they think that's going to stop me. I sometimes wonder if there aren't two groups. The real one, the Negro—and then a bunch of fools trying to stick their noses in and making mistake after mistake."

He made his hand jump up from the arm of the chair and looked at it happily.

"I can get through walls. What did you tell them?" he asked, turning to Eve with curiosity.

"Not to lock you up."

He shrugged. "You shouldn't have said that. You made a mistake too . . . unless you did it on purpose. You've got to call their bluff."

He was silent! Eve lowered her head sadly: *"They grab things!" How scornfully he said that—and he was right. Do I grab things too? It doesn't do any good to watch myself, I think most of my movements annoy him. But he doesn't say anything.* Suddenly she felt as miserable as when she was fourteen and Mme. Darbedat told her: "You don't know what to do with your hands." She didn't dare make a move and just at that time she had an irresistible desire to change her position. Quietly she put her feet under the chair, barely touching the rug. She watched the lamp on the table—the lamp whose base Pierre had painted black—and the chess set. Pierre had left only the black pawns on the board. Sometimes he would get up, go to the table and take the pawns in his hands one by one. He spoke to them, called them Robots and they seemed to stir with a mute life under his fingers. When he set them down, Eve went and touched them in her turn (she always felt somewhat ridiculous about it). They had become little bits of dead wood again but something vague and incomprehensible stayed in them, something like understanding. *These are his things*, she thought. *There is nothing of mine in the room.* She had had a few pieces of furniture before; the mirror and the little inlaid dresser handed down from her grandmother and which Pierre jokingly called *"your* dresser." Pierre had carried them away with him; things showed their true face to Pierre alone. Eve could watch them for hours: they were unflaggingly stubborn and determined to deceive her, offering her nothing but their appearance—as they did to Dr. Franchot and M. Darbedat. *Yet,* she told herself with anguish, *I don't see them quite like my father. It isn't possible for me to see them exactly like him.*

She moved her knees a little: her legs felt as though they were crawling with ants. Her body was stiff and taut and hurt her; she felt it too alive, too demanding. *I would like to be invisible and stay here seeing him without his seeing me. He doesn't need me; I am useless in this room.* She turned her head slightly and looked at the wall above Pierre. Threats were written on the wall. Eve knew it but she could not read them. She often watched the big red roses on the wallpaper until they began to dance before her eyes. The roses flamed in shadow. Most of the time the threat was written near the ceiling, a little to the left of the bed; but sometimes it moved. *I must get up. I can't . . . I can't sit down any longer.* There were also white discs on the wall that looked like slices of onion. The discs spun and Eve's hands began to tremble: *Sometimes I think I'm going mad. But no,* she thought, *I can't go mad. I get nervous, that's all.*

Suddenly she felt Pierre's hand on hers.

"Agatha," Pierre said tenderly.

He smiled at her but he held her hand by the ends of his fingers with a sort of revulsion, as though he had picked up a crab by the back and wanted to avoid its claws.

"Agatha," he said, "I would so much like to have confidence in you."

She closed her eyes and her breast heaved. *I mustn't answer anything, if I do he'll get angry, he won't say anything more.*

Pierre had dropped her hand. "I like you, Agatha," he said, "but I can't understand you. Why do you stay in the room all the time?"

Eve did not answer.

"Tell me why."

"You know I love you," she said dryly.

"I don't believe you," Pierre said. "Why should you love me? I must frighten you: I'm haunted." He smiled but suddenly became serious. "There is a wall between you and me. I see you, I speak to you, but you're on the other side. What keeps us from loving? I think it was easier before. In Hamburg."

"Yes," Eve said sadly. Always Hamburg. He never spoke of their real past. Neither Eve nor he had ever been to Hamburg.

"We used to walk along the canal. There was a barge, remember? The barge was black; there was a dog on the deck."

He made it up as he went along; it sounded false.

"I held your hand. You had another skin. I believed all you told me. Be quiet!" he shouted.

He listened for a moment. "They're coming," he said mournfully.

Eve jumped up. "They're coming? I thought they wouldn't ever come again."

Pierre had been calmer for the past three days; the statues did not come. Pierre was terribly afraid of the statues even though he would never admit it. Eve was not afraid: but when they began to fly, buzzing, around the room, she was afraid of Pierre.

"Give me the ziuthre," Pierre said.

Eve got up and took the ziuthre: it was a collection of pieces of cardboard Pierre had glued together; he used it to conjure the statues. The ziuthre looked like a spider. On one of the cardboards Pierre had written, "Power over ambush," and on the other, "Black." On a third he had drawn a laughing face with wrinkled eyes: it was Voltaire.

Pierre seized the ziuthre by one end and looked at it darkly.

"I can't use it any more," he said.

"Why?"

"They turned it upside down."

"Will you make another?"

He looked at her for a long while. "You'd like me to, wouldn't you," he said between his teeth.

Eve was angry at Pierre. *He's warned every time they come: how does he do it? He's never wrong.*

35

The ziuthre dangled pitifully from the ends of Pierre's fingers. *He always finds a good reason not to use it. Sunday when they came he pretended he'd lost it but I saw it behind the paste pot and he couldn't fail to see it. I wonder if he isn't the one who brings them.* One could never tell if he were completely sincere. Sometimes Eve had the impression that despite himself Pierre was surrounded by a swarm of unhealthy thoughts and visions. But at other times Pierre seemed to invent them. *He suffers. But how much does he believe in the statues and the Negro? Anyhow, I know he doesn't see the statues, he only hears them: when they pass he turns his head away; but he still says he sees them; he describes them.* She remembered the red face of Dr. Franchot: "But my dear madame, all mentally unbalanced persons are liars; you're wasting your time if you're trying to distinguish between what they really feel and what they pretend to feel." She gave a start. *What is Franchot doing here? I don't want to start thinking like him.*

Pierre had gotten up. He went to throw the ziuthre into the wastebasket: *I want to think like you,* she murmured. He walked with tiny steps, on tiptoe, pressing his elbows against his hips so as to take up the least possible space. He came back and sat down and looked at Eve with a closed expression.

"We'll have to put up black wallpaper," he said. "There isn't enough black in this room."

He was crouched in the armchair. Sadly Eve watched his meager body, always ready to withdraw, to shrink: the arms, legs, and head looked like retractable organs. The clock struck six. The piano downstairs was silent. Eve sighed: the statues would not come right away; they had to wait for them.

"Do you want me to turn on the light?"

She would rather not wait for them in darkness.

"Do as you please," Pierre said.

Eve lit the small lamp on the bureau and a red mist filled the room. Pierre was waiting too.

He did not speak but his lips were moving, making two dark stains in the red mist. Eve loved Pierre's lips. Before, they had been moving and sensual; but they had lost their sensuality. They were wide apart, trembling a little, coming together incessantly, crushing against each other only to separate again. They were the only living things in this blank face; they looked like two frightened animals. Pierre could mutter like that for hours without a sound leaving his mouth and Eve often let herself be fascinated by this tiny, obstinate movement. *I love his mouth.* He never kissed her any more; he was horrified at contacts: at night they touched him—the hands of men, hard and dry, pinched him all over; the long-nailed hands of women caressed him. Often he went to bed with his clothes on but the hands slipped under the clothes and tugged at his shirt. Once he heard laughter and puffy lips were placed on his mouth. He never kissed Eve after that night.

"Agatha," Pierre said, "don't look at my mouth."

Eve lowered her eyes.

"I am not unaware that people can learn to read lips," he went on insolently.

His hands trembled on the arm of the chair. The index finger stretched out, tapped three times on the thumb and the other fingers curled: this was a spell. *It's going to start,* she thought. She wanted to take Pierre in her arms.

Pierre began to speak at the top of his voice in a very sophisticated tone.

"Do you remember Sao Paulo?"

No answer. Perhaps it was a trap.

"I met you there," he said, satisfied. "I took you away from a Danish sailor. We almost fought but I paid for a round of drinks and he let me take you away. All that was only a joke."

He's lying, he doesn't believe a word of what he says. He knows my name isn't Agatha. I hate him when he lies. But she saw his staring eyes and her rage melted. *He isn't lying,* she thought, *he can't stand it any more. He feels them coming; he's talking to keep from hearing them.* Pierre dug both hands into the arm of the chair. His face was pale; he was smiling.

"These meetings are often strange," he said, "but I don't believe it's by chance. I'm not asking who sent you. I know you wouldn't answer. Anyhow, you've been smart enough to bluff me."

He spoke with great difficulty, in a sharp, hurried voice. There were words he could not pronounce and which left his mouth like some soft and shapeless substance.

"You dragged me away right in the middle of the party, between the rows of black automobiles, but behind the cars there was an army with red eyes which glowed as soon as I turned my back. I think you made signs to them, all the time hanging on my arm, but I didn't see a thing. I was too absorbed by the great ceremonies of the Coronation."

He looked straight ahead, his eyes wide open. He passed his hand over his forehead very rapidly, in one spare gesture, without stopping his talking. He did not want to stop talking.

"It was the Coronation of the Republic," he said stridently, "an impressive spectacle of its kind because of all the species of animals that the colonies sent for the ceremony. You were afraid to get lost among the monkeys. I said among the monkeys," he repeated arrogantly, looking around him, "I could say *among the Negroes!* The abortions sliding under the tables, trying to pass unseen, are discovered and nailed to the spot by my Look. The password is silence. To be silent. Everything in place and attention for the entrance of the statues, that's the countersign. Tralala . . . ," he shrieked and cupped his hands to his mouth. "Tralalala, tralalalala!"

He was silent and Eve knew that the statues had come into the room. He was stiff, pale and distrustful. Eve stiffened too and both waited in silence. Someone was walking in the corridor: it was Marie the housecleaner, she had undoubtedly just arrived. Eve thought, *I have to give her money for the gas.* And then the statues began to fly; they passed between Eve and Pierre.

Pierre went "Ah!" and sank down in the armchair, folding his legs beneath him. He turned his face away; sometimes he grinned, but drops of sweat pearled his forehead. Eve could stand the sight no longer, this pale cheek, this mouth deformed by a trembling grimace; she closed her eyes. Gold threads began to dance on the red background of her eyelids; she felt old and heavy. Not far from her Pierre was breathing violently. *They're flying, they're buzzing, they're bending over him.* She felt a slight tickling, a pain in the shoulder and right side. Instinctively her body bent to the left as if to avoid some disagreeable contact, as if to let a heavy, awkward object pass. Suddenly the floor creaked and she had an insane desire to open her eyes, to look to her right, sweeping the air with her hand.

She did nothing; she kept her eyes closed and a bitter joy made her tremble: *I am afraid too,* she thought. Her entire life had taken refuge in her right side. She leaned towards Pierre without opening her eyes. The slightest effort would be enough and she would enter this tragic world for the first time. *I'm afraid of the statues,* she thought. It was a violent, blind affirmation, an incantation. She wanted to believe in their presence with all her strength. She tried to make a new sense, a sense of touch out of the anguish which paralyzed her right side. She *felt* their passage in her arm, in her side and shoulder.

The statues flew low and gently; they buzzed. Eve knew that they had an evil look and that eyelashes stuck out from the stone around their eyes; but she pictured them badly. She knew, too, that they were not quite alive but that slabs of flesh, warm scales appeared on their great bodies; the stone peeled from the ends of their fingers and their palms were eaten away. Eve could not *see* all that: she simply thought of enormous women sliding against her, solemn and grotesque, with a human look and compact heads of stone. *They are bending over Pierre*—Eve made such a violent effort that her hands began trembling—*they are bending over me*. A horrible cry suddenly chilled her. They had touched him. She opened her eyes: Pierre's head was in his hands, he was breathing heavily. Eve felt exhausted: *a game*, she thought with remorse; *it was only a game. I didn't sincerely believe it for an instant. And all that time he suffered as if it were real.*

Pierre relaxed and breathed freely. But his pupils were strangely dilated and he was perspiring.

"Did you see them?" he asked.

"I can't see them."

"Better for you. They'd frighten you," he said. "I am used to them."

Eve's hands were still shaking and the blood had rushed to her head. Pierre took a cigarette from his pocket and brought it up to his mouth. But he did not light it:

"I don't care whether I see them or not," he said, "but I don't want them to touch me: I'm afraid they'll give me pimples."

He thought for an instant, then asked, "Did you hear them?"

"Yes," Eve said, "it's like an airplane engine." (Pierre had told her this the previous Sunday.)

Pierre smiled with condescension. "You exaggerate," he said. But he was still pale. He looked at Eve's hands. "Your hands are trembling. That made quite an impression on you, my poor Agatha. But don't worry. They won't come back again before tomorrow." Eve could not speak. Her teeth were chattering and she was afraid Pierre would notice it. Pierre watched her for a long time.

"You're tremendously beautiful," he said, nodding his head. "It's too bad, too bad."

He put out his hand quickly and toyed with her ear. "My lovely devil-woman. You disturb me a little, you are too beautiful: that distracts me. If it weren't a question of recapitulation. . . ."

He stopped and looked at Eve with surprise.

"That's not the word . . . it came . . . it came," he said, smiling vaguely. "I had another on the tip of my tongue . . . but this one . . . came in its place. I forget what I was telling you."

He thought for a moment, then shook his head.

"Come," he said, "I want to sleep." He added in a childish voice, "You know, Agatha, I'm tired. I can't collect my thoughts any more."

He threw away his cigarette and looked at the rug anxiously. Eve slipped a pillow under his head.

"You can sleep too," he told her, "they won't be back."

. . . *Recapitulation.* . . .

Pierre was asleep, a candid half-smile on his face; his head was turned to one side: one might have thought he wanted to caress his cheek with his shoulder. Eve was not sleepy, she was thoughtful: *Recapitulation.* Pierre had suddenly looked stupid and the word had slipped out of his mouth, long and whitish. Pierre had stared ahead of him in astonishment, as if he had seen the word and didn't recognize it; his mouth was open, soft: something seemed broken in it. He stammered. *That's the first time it ever happened to him: he noticed it, too. He said he couldn't collect his thoughts any more.* Pierre gave a voluptuous little whimper and his hand made a vague movement. Eve watched him harshly: *how is he going to wake up?* It gnawed at her. As soon as Pierre was asleep she had to think about it. She was afraid he would wake up wild-eyed and stammering. *I'm stupid,* she thought, *it can't start before a year; Franchot said so.* But the anguish did not leave her; a year: a winter, a springtime, a summer, the beginning of another autumn. One day his features would grow confused, his jaw would hang loose, he would half open his weeping eyes. Eve bent over Pierre's hand and pressed her lips against it: *I'll kill you before that.*

EROSTRATUS

You really have to see men from above. I put out the light and went to the window: they never suspected for a moment you could watch them from up there. They're careful of their fronts, sometimes of their backs, but their whole effect is calculated for spectators of about five feet eight. Who ever thought about the shape of a derby hat seen from the seventh floor? They neglect protecting their heads and shoulders with bright colors and garish clothes, they don't know how to fight this great enemy of Humanity, the downward perspective. I leaned on the window sill and began to laugh: where was this wonderful upright stance they're so proud of: they were crushed against the sidewalk and two long legs jumped out from under their shoulders.

On a seventh floor balcony: that's where I should have spent my whole life. You have to prop up moral superiorities with material symbols or else they'll tumble. But exactly what is my superiority over men? Superiority of position, nothing more: I have placed myself above the human within me and I study it. That's why I always liked the towers of Notre-Dame, the platforms of the Eiffel Tower, the Sacré-Coeur, my seventh floor on the Rue Delambre. These are excellent symbols.

Sometimes I had to go down into the street. To the office, for example. I stifled. It's much harder to consider people as ants when you're on the same plane as they are: they *touch* you. Once I saw a dead man in the street. He had fallen on his face. They turned him over, he was bleeding. I saw his open eyes and his cockeyed look and all the blood. I said to myself, "It's nothing, it's no more touching then wet paint. They painted his nose red, that's all." But I felt a nasty softness in my legs and neck and I fainted. They took me into a drugstore, gave me a few slaps on the face and a drink. I could have killed them.

I knew they were my enemies but they didn't know it. They liked each other, they rubbed elbows; they would even have given me a hand, here and there, because they thought I was like them. But if they could have guessed the least bit of the truth, they would have beaten me. They did later, anyhow. When they got me and knew *who* I was, they gave me the works; they beat me up for two hours in the station house, they slapped me and punched me and twisted my arms, they ripped off my pants and to finish they threw my glasses on the floor and while I looked for them, on all fours, they laughed and kicked me. I always knew they'd end up beating me; I'm not strong and I can't defend myself. Some of them had been on the lookout for me for a long time: the big ones. In the street they'd bump into me to see what I'd do. I said nothing. I acted as if I didn't understand. But they still got me. I was afraid of them: it was a foreboding. But don't think I didn't have more serious reasons for hating them.

As far as that was concerned, everything went along much better starting from the day I bought a revolver. You feel strong when you assiduously carry on your person something that can explode and make a noise. I took it every Sunday, I simply put it in my pants pocket and then went out for a walk—generally along the boulevards. I felt it pulling at my pants like a crab, I felt it cold against my thigh. But little by little it got warmer with the contact of my body. I walked with a certain stiffness, I looked like a man with a hard-on, with his thing sticking out at every step. I slipped my hand in my pocket and felt the *object*. From time to time I went into a *urinoir*—even in there I had to be careful because I often had neighbors—I took out my revolver, I felt the weight of it, I looked at its black checkered butt and its trigger that looked like a half-closed eyelid. The others, the ones who saw me from the outside, thought I was pissing. But I never piss in the *urinoirs*.

One night I got the idea of shooting people. It was a Saturday evening, I had gone out to pick up Lea, a blonde who works out in front of a hotel on the Rue Montparnasse. I never had intercourse with a woman: I would have felt robbed. You get on top of them, of course, but they eat you up with their big hairy mouth and, from what I hear, they're the ones—by a long shot—who gain on the deal. I don't ask anybody for anything, but I don't give anything, either. Or else I'd have to have a cold, pious woman who would give in to me with disgust. The first Saturday of every month I went to one of the rooms in the Hotel Duquesne with Lea. She undressed and I watched her without touching her. Sometimes I went off in my pants all by myself, other times I had time to get home and finish it. That night I didn't find her.

I waited for a little while and, as I didn't see her coming, I supposed she had a cold. It was the beginning of January and it was very cold. I was desolated: I'm the imaginative kind and I had pictured to myself all the pleasure I would have gotten from the evening. On the Rue Odessa there was a brunette I had often noticed, a little ripe but firm and plump: I don't exactly despise ripe women: when they're undressed they look more naked than the others. But she didn't know anything of my wants and I was a little scared to ask her right off the bat. And then I don't care too much for new acquaintances: these women can be hiding some thug behind a door, and after, the man suddenly jumps out and takes your money. You're lucky if you get off without a beating. Still, that evening I had nerve, I decided to go back to my place, pick up the revolver and try my luck.

So when I went up to this woman, fifteen minutes later, my gun was in my pocket and I wasn't afraid of anything. Looking at her closely, she seemed rather miserable. She looked like my neighbor across the way, the wife of the police sergeant, and I was very pleased because I'd been wanting to see her naked for a long time. She dressed with the window open when the sergeant wasn't there, and I often stayed behind my curtain to catch a glimpse of her. But she always dressed in the back of the room.

There was only one free room in the Hotel Stella, on the fifth floor. We went up. The woman was fairly heavy and stopped to catch her breath after each step. I felt good: I have a wiry body, in spite of my belly, and it takes more than five floors to wind me. On the fifth floor landing, she stopped and put her right hand to her heart and breathed heavily. She had the key to the room in her left hand.

"It's a long way up," she said, trying to smile at me. Without answering, I took the key from her and opened the door. I held my revolver in my left hand, pointing straight ahead through the pocket, and I didn't let go of it until I switched the light on. The room was empty. They had a little square of green soap on the washbasin, for a one-shot. I smiled: I don't have much to do with bidets and little squares of soap. The woman was still breathing heavily behind me and that excited me. I turned; she put out her lips towards me. I pushed her away.

"Undress," I told her.

There was an upholstered armchair; I sat down and made myself comfortable. It's at times like this I wish I smoked. The woman took off her dress and stopped, looking at me distrustfully.

"What's your name?" I asked, leaning back.

"Renée."

"All right, Renée, hurry up. I'm waiting."

"You aren't going to undress?"

"Go on," I said, "don't worry about me."

She dropped her panties, then picked them up and put them carefully on top of her dress along with her brassiere.

"So you're a little lazybones, honey?" she asked me. "You want your little girl to do all the work?"

At the same time she took a step towards me, and, leaning her hands on the arm of the chair, tried heavily to kneel between my legs. I got up brusquely.

"None of that," I told her.

She looked at me with surprise.

"Well, what do you want me to do?"

"Nothing. Just walk. Walk around. I don't want any more from you."

She began to walk back and forth awkwardly. Nothing annoys women more than walking when they're naked. They don't have the habit of putting their heels down flat. The whore arched her back and let her arms hang. I was in heaven: there I was, calmly sitting in an armchair, dressed up to my neck, I had even kept my gloves on and this ripe woman had stripped herself naked at my command and was turning back and forth in front of me. She turned her head towards me, and, for appearance, smiled coquettishly.

"You think I'm pretty? You're getting an eyeful?"

"Don't worry about that."

"Say," she asked with sudden indignation, "do you think you're going to make me walk up and down like this very long?"

"Sit down."

She sat on the bed and we watched each other in silence. She had gooseflesh. I could hear the ticking of an alarm clock from the other side of the wall. Suddenly I told her:

"Spread your legs."

She hesitated a fraction of a second then obeyed. I looked between her legs and turned up my nose. Then I began to laugh so hard that tears came to my eyes. I said, simply, "Look at that!"

And I started laughing again.

She looked at me, stupefied, then blushed violently and clapped her legs shut.

"Bastard," she said between her teeth.

44

But I laughed louder, then she jumped up and took her brassiere from the chair.

"Hey!" I said, "it isn't over. I'm going to give you fifty francs after a while, but I want my money's worth."

She picked up her panties nervously.

"I've had enough, get it? I don't know what you want. And if you had me come up here to make a fool out of me. . . ."

Then I took out my revolver and showed it to her. She looked at me seriously and dropped the panties without a word.

"Walk," I told her, "walk around."

She walked around for another five minutes. Then I gave her my cane and made her do exercises. When I felt my drawers were wet I got up and gave her a fifty-franc note. She took it.

"So long," I added. "I don't think I tired you out very much for the money."

I went out, I left her naked in the middle of the room, the brassiere in one hand and the fifty-franc note in the other. I didn't regret the money I spent; I had dumbfounded her and it isn't easy to surprise a whore. Going down the stairs I thought, "That's what I want. To surprise them all." I was happy as a child. I had brought along the green soap and after I reached home I rubbed it under the hot water for a long time until there was nothing left of it but a thin film between my fingers and it looked like a mint candy someone had sucked on for a long time.

But that night I woke up with a start and I saw her face again, her eyes when I showed her my gun, and her fat belly that bounced up and down at every step.

What a fool, I though. And I felt bitter remorse: I should have shot her while I was at it, shot that belly full of holes. That night and three nights afterward, I dreamed of six little red holes grouped in a circle about the navel.

As a result, I never went out without my revolver. I looked at people's backs, and I imagined, from their walk, the way they would fall if I shot them. I was in the habit of hanging around the Châtelet every Sunday when the classical concerts let out. About six o'clock I heard a bell ring and the ushers came to fasten back the plate glass doors with hooks. This was the beginning: the crowd came out slowly; the people walked with floating steps, their eyes still full of dreams, their hearts still full of pretty sentiments. There were a lot of them who looked around in amazement: the street must have seemed quite strange to them. Then they smiled mysteriously: they were passing from one world to another. I was waiting for them in this other world. I slid my right hand into my pocket and gripped the gun butt with all my strength. After a while, I *saw* myself shooting them. I knocked them off like clay pipes, they fell, one after the other and the panic-stricken survivors streamed back into the theatre, breaking the glass in the doors. It was an exciting game: when it was over, my hands were trembling and I had to go to Dreher's and drink a cognac to get myself in shape.

I wouldn't have killed the women. I would have shot them in the kidneys. Or in the calves, to make them dance.

I still hadn't decided anything. But I did everything just as though my power of decision had stopped. I began with minor details. I went to practice in a shooting gallery at Denfert-Rochereau. My scores weren't tremendous, but men are bigger targets, especially when you shoot point-blank. Then I arranged my publicity. I chose a day when all my colleagues would be together in the office. On Monday morning. I was always very friendly with them, even though I had a horror of shaking their hands. They took off their gloves to greet you; they had an obscene way of undressing their hand, pulling the glove back and sliding it slowly along the fingers, unveiling the fat, wrinkled nakedness of the palm. I always kept my gloves on.

We never did much on Mondays. The typist from the commercial service came to bring us receipts. Lemercier joked pleasantly with her and when she had gone, they described her charms with a blasé competence. Then they talked about Lindbergh. They liked Lindbergh. I told them:

"I like the black heroes."

"Negroes?" Masse asked.

"No, black as in Black Magic. Lindbergh is a white hero. He doesn't interest me."

"Go see if it's easy to cross the Atlantic," Bouxin said sourly.

I told them my conception of the black hero.

"An anarchist," Lemercier said.

"No," I said quietly, "the anarchists like their own kind of men."

"Then it must be a crazy man."

But Masse, who had some education, intervened just then.

"I know your character," he said to me. "His name is Erostratus. He wanted to become famous and he couldn't find anything better to do than to burn down the temple of Ephesus, one of the seven wonders of the world."

"And what was the name of the man who built the temple?"

"I don't remember," he confessed. "I don't believe anybody knows his name."

"Really? But you remember the name of Erostratus? You see, he didn't figure things out too badly."

The conversation ended on these words, but I was quite calm. They would remember it when the time came. For myself, who, until then, had never heard of Erostratus, his story was encouraging. He had been dead for more than two thousand years and his act was still shining like a black diamond. I began to think that my destiny would be short and tragic. First it frightened me but I got used to it. If you look at it a certain way, it's terrible, but on the other hand, it gives the passing moment considerable force and beauty. I felt a strange power in my body when I went down into the street. I had my revolver on me, the thing that explodes and makes noise. But I no longer drew my assurance from that, it was from myself: I was a being like a revolver, a torpedo or a bomb. I too, one day at the end of my somber life, would explode and light the world with a flash as short and violent as magnesium. At that time I had the same dream several nights in a row. I was an anarchist. I had put myself in the path of the Tsar and I carried an infernal machine on me. At the appointed hour, the cortège passed, the bomb exploded and we were thrown into the air, myself, the Tsar, and three gold-braided officers, before the eyes of the crowd.

I now went for weeks on end without showing up at the office. I walked the boulevards in the midst of my future victims or locked myself in my room and made my plans. They fired me at the beginning of October. Then I spent my leisure working on the following letter, of which I made 102 copies:

Monsieur:

You are a famous man and your works sell by the thousands. I am going to tell you why: because you love men. You have humanism in your blood: you are lucky. You expand when you are with people; as soon as you see one of your fellows, even without knowing him, you feel sympathy for him. You have a taste for his body, for the way he is jointed, for his legs which open and close at will, and above all for his hands: it pleases you because he has five fingers on each hand and he can set his thumb against the other fingers. You are delighted when your neighbor takes

47

a cup from the table because there is a way of taking it which is strictly human and which you have often described in your works; less supple, less rapid than that of a monkey, but is it not so much more intelligent? You also love the flesh of man, his look of being heavily wounded with re-education, seeming to re-invent walking at every step, and his famous look which even wild beasts cannot bear. So it has been easy for you to find the proper accent for speaking to man about himself: a modest, yet frenzied accent. People throw themselves greedily upon your books, they read them in a good armchair, they think of a great love, discreet and unhappy, which you bring them and that makes up for many things, for being ugly, for being cowardly, for being cuckolded, for not getting a raise on the first of January. And they say willingly of your latest book: it's a good deed.

I suppose you might be curious to know what a man can be like who does not love men. Very well, I am such a man, and I love them so little that soon I am going out and kill half a dozen of them: perhaps you might wonder why *only* half a dozen? Because my revolver has only six cartridges. A monstrosity, isn't it? And moreover, an act strictly impolitic? But I tell you I *cannot* love them. I understand very well the way you feel. But what attracts you to them disgusts me. I have seen, as you, men chewing slowly, all the while keeping an eye on everything, the left hand leafing through an economic review. Is it my fault I prefer to watch the sea-lions feeding? Man can do nothing with his face without its turning into a game of physiognomy. When he chews, keeping his mouth shut, the corners of his mouth go up and down, he looks as though he were passing incessantly from serenity to tearful surprise. You love this, I know, you call it the watchfulness of the Spirit. But it makes me sick; I don't know why; I was born like that.

If there were only a difference of taste between us I would not trouble you. But everything happens as if you had grace and I had none. I am free to like or dislike lobster Newburg, but if I do not like men I am a wretch and can find no place in the sun. They have monopolized the sense of life. I hope you will understand what I mean. For the past 33 years I have been beating against closed doors above which is written: "No entrance if not a humanist." I have had to abandon all I have undertaken; I had to choose: either it was an absurd and ill-fated attempt, or sooner or later it had to turn to their profit. I could not succeed in detaching from myself thoughts I did not expressly destine for them, in formulating them: they remained in me as slight organic movements. Even the tools I used I felt belonged to them; words, for example: I wanted *my own* words. But the ones I use have dragged through I don't know how many consciences; they arrange themselves in my head by virtue of the habits I have picked up from the others and it is not without repugnance that I use them in writing to you. But this is the last time. I say to you: love men or it is only right for them to let you sneak out of it. Well, I do not want to sneak out. Soon I am going to take my revolver, I am going down into the street and see if anybody can do anything to *them*. Goodbye, perhaps it will be you I shall meet. You will never know then with what pleasure I shall blow your brains out. If not—and this is more likely—read tomorrow's papers. There you will see that an individual named Paul Hilbert has killed, in a moment of fury, six passers-by on the Boulevard Edgar-Quinet. You know better than anyone the value of newspaper prose. You understand then that I am not "furious." I am, on the contrary, quite calm and I pray you to accept, Monsieur, the assurance of my distinguished sentiments.

PAUL HILBERT

I slipped the 102 letters in 102 envelopes and on the envelopes I wrote the addresses of 102 French writers. Then I put the whole business in my table drawer along with six books of stamps.

I went out very little during the two weeks that followed. I let myself become slowly occupied by my crime. In the mirror, to which I often went to look at myself, I noticed the changes in my face with pleasure. The eyes had grown larger, they seemed to be eating up the whole face. They were black and tender behind the glasses and I rolled them like planets. The fine eyes of an artist or assassin. But I counted on changing even more profoundly after the massacre. I have seen photographs of two beautiful girls—those servants who killed and plundered their mistress. I saw their photos *before* and *after*. *Before*, their faces poised like sky flowers above piqué collars. They smelled of hygiene and appetizing honesty. A discreet curling iron had

49

waved their hair exactly alike. And, even more reassuringly than their curled hair, their collars and their look of being at the photographer's, there was their resemblance as sisters, their well considered resemblance which immediately put the bonds of blood and natural roots of the family circle to the fore. *After*, their faces were resplendent as fire. They had the bare neck of prisoners about to be beheaded. Everywhere wrinkles, horrible wrinkles of fear and hatred, folds, holes in the flesh as though a beast with claws had walked over their faces. And those eyes, always those black, depthless eyes—like mine. Yet they did not resemble one another. Each one, in her own way, bore the memory of the common crime. "If it is enough," I told myself, "for a crime which was mostly chance, to transform these orphans' faces, what can I not hope for from a crime entirely conceived and organized by myself." It would possess me, overturning my all-too-human ugliness . . . a crime, cutting the life of him who commits it in two. There must be times when one would like to turn back, but this shining object is there behind you, barring the way. I asked only an hour to enjoy mine, to feel its crushing weight. This time, I would arrange to have everything my way: I decided to carry out the execution at the top of the Rue Odessa. I would profit by the confusion to escape, leaving them to pick up their dead. I would run, I would cross the Boulevard Edgar-Quinet and turn quickly into the Rue Delambre. I would need only 30 seconds to reach the door of my building. My pursuers would still be on the Boulevard Edgar-Quinet, they would lose my trail and it would surely take them more than an hour to find it again. I would wait for them in my room, and when I would hear the beating on the door I would re-load my revolver and shoot myself in the mouth.

I began to live more expensively; I made an arrangement with the proprietor of a restaurant on the Rue Vavin who had a tray sent up every morning and evening. The boy rang, but I didn't open, I waited a few minutes then opened the door halfway and saw full plates steaming in a long basket set on the floor.

On October 27, at six in the evening, I had only 17 and a half francs left. I took my revolver and the packet of letters and went downstairs. I took care not to close the door, so as to re-enter more rapidly once I had finished. I didn't feel well, my hands were cold and blood was rushing to my head, my eyes tickled me. I looked at the stores, the Hotel de l'Ecole, the stationer's where I buy my pencils, and I didn't recognize them. I wondered, "What street is this?" The Boulevard Montparnasse was full of people. They jostled me, pushed me, bumped me with their elbows or shoulders. I let myself be shoved around, I didn't have the strength to slip in between them. Suddenly I saw myself in the heart of this mob, horribly alone and little. How they could have hurt me if they wanted! I was afraid because of the gun in my pocket. It seemed to me they could guess it was there. They would look at me with their hard eyes and would say: "Hey there . . . hey . . . !" with happy indignation, harpooning me with their men's paws. Lynched! They would throw me above their heads and I would fall back in their arms like a marionette. I thought it wiser to put off the execution of my plan until the next day. I went to eat at the *Cupole* for 16 francs 80. I had 70 centimes left and I threw them in the gutter.

I stayed three days in my room, without eating, without sleeping. I had drawn the blinds and I didn't dare go near the window or make a light. On Monday, someone rang at my door. I held my breath and waited. After a minute they rang again. I went on tiptoe and glued my eye to the keyhole. I could only see a piece of black cloth and a button. The man rang again and then went away. I don't know who it was. At night I had refreshing visions, palm trees, running water, a purple sky above a dome. I wasn't thirsty because hour after hour I went and drank at the spigot. But I was hungry. I saw the whore again. It was in a castle I had built in Causses Noires, about 60 miles from any town. She was naked and alone with me. Threatening her with my revolver I forced her to kneel and then run on all fours; then I tied her to a pillar and after I explained at great length what I was going to do, I riddled her with bullets. These images troubled me so much that I had to satisfy myself. Afterwards, I lay motionless in the darkness, my head absolutely empty. The furniture began to creak. It was five in the morning. I would have given anything to leave the room, but I couldn't go out because of the people walking in the street.

Day came, I didn't feel hungry any more, but I began to sweat: my shirt was soaked. Outside there was sunlight. Then I thought: "He is crouched in blackness, in a closed room, for three days. He has neither eaten nor slept. They rang and He didn't open. Soon, He is going into the street and He will kill."

I frightened myself. At six o'clock in the evening hunger struck me again. I was mad with rage. I bumped into the furniture, then I turned lights on in the rooms, the kitchen, the bathroom. I began to sing at the top of my voice. I washed my hands and I went out. It took me a good two minutes to put all the letters in the box. I shoved them in by tens. I must have crumpled a few envelopes. Then I followed the Boulevard Montparnasse as far as the Rue Odessa. I stopped in front of a haberdasher's window and when I saw my face I thought, "Tonight."

I posted myself at the to of the Rue Odessa, not far from the street lamp, and waited. Two women passed, arm in arm.

I was cold but I was sweating freely. After a while I saw three men come up; I let them by: I needed six. The one on the left looked at me and clicked his tongue. I turned my eyes away.

At seven-five, two groups, followed each other closely, came out onto the Boulevard Edgar-Quinet. There was a man and a woman with two children. Behind them came three old women. I took a step forward. The woman looked angry and was shaking the little boy's arm. The man drawled,

"What a little bastard he is."

My heart was beating so hard it hurt my arms. I advanced and stood in front of them, motionless. My fingers, in my pocket, were all soft around the trigger.

"Pardon," the man said, bumping into me.

I remembered I had closed the door of the apartment and that provoked me. I would have to lose precious time opening it. The people were getting further away. I turned around and followed them mechanically. But I didn't feel like shooting them any more. They were lost in the crowd on the boulevard. I leaned against the wall. I heard eight and nine o'clock strike. I repeated to myself, "Why must I kill all these people who are dead *already?*" and I wanted to laugh. A dog came and sniffed at my feet.

When the big man passed me, I jumped and followed him. I could see the fold of his red neck between his derby and the collar of his overcoat. He bounced a little in walking and breathed heavily, he looked husky. I took out my revolver: it was cold and bright, it disgusted me, I couldn't remember very well what I was supposed to do with it. Sometimes I looked at it and sometimes I looked at his neck. The fold in the neck smiled at me like a smiling, bitter mouth. I wondered if I wasn't going to throw my revolver into the sewer.

Suddenly, the man turned around and looked at me, irritated. I stepped back.

"I wanted to ask you. . . ."

He didn't seem to be listening, he was looking at my hands.

"Can you tell me how to get to the Rue de la Gaité?"

His face was thick and his lips trembled. He said nothing. He stretched out his hand. I drew back further and said:

"I'd like. . . ."

Then I *knew* I was going to start screaming. I didn't want to: I shot him three times in the belly. He fell with an idiotic look on his face, dropped to his knees and his head rolled on his left shoulder.

"Bastard," I said, "rotten bastard!"

I ran. I heard him coughing. I also heard shouts and feet clattering behind me. Somebody asked, "Is it a fight?" then right after that someone shouted, "Murder! Murder!" I didn't think these shouts concerned me. But they seemed sinister, like the sirens of the fire engines when I was a child. Sinister and slightly ridiculous. I ran as fast as my legs could carry me.

Only I had committed an unpardonable error: instead of going up the Rue Odessa to the Boulevard Edgar-Quinet, *I was running down it toward the Boulevard Montparnasse.* When I realized it, it was too late: I was already in the midst of the crowd, astonished faces turned toward me (I remember the face of a heavily rouged woman wearing a green hat with an aigrette) and I heard the fools in the Rue Odessa shouting "murder" after me. A hand took me by the shoulder. I lost my head then: I didn't want to die stifled by this mob. I shot twice. People began to scream and scatter. I ran into a café. The drinkers jumped up as I ran through but made no attempt to stop me, I crossed the whole length of the café and locked myself in the lavatory. There was still one bullet in my revolver.

A moment went by. I was out of breath and gasping. Everything was extraordinarily silent, as though the people were keeping quiet on purpose. I raised the gun to my eyes and I saw its small hole, round and black: the bullet would come out there; the powder would burn my face. I dropped my arm and waited. After a while they came; there must have been a crowd of them, judging by the scuffling on the floor. They whispered a little and then were quiet. I was still breathing heavily and I thought they must hear me breathing from the other side of the partition. Someone advanced quietly and rattled the doorknob. He must have been flattened beside the door to avoid my bullets. I still wanted to shoot—but the last bullet was for me.

"What are they waiting for?" I wondered. "If they pushed

against the door and broke it down *right away* I wouldn't have time to kill myself and they would take me alive." But they were in no hurry; they gave me all the time in the world to die. The bastards, they were afraid.

After a while, a voice said, "All right, open up. We won't hurt you."

There was silence and the same voice went on, "You know you can't get away."

I didn't answer, I was still gasping for breath. To encourage myself to shoot, I told myself, "If they get me, they're going to beat me, break my teeth, maybe put an eye out." I wanted to know if the big man was dead. Maybe I only wounded him. . . . They were getting something ready, they were dragging something heavy across the floor. I hurriedly put the barrel of the gun in my mouth, and I bit hard on it. But I couldn't shoot, I couldn't even put my finger on the trigger. Everything was dead silent.

I threw away the revolver and opened the door.

INTIMACY

Lulu slept naked because she liked to feel the sheets caressing her body and also because laundry was expensive.

In the beginning Henri protested: you shouldn't go to bed naked like that, it isn't nice, it's dirty. Anyhow, he finally followed her example, though in his case it was merely laziness; he was stiff as a poker when there was company (he admired the Swiss, particularly the Genevans: he thought them high-class because they were so wooden) but he was negligent in small matters, for example, he wasn't very clean, he didn't change his underwear often enough; when Lulu put it in the dirty laundry bag she couldn't help noticing the bottoms were yellow from rubbing between his legs. Personally, Lulu did not despise uncleanliness: it was more intimate and made such tender shadows; in the crook of the arm, for instance; she couldn't stand the English with their impersonal bodies which smelt of nothing. But she couldn't bear the negligence of her husband, because it was a way of getting himself coddled. In the morning, he was always very tender toward himself, his head full of dreams, and broad daylight, cold water, the coarse bristles of the brush made him suffer brutal injustices.

Lulu was sleeping on her back, she had thrust the great toe of her left foot into a tear in the sheet: it wasn't a tear, it was only the hem coming apart. But it annoyed her; I have to fix that tomorrow, but still she pushed against the threads so as to feel them break. Henri was not sleeping yet, but he was quiet. He often told Lulu that as soon as he closed his eyes he felt bound by tight, resistant bonds, he could not even move his little finger. A great fly caught in a spider web. Lulu loved to feel this gross, captive body against her. If he could only stay like that, paralyzed, I would take care of him, clean him like a child and sometimes I'd turn him over on his stomach and give him a spanking, and other times when his mother came to see him, I'd find some reason to uncover him, I'd pull back the sheet and his mother

55

would see him all naked. I think she'd fall flat on her face, it must be fifteen years since she's seen him like that. Lulu passed a light hand over her husband's hip and pinched him a little in the groin. Henri muttered but did not move. Reduced to impotence. Lulu smiled; the word "impotence" always made her smile. When she still loved Henri, and when he slept, thus, she liked to imagine he had been patiently tied up by little men like the ones she had seen in a picture when she was a child and reading *Gulliver's Travels*. She often called Henri "Gulliver" and Henri liked that because it was an English name and it made her seem educated, only he would have rather had her pronounce it with the accent. God, how they annoyed me: if he wanted someone educated all he had to do was marry Jeanne Beder, she's got breasts like hunting horns but she knows five languages. When we were still at Sceaux, on Sundays, I got so annoyed with his family I read books, any book; there was always somebody who came and watched what I was reading and his little sister asked me, "Do you understand, Lucie?" The trouble is, he doesn't think I'm distinguished enough. The Swiss, yes, they're distinguished all right because his older sister married a Swiss who gave her five children and then they impress him with their mountains. I can't have a child because of my constitution, but I never thought it was distinguished, what he does, when he goes out with me, always going into the *urinoirs* and I have to look at the store windows waiting for him, what does that make me look like? and he comes out pulling at his pants and bending his legs like an old man.

Lulu took her toe out of the slit in the sheet and wiggled her feet for the pleasure of feeling herself alert next to this soft, captive flesh. She heard rumblings: a gurgling stomach, I hate it, I can never tell whether it's his stomach or mine. She closed her eyes; liquids do it. bubbling through packs of soft pipes, everybody has them, Rirette has them, I have them (I don't like to think about it, it makes my stomach hurt). He loves me, he doesn't love my bowels, if they showed him my appendix in a glass he wouldn't recognize it, he's always feeling me, but if they put the glass in his hands he wouldn't touch it, he wouldn't think, "that's hers," you ought to love all of somebody, the esophagus, the liver, the intestines. Maybe we don't love them because we aren't used to them, if we saw them the way we saw our hands and arms maybe we'd love them; the starfish must love each other better than we do. They stretch out on the beach when there's sunlight and they poke out their stomachs to get the air and everybody can see them; I wonder where we could stick ours out, through the navel. She had closed her eyes and blue circles began to turn, like a carnival; yesterday I was shooting those circles with rubber arrows and letters lit up, one at every shot and they made the name of a city, he kept me from finishing Dijon with his mania for pressing himself up behind me, I hate people to touch me from behind, I'd rather not have a back, I don't like people to do things to me when I can't see them, they can grab a handful and then you don't see their hands, you can feel them going up and down but you can't tell where they're going, they look at you with all their eyes and you don't see them, he loves that; Henri would never think of it but he, all he thinks about is getting behind me and I know he does it on purpose to touch my behind because he knows I practically die of shame because I have one, when I'm ashamed it excites him but I don't want to think about him (she was afraid) I want to think about Rirette. She thought about Rirette every evening at the same time, just at the moment when Henri began to snuffle and grunt. But there was resistance to the thought and someone else came in her place, she even caught a glimpse of crisp black hair and she thought here it comes and she shuddered because you never know what's coming, if it's the face it's all right, that can still pass, but there were nights she spent without closing her eyes because of those horrible memories coming to the surface, it's terrible when you know all of a man and especially *that*. It isn't the same thing with Henri, I can imagine him from head to foot and it touches me because he's soft with flesh that's all grey except the belly and that's pink, he says when a well built man sits down, his belly makes three folds, but he has six, only he counts by twos and he doesn't want to see the others. She felt annoyed thinking about Rirette: "Lulu, you don't know what the body of a handsome man is like." It's ridiculous, naturally I know, she means a body hard as rock, with muscles, I don't like that, and I felt soft as a caterpillar when he hugged me against him; I married Henri because he was soft, because he looked like a priest. The priests are soft as women with their cassocks and it seems they wear stockings. When I was fifteen I wanted to lift up their skirts quietly and see their men's knees and their drawers, it was so funny they had something between their legs; I would have taken the skirt in one hand and slipped the other up their legs as far as you think, it's not that I like women so much but a man's thing when it's under a skirt is so soft, like a big flower. The trouble is you can never really hold it in your hands, if it would only stay quiet, but it starts moving like an animal, it gets hard, it frightens me when it's hard and sticking up in the air, it's brutal; God, how rotten love is. I loved Henri because his little thing never got hard, never raised its head, I laughed, sometimes I embarrassed him, I wasn't any more afraid of his than of a child's; in the evening I always took his soft little thing between my fingers, he blushed and turned his head away, sighing, but it didn't move, it behaved itself in my hand, I didn't squeeze it, we always stayed like that for a long time and then he went to sleep. Then I stretched out on my back and thought about priests and pure things, about women, and I stroked my stomach first, my beautiful flat stomach, then I slid my hands down and it was pleasure; the pleasure only I know how to give myself.

The crisp hair, the hair of a Negro. And anguish in her throat like a ball. But she closed her eyes tightly and finally the ear of Rirette appeared, a small ear, all red and golden, looking like a sugar candy. Lulu had not as much pleasure as usual at the sight of it because she heard Rirette's voice at the same time. It was a sharp, precise voice which Lulu didn't like. "You *should* go away with Pierre, Lulu; it's the only intelligent thing to do." I like Rirette very much, but she annoys me a little when she acts important and gets carried away by what she says. The night before, at the *Cupole*, Rirette was bent over her with a reasonable and somewhat haggard look. "You *can't* stay with Henri, because you don't love him, it would be a crime." She doesn't lose a chance to say something bad about him, I don't think it's very nice, he's always been perfect with her; maybe I don't love him any more, but it isn't up to Rirette to tell me; everything looks so simple and easy to her: you love or you don't love any more: but I'm not simple. First I'm used to it here and then I do like him, he's my husband. I wanted to beat her, I always wanted to hurt her because she's fat. "It would be a crime." She raised her arms, I saw her armpit, I always like her better when she has bare arms. The armpit. It was half-open, you might have thought it was a mouth; Lulu saw purple wrinkled flesh beneath the curly hairs. Pierre calls her "Minerva the Plump," she doesn't like that at all, Lulu smiled because she thought of her little brother Robert who asked her one day when she had on nothing but her slip, "Why do you have hair under your arms?" and she answered, "It's a sickness." She liked to dress in front of her little brother because he made such funny remarks, and you wondered where he picked them up. He always felt her clothes and folded her dresses carefully, his hands were so deft: one day he'll be a great dressmaker. That's a charming business, I'll design the materials for him. It's odd for a little boy to want to be a dressmaker; if I had been a boy I would have wanted to be an explorer or an actor, but not a dressmaker; but he always was a dreamer, he doesn't talk enough, he sticks to his own ideas; I wanted to be a nun and take up collections in beautiful houses. My eyes feel all soft, all soft as flesh, I'm going to sleep. My lovely pale face under the stiff head-dress, I would have looked distinguished. I would have seen hundreds of dark hallways. But the maid would have turned the light on right away; then I'd have seen family portraits, bronze statues on the tables. And closets. The woman comes with a little book and a fifty-franc note "Here you are, Sister." "Thank you, madame, God bless you. Until the next time." But I wouldn't have been a real nun. In the bus, sometimes, I'd have made eyes at some fellow, first he'd be dumbfounded, then he'd follow me, telling me a lot of nonsense and I'd have a policeman lock him up. I would have kept the collection money myself. What would I have bought? *Antidote*. It's silly. My eyes are getting softer, I like that, you'd think they were soaked in water and my whole body's comfortable. The beautiful green tiara with emeralds and lapis lazuli. The tiara turned and it was a horrible bull's head, but Lulu was not afraid, she said, "Birds of Cantal. Attention." A long red river dragged across arid countrysides. Lulu thought of her meat-grinder, then of hair grease.

"It would be a crime." She jumped bolt upright in the blackness, her eyes hard. They're torturing me. "You'll come to my house, I want you all for good intentions but she who's so reasonable for other people, she ought to know I need to think it over. He said, "You'll come!" making fiery eyes at me. "You'll come into my house, I want you all for myself!" His eyes terrify me when he wants to hypnotize; he kneaded my arms; when I see him with eyes like that I always think of the hair he has on his chest. You will come, I want you all for myself; how can he say things like that? I'm not a dog.

When I sat down, I smiled at him. I had changed my powder for him and I made up my eyes because he likes that, but he didn't see a thing, he doesn't look at my face, he looks at my breasts and I wish they'd dry up, just to annoy him, even though

I don't have too much, they're so small. You will come to my
villa in Nice. He said it was white with a marble staircase, that
it looked out on the sea, and we'd live naked all day, it must be
funny to go up a stairway when you're naked; I'd make him go
up ahead of me so that he wouldn't look at me; or else I wouldn't
be able to move a foot, I'd stay motionless, wishing with all my
heart he'd go blind; anyhow, that would hardly change anything;
when he's there I always think I'm naked. He took me by the
arm, he looked wicked, he told me, "You've got me under your
skin!" and I was afraid and said, "Yes"; I want to make you happy,
we'll go riding in the car, in the boat, we'll go to Italy and I'll
give you everything you want. But his villa is almost unfurnished
and we'd have to sleep on a mattress on the floor. He wants me
to sleep in his arms and I'll smell his odor; I'd like his chest
because it's brown and wide, but there's a pile of hair on it, I
wish men didn't have hair, his is black and soft as moss, sometimes
I stroke it and sometimes I'm horrified by it, I pull back as far as
possible but he hugs me against him. He'll want me to sleep in
his arms, he'll hug me in his arms and I'll smell his odor; and
when it's dark we'll hear the noise of the sea and he may wake
me up in the middle of the night if he wants to do it: I'll never
be able to sleep peacefully except when I have my sickness
because, then, he'll shut up but even so it seems there are men
who do it with women then and afterwards they have blood on
them, blood that isn't theirs, and there must be some on the
sheets, everywhere, it's disgusting, why must we have bodies?

Lulu opened her eyes, the curtains were colored red by a
light coming from the street, there was a red reflection in the
mirror: Lulu loved this red light and there was an armchair which
made funny shadows against the window. Henri had put his
pants on the arm of the chair, and his suspenders were hanging
in emptiness. I have to buy him new suspenders. Oh I don't
want to, I don't want to leave. He'll kiss me all day and I'll be
his, I'll be his pleasure, he'll look at me, he'll think, "this is my
pleasure, I touched her there and there and I can do it again if
it pleases me." At Port-Royal. Lulu kicked her feet in the sheets,
she hated Pierre when she remembered what happened at Port-
Royal. She was behind the hedge, she thought he had stayed in
the car, looking at the map, and suddenly she saw him, running
up behind her, he looked at her. Lulu kicked Henri. He's going
to wake up. But Henri said, "Humph," and didn't waken. I'd
like to know a handsome young man, pure as a girl, and we

wouldn't touch each other, we'd walk along the seashore and we'd hold hands, and at night we'd sleep in twin beds, we'd stay like brother and sister and talk till morning. I'd like to live with Rirette, it's so charming, women living together; she has fat, smooth shoulders; I was miserable when she was in love with Fresnel, and it worried me to think he petted her, that he passed his hands slowly over her shoulders and thighs and she sighed. I wonder what her face must look like when she's stretched out like that, all naked, under a man, feeling hands on her flesh. I wouldn't touch her for all the money in the world, I wouldn't know what to do with her, even if she wanted, even if she said, "I want it!" I wouldn't know how, but if I were invisible I'd like to be there when somebody was doing it to her and watch her face (I'd be surprised if she still looked like Minerva) and stroke her spread knees gently, her pink knees and hear her groan. Dry throated, Lulu gave a short laugh: sometimes you think about things like that. Once she pretended Pierre wanted to rape Rirette. And I helped him, I held Rirette in my arms. Yesterday. She had fire in her cheeks, we were sitting on her sofa, one against the other, her legs were pressed together, but we didn't say anything, we'll never say anything. Henri began to snore and Lulu hissed. I'm here, I can't sleep, I'm upset and he snores, the fool. If he were to take me in his arms, beg me, if he told me, "You are all mine, Lulu, I love you, don't go!" I'd make the sacrifice for him, I'd stay, yes, I'd stay with him all my life to give him pleasure.

II

Rirette sat on the terrace of the *Dôme* and ordered a glass of port. She felt weary and angry at Lulu:

And their port has a taste of cork, Lulu doesn't care because she drinks coffee, but still you can't drink coffee at aperitif time; here they drink coffee all day or café-crême because they don't have a cent, God that must annoy them, I couldn't do it, I'd chuck the whole place in the customer's faces, these people don't need to keep up with anybody. I don't know why she always meets me in Montparnasse, it would be just as close if she met me at the Café de la Paix or the Pam-Pam, and it wouldn't take me so far from my work; impossible to imagine how sad it makes me feel to see these faces all the time, as soon as I have a minute to spare, I have to come here, it's not so bad on the terrace, but inside it smells like dirty underwear and I don't like failures.

Even on the terrace I feel out of place because I'm clean, it must surprise everybody that passes to see me in the middle of these people here who don't even shave and women who look like I don't know what. They must wonder, "What's she doing there?" I know rich Americans sometimes come in the summer, but it seems they're stopping in England now, what with the government we've got, that's why the commerce-de-luxe isn't going so well, I sold a half less than last year at this same time, and I wonder how the others make out, because I'm the best salesgirl, Mme. Dubech told me so, I feel sorry for the little Yonnel girl, she doesn't know how to sell, she can't have made a cent commission this month, and when you're on your feet all day you like to relax a little in a nice place, with a little luxury and a little art and stylish help. You like to close your eyes and let yourself go and then you like to have nice soft music, it wouldn't cost so much to go dancing at the *Ambassadeurs* sometimes; but the waiters here are so impudent, you can tell they're used to handling a cheap crowd, except the little one with brown hair who serves me, he's nice; I think Lulu must like to be surrounded with all these failures, it would scare her to go into a chic place, fundamentally, she isn't sure of herself, it frightens her as soon as there's a man with good manners, she didn't like Louis; well, she ought to be comfortable here, some of them don't even have collars, with their shoddy appearance and their pipes and the way they look at you, they don't even try to hide it, you can see they don't have enough money to pay for a woman, but that isn't what's lacking in the neighborhood, it's disgusting; you'd think they're going to eat you and they couldn't even tell you nicely that they want you, to carry it off in a way to make you feel good.

The waiter came: "Did you want dry port, mademoiselle?"

"Yes, please."

He spoke again, looking friendly, "Nice weather we're having."

"Not too soon for it," Rirette said.

"That's right. You'd think winter wouldn't ever end."

He left and Rirette followed him with her eyes. "I like that waiter," she thought, he knows his place, he doesn't get familiar, but he always has something to say to me, a little special attention.

A thin, bent young man was watching her steadily; Rirette shrugged her shoulders and turned her back on him: When they want to make eyes at a woman they could at least change their underwear. I'll tell him that if he says anything to me. I wonder why she doesn't leave. She doesn't want to hurt Henri, I think that's too stupid: a woman doesn't have the right to spoil her life for some impotent. Rirette hated impotents, it was physical. She's got to leave, she decided, her happiness is at stake, I'll tell her she can't gamble with her happiness. Lulu, you don't have the right to gamble with your happiness. I won't say anything to her, it's finished, I told her a hundred times, you can't make people happy if they don't want to be. Rirette felt a great emptiness in her head, because she was so tired, she looked at the port, all sticky in the glass, like a liquid caramel and a voice in her repeated, "Happiness, happiness," and it was a beautifully grave and tender world. And she thought that if anybody had asked her opinion in the *Paris-Soir* contest she would have said it was the most beautiful word in the French language. Did anyone think of it? They said energy, courage, but that's because they were men, there should have been a woman, the women could find it, there should have been two prizes, one for men and one for women and the most beautiful name would have been Honor; one for the women and I'd have won, I'd have said Happiness. Happiness and Honor. I'll tell her, Lulu, you don't have the right to miss out on your happiness. Your Happiness, Lulu, your Happiness. Personally, I think Pierre is very nice, first, he's a real man, and besides, he's intelligent and that never spoils anything, he has money, he'd do anything for her. He's one of those men who knows how to smooth out life's little difficulties, that's nice for a woman; I like people who know how to command, it's a knack, but he knows how to speak to waiters and head waiters; they obey him, I call that a dominant personality. Maybe that's the thing that's most lacking in Henri. And then there's the question of health, with the father she had, she should take care, it's charming to be slender and light and never to be hungry or sleepy, to sleep four hours a night and run all over Paris all day selling material but it's silly, she ought to follow a sensible diet, not eat too much at one time, but more often and at regular hours. She'll see when they send her to the sanitorium for ten years.

She stared perplexedly at the clock over the Montparnasse intersection, it said 11:20. I don't understand Lulu, she's got a funny temperament, I could never find out whether she liked men or whether they disgusted her; still, she ought to be happy with Pierre, that gives her a change, anyhow, from the one she had last year, from her Rabut, *Rebut* I called him. This memory amused her but she held back her smile because the thin young man was still watching her, she caught him by surprise when she turned her head. Rabut had a face dotted with blackheads and Lulu amused herself by removing them for him, pressed on the skin with her nails: It's sickening, but it's not her fault, Lulu doesn't know what a good-looking man is, I love cute men, first, their things are so pretty, their men's shirts, their shoes, their shiny ties, it may be crude, but it's so sweet, so strong, a sweet strength, it's like the smell of English tobacco and eau de cologne and their skin when they've just shaved, it isn't . . . it isn't like a woman's skin, you'd think it was cordova leather, and their strong arms close around you and you put your head on their chest, you smell their sweet strong odor of well-groomed men, they whisper sweet words to you; they have nice things, nice rough cowhide shoes, they whisper, "Darling, dearest darling," and you feel yourself fainting; Rirette thought of Louis who left her last year and her heart tightened; A man in love with himself, with a pile of little mannerisms, a ring and gold cigarette case and full of little manias . . . but they can be rough sometimes, worse than women. The best thing would be a man about forty, someone who still took care of himself, with grey hair on the sides, brushed back, very dry, with broad shoulders, athletic, but who'd know life and who'd be good because he'd suffered. Lulu is only a kid, she's lucky to have a friend like me, because Pierre's beginning to get tired and some people would take advantage of it if they were in my place; I always tell him to be patient, and when he gets a little sweet on me I act like I'm not paying attention, I begin to talk about Lulu and I always have a good word for her, but she doesn't deserve the luck she has, she doesn't realize; I wanted her to live alone a little the way I did when Louis went away, she'd see what it was like to go back alone to her room every evening, when you've worked all day and find the room empty and dying to put your head on a shoulder. Sometimes you wonder where you find the courage to get up the next morning and go back to work and be seductive and gay and make everybody feel good when you'd rather die than keep on with that life.

The clock struck 11:30. Rirette thought of happiness, the bluebird, the bird of happiness, the rebel bird of love. She gave a start. Lulu is half an hour late, that's usual. She'll never leave her husband, she doesn't have enough will power for that. At heart, it's mainly because of respectability that she stays with

Henri: she cheats on him but so long as they call her "Madame," she doesn't think it matters. She can say anything against him she wants but you can't repeat it the next day, she'd burn up. I did everything I could and I've told her everything I had to tell her, too bad for her.

A taxi stopped in front of the *Dôme* and Lulu stepped out. She was carrying a large valise and her face was solemn.

"I left Henri," she called.

She came nearer, bent under the weight of the valise. She was smiling.

"What?" Rirette gasped, "you don't mean. . . ."

"Yes," Lulu said. "Finished, I dropped him."

Rirette was still incredulous. "He knows? You told him?"

Lulu's eyes clouded. "And how!" she said.

"Well, well . . . my own little Lulu!"

Rirette did not know what to think, but in any case, she supposed Lulu needed encouragement.

"That's good news," she said. "How brave you were."

She felt like adding: you see, it wasn't so hard. But she restrained herself. Lulu let herself be admired: she had rouged her cheeks and her eyes were bright. She sat and put the valise down near her. She was wearing a grey wool coat with a leather belt, a light yellow sweater with a rolled collar. She was bare-headed. She recognized immediately the blend of guilt and amusement she was plunged in; Lulu always made that impression on her. What I like about her, Rirette thought, is her vitality.

"In two shakes," Lulu said, "I told him what I thought. He was struck dumb."

"I can't get over it," said Rirette. "But what came over you, darling? Yesterday evening I'd have bet my last franc you'd never leave him."

"It's on account of my kid brother, I don't mind him getting stuck up with me but I can't stand it when he starts on my family."

"But how did it happen?"

"Where's the waiter?" Lulu asked, stirring restlessly on the chair. "The Dôme waiters aren't ever there when you want them. Is the little brown-haired one serving us?"

"Yes," Rirette said, "did you know he's mad about me?"

"Oh? Look out for the woman in the washroom then, he's always mixed up with her. He makes passes at her but I think he just does it to see the women go into the toilets; when they

65

come out he looks hard enough to make you blush. By the way, I've got to leave you for a minute, I have to go down and call Pierre, I'd like to see his face! If you see the waiter, order a café-crême for me: I'll only be a minute and then I'll tell you everything."

She got up, took a few steps and came back towards Rirette. "Dearest Lulu," said Rirette, taking her by the hands.

Lulu left her and stepped lightly across the terrace. Rirette watched her. I never thought she could do it. How gay she is, she thought, a little scandalized, it's good for her to walk out on her husband. If she had listened to me she'd have done it long ago. Anyhow, it's thanks to me; fundamentally, I have a lot of influence on her.

Lulu was back a few minutes later.

"Pierre was bowled over," she said, "He wanted the details but I'll give them to him later, I'm lunching with him. He says maybe we can leave tomorrow night."

"How glad I am, Lulu," Rirette said. "Tell me quickly. Did you decide last night?"

"You know, I didn't decide anything," Lulu said modestly, "It was decided all by itself." She tapped nervously on the table. "Waiter! Waiter! God, he annoys me. I'd like a café-crême."

Rirette was shocked. In Lulu's place and under circumstances as serious as this she wouldn't have lost time running after a café-crême. Lulu was charming, but it was amazing how futile she could be, like a bird.

Lulu burst out laughing. "If you'd seen Henri's face!

"I wonder what your mother will say?" said Rirette seriously.

"My mother? She'll be en-chan-ted," Lulu said with assurance. "He was impolite with her, you know, she was fed up. Always complaining because she didn't bring me up right, that I was this, I was that, that you could see I was brought up in a barn. You know, what I did was a little because of her."

"But what happened?"

"Well, he slapped Robert."

"You mean Robert was in your place?"

"Yes, just passing by this morning because mother wants to apprentice him with Gompez. I think I told you. So, he stopped in while we were eating breakfast and Henri slapped him."

"But why?" Rirette asked, slightly annoyed. She hated the way Lulu told stories.

"They had an argument," Lulu said vaguely, "and the boy

66

wouldn't let himself be insulted. He stood right up to him. 'Old asshole,' he called him, right to his face. Because Henri said he was poorly raised, naturally, that's all he can say. I thought I'd die laughing. Then Henri got up, we were eating in the kitchenette, and smacked him, I could have killed him!"

"So you left?"

"Left?" Lulu asked, amazed. "Where?"

"I thought you left him then. Look, Lulu, you've got to tell me these things in order, otherwise I don't understand. Tell me," she added, suspiciously, "you really left him, that's all true?"

"Of course. I've been explaining to you for an hour."

"Good. So Henri slapped Robert. Then what?"

"Then," Lulu said, "I locked him on the balcony, it was too funny! He was still in his pajamas, tapping on the window but he didn't dare break the glass because he's as mean as dirt. If I had been in his place, I'd have broken up everything, even if I had to cut my hands to pieces. And the Texiers came in. Then he started smiling through the window acting as if it were a joke."

The waiter passed; Lulu seized his arm:

"So there you are, waiter. Would it trouble you too much to get me a café-crème?"

Rirette was annoyed and she smiled knowingly at the waiter but the waiter remained solemn and bowed with guilty obsequiousness. Rirette was a little angry at Lulu: she never knew the right tone to use on inferiors, sometimes she was too familiar, sometimes too dry and demanding.

Lulu began to laugh.

"I'm laughing because I can still see Henri in his pajamas on the balcony; he was shivering with cold. Do you know how I managed to lock him out? He was in the back of the kitchenette, Robert was crying and he was making a sermon. I opened the window and told him, 'Look, Henri! There's a taxi that just knocked over the flower woman.' He came right out; he likes the flower woman because she told him she was Swiss and he thinks she's in love with him. 'Where? Where?' he kept saying. I stepped back quietly, into the room, and closed the window. Then I shouted through the glass, 'That'll teach you to be a brute to my brother.' I left him on the balcony more than an hour, he kept watching us with big round eyes, he was green with rage. I stuck my tongue out at him and gave Robert candy; after that I brought my things into the kitchenette and got dressed in front of Robert because I know Henri hates that: Robert kissed my arms and neck like a little man, he's so charming, we acted as if Henri weren't there. On top of all that, I forgot to wash."

"And Henri outside the window. It's too funny for words," Rirette said, bursting with laughter.

Lulu stopped laughing. "I'm afraid he'll catch cold," she said seriously. "You don't think when you're mad." She went on gaily, "He shook his fist at us and kept talking all the time but I didn't understand half of what he said. Then Robert left and right after that the Texiers rang and I let them in. When he saw them he was all smiles and bowing at them and I told them, 'Look at my husband, my big darling, doesn't he look like a fish in an aquarium?' The Texiers waved at him through the glass, they were a little surprised but they didn't let on."

"I can see it all," Rirette said, laughing. "Haha! Your husband on the balcony and the Texiers in the kitchenette. . . ." She wanted to find the right comic and picturesque words to describe the scene to Lulu, she thought Lulu did not have a real sense of humor, but the words did not come.

"I opened the window," Lulu said, "and Henri came in. He kissed me in front of the Texiers and called me a little clown. 'Oh, the little clown,' he said, 'she wanted to play a trick on me.' And I smiled and the Texiers smiled politely, everybody smiled. But when they left he hit me on the ear. Then I took a brush and hit him in the corner of the mouth with it: I split his lip."

"Poor girl," Rirette said with tenderness.

But with a gesture Lulu dismissed all compassion. She held herself straight, shaking her brown curls combatively and her eyes flashed lightning.

"Then we talked it over: I washed his mouth with a towel and then I told him I was sick of it, that I didn't love him any more and that I was leaving. He began to cry. He said he'd kill himself. But that didn't work any more: you remember, Rirette, last year, when there was all that trouble in the Rhineland, he sang the same tune every day: 'There's going to be a war, I'm going to enlist and I'll be killed and you'll be sorry, you'll regret all the sorrow you've caused me.' 'That's enough,' I told him, 'you're impotent, they wouldn't take you.' Anyhow, I calmed him down because he was talking about locking me up in the kitchenette, I swore I wouldn't leave before a month. After that he went to the office, his eyes were all red and there was a piece of cloth sticking to his lip, he didn't look too good. I did the housework, I put the lentils on the stove and packed my bag. I left him a note on the kitchen table."

"What did you write?"

"I said," Lulu said proudly, "The lentils are on the stove. Help yourself and turn off the gas. There's ham in the icebox. I'm fed up and I'm leaving. Goodbye."

They both laughed and two passers-by turned around. Rirette thought they must present a charming sight and was sorry they weren't sitting on the terrace of the *Viel* or the *Café de la Paix*. When they finished laughing, they were silent a moment and Rirette realized they had nothing more to say to each other. She was a little disappointed.

"I've got to run," Lulu said, rising; "I meet Pierre at noon. What am I going to do with my bag?"

"Leave it with me," Rirette said, "I'll check it with the woman in the ladies' room. When will I see you again?"

"I'll pick you up at your place at two, I have a pile of errands to do: I didn't take half my things, Pierre's going to have to give me money."

Lulu left and Rirette called the waiter. She felt grave and sad enough for two. The waiter ran up: Rirete already noticed that he always hurried when she called him.

"That's five francs," he said. He added a little dryly, "You two were pretty gay, I could hear you laughing all the way back there."

Lulu hurt his feelings, thought Rirette, spitefully. Blushing, she said, "My friend is a little nervous this morning."

"She's very charming," the waiter said soulfully. "Thank you very much, mademoiselle."

He pocketed the six francs and went off. Rirette was a little amazed, but noon struck and she thought it was time for Henri to come back and find Lulu's note: this was a moment full of sweetness for her.

III

"I'd like all that to be sent *before tomorrow evening*, to the Hotel du Théatre, Rue Vandamme." Lulu told the cashier, putting on the air of a great lady. She turned to Rirette:

"It's all over. Let's go."

"What name?" the cashier asked.

"Mme. Lucienne Crispin."

Lulu threw her coat over her arm and began to run; she ran down the wide staircase of the Samaritain. Rirette followed her, almost falling several times because she didn't watch her step: she had eyes only for the slender silhouette of blue and canary yellow dancing before her! It's true, she does have an obscene body . . . Each time Rirette saw Lulu from behind or in profile, she was struck by the obscenity of her shape though she could not explain why; it was an impression. She's supple and slender, but there's something indecent about her, I don't know what. She does everything she can do to display herself, that must be it. She says she's ashamed of her behind and still she wears skirts that cling to her rump. Her tail is small, yes, a lot smaller than mine, but you can see more of it. It's all around, under her thin back, it fills the skirt, you'd think it was poured in, and besides it jiggles.

Lulu turned around and they smiled at each other. Rirette thought of her friend's indiscreet body with a mixture of reprobation and languor: tight little breasts, a polished flesh, all yellow —when you touched it you'd swear it was rubber—long thighs, a long, common body with long legs: the body of a Negress, Rirette thought, she looks like a Negress dancing the rumba. Near the revolving door a mirror gave Rirette the reflection of her own full body. I'm more the athletic type, she thought, taking Lulu's arm, she makes a better impression than I do when we're dressed, but naked, I'm sure I'm better than she is.

They stayed silent for a moment, then Lulu said:

"Pierre was simply charming. You've been charming too, Rirette, and I'm very grateful to both of you."

She said that with a constrained air, but Rirette paid no attention: Lulu never knew how to thank people, she was too timid.

"What a bore," Lulu said suddenly, "I have to buy a brassiere."

"Here?" Rirette asked. They were just passing a lingerie shop.

"No. But I thought of it because I saw them. I go to Fisher's for my brassieres."

"Boulevard Montparnasse?" Rirette cried. "Look out, Lulu," she went on gravely, "better not hang around the Boulevard Montparnasse, especially now: we'd run into Henri and that would be most unpleasant."

"Henri?" said Lulu, shrugging her shoulders; "Of course not. Why?"

Indignation flushed purple on Rirette's cheeks and temples.

"You're still the same, Lulu, when you don't like something, you deny it, pure and simple. You want to go to Fisher's so you insist Henri won't be on the Boulevard Montparnasse. You know very well he goes by every day at six, it's his way home. You told me that yourself: he goes up the Rue de Rennes and waits for the bus at the corner of the Boulevard Raspail."

"First, it's only five o'clock," Lulu said, "and besides, maybe he didn't go to the office: the note I wrote must have knocked him out."

"But, Lulu," Rirette said suddenly, "You know there's another Fisher's not far from the Opera, on the Rue du Quartre Septembre."

"Yes," Lulu said weakly, "but it's so far to go there."

"Well, I like that; so far to go. It's only two minutes from here. it's a lot closer than Montparnasse."

"I don't like their things."

Rirette thought with amusement that all the Fishers sold the same things.

But Lulu was incomprehensibly obstinate: Henri was positively the last person on earth she would want to meet now and you'd think she was purposely throwing herself in his way.

"Well," she said indulgently, "if we meet him, we meet him, that's all. He isn't going to eat us."

Lulu insisted on going to Montparnasse on foot; she said she needed air. They followed the Rue de Seine, then the Rue de L'Odéon and the Rue de Vaugirard. Rirette praised Pierre and showed Lulu how perfect he had been under the circumstances.

"How I love Paris," Lulu said, "I'm going to miss it!"

"Oh be quiet, Lulu, when I think how lucky you are to go to Nice and then you say how much you'll miss Paris."

Lulu did not answer, she began looking right and left sadly, searching.

When they came out of Fisher's they heard six o'clock strike. Rirette took Lulu's elbow and tried to hurry her along, but Lulu stopped before Baumann the florist.

"Look at those azaleas, Rirette. If I had a nice living room I'd have them everywhere."

"I don't like potted plants," Rirette said.

She was exasperated. She turned her head toward the Rue

de Rennes and sure enough, after a minute, she saw Henri's great stupid silhouette appear. He was bare-headed, and wearing a brown tweed sport coat. Rirette hated brown: "There he is, Lulu, there he is," she said hurriedly.

"Where?" Lulu asked. "Where is he?"

She was scarcely more calm than Rirette.

"Behind us, on the other side of the street. Run and don't turn around."

Lulu turned around anyhow.

"I see him," she said.

Rirette tried to drag her away, but Lulu stiffened and stared at Henri. At last she said, "I think he saw us."

She seemed frightened, suddenly yielded to Rirette and let herself be taken away quietly.

"Now for Heaven's sake, Lulu, don't turn around again," Rirette said breathlessly. "We'll turn down the first street on the right, Rue Delambre."

They walked very quickly, jostling the passers-by. At times Lulu held back a little, or sometimes it was she who dragged Rirette. But they had not quite reached the corner of the Rue Delambre when Rirette saw a large brown shadow behind Lulu; she knew it was Henri and began shaking with anger. Lulu kept her eyes lowered, she looked sly and determined. She's regretting her mistake, but it's too late. Too bad for her.

They hurried on; Henri followed them without a word. They passed the Rue Delambre and kept walking in the direction of the Observatoire. Rirette heard the squeak of Henri's shoes; there was also a sort of light, regular rattle that kept time with their steps: it was his breathing (Henri always breathed heavily, but never that much; he must have run to catch up with them or else it was emotion).

We must act as if he weren't there, Rirette thought. Pretend not to notice his existence. But she could not keep from looking out of the corner of her eye. He was white as a sheet and his eyelids were so lowered they seemed shut. Almost looks like a sleepwalker, thought Rirette with a sort of horror. Henri's lips were trembling and a little bit of pink gauze trembled on the lower lip. And the breathing—that hoarse, even breathing, now ending with a sort of nasal music. Rirette felt uncomfortable: she was not afraid of Henri, but sickness and passion always frightened her a little. After a moment, Henri put his hand out gently and took Lulu's arm. Lulu twisted her mouth as if she were going to cry and pulled it away, shuddering.

Henri went "Phew!"

Rirette had a mad desire to stop: she had a stitch in the side and her ears were ringing. But Lulu was almost running; she too looked like a sleepwalker. Rirette had the feeling that if she let go of Lulu's arm and stopped, they would both keep on running side by side, mute, pale as death, their eyes closed.

Henri began to speak. With a strange, hoarse voice he said: "Come back with me."

Lulu did not answer. Henri said again, in the same toneless voice:

"You are my wife. Come back with me."

"You can see she doesn't want to go back," Rirette answered between her teeth. "Leave her alone."

He did not seem to hear her. "I am your husband," he repeated. "I want you to come back with me."

"For God's sake let her alone," Rirette said sharply. "Bothering her like that won't do any good, so shut up and let her be."

"She is my wife," he said, "she belongs to me, I want her to come back with me."

He had taken Lulu's arm and this time Lulu did not shake him off.

"Go away," Rirette said.

"I won't go away, I'll follow her everywhere, I want her to come back home."

He spoke with effort. Suddenly he made a grimace which showed his teeth and shouted with all his might:

"You belong to me!"

Some people turned around, laughing. Henri shook Lulu's arm, curled back his lips and howled like an animal. Luckily an empty taxi passed. Rirette waved at it and the taxi stopped. Henri stopped too. Lulu wanted to keep on walking but they held her firmly, each by one arm.

"You ought to know," said Rirette, pulling Lulu towards the street, "You'll never get her back with violence."

"Let her alone, let my wife alone," Henri said, pulling in the opposite direction. Lulu was limp as a bag of laundry.

"Are you getting in or not?" the taxi driver called impatiently.

Rirette dropped Lulu's arm and rained blows on Henri's hand. But he did not seem to feel them. After a moment he let go and began to look at Rirette stupidly. Rirette looked at him

73

too. She could barely collect her thoughts, an immense sickness filled her. They stayed, eye to eye, for a few seconds, both breathing heavily. Then Rirette pulled herself together, took Lulu by the waist and drew her to the taxi.

"Where to?" the driver asked.

Henri had followed. He wanted to get in with them. But Rirette pushed him back with all her strength and closed the door quickly.

"Drive, drive!" she told the chauffeur. "We'll tell you the address later."

The taxi started up and Rirette dropped to the back of the car. How vulgar it all was, she thought. She hated Lulu.

Where do you want to go, Lulu?" she asked sweetly.

Lulu did not answer. Rirette put her arms around her and became persuasive.

"You must answer me. Do you want me to drop you off at Pierre's?"

Lulu made a movement Rirette took for acquiescence. She leaned forward: "11 Rue Messine."

When Rirette turned around again, Lulu was watching her strangely.

"What the . . . ," Rirette began.

"I hate you," Lulu screamed, "I hate Pierre, I hate Henri. What do you all have against me? You're torturing me."

She stopped short and her features clouded.

"Cry," Rirette said with calm dignity, "cry, it'll do you good."

Lulu bent double and began to sob. Rirette took her in her arms and held her close. From time to time she stroked her hair. But inside she felt cold and distrustful. Lulu was calm when the cab stopped. She wiped her eyes and powdered her nose.

"Excuse me," she said gently, "it was nerves. I couldn't bear seeing him like that, it hurt me."

"He looked like an orangoutang," said Rirette, once more serene.

Lulu smiled.

"When will I see you again?" Rirette asked.

"Oh, not before tomorrow. You know Pierre can't put me up because of his mother. I'll be at the Hotel du Théatre. You could come early, around nine, if it doesn't put you out, because after that I'm going to see Mama."

She was pale and Rirette thought sadly of the terrible ease with which she could break down.

"Don't worry too much tonight," she said.

"I'm awfully tired," Lulu said, "I hope Pierre will let me go back early, but he never understands those things."

Rirette kept the taxi and was driven home. For a moment she thought she'd go to the movies, but she had no heart for it. She threw her hat on a chair and took a step towards the window. But the bed attracted her, all white, all soft and moist in its shadowy hollows. To throw herself on it, to feel the caress of the pillow against her burning cheeks. I'm strong. I did everything for Lulu and now I'm all alone and no one does anything for me. She had so much pity for herself that she felt a flood of sobs mounting in her throat. They're going to go to Nice and I won't see them any more. I'm the one who made them happy but they won't think about me. And I'll stay here working eight hours a day selling artificial pearls in Burma's. When the first tears rolled down her cheeks she let herself fall softly on the bed. "Nice," she repeated, weeping bitterly, "Nice . . . in the sunlight . . . on the Riviera. . . ."

IV

"Phew!"

Black night. You'd think somebody was walking around the room: a man in slippers. He put one foot out cautiously, then the other, unable to avoid a light cracking of the floor. He stopped, there was a moment of silence, then, suddenly transported to the other end of the room, he began his aimless, idiotic walking again. Lulu was cold, the blankets were much too light. She said *Phew* aloud and the sound of her voice frightened her.

Phew! I'm sure he's looking at the sky and the stars now, he's lighting a cigarette, he's outside, he said he liked the purple color of the Paris sky. With little steps, he goes back, with little steps: he feels poetic just after he's done it, he told me, and light as a cow that's just been milked, he doesn't think any more about it—and me, I'm defiled. It doesn't surprise me that he's pure now that he left his own dirt here, in the blackness, there's a hand towel full of it and the sheet's wet in the middle of the bed, I can't stretch out my legs because I'll feel the wet on my skin, what filth and him all dry, I heard him whistle under my window when he left; he was down there dry and fresh in his fine clothes and topcoat, you must admit he knows how to dress, a woman would be proud to go out with him, he was under the window and I was naked in the blackness and I was cold and rubbed my belly with my hands because I thought I was still wet. I'll come up for a minute, he said, just to see your room. He stayed two hours and the bed creaked—this rotten little iron bed. I wonder where he found out about this hotel, he told me he spent two weeks here once, that I'd be all right here, these are funny rooms, I saw two of them, I never saw such little rooms cluttered up with furniture, cushions and couches and little tables, it stinks of love, I don't know whether he stayed here two weeks but he surely didn't stay alone; he can't have much respect for me to stick me in here. The bellboy laughed when we went up, an Algerian, I hate those people, he looked at my legs, then he went into the office, he must have thought, That's it, they're going to do it, and imagined all sorts of dirty things, they say it's terrible what they do with women down there; if they ever get hold of one she limps for the rest of her life; and all the time Pierre was bothering me I was thinking about that Algerian who was thinking about what I was doing and thinking a lot of dirtiness worse than it was. Somebody's in this room!

Lulu held her breath but the creaking stopped immediately. I have a pain between my thighs, it itches, I want to cry and it will be like that every night except tomorrow night because we'll be on the train. Lulu bit her lip and shuddered because she remembered she had groaned. It's not true, I didn't groan, I simply breathed hard a little because he's so heavy, when he's on me he takes my breath away. He said, "You're groaning, you're coming." I hate people to talk to me when I'm doing that, I wish they'd forget but he never stops saying a lot of dirty things. I didn't groan, in the first place, I can't have any pleasure, it's a fact, the doctor said so, unless I do it to myself. He won't believe it, they never want to believe it, they all said: "It's because you got off to a bad start, I'll teach you"; I let them talk, I knew what the trouble was, it's medical; but that provokes them.

Someone was coming up the stairs. Someone coming back. God, don't let him come back. He's capable of doing it if he feels like it again. It isn't him, those are heavy steps—or else—Lulu's heart jumped in her breast—if it was the Algerian, he knows I'm alone, he's going to knock on the door, I can't, I can't stand that, no, it's the floor below, it's a man going in, he's putting his key in the lock, he's taking his time, he's drunk, I wonder who lives in this hotel, it must be a fine bunch; I met a redhead this afternoon, on the stairs, she had eyes like a dope fiend. I didn't groan.

Of course, he did manage to bother me with all his feeling around, he knows how; I have a horror of men who know how, I'd rather sleep with a virgin. Those hands going right to where they want, pressing a little, not too much . . . they take you for an instrument they're proud of knowing how to play. I hate people to bother me, my throat's dry, I'm afraid and I have a bad taste in my mouth and I'm humiliated because they think he dominates me, I'd like to slap Pierre when he put on his elegant airs and says, "I've got technique." My God, to think that's life, that's why you get dressed and wash and make yourself pretty and all the books are written about that and you think about it all the time and finally that's what it is, you go to a room with somebody who half smothers you and ends up by wetting your stomach. I want to sleep. Oh, if I could only sleep a little bit, tomorrow I'll travel all night, I'll be all in. Still I'd like to be a little fresh to walk around Nice; they say it's so lovely, little Italian streets and colored clothes drying in the sun, I'll set myself up with my easel and I'll paint and the little girls will come to see what I'm doing. Rot! (She had stretched out a little and her hip touched the damp spot in the sheet.) That's all he brought me here for. Nobody, nobody loves me. He walked beside me and I almost fainted and I waited for one tender word, he could have said, "I love you." I wouldn't have gone back to him, of course, but I'd have said something nice, we would have parted good friends, I waited and waited, he took my arm and I let him, Rirette was furious, it's not true he looked like an orangoutang but I knew she was thinking something like that, she was watching him out of the corner of her eye, nastily, it's amazing how nasty she can be, well, in spite of that, when he took my arm I didn't resist but it wasn't *me* he wanted, he wanted his wife because he married me and he's my husband; he always depreciated me, he said he was more intelligent than I and everything that happened is all his fault, he didn't need to treat me so high and mighty, I'd still be with him. I'm sure he doesn't miss me now, he isn't crying, he's raving, that's what he's doing and he's glad to have the bed all to himself so he can stretch his long legs out. I'd like to die. I'm so afraid he'll think badly of me; I couldn't explain anything to him because Rirette was between us, talking, talking, she looked hysterical. Now she's glad, she's complimenting herself on her courage, how rotten that is with Henri who's gentle as a lamb. I'll go. They can't make me leave him like a dog. She jumped out of bed and turned the switch. My stockings and slip are enough. She was in such a hurry that she did not even take the trouble to comb her hair. And the people who see me won't know I'm naked under my heavy grey coat, it comes down to my feet. The Algerian— she stopped, her heart pounding—I'll have to wake him up to open the door. She went down on tiptoe—but the steps creaked one by one; she knocked at the office window.

"Who is it?" the Algerian asked. His eyes were red and his hair tousled, he didn't look very frightening.

"Open the door for me," Lulu said dryly.

Fifteen minutes later she rang at Henri's door.

V

"Who's there?" Henri asked through the door.

"It's me."

He doesn't answer, he doesn't want to let me in my own home. But I'll knock on the door till he opens, he'll give in because of the neighbors. After a minute the door was half opened and Henri appeared, pale, with a pimple on his nose; he was in pajamas. He hasn't slept, Lulu thought tenderly.

"I didn't want to leave like that, I wanted to see you again."

Henri still said nothing. Lulu entered, pushing him aside a little. How stupid he is, he's always in your way, he's looking at me with round eyes with his arms hanging, he doesn't know what to do with his body. Shut up, shut up, I see you're moved and you can't speak. He made an effort to swallow his saliva and Lulu had to close the door.

"I want us to part good friends," she said.

He opened his mouth as if to speak, turned suddenly and fled. What's he doing? She dared not follow him. Is he crying? Suddenly she heard him cough: he's in the bathroom. When he came back she hung about his neck and pressed her mouth against his: he smelled of vomit. Lulu burst out sobbing.

"I'm cold," Henri said.

"Let's go to bed," she said, weeping. "I can stay till tomorrow morning."

They went to bed and Lulu was shaken with enormous sobs because she found her room and bed clean and the red glow in the window. She thought Henri would take her in his arms but he did nothing: he was sleeping stretched out full length as if someone had put a poker in the bed. He's as stiff as when he talks to a Swiss. She took his head in her two hands and stared at him. "You are pure, pure." He began to cry.

"I'm miserable," he said, "I've never been so miserable."

"I haven't either," Lulu said.

They wept for a long time. After a while she put out the light and laid her head on his shoulder. If we could stay like that forever: pure and sad as two orphans; but it isn't possible, it doesn't happen in life. Life was an enormous wave breaking on Lulu, tearing her from the arms of Henri. Your hand, your big hand. He's proud of them because they're big, he says that descendants of old families always have big limbs. He won't take my waist in his hand any more. He tickled me a little but I was proud because he could almost make his fingers meet. It isn't true that he's impotent—he's pure, pure and a little lazy. She smiled through her tears and kissed him under the chin.

"What am I going to tell my parents?" Henri asked. "My mother'll die when she hears."

Mme. Crispin would not die, on the contrary, she would triumph. They'll talk about me, at meals, all five of them, blaming me, like people who know a lot about things but don't want to say everything because of the kid who's sixteen and she's too young to talk about certain things in front of her. She'll laugh inside herself because she knows it all, she always knows it all and she detests me. All this muck. And appearances are against me.

"Don't tell them right away," she pleaded, "tell them I'm at Nice for my health."

"They won't believe me."

She kissed Henri quickly all over his face.

"Henri, you weren't nice enough to me."

"That's true," Henri said, "I wasn't nice enough. Neither were you," he reflected, "you weren't nice enough."

"I wasn't. Ah!" Lulu said, "how miserable we are!" She cried so loudly she thought she would suffocate: soon it would be day and she would leave. You never, never do what you want, you're carried away.

"You shouldn't have left like that," said Henri.

Lulu sighed. "I loved you a lot, Henri."

"And now you don't?"

"It isn't the same."

"Who are you leaving with?"

"People you don't know."

"How do you know people I don't know?" Henri asked angrily, "Where did you meet them?"

"Never mind, darling, my little Gulliver, you aren't going to act like a husband now?"

"You're leaving with a man," Henri said, weeping.

"Listen, Henri, I swear I'm not, I swear, men disgust me now. I'm leaving with a family, with friends of Rirette, old people. I want to live alone, they'll find a job for me; Oh Henri, if you knew how much I needed to live alone, how it all disgusts me."

"What?" Henri asked, "what disgusts you?"

"Everything!" She kissed him. "You're the only one that doesn't disgust me, darling."

She passed her hands under Henri's pajamas and caressed his whole body. He shuddered under her icy hands but he did not turn away, he said only, "I'm going to get sick."

Surely, something was broken in him.

At seven o'clock, Lulu got up, her eyes swollen with tears. She said wearily, "I have to go back there."

"Back where?"

"Hotel du Théâtre, Rue Vandamme. A rotten hotel."

"Stay with me."

"No, Henri, please, don't insist. I told you it was impossible."

The flood carries you away; that's life; we can't judge or understand, we can only let ourselves drift. Tomorrow I'll be in Nice. She went to the bathroom to wash her eyes with warm water. She put on her coat, shivering. It's like fate. I only hope I can sleep on the train tonight, or else I'll be completely knocked out when I get to Nice. I hope he got first-class tickets; that'll be the first time I ever rode first class. Everything is always like that: for years I've wanted to take a long trip first class, and the day it happens it works out so that I can't enjoy it. She was in a hurry to leave now, for these last moments had been unbearable.

"What are you going to do with that Gallois person?" she asked.

Gallois had ordered a poster from Henri, Henri had made it and now Gallois didn't want it any more.

"I don't know," Henri said.

He was crouched under the covers, only his hair and the end of his ear was visible. Slowly and softly, he said, "I'd like to sleep for a week."

"Goodbye, darling," Lulu said.

"Goodbye."

She bent over him, drawing aside the covers a little, and kissed him on the forehead. She stayed a long while on the landing without deciding to close the door of the apartment. After a moment, she turned her eyes away and pulled the knob violently. She heard a dry noise and thought she was going to faint: she had felt like that when they threw the first shovelful of earth on her father's casket.

Henri hasn't been nice. He could have gotten up and gone as far as the door with me. I think I would have minded less if he had been the one who closed it.

VI

"She did that!" said Rirette, with a far-off look. "She did that!"

It was evening. About six Pierre had called Rirette and she had met him at the *Dôme*.

"But you," Pierre said, "weren't you supposed to see her this morning at nine?"

"I saw her."

"She didn't look strange?"

"No indeed," Rirette said, "I didn't notice anything. She was a little tired but she told me she hadn't slept after you left because she was so excited about seeing Nice and she was a little afraid of the Algerian bellboy. . . . Wait . . . she even asked me if I thought you'd bought first-class tickets on the train, she said it was the dream of her life to travel first class. No," Rirette decided, "I'm sure she didn't have anything like that in mind; at least not while I was there. I stayed with her for two hours and I can tell those things, I'd be surprised if I missed anything. You tell me she's very close-mouthed but I've known her for four years and I've seen her in all sort of situations. I know Lulu through and through."

"Then the Texiers made her mind up. It's funny. . . ." He mused a few moments and suddenly began again. "I wonder who gave them Lulu's address. I picked out the hotel and she'd never heard of it before."

He toyed distractedly with Lulu's letter and Rirette was annoyed because she wanted to read it and he hadn't offered it to her.

"When did you get it?" she asked, finally.

"The letter? . . ." He handed it to her with simplicity. "Here, you can read it. She must have given it to the concierge around one o'clock."

It was a thin, violet sheet such as is sold in cigar stores:

Dearest Darling.

The Texiers came (I don't know who gave them the address) and I'm going to cause you a lot of sorrow, but I'm not going, dearest, darling Pierre; I am staying with Henri because he is too unhappy. They went to see him this morning, he didn't want to open the door and Mme. Texier said he didn't look human. They were very nice and they understood my reasons, they said all the wrong was on his side, that he was a bear but at heart he wasn't bad. She said he needed that to make him understand how much he needed me. I don't know who gave them the address, they didn't say, they must have happened to see me when I was leaving the hotel this morning with Rirette. Mme. Texier said she knew she was asking me to make an enormous sacrifice but that she knew me well enough to know that I wouldn't sneak out. I'll miss our lovely trip to Nice very much, darling, but I thought you would be less unhappy because I am still yours. I am yours with all my heart and all my body and we shall see each other as often as before. But Henri would kill himself if he didn't have me any more. I am indispensable to him; I assure you that it doesn't amuse me to feel such a responsibility. I hope you won't make your naughty little face which frightens me so, you wouldn't want me to be sorry, would you? I am going back to Henri soon, I'm a little sick when I think that I'm going to see him in such a state but I will have the courage to name my own conditions. First, I want more freedom because I love you and I want him to leave Robert alone and not say anything bad about Mama any more, ever. Dearest, I am so sad, I wish you could be here, I want you, I press myself against you and I feel your caresses in all my body. I will be at the Dôme tomorrow at five.

LULU

"Poor Pierre."
Rirette took his hand.

"I'll tell you," Pierre said, "I feel sorry for her. She needed air and sunshine. But since she decided that way. . . . My mother made a frightful scene," he went on. "The villa belongs to her, she didn't want me to take a woman there."

"Ah?" Rirette said, in a broken voice, "Ah? So everything's all right, then, everybody's happy!"

She dropped Pierre's hand: without knowing why she felt flooded with bitter regret.

THE CHILDHOOD
OF A LEADER

"I look adorable in my little angel's costume." Mme. Portier told mamma: "Your little boy looks good enough to eat. He's simply adorable in his little angel's costume." M. Bouffardier drew Lucien between his knees and stroked his arm: "A real little girl," he said, smiling. "What's your name? Jacqueline, Lucienne, Margot?" Lucien turned red and said, "My name is Lucien." He was no longer quite sure about not being a little girl: a lot of people had kissed him and called him mademoiselle, everybody thought he was so charming with his gauze wings, his long blue robe, small bare arms and blond curls: he was afraid that the people would suddenly decide he wasn't a little boy any more; he would have protested in vain, no one would listen to him, they wouldn't let him take off his dress any more except to sleep and every morning when he woke up he would find it at the foot of his bed and when he wanted to wee-wee during the day, he'd have to lift it up like Nenette and sit on his heels. Everybody would say: my sweet little darling; maybe it's happened already and I *am* a little girl; he felt so soft inside that it made him a little sick and his voice came out of his mouth like a flute and he offered flowers to everybody in rounded, curved gestures; he wanted to kiss his soft upper arm. He thought: it isn't real. He liked things that weren't real, but he had a better time on Mardi Gras: they dressed him up as Pierrot, he ran and jumped and shouted with Riri and they hid under the tables. His mother gave him a light tap with her lorgnette. "I'm proud of my little boy." She was impressive and beautiful, the fattest and biggest of all these ladies. When he passed in front of the long buffet covered with a white tablecloth, his papa who was drinking a glass of champagne, lifted him up and said, "Little man!" Lucien felt like crying and saying, "Nah!" He asked for orangeade because it was cold and they had forbidden him to drink it. But they poured him some in a tiny glass. It had a pithy taste and wasn't as cold as they said: Lucien began to think about the orangeade with castor oil he swallowed when he was sick. He burst out sobbing and found it comforting to sit between papa and mama in the car. Mama pressed Lucien against her, she was hot and perfumed and all in silk. From time to time the inside of the car grew white as chalk, Lucien blinked his eyes, the violets mama was wearing on her corsage came out of the shadows and Lucien suddenly smelled their perfume. He was still sobbing a little but he felt moist and itchy, somewhat pithy like the orangeade; he would have liked to splash in his little bathtub and have mama wash him with the rubber sponge. They let him sleep in papa and mama's room because he was a little baby; he laughed and made the springs of his little bed jingle and papa said, "The child is over-excited." He drank a little orange-blossom water and saw papa in shirtsleeves.

The next day Lucien was sure he had forgotten something. He remembered the dream he had very clearly: papa and mama were wearing angels' robes, Lucien was sitting all naked on his pot beating a drum, papa and mama flew around him; it was a nightmare. But there had been something before the dream, Lucien must have wakened. When he tried to remember, he saw a long black tunnel lit by a small blue lamp like the night-light they turned on in his parents' room every evening. At the very bottom of this dark blue night something went past—something white. He sat on the ground at mama's feet and took his drum. Mama asked him, "Why are you looking at me like that, darling?" He lowered his eyes and beat on his drum, crying, "Boom, boom, taraboom." But when she turned her head he began to scrutinize her minutely as if he were seeing her for the first time. He recognized the blue robe with the pink stuff and the face too. Yet it wasn't the same. Suddenly he thought he had it; if he thought about it a tiny bit more, he would find what he was looking for. The tunnel lit up with a pale grey light and he could see something moving. Lucien was afraid and cried out. The tunnel disappeared. "What's the matter, little darling?" Mama asked. She was kneeling close to him and looked worried. "I'm having fun," Lucien said. Mama smelled good but he was afraid she would touch him: she looked funny to him, papa too. He decided he would never sleep in their room any more.

Mama noticed nothing the following day. Lucien was always under her feet, as usual, and he gossiped with her like a real little man. He asked her to tell him Little Red Riding-hood and mama took him on her knees. She talked about the wolf and Little Red Riding-hood's grandmother, with finger raised, smiling and grave, Lucien looked at her and said, "And then what?" And sometimes he touched the little hairs on the back of her neck; but he wasn't listening, he was wondering if she were his real mother. When she finished, he said, "Mama, tell me about when you were a little girl." And mama told him; but maybe she was lying. Maybe she was a little boy before and they put dresses on her—like Lucien, the other night—and she kept on wearing them to act like a little girl. Gently he felt her beautiful fat arms which were soft as butter under the silk. What would happen if they took off mama's dress and she put on papa's pants? Maybe right away she'd grow a black moustache. He clasped mama's arms with all his might; he had a feeling she was going to be transformed into a horrible beast before his eyes—or maybe turn into a bearded lady like the one in the carnival. She laughed, opening her mouth wide, and Lucien saw her pink tongue and the back of her throat: it was dirty, he wanted to spit in it. "Hahaha!" Mama said, "how you hug me, little man. Hug me tight. As tight as you love me." Lucien took one of her lovely hands with the silver rings on it and covered it with kisses. But the next day when she was sitting near him holding his hands while he was on the pot and said to him, "Push, Lucien, push, little darling . . . please." He suddenly stopped pushing and asked her, a little breathlessly, "But you're my real mother, aren't you?" She said, "Silly," and asked him if it wasn't going to come soon. From the day Lucien was sure she was playing a joke on him and he never again told her he would marry her when he grew up. But he was not quite sure what the joke was: maybe one night in the tunnel, robbers came and took papa and mama and put those two in their place. Or maybe it was really papa and mama but during the day they played one part and at night they were all different. Lucien was hardly surprised on Christmas Eve when he suddenly woke up and saw them putting toys in front of the fireplace. The next day they talked about Père Noël and Lucien pretended he believed them: he thought it was their role, they must have stolen the toys. He had scarlatina in February and had a lot of fun.

After he was cured, he got in the habit of playing orphan. He sat under the chestnut tree in the middle of the lawn, filling his hands with earth, and thought: I'm an orphan. I'm going to call myself Louis. I haven't eaten for six days. Germaine, the maid, called him to lunch and at table he kept on playing; papa and mama noticed nothing. He had been picked up by robbers who wanted to make a pickpocket out of him. After he had eaten he would run away and denounce them. He ate and drank very little; he had read in *L'Auberge de l'Ange Gardien* that the first meal of a starving man should be light. It was amusing because everybody was playing. Papa and mama were playing papa and mama; mama was playing worried because her little darling wasn't eating, papa was playing at reading the paper and sometimes shaking his finger in Lucien's face saying, "Badaboom, little man!" And Lucien was playing too, but finally he didn't know at what. Orphan? Or Lucien? He looked at the water bottle. There was a little red light dancing in the bottom of the water and he would have sworn papa's hand was in the water bottle, enormous, luminous, with little black hairs on the fingers. Lucien suddenly felt that the water bottle was playing at being a water bottle. He barely touched his food and he was so hungry in the afternoon that he stole a dozen plums and almost had indigestion. He thought he had enough of playing Lucien.

Still, he could not stop himself and it seemed to him that he was always playing. He wanted to be like M. Bouffardier who was so ugly and serious. When M. Bouffardier came to dinner, he bent over mama's hand and said, "Your servant, dear madame," and Lucien planted himself in the middle of the salon and watched him with admiration. But nothing serious happened to Lucien. When he fell down and bumped himself, he sometimes stopped crying and wondered, "Do I really hurt?" Then he felt even sadder and his tears flowed more than ever. When he kissed mama's hand and said, "Your servant, dear madame," she rumpled his hair and said, "It isn't nice, little mouse, you mustn't make fun of grown-ups," and felt all discouraged. The only important things he could find were the first and third Fridays of the month. Those days a lot of ladies came to see mama and two or three were always in mourning; Lucien loved ladies in mourning especially when they had big feet. Generally, he liked grown-ups because they were so respectable—and you could never imagine they forgot themselves in bed or did all the other things little boys do, because they have so many dark clothes on their bodies and you can't imagine what's underneath. When they're all together they eat everything and talk and even their laughs are serious, it's beautiful, like at mass. They treated Lucien like a grown-up person. Mme. Couffin took Lucien on her lap and felt his calves, declaring, "He's the prettiest, cutest one I've seen." Then she questioned him about his likes and dislikes, kissed him and asked him what he would do when he was big. And sometimes he answered he'd be a great general like Joan of Arc and he'd take back Alsace-Lorraine from the Germans, or sometimes he wanted to be a missionary. As he spoke, he believed what he said. Mme. Besse was a large, strong woman with a slight moustache. She romped with Lucien, tickled him and called him "my little doll." Lucien was overjoyed, he laughed easily and squirmed under the ticklings; he thought he was a little doll, a charming little doll for the grown-ups and he would have liked Mme. Besse to undress him and wash him like a rubber doll and send him bye-bye in a tiny little cradle. And sometimes Mme. Besse asked, "And does my little doll talk?" and she squeezed his stomach suddenly. Then Lucien pretended to be a mechanical doll and said, "Crick!" in a muffled voice and they both laughed.

The curé who came to the house every Saturday asked him if he loved his mother. Lucien adored his pretty mama and his papa who was so strong and good. He answered, "Yes," looking the curé straight in the eyes with a little air of boldness that made everybody laugh. The curé had a face like a raspberry, red and lumpy with a hair on each lump. He told Lucien it was very nice and that he should always love his mama; then he asked who Lucien preferred, his mother or God. Lucien could not guess the answer on the spot and he began to shake his curls and stamp his feet shouting, "Baroom, tarataraboom!" and the grown-ups continued their conversation as though he did not exist. He ran to the garden and slipped out by the back door; he had brought his little reed cane with him. Naturally, Lucien was never supposed to leave the garden, it was forbidden; usually Lucien was a good little boy but that day he felt like disobeying. He looked defiantly at the big nettle patch; you could see it was a forbidden place; the wall was black, the nettles were naughty, harmful plants, a dog had done his business just at the foot of the nettles; it smelled of plants, dog dirt and hot wine. Lucien lashed at the nettles with his cane crying "I love my mama, I love my mama." He saw the broken nettles hanging sadly, oozing a white juice, their whitish, down necks had unravelled in breaking, he heard a small solitary voice which cried, "I love my mama, I love my mama"; a big blue fly was buzzing around: a horsefly, Lucien was afraid of it—and a forbidden, powerful odor, putrid and peaceful, filled his nostrils. He repeated, "I love my mama," but his voice seemed strange, he felt deep terror and ran back into the salon, like a flash. From that day on, Lucien understood that he did not love his mama. He did not feel guilty but redoubled his niceties because he thought he should pretend to love his parents all his life, or else he was a naughty little boy. Mme. Fleurier found Lucien more and more tender and just then there was the war and papa went off to fight and mama was glad, in her sorrow, that Lucien was so full of attention; in the afternoons, when she rested on her beach chair in the garden because she was so full of sorrow, he ran to get her a cushion and slipped it beneath her head or put a blanket over her legs and she protested, laughing, "But I'll be too hot, my little man, how sweet you are!" He kissed her furiously, all out of breath, saying, "My own mama," and sat down at the foot of the chestnut tree.

He said, "chestnut tree," and waited. But nothing happened. Mama was stretched out on the verandah, all tiny at the bottom of a heavy stifling silence. There was a smell of hot grass, you could play explorer in the jungle; but Lucien did not feel like playing. The air trembled about the red crest of the wall and the sunlight made burning spots on the earth and on Lucien's hands. "Chestnut tree!" It was shocking: when Lucien told mama, "My pretty little mama" she smiled and when he called Germaine "stinkweed" she cried and went complaining to mama. But when he said "chestnut tree," nothing at all happened. He muttered between his teeth, "Nasty old tree," and was not reassured, but since the tree did not move he repeated, louder, "Nasty old tree, nasty old chestnut tree, you wait, you just wait and see!" and he kicked it. But the tree stayed still—just as though it were made of wood. That evening at dinner Lucien told mama, "You know, mama, the trees, well . . . they're made out of wood," making a surprised little face which mama liked. But Mme. Fleurier had received no mail at noon. She said dryly, "Don't act like a fool." Lucien became a little roughneck. He broke his toys to see how they were made, he whittled the arm of a chair with one of papa's old razors, he knocked down a tanagra figure in the living room to see if it were hollow and if there were anything inside; when he walked he struck the heads from plants and flowers with his cane: each time he was deeply disappointed, things were stupid, nothing really and truly existed. Often mama showed him flowers and asked him, "What's the name of this?" But Lucien shook his head and answered, "That isn't anything, that doesn't have any name." All that wasn't worth bothering with. It was much more fun to pull the legs off a grasshopper because they throbbed between your fingers like a top and a yellow cream came out when you pressed its stomach. But even so, the grasshoppers didn't make any noise. Lucien would have liked to torture an animal that cried when it was hurt, a chicken for instance, but he didn't dare go near them. M. Fleurier came back in March because he was a manager and the general told him he would be much more useful at the head of his factory than in the trenches like just anybody. He thought Lucien had changed very much and said he didn't recognize his little man any more. Lucien had fallen into a sort of somnolence; he answered quickly, he always had a finger in his nose or else he breathed on his fingers and smelled them and he had to be begged to do his little business. Now he went alone to the bathroom; he had only to leave the door half open and from time to time, mama or Germaine came to encourage him. He stayed whole hours on the throne and once he was so bored he went to sleep. The doctor said he was growing too quickly and prescribed a tonic. Mama wanted to teach Lucien new games but Lucien thought he played enough as it was and anyhow all games were the same, it was always the same thing. He often pouted: it was also a game and rather amusing. It hurt mama, you felt all sad and resentful, you got a little deaf and your mouth was pursed up and your eyes misty, inside it was warm and soft like when you're under the sheets at night and smell your own odor; you were alone in the world. Lucien could no longer leave his broodings and when papa put on his mocking voice to tell him, "You're going to hatch chickens," Lucien rolled on the ground and sobbed. He still went to the salon when mama was having visitors, but since they had cut off his curls the grown-ups paid less attention to him unless it was to point out a moral for him and tell him instructive stories. When his cousin Riri and Aunt Bertha, his pretty mama, came to Ferolles because of the bombings, Lucien was very glad and tried to teach him how to play. But Riri was too busy hating the Boches and he still smelled like a baby even though he was six months older than Lucien; he had freckles and didn't always understand things very well. However, Lucien confided to him that he walked in his sleep. Some people get up at night and talk and walk around still sleeping: Lucien had read that in the *Petit Explorateur* and he thought there must be a real Lucien who talked, walked, and really loved his parents at night, only as soon as morning came, he forgot everything and began to pretend to be Lucien. In the beginning Lucien only half believed this story but one day they went near the nettles and Riri showed Lucien his wee-wee and told him, "Look how big it is, I'm a big boy. When it'll be all big I'll be a man and I'll go and fight the Boches in the trenches." Lucien thought Riri was funny and he burst out laughing. "Let's see yours," Riri said. They compared and Lucien's was smaller but Riri cheated: he pulled his to make it longer. "I have the biggest," Riri said. "Yes, but I'm a sleepwalker," Lucien said calmly. Riri didn't know what a sleepwalker was and Lucien had to explain it to him. When he finished, he thought, "Then it's true I'm a sleepwalker," and he had a terrible desire to cry. Since they slept in the same bed they agreed that Riri would stay up the next night and watch Lucien when Lucien got up and remember all he said. "You wake me up after a while," Lucien said, "to see if I remember anything I did." That night, Lucien, unable to sleep, heard sharp snores and had to wake up Riri. "Zanzibar!" Riri said. "Wake up, Riri, you have to watch me when I get up." "Let me sleep," Riri said in a thick, pasty voice. Lucien shook him and pinched him under his shirt and Riri began to jump around and he stayed awake, his eyes open and a funny smile on his lips. Lucien thought about a bicycle his father was to buy him, he heard a train whistle and suddenly the maid came in and opened the curtains, it was eight o'clock in the morning. Lucien never knew what he did during the night. But God knew because God knew everything. Lucien knelt on the prie-dieu and forced himself to behave so that his mama would congratulate him after mass but he hated God: God knew more about Lucien than Lucien himself. God knew that Lucien didn't love his mama or papa and that he pretended to be good and touched his wee-wee in bed at night. Luckily, God couldn't remember everything because there were so many little boys in the world. When Lucien tapped his forehead and said, "Picotin," right away God forgot everything he had seen. Lucien also undertook to persuade God that he loved his mama. From time to time he said in his head, "How I love my dear mama!" There was always a little corner in him which wasn't quite persuaded and of course God saw that corner. In that case, He won. But sometimes you could absorb yourself so completely in what you were saying. You said very quickly, "Oh how I love my mama," pronouncing it carefully and you saw mama's face and felt all tender, you thought vaguely, vaguely, that God was watching you and afterwards you didn't think about it any more, you were all creamy with tenderness and then there were words dancing in your ears: mama, MAMA, MAMA. That only lasted an instant, of course, it was like Lucien trying to balance a chair on his feet. But if, at that moment, you said, "Pacota," God had lost: He had only seen Good and what he saw engraved itself in His memory forever. But Lucien tired of this game because he had to make too much effort and besides you never knew whether God had won or lost. Lucien had nothing more to do with God. When he made his first communion, the curé said he was the best behaved little boy and the most pious of all the catechism class. Lucien grasped things quickly and he had a good memory but his head was full of fog.

Sundays were a bright spot. The fog lifted when Lucien went walking with his father on the Paris road. He had on his handsome sailor suit and they met workers who saluted papa and Lucien. Papa went up to them and they said, "Good morning, M. Fleurier," and also, "Good morning, Master Fleurier." Lucien liked the workers because they were grown-ups but not like the others. First, they called him master. And they wore caps and had short nails and big hands which always looked chapped and hurt. They were responsible and respectful. You mustn't pull old Bouligaud's moustache: papa would have scolded Lucien. But when he spoke to papa, old Bouligaud took off his cap and papa and Lucien kept their hats on and papa spoke in a loud voice, smiling and somewhat testy. "So, we're waiting for our boy, are we, Bouligaud? When does he get leave?" "At the end of the month, Monsieur Fleurier, thank you, Monsieur Fleurier." Old Bouligaud looked happy and he wasn't allowed to slap Lucien on the rear and call him Toad, like M. Bouffardier. Lucien hated M. Bouffardier because he was so ugly. But when he saw old Bouligaud he felt all tender and wanted to be good. Once, coming back from the walk, papa took Lucien on his knees and explained to him what it was to be a boss. Lucien wanted to know how papa talked to the workers when he was at the factory and papa showed him how you had to do it and his voice was all changed. "Will I be a boss too?" Lucien asked. "Yes, indeed, my little man, that's what I made you for." "And who will I command?" "Well, when I'm dead you'll be the boss of my factory and you'll command my workers." "But they'll be dead too." "Well, you'll command their children and you must know how to make yourself obeyed and liked." "And how will I make myself be liked, papa?" Papa thought a little and said, "First, you must know them all by name." Lucien was deeply touched and when the foreman Morel's son came to the house to announce that his father had two fingers cut off, Lucien spoke seriously and gently with him, looking him straight in the eye and calling him Morel. Mama said she was proud to have such a good, sensitive little boy. After that came the armistice, papa read the papers aloud every evening, everybody was talking about the Russians and the German government and reparations and papa showed Lucien the countries on the map: Lucien spent the most boring year of his life, he liked it better when the war was still going on; now everybody looked lost and the light you saw in Mme. Coffin's eyes went out. In October, 1919, Mme. Fleurier made him attend the Ecole Saint-Joseph as a day student.

It was hot in Abbé Geromet's office. Lucien was standing near the abbé's armchair, he had his hands clasped behind him and was deeply bored. "Isn't mama going to go soon?" But Mme. Fleurier had not yet thought of leaving. She was seated on the very edge of a green armchair and stretched out her ample bosom to the abbé; she spoke quickly and she had her musical voice she used when she was angry and didn't want to show it. The abbé spoke slowly and the words seemed much longer in his mouth than in other people's, you might think he was sucking them the way you suck barley sugar before swallowing it. He explained to mama that Lucien was a good little boy and polite and a good worker but so terribly indifferent to everything and Mme. Fleurier said that she was very disappointed because she thought a change would do him good. She asked if he played, at least, during recess. "Alas, madame," the old priest answered, "even games do not seem to interest him. He is sometimes turbulent and even violent but he tires quickly; I believe he lacks perseverance." Lucien thought: they're talking about me. They were two grownups and he was the subject of their conversation, just like the war, the German government or M. Poincaré; they looked serious and they reasoned out his case. But even this thought did not please him. His ears were full of his mother's little singing words, the sucked and sticky words of the abbé, he wanted to cry. Luckily the bell rang and they let him go. But during geography class he felt enervated and asked Abbé Jacquin permission to leave the room because he needed to move around.

First, the coolness, the solitude and the good smell of the toilet calmed him. He squatted down simply to clear his conscience but he didn't feel like it; he raised his head and began reading the inscriptions which covered the door. Someone had written in blue pencil *Barataud is a louse*. Lucien smiled: it was true, Barataud was a louse, he was small and they said he'd grow a little but not much because his father was little, almost a dwarf. Lucien wondered if Barataud had read this inscription and he thought not: otherwise it would be rubbed out. Barataud would have wet his finger and rubbed the letters until they disappeared. Lucien rejoiced a little imagining that Barataud would go to the toilet around four o'clock and that he would take down his velvet pants and read *Barataud is a louse*. Maybe he had never thought he was so small . . . Lucien promised himself to call him a louse starting the next day at recess. He got up on the right hand wall, read another inscription written in the same blue pencil: *Lucien Fleurier is a big beanpole*. He wiped it out carefully and went back to class. It's true, he thought, looking around at his schoolmates, they're all smaller than I am. He felt uncomfortable. Big beanpole. He was sitting at his little desk of holly-wood. Germaine was in the kitchen, mama hadn't come home yet. He wrote "big beanstalk" on a sheet of white paper to re-establish the spelling. But the words seemed too well known and made no effect on him. He called, "Germaine! Germaine!" "What do you want now?" Germaine asked. "Germaine, I'd like you to write on this paper: Lucien Fleurier is a big beanpole." "Have you gone out of your mind, Monsieur Lucien?" He put his arms around her neck. "Be nice, Germaine." Germaine began to laugh and wiped her fat fingers on her apron. He did not look while she was writing, but afterwards he carried the paper to his room and studied it for a long time. Germaine's writing was pointed, Lucien thought he heard a dry voice saying in his ear: big beanpole. He thought, "I'm big." He was crushed with shame: big as Barataud was small and the others laughed behind his back. It was as if someone had cast a spell over him: until then it had seemed natural to see his friends from above. But now it seemed he had been suddenly condemned to be big for the rest of his life. That evening he asked his father if a person could shrink if he wanted to with all his might. M. Fleurier said no: all the Fleuriers had been big and strong and Lucien would grow still bigger. Lucien was without hope. After his mother tucked him in he got up and went to look at himself in the mirror. "I'm big." But he looked in vain, he could not see it, he seemed neither big nor little. He lifted up his nightshirt a little and saw his legs; then he imagined

Costil saying to Hebrard: Say, look at those long beanpoles, and it made him feel funny. He was cold, he shivered and someone said, the beanpole has gooseflesh! Lucien lifted his shirt-tail very high and they all saw his naval and his whole business and then he ran and slipped into bed. When he put his hand under his shirt he thought that Costil saw him and was saying, Look what the big beanpole's doing! He squirmed and turned in bed, breathing heavily. Big beanpole! Big beanpole! until he made a little acid itching come beneath his fingers.

The following days, he wanted to ask the abbé's permission to sit in the rear of the class. It was because of Boisset, Winckelmann and Costil who were behind him and could look at the back of his neck. Lucien felt the back of his neck but he could not see it and often even forgot about it. But while he was answering the abbé as well as he could and was reciting the tirade from *Don Diego,* the others were behind him watching the back of his neck." Lucien forced himself to make his voice swell and express the humiliation of Don Diego. He could do what he wanted with his voice; but the back of his neck was always there, peaceful, inexpressive, like someone resting and Boisset saw it. He dared not change his seat because the last row was reserved for the dunces, but the back of his neck and his shoulder blades were constantly itching and he was obliged to scratch unceasingly. Lucien invented a new game: in the morning, when he took his bath, he imagined someone was watching him through the keyhole, sometimes Costil, sometimes old Bouligaud, sometimes Germaine. Then he turned all around for them to see him from all sides and sometimes he turned his rear toward the door, going down on all fours so that it would look all plump and ridiculous; M. Bouffardier was coming on tiptoe to give him an enema. One day when he was in the bathroom he heard sounds; it was Germaine rubbing polish on the buffet in the hall. His heart stopped beating, he opened the door quietly and went out, his trousers round his heels, his shirt rolled up around his back. He was obliged to make little hops in order to go forward without losing his balance. Germaine looked at him calmly: "What are you doing, running a sack race?" she asked. Enraged, he pulled up his trousers and ran and threw himself on his bed. Mme. Fleurier was heartbroken. She often told her husband, "He was so graceful when he was little and now look how awkward he is, if that isn't a shame." M. Fleurier glanced carelessly at Lucien and answered "It's his age." Lucien did not know what to do with his body; no matter what he did, he felt this body existing on all sides at once, without consulting him. Lucien indulged himself by imagining he was invisible and then he took the habit of looking through keyholes to see how the others were made without their knowing it. He saw his mother while she was washing. She was seated on the *bidet*, she seemed asleep and she had surely forgotten her body and her face, because she thought that no one saw her. The sponge went back and forth by itself over this abandoned flesh; she moved lazily and he felt she was going to stop somewhere along the way. Mama rubbed a washcloth with a piece of soap and her hand disappeared between her legs. Her face was restful, almost sad, surely she was thinking of something else, about Lucien's education or M. Poincaré. But during this time she *was* this gross pink mass, this voluminous body hanging over the porcelain *bidet*. Another time, Lucien removed his shoes and climbed all the way up to the eaves. He saw Germaine. She had on a long green chemise which fell to her feet, she was combing her hair before a small round mirror and she smiled softly at her image. Lucien began to laugh uncontrolledly and had to climb down hurriedly. After that he smiled and made faces at himself in front of the mirror in the salon and after a moment was seized with terrible fears.

Lucien finally went completely asleep but no one noticed except Mme. Coffin who called him her sleeping beauty; a great air bubble he could neither swallow nor spit out was always in his half open mouth: it was his *yawning;* when he was alone the bubble grew larger, caressing his palate and tongue; his mouth opened wide and tears ran down his cheeks: these were very pleasant moments. He did not amuse himself as much in the bathroom but to make up for it he liked very much to sneeze, it woke him up and for an instant he looked around him, exhilarated, then dozed off again. He learned to recognize different sorts of sleep: in winter, he sat before the fireplace and stretched his head toward the blaze; when it was quite red and roasted it suddenly emptied; he called that "head sleeping." Sunday morning, on the other hand, he went to sleep by the feet: he got into his bath, slowly lowered himself and sleep climbed in ripples all along his legs and thighs. Above the sleeping body, all white and swollen like a stewed chicken at the bottom of the water, a little blond head was enthroned, full of wise words, templum, templi, templo, iconoclasts. In class sleep was white and riddled with flashes: First: Lucien Fleurier. "What was the third estate?

Nothing." First, Lucien Fleurier, second, Winckelmann, Pellereau was first in algebra; he had only one testicle, the other one hadn't come down; he made them pay two sous to see and ten to touch. Lucien gave the ten sous, hesitated, stretched out his hand and left without touching, but afterwards his regrets were so great that sometimes they kept him awake for more than an hour. He was less good in geology than in history. First, Winckelmann, second, Fleurier. On Sundays he went bicycling with Costil and Winckelmann. Through russet, heat-crushed countrysides, the bicycles skidded in the marrowy dust; Lucien's legs were active and muscular but the sleepy odor of the roads went to his head, he bent over the handlebars, his eyes grew pink and half closed. He won the honor prize three times in a row. They gave him *Fabiola, or The Church in the Catacombs,* the *Genie du Christianisme* and the *Life of Cardinal Lavigerie.* Costil, back from the long vacation, taught them all *De Profondis Morpionibus* and the *Artilleur de Metz.* Lucien decided to do better and consulted his father's *Larousse Medical Dictionary* on the article "Uterus," then he explained to them how women were made, he even made a sketch on the board and Costil declared it disgusting; but after that they could hear no mention of "tubes" without bursting out laughing and Lucine thought with satisfaction that in all of France you coudn't find a second class student and perhaps even a rhetoric student who knew female organs as well as he.

It was like a flash of magnesium when the Fleuriers moved to Paris. Lucien could no longer sleep because of the movies, cars and streets. He learned to distinguish a Voisin from a Packard, a Hispano-Suiza from a Rolls and he spoke frequently of cars. He had been wearing long pants for more than a year. His father sent him to England as a reward for his success in the first part of the baccalaureat; Lucien saw plains swollen with water and white cliffs, he boxed with John Latimer and learned the overarm stroke but, one fine day, he woke up to find himself asleep, it had come back; he went somnolently back to Paris. The elementary mathematics class in the Lycée Condorcet had 37 pupils. Eight of these pupils said they knew all about women and called the others virgins. The Enlightened scorned Lucien until the first of November, but on All Saint's Day, Lucien went walking with Garry, the most experienced of all of them and negligently showed him proof of such anatomical knowledge that Garry was astonished. Lucien did not enter the group of the enlightened because his parents did not allow him out at night, but he had a deeper and deeper understanding.

On Thursday, Aunt Berthe and Riri came to lunch at Rue Raynouard. She had grown enormous and sad and spent her time sighing; but since her skin had remained very fine and white, Lucien would have liked to see her naked. He thought about it that night in bed; it would be a winter day, in the Bois de Boulogne, he would come upon her naked in a copse, her arms crossed on her breast, shivering with gooseflesh. He imagined that a nearsighted passer-by touched her with his cane and said, "Well, what can that be?" Lucien did not get along too well with his cousin: Riri had become a very handsome young man, a little too elegant. He was taking philosophy at Lakanal and understood nothing of mathematics. Lucien could not keep himself from thinking that Riri, seven years ago, still did number two in his pants and after that walked with his legs wide apart like a duck and looked at his mother with candid eyes saying, "No, mama, I didn't do it, I promise." And he had some repugnance about touching Riri's hand. Yet he was very nice to him and explained his mathematics courses; sometimes he had to make a great effort not to lose patience because Riri was not very intelligent. But he never let himself be carried away and always kept a calm, poised voice. Mme. Fleurier thought Lucien had much tact but Aunt Berthe showed him no gratitude. When Lucien proposed to give Riri a lesson she blushed a little, moved about on her chair, saying, "No, you're very kind, my little Lucien, but Riri is too big a boy. He can if he wants; but he must not get in the habit of counting on others." One night Mme. Fleurier told Lucien brusquely, "You think Riri's grateful for what you're doing for him? Well, don't kid yourself, my boy: he thinks you're stuck-up, your Aunt Berthe told me so." She had assumed her musical voice and familiar air; Lucien realized she was mad with rage. He felt vaguely intrigued but could find nothing to answer. The next day and the day after that he had a lot of work and the whole episode left his mind.

Sunday morning he set his pen down brusquely and wondered, "Am I stuck-up?" It was eleven o'clock; sitting in his study Lucien watched the pink cretonne designs of the cretons which lined the walls; on his left cheek he felt the dry and dusty warmth of the first April sunlight, on his right cheek he felt the heavy, stifling heat of the radiator. "Am I stuck-up?" It was hard to answer. Lucien first tried to remember his last conversation with Riri and to judge his own attitude impartially. He had bent over Riri and smiled at him, saying, "You get it? If you don't catch on, don't be afraid to say so, and we'll start over." A little later he had made an error in a delicate problem and said, gaily, "That's one on me." It was an expression he had taken from M. Fleurier which amused him: "But was I stuck-up when I said that?" By dint of searching, he suddenly made something round and white appear, soft as a bit of cloud: it was his thought of the other day: he had said, "Do you get it?" and it was in his head but it couldn't be described. Lucien made desperate efforts to *look* at this bit of cloud and he suddenly felt as though he were falling into it head first, he found himself in the mist and became mist himself, he was no more than a damp white warmth which smelled of linen. He wanted to tear himself from this mist and come back but it came with him. He thought, "I'm Lucien Fleurier, I'm in my room, I'm doing a problem in physics, it's Sunday." But his thoughts melted into banks of white fog. He shook himself and began counting the cretonne characters, two shepherdesses, two shepherds and Cupid. Then suddenly he told himself, "I am . . ." and there was a slight click: he had awakened from his long somnolence.

It was not pleasant. The shepherds had jumped back, it seemed to Lucien that he was looking at them from the wrong end of a telescope. In place of his stupor so sweet to him and which lost itself in its own folds, there was now a small, wide-awake perplexity which wondered, "Who am I?"

"Who am I? I look at the bureau, I look at the notebook. My name is Lucien Fleurier but that's only a name. I'm stuck-up. I'm not stuck-up. I don't know, but it doesn't make sense."

"I'm a good student. No. That's a lie: a good student likes to work—not me. I have good marks but I don't like to work. I don't hate it, either, I don't give a damn. I don't give a damn about anything. I'll never be a boss." He thought with anguish "But what will I be?" A moment passed; he scratched his cheek and shut his left eye because the sun was in it: "What am I, I . . . ?" There was this fog rolling back on itself, indefinite. "I!" He looked into the distance; the word rang in his head and then perhaps it was possible to make out something, like the top of a pyramid whose side vanished, far off, into the fog. Lucien shuddered and his hands trembled. "Now I have it!" he thought, "now I have it! I was sure of it: *I don't exist!*"

During the months that followed, Lucien often tried to go

back to sleep but did not succeed: he slept well and regularly nine hours a night and the rest of the time was more lively and more and more perplexed: his parents said he had never been so healthy. When he happened to think he did not have the stuff to make a boss he felt romantic and wanted to walk for hours under the moon; but his parents still did not allow him out at night. Often, then, he would stretch out on his bed and take his temperature: the thermometer showed 98.6 or 98.7 and Lucien thought with bitter pleasure that his parents found him looking fine. "I don't exist." He closed his eyes and let himself drift: existence is an illusion because I *know* I don't exist, all I have to do is plug my ears and not think about anything and I'll become nothingness." But the illusion was tenacious. Over other people, at least, he had the malicious superiority of possessing a secret: Garry, for instance, didn't exist any more than Lucien. But it was enough to see him snorting tempestuously in the midst of his admirers: you could see right away he thought his own existence as solid as iron. Neither did M. Fleurier exist—nor Riri—nor anyone—the world was a comedy without actors. Lucien, who had been given an "A" for his dissertation on "Morality and Science," dreamed of writing a "Treatise on Nothingness" and he imagined that people, reading it, would disappear one after the other like vampires at cockcrow. Before beginning this treatise, he wanted the advice of The Baboon, his philosophy prof. "Excuse me, sir," he said at the end of a class, "could anyone claim that we don't exist?" The Baboon said no. "Goghito," he said, "ergo zum. You exist because you doubt your existence." Lucien was not convinced but he gave up his work. In July, he was given, without fanfare, his baccalaureat in mathematics and left for Férolles with his parents. The perplexity still did not leave him: it was like wanting to sneeze.

Old Bouligaud had died and the mentality of M. Fleurier's workers had changed a lot. Now they were drawing large salaries and their wives bought silk stockings. Mme. Bouffardier cited frightful examples to Mme. Fleurier: "My maid tells me she saw that little Ansiaume girl in the cook-shop. She's the daughter of one of your husband's best workers, the one we took care of when she lost her mother. She married a fitter from Beaupertuis. Well, she ordered a 20-franc chicken. And so arrogant! Nothing's good enough for them: they want to have everything we have." Now, when Lucien took short Sunday walks with his father, the workers barely touched their caps on seeing them and there were even some who crossed over so as not to salute them. One day Lucien met Bouligaud's son who did not even seem to recognize him. Lucien was a little excited about it: here was a chance to prove himself a boss. He threw an eagle eye on Jules Bouligaud and went toward him, his hands behind his back. But Bouligaud did not seem intimidated: he turned vacant eyes to Lucien and passed by him, whistling. "He didn't recognize me," Lucien told himself. But he was deeply disappointed and, in the following days, thought more than ever that the world did not exist.

Mme. Fleurier's little revolver was put away in the left-hand drawer of her dressing table. Her husband made her a present of it in September, 1914, before he left for the front. Lucien took it and turned it around in his hand for a long while: it was a little jewel, with a gilded barrel and a butt inlaid with mother of pearl. He could not rely on a philosophical treatise to persuade people they did not exist. Action was needed, a really desperate act which would dissolve appearances and show the nothingness of the world in full light. A shot, a young body bleeding on the carpet, a few words scribbled on a piece of paper: "I kill myself because I do not exist. And you too, my brothers, you are nothingness!" People would read the newspaper in the morning and would see "An adolescent has dared!" And each would feel himself terribly troubled and would wonder, "And what about me? Do I exist?" There had been similar epidemics of suicide in history, among others after the publication of Werther. Lucien thought how "martyr" in Greek meant "witness." He was too sensitive for a boss but not for a martyr. As a result, he often entered his mother's room and looked at the revolver; he was filled with agony. Once he even bit the gilded barrel, gripping his fingers tightly around the butt. The rest of the time he was very gay for he thought that all true leaders had known the temptation of suicide. Napoleon, for example. Lucien did not hide from himself the fact that he was touching the depths of despair but he hoped to leave this crisis with a tempered soul and he read the *Mémorial de Saint-Hélène* with interest. Yet he had to make a decision: Lucien set September 30 as the end of his hesitations. The last days were extremely difficult: surely the crisis was salutary, but it required of Lucien a tension so strong that he thought he would break, one day, like a glass. He no longer dared to touch the revolver; he contented himself with opening the drawer, lifting up his mother's slips a little and studying at great length the icy, headstrong little monster which rested in a hollow of pink silk. Yet he felt a sharp disappointment when he decided to live and found himself completely unoccupied. Fortunately, the multiple cares of going back to school absorbed him: his parents sent him to the Lycée Saint-Louis to take prepartory courses for the Ecole Centrale. He wore a fine red-bordered cap with an insignia and sang:

> C'est le piston qui fait marcher les machines
> C'est le piston qui fait marcher les wagons . . .

This new dignity of *piston* filled Lucien with pride; and then his class was not like the others: it had traditions and a ceremonial; it was a force. For instance, it was the usual thing at the end of the French class for a voice to ask, "What's a *cyrard?*" and everybody answered softly, "A *con!*" After which the voice repeated, "What's an *agro?*" and they answered a little louder, "A *con!*" Then M. Béthune, who was almost blind and wore dark glasses, said wearily, "Please, gentlemen!" There were a few moments of absolute silence and the students looked at each other with smiles of intelligence, then someone shouted, "What's a *piston?*" and they all roared, "A great man!" At those times Lucien felt galvanized. In the evening he told his parents the various incidents of the day in great detail and when he said, "Then the whole class started laughing . . ." or "the whole class decided to put Meyrinez in quarantine," the words, in passing, warmed his mouth like a drink of liquor. Yet the first months were very hard: Lucien missed his math and physics and then, individually, his schoolmates were not too sympathetic: they were on scholarships, mostly grinds, untidy and ill-mannered. "There isn't one," he told his father, "I could make a friend of." "Young men on scholarships," M. Fleurier said dreamily, "represent an intellectual elite and yet they're poor leaders: they have missed one thing." Hearing him talk about "poor leaders," Lucien felt a disagreeable pinching in his heart and again thought of killing himself during the weeks that followed, but he had not the same enthusiasm as he had during vacation. In January, a new student named Berliac scandalized the whole class: he wore coats ringed in green or purple, in the latest styles, little round collars and trousers that are seen in tailors' engravings, so narrow that one wondered how he could even get into them. From the beginning, he was classed last in mathematics. "I don't give a damn," he said, "I'm literary, I take math to mortify myself." After a month he had won everyone's heart: he distributed contraband cigarettes and told them he had women and showed letters they sent him. The whole class decided he was all right and it would be best to let him alone. Lucien greatly admired his elegance and manners, but Berliac treated Lucien with condescension and called him a "rich kid." "After all," Lucien said one day, "it's better than being a poor kid." Berliac smiled. "You're a little cynic!" he told him and the next day he let him read one of his poems: "Caruso gobbled raw eyes every evening, otherwise he was sober as a camel. A lady made a bouquet with the eyes of her family and threw it on the stage. Everyone bows before this exemplary gesture. But do not forget that her hour of glory lasts only 27 minutes: precisely from the first bravo to the extinction of the great chandelier in the Opera (after that she must keep her husband on a leash, winner of several contests, who filled the pink cavities of his orbits with two croix-de-guerre). And note well: all those among us who eat too much canned human flesh shall perish with scurvy." "It's very good," Lucien said, taken aback—"I get them by a new technique called automatic writing." Some time later Lucien had a violent desire to kill himself and decided to ask Berliac's advice. "What must I do?" he asked after he had explained the case. Berliac listened attentively; he was in the habit of sucking his fingers and then coating the pimples on his face with saliva, so that his skin glistened in spots like a road after a rainstorm. "Do what you want," he said, "it makes absolutely no difference." Lucien was a little disappointed but he realized Berliac had been profoundly touched when he asked Lucien to have tea with his mother the next Thursday. Mme. Berliac was very friendly; she had warts and a wine-colored birthmark on her left cheek: "You see," Berliac told Lucien, "we are the real victims of the war." That was also the opinion of Lucien and they agreed that they both belonged to the same sacrificed generation. Night fell, Berliac was lying on his bed, his hands knotted behind his head. They smoked English cigarettes, played phonograph records and Lucien heard the voice of Sophie Tucker and Al Jolson. They grew melancholy and Lucien thought Berliac was his best friend. Berliac asked him if he knew about psychoanalysis; his voice was serious and he looked at Lucien with gravity. "I desired my mother until I was fifteen," he confided. Lucien felt uncomfortable; he was afraid of blushing and remembered Mme. Berliac's moles and could not understand how anyone could desire her. Yet when she came to bring them toast, he was vaguely troubled and tried to imagine her breasts through the yellow sweater she wore. When she left, Berliac said in a positive voice, "Naturally, you've wanted to sleep with your mother too." He did not question, he affirmed. Lucien shrugged. "Naturally," he said. The next day he was worried, he was afraid Berliac would repeat their conversation. But he reassured himself quickly: After all, he thought, he's compromised himself more than I. He was quite taken by the scientific turn their confidences had taken and on the following Thursday he read a book on dreams by Freud he found in the Sainte-Geneviève Library. It was a revelation. "So that's it," Lucien repeated, roaming the streets, "so that's it." Next he bought *Introduction to Psychoanalysis* and *Psychopathology of Everyday Life,* and everything became clear to him. This strange feeling of not existing, this long emptiness in his conscience, his somnolence, his perplexities, his vain efforts to know himself which met only a curtain of fog . . . "My God," he thought, "I have a complex." He told Berliac how he was when he was a child, imagining he was a sleepwalker and how objects never seemed quite real to him. "I must have," he concluded, "a very extraordinary complex." "Just like me," said Berliac, "we both have terrific complexes!" They got the habit of interpreting their dreams and their slightest gestures; Berliac always had so many stories to tell that Lucien suspected him of inventing them, or at least enlarging them. But they got along well and approached the most delicate subjects with objectivity; they confessed to each other that they wore a mask of gaiety to deceive their associates but at heart were terribly tormented. Lucien was freed from his worries. He threw himself greedily into psychoanalysis because he realized it was something that agreed with him and now he felt reassured, he no longer needed to worry or to be always searching his conscience for palpable manifestations of his character. The true Lucien was deeply buried in his subconscious; he had to dream of him without ever seeing him, as an absent friend. All day Lucien thought of his complexes and with a certain pride he imagined the obscure world, cruel and violent, that rumbled beneath the mists of his consciousness. "You understand," he told Berliac, "in appearance I was a sleepy kid, indifferent to everything, somebody not too interesting. And even inside, you know, it seemed to be so much like that that I almost let myself be caught. But I knew there was something else." "There's *always* something else," Berliac answered. They smiled proudly at each other, Lucien wrote a poem called "When the Fog Lifts" and Berliac found it excellent, but he reproached

Lucien for having written it in regular verse. Still, they learned it by heart and when they wished to speak of their libidos they said willingly:

"The great crabs wrapped in the mantle of fog," then simply, "crabs," winking an eye. But after a while, Lucien, when he was alone at night, began to find all that a little terrifying. He no longer dared look his mother in the face and when he kissed her before going to bed he was afraid some shadowy power would deviate his kiss and drop it on Mme. Fleurier's mouth, it was as if he carried a volcano within himself. Lucien treated himself with caution in order not to violate the sumptuous, sinister soul he had discovered. Now he knew the price of everything and dreaded the terrible awakening. "I'm afraid of myself," he said. For six months he had renounced solitary practices because they annoyed him and he had too much work but he returned to them: everyone had to follow their bent, the books of Freud were filled with stories of unfortunate young people who became neurotic because they broke too quickly with their habits. "Are we going to go crazy?" he asked Berliac. And in fact, on certain Thursdays they felt strange; shadows had cunningly slipped into Berliac's room, they smoked whole packs of scented cigarettes, and their hands trembled. Then one of them would rise without a word, tiptoe to the door and turn the switch. A yellow light flooded the room and they looked at each other with defiance.

Lucien was not late in noticing that his friendship with Berliac was based on a misunderstanding; surely no one was more sensitive than he to the pathetic beauty of the Oedipus complex but in it he saw especially the sign of a power for passion which later he would like to use toward different ends. On the other hand, Berliac seemed to be content with his state and had no desire to leave it. "We're screwed," he said proudly, "We're flops. We'll never do anything." "Never anything." Lucien answered in echo. But he was furious. After Easter vacation Berliac told him he had shared his mother's room in a hotel in Dijon: he had risen very early in the morning, went to the bed on which his mother still was sleeping and gently lifted up the covers. "Her nightgown was up," he grinned. Hearing these words, Lucien could not keep himself from scorning Berliac a little and he felt quite alone. It was fine to have complexes but you had to know how to get rid of them eventually. How would a man be able to assume responsibilities and take command if he still had an infantile sexuality? Lucien began to worry seriously: he would have liked to take the advice of some competent person but he did not know whom to see. Berliac often spoke to him about a surrealist named Bergère who was well versed in psychoanalysis and who seemed to have a great ascendancy over him; but he had never offered to introduce him to Lucien. Lucien was also very disappointed because he had counted on Berliac to get women for him; he thought that the possession of a pretty mistress would naturally change the course of his ideas. But Berliac spoke no more of his lady friends. Sometimes they went along the boulevards and followed women, never daring to speak to them: "What do you expect, old man?" Berliac said. "We aren't the kind that pleases. Women feel something frightening in us." Lucien did not answer; Berliac began to annoy him. He often made jokes in very bad taste about Lucien's parents, he called them M. and Mme. Dumollet. Lucien understood very well that a surrealist scorned the bourgeoisie in general, but Berliac had been invited several times by Mme. Fleurier who had treated him with confidence and friendship: lacking gratitude, a simple attention to decency would have kept him from speaking of her in that manner. And then Berliac was terrible with his mania for borrowing money and never returning it, in a café he only proposed to pay the round once out of five. Lucien told him plainly one day that he didn't understand, and that between friends, they should share all expenses. Berliac looked at him deeply and said, "I thought so: you're an anal," and he explained the Freudian relation to him; feces equal gold and the Freudian theory of guilt. "I'd like to know one thing," he said, "until what age did your mother wipe you?" They almost fought.

From the beginning of May, Berliac began to cut school: Lucien went to meet him after class, in a bar on Rue des Petits-Champs where they drank Crucifix Vermouths. One Tuesday afternoon Lucien found Berliac sitting in front of an empty glass. "Oh, there you are," Berliac said. "Listen, I've got to beat it, I have an appointment with the dentist at five. Wait for me, he lives near here and it'll only take a half hour." "OK," Lucien answered, dropping into a chair. "François, give me a white vermouth." Just then a man came into the bar and smiled surprisedly at seeing them. Berliac blushed and got up hurriedly. "Who can that be?" Lucien wondered. Berliac, shaking hands with the stranger, stood so as to hide Lucien; he spoke in a low, rapid voice, the other answered clearly, "Indeed not, my friend, you'll always be a fool." At the same time he raised himself on tiptoe and looked at Lucien over Berliac's head with calm assurance. He could have been 35; he had a pale face and magnificent white hair: "It's surely Bergère," Lucien thought, his heart pounding, "how handsome he is."

Berliac had taken the man with white hair by the elbow with an air of timid authority.

"Come with me," he said, "I'm going to the dentist, just across the way."

"But you were with a friend, weren't you?" the other answered, his eyes not leaving Lucien's face. "You should introduce us."

Lucien got up, smiling, "Caught!" he thought; his cheeks were burning. Berliac's neck disappeared into his shoulders and for a second Lucien thought he was going to refuse. "So introduce me," he said gaily. But as soon as he had spoken the blood rushed to his temples and he wished the ground would swallow him. Berliac turned around and without looking at anyone, muttered "Lucien Fleurier, a friend from the lycée, Monsieur Achille Bergère."

"I admire your works," Lucien said feebly. Bergère took his hand in his own long, delicate fingers and motioned him to sit down. Bergère enveloped Lucien with a tender, warm look; he was still holding his hand. "Are you worried?" he asked gently.

"I am worried," he answered distinctly. It seemed he had just undergone the trials of an initiation. Berliac hesitated an instant then angrily sat down again, throwing his hat on the table. Lucien burned with a desire to tell Bergère of his attempted suicide; this was someone to whom one had to speak of things abruptly and without preparation. He dared not say anything because of Berliac; he hated Berliac.

"Do you have any *raki*?" Bergère asked the waiter.

"No, they don't," Berliac said quickly; "It's a nice little place but all they have to drink is vermouth."

"What's that yellow stuff you have in the bottle?" Bergère asked with an ease full of softness.

"White Crucifix," the waiter answered.

"All right, I'll have some of that."

Berliac squirmed on his chair: he seemed caught between a desire to show off his friends and the fear of making Lucien shine at his expense. Finally, he said, in a proud and dismal voice, "He wanted to kill himself."

"My God!" Bergère said, "I should hope so!"

There was another silence: Lucien had lowered his eyes modestly but he wondered if Berliac wasn't soon going to clear out: Bergère suddenly looked at his watch. "What about your dentist?" he asked.

Berliac rose ungraciously. "Come with me, Bergère," he begged, "it isn't fair."

"No, you'll be back. I'll keep your friend company."

Berliac stayed for another moment, shifting from one foot to the other.

"Go on," Bergère said imperiously, "You'll meet us here."

When Berliac had gone, Bergère got up and sat next to Lucien. Lucien told him of his suicide at great length; he also explained to him that he had desired his mother and that he was a sadico-anal and that fundamentally he didn't love anything and that everything in him was a comedy. Bergère listened without a word, watching him closely and Lucien found it delicious to be understood. When he finished, Bergère passed his arm familiarly around his shoulders and Lucien smelled a scent of eau-de-cologne and English tobacco.

"Do you know, Lucien, how I would describe your condition?" Lucien looked at Bergère hopefully; he was not disappointed.

"I call it," Bergère said, "disorder."

Disorder: the word had begun tender and white as moonlight but the final "order" had the coppered flash of a trumpet.

"Disorder," Lucien said.

He felt as grave and uneasy as the time he told Riri he was a sleepwalker. The bar was dark but the door opened wide on the street, on the luminous springtime mist; under the discreet perfume Bergère gave off, Lucien perceived the heavy odor of the obscure room, an odor of red wine and damp wood. "Disorder," he thought; what good will that do me? He did not know whether a dignity or new sickness had been discovered in him; near his eyes he saw the quick lips of Bergère veiling and unveiling incessantly the sparkle of a gold tooth.

"I like people in disorder," Bergère said, "and I think you are extraordinarily lucky. For after all, that has been given you. You see all these swine? They're pedestrian. You'd have to give them to the red ants to stir them up a little. Do you know they have the consciousness of beasts?"

"They eat men," Lucien said.

"Yes, they strip skeletons of the human meat."

"I see," Lucien said. He added, "And I? What must I do?"

"Nothing, for God's sake," Bergère said with a look of comic fear. "Above all, don't sit down. Unless," he said laughing, "it's on a tack. Have you read Rimbaud?"

"N-no," Lucien said.

"I'll lend you *The Illuminations*. Listen, we must see each other again. If you're free Thursday, stop in and see me around 3, I live in Montparnasse, 9 Rue Campagne-Première."

The next Thursday Lucien went to see Bergère and he went back almost every day throughout May. They agreed to tell Berliac that they saw each other once a week, because they wanted to be frank with him and yet avoid hurting his feelings. Berliac showed himself to be completely out of sorts; he asked Lucien, grinning, "So, are you going steady? He gave you the worry business and you gave him the suicide business: a great game, what?" Lucien protested, "I'd like to have you know that it was you who talked about my suicide first." "Oh," Berliac said, "it was only to spare you the shame of telling it yourself." Their meetings became more infrequent. "Everything I liked about him," Lucien told Bergère one day, "he borrowed from you, I realize it now." "Berliac is a monkey," Bergère said, laughing, "that's what always attracted me. Did you know his maternal grandmother was a Jewess? That explains a lot of things." "Rather," Lucien answered. After an instant he added, "Besides, he's very charming." Bergère's apartment was filled with strange and comical objects: hassocks whose red velvet seats rested on the legs of painted wooden women, Negro statuettes, a studded chastity belt of forged iron, plaster breasts in which little spoons had been planted, on the desk a gigantic bronze louse and a monk's skull stolen from the Mistra Ossuary served as paper weights. The walls were papered with notices announcing the death of the surrealist Bergère. In spite of all this, the apartment gave the impression of intelligent comfort and Lucien liked to stretch out on the deep divan in the den. What particularly surprised Lucien was the enormous quantity of practical jokes Bergère had accumulated on a shelf: solid liquids, sneezing powder, itching powder, floating sugar, an imitation turd and a bride's garter. While Bergère spoke, he took the artificial turd between his fingers and considered it with gravity. "These jokes," he said, "have a revolutionary value. They disturb. There is more destructive power in them than in all the works of Lenin." Lucien, surprised and charmed, looked by turns at this handsome tormented face with hollow eyes and these long delicate fingers gracefully holding a perfectly imitated excrement. Bergère spoke often of Rimbaud and the "systematic disordering of all the senses." "When you will be able, in crossing the Place de la Concorde, to see distinctly and at will a kneeling Negress sucking the obelisk, you will be able to tell yourself that you have torn down the scenery and you are saved." He lent him *The Illuminations*, the *Chants de Maldoror* and the works of the Marquis de Sade. Lucien tried conscientiously to understand them, but many things escaped him and he was shocked because Rimbaud was a pederast. He told Bergère who began to laugh. "Why not, my little friend?" Lucien was very embarrassed. He blushed and for a minute began to hate Bergère with all his might, but he mastered it, raised his head and said with simple frankness, "I'm talking nonsense." Bergère stroked his hair; he seemed moved; "These great eyes full of trouble," he said, "these doe's eyes. . . . Yes, Lucien, you talked nonsense. Rimbaud's pederasty is the first and genial disordering of his sensitivity. We owe his poems to it. To think that there are specific objects of sexual desire and that these objects are women because they have a hole between their legs, is the hideous and wilful error of the pedestrian. Look!" He took from his desk a dozen yellowing photos and threw them on Lucien's knees. Lucien gazed on horrible naked whores, laughing with toothless mouths, spreading their legs like lips and darting between their thighs something like a mossy tongue. "I got the collection for 3 francs at Bou-Saada," Bergère said. "If you kiss the behind of one of those women, you're a regular guy and everybody will say you're a he-man. Because they're women, do you understand? I tell you the first thing to convince yourself of is that *everything* can be an object of sexual desire, a sewing machine, a measuring glass, a horse or a shoe. I," he smiled, "have made love with flies. I know a marine who used to sleep with ducks. He put the head in a drawer, held them firmly by the feet and hoop-la!" Bergère pinched Lucien's ear distractedly and concluded, "The duck died and the battalion ate it." Lucien emerged from these conversations with his face on fire, he thought Bergère was a genius but sometimes he woke up at night, drenched in sweat, his head filled with monstrous obscene visions and he wondered if Bergère was a good influence on him. "To be alone," he cried, wringing his hands, "to have no one to advise me, to tell me if I'm on the right path." If he went to the very end, if he really practiced the disordering of the senses, would he lose his footing and drown? One day Bergère had spoken to him of André Breton; Lucien murmured, as if in a dream, "Yes, but afterwards, if I could never come back." Bergère started. "Come back? Who's talking about coming back? If you go insane, so much the better. After that, as Rimbaud says, *'viendront d'autres horribles travailleurs.'*" "That's what I thought," Lucien said sadly. He had noticed that these long chats had the opposite effect from the one wished for by Bergère: as soon as Lucien caught himself showing the beginnings of a fine sensation or an original impression, he began to tremble: "Now it's starting," he thought. He would willingly have wished to have only the most banal, stupid perception; he only felt comfortable in the evenings with his parents: that was his refuge. They talked about Briand, the bad faith of the Germans, of cousin Jeanne's confinements, and the cost of living; Lucien voluptuously exchanged good common sense with them. One day after leaving Bergère, he was entering his room and mechanically locked the door and slid the bolt. When he noticed this gesture he forced himself to laugh at it but that night he could not sleep: he had just understood he was afraid.

However, nothing in the world would have stopped him from seeing Bergère. "He fascinates me," he told himself. And then he had a lively appreciation of the friendship so delicate and so particular which Bergère had been able to establish between them. Without dropping a virile, almost rude tone of voice, Bergère had the artistry to make Lucien feel, and, in a way of speaking, touch his tenderness: for instance, he re-knotted his tie and scolded him for being so untidy, he combed his hair with a gold comb from Cambodia. He made Lucien discover his own body and explained to him the harsh and pathetic beauty of Youth: "You are Rimbaud," he told him, "he had your big hands when he came to Paris to see Verlaine. He had this pink face of a young healthy peasant and this long slim body of a fair-haired girl." He made Lucien unbutton his collar and open his shirt, then led him, confused, before a mirror and made him admire the charming harmony of his red cheeks and white throat; then he caressed Lucien's hips with a light hand and added, sadly, "We should kill ourselves at twenty." Often now, Lucien looked at himself in mirrors and he learned to enjoy his young awkward grace. "I am Rimbaud," he thought, in the evenings, removing his clothing with gestures full of gentleness and he began to believe that he would have the short and tragic life of a too-beautiful flower. At these times, it seemed to him that he had known, long before, similar impressions and an absurd image came to his mind: he saw himself again, small, with a long blue robe and angel's wings, distributing flowers at a charity sale. He looked at his long legs. "Is it true I have such a soft skin?" he thought with amusement. And once he ran his lips over his forearm from the wrist to the elbow, along a charming blue vein.

One day, he had an unpleasant surprise going to Bergère's: Berliac was there, busy cutting with a knife fragments of a blackish substance that looked like a clod of earth. The two young people had not seen each other for ten days: they shook hands coldly. "See that?" Berliac said, "that's hasheesh. We're going to put it in these pipes, between two layers of light tobacco, it gives a surprising effect. There's some for you," he added. "No thanks," Lucien said, "I don't care for it." The other two laughed and Berliac insisted, looking ugly: "But you're crazy, old man, you've got to take some. You can't imagine how pleasant it is." "I told you no," Lucien said. Berliac said no more, merely smiled with a superior air and Lucien saw Bergère was smiling too. He tapped his foot and said "I don't want any, I don't want to knock myself out, I think it's crazy to stupefy yourself with that stuff." He had let that go in spite of himself, but when he realized the range of what he had just said and imagined what Bergère must think of him, he wanted to kill Berliac and tears came to his eyes. "You're a bourgeois," said Berliac, shrugging his shoulders, "you pretend to swim but you're much too afraid of going out of your depth." "I don't want to get in the drug habit," Lucien said in a calmer voice; "one slavery is like another and I want to stay clear." "Say you're afraid to get into it," Berliac answered violently. Lucien was going to slap him when he heard the imperious voice of Bergère. "Let him alone, Charles," he told Berliac, "he's right. His fear of being involved is *also* disorder." They both smoked, stretched out on the divan and an odor of Armenian paper filled the room. Lucien sat on a red velvet hassock and watched them in silence. After a time, Berliac let his head fall back and fluttered his eyelids with a moist smile. Lucien watched him with rancor and felt humiliated. At last Berliac got up and walked unsteadily out of the room: to the end he had the funny, sleeping and voluptuous smile on his lips. "Give me a pipe," Lucien said hoarsely. Bergère began to laugh. "Don't bother," he said, "don't worry about Berliac. Do you know what he's doing now?" "I don't give a damn," Lucien said. "Well, I'll tell you anyhow. He's vomiting," Bergère said calmly. "That's the only effect hasheesh ever

had on him. The rest is a joke, but I make him smoke it sometimes because he wants to show off and it amuses me." The next
day Berliac came to the lycée and wanted to show off in front of
Lucien. "You don't exactly go out on a limb, do you?" he said.
But he found out to whom he was talking. "You're a little show-
off," Lucien answered, "maybe you think I don't know what you
were doing in the bathroom yesterday? You were puking, old
man!" Berliac grew livid. "Bergère told you?" "Who do you
think?" "All right," Berliac stammered, "but I wouldn't have
thought Bergère would screw his old friends with new ones."
Lucien was a little worried. He had promised Bergère not to repeat anything. "All right, all right," he said, "he didn't screw
you, he just wanted to show me it didn't work." But Berliac turned
his back and left without shaking hands. Lucien was not too
glad when he met Bergère. "What did you say to Berliac?" Bergère asked him neutrally. Lucien lowered his head without answering: he felt overwhelmed. But suddenly he felt Bergère's
hand on his neck: "It doesn't make any difference. In any case,
it had to end: comedians don't amuse me very long." Lucien took
heart; he raised his head and smiled: "But I'm a comedian, too,"
he said, blinking his eyes. "Yes, but you're pretty," Bergère answered, drawing him close. Lucien let himself go; he felt soft as
a girl and tears were in his eyes. Bergère kissed his cheeks and
bit his ear sometimes calling him "my lovely little scoundrel" and
sometimes "my little brother," and Lucien thought it was quite
pleasant to have a big brother who was so indulgent and understanding.

M. and Mme. Fleurier wanted to meet this Bergère of whom
Lucien spoke so much and they invited him to dinner. Everyone
found him charming, including Germaine who had never seen
such a handsome man; M. Fleurier had known General Nizan
who was Bergère's uncle and he spoke of him at great length.
Also, Mme. Fleurier was only too glad to confide Lucien to Bergère for the spring vacation. They went to Rouen by car; Lucien
wanted to see the cathedral and the hôtel-de-ville, but Bergère
flatly refused. "That rubbish?" he asked insolently. Finally, they
spent two hours in a brothel on Rue des Cordeliers and Bergère
was a scream: he called all the chippies "mademoiselle," nudging
Lucien under the table, then he agreed to go up with one of them
but came back after five minutes: "Get the hell out," he gasped,
"it's going to be rough." They paid quickly and left. In the street
Bergère told what happened; while the woman had her back

turned he threw a handful of itching powder on the bed, then told her he was impotent and came down again. Lucien had drunk two whiskeys and was a little tight; he sang the *Artilleur de Metz* and *De Profondis Morpionibus*; he thought it wonderful that Bergère was at the same time so profound and so childish.

"I only reserved one room," Bergère said when they arrived at the hotel, "but there's a big bathroom." Lucien was not surprised: he had vaguely thought during the trip that he would share the room with Bergère without dwelling too much on the idea. Now that he could no longer retreat he found the thing a little disagreeable, especially because his feet were not clean. As the bags were being brought up, he imagined that Bergère would tell him, "How dirty you are, you'll make the sheets black." And he would answer insolently, "Your ideas of cleanliness are really bourgeois." But Bergère shoved him into the bathroom with his bag, saying, "Get yourself ready in there, I'm going to undress in the room." Lucien took a footbath and a sitz bath. He wanted to go to the toilet but he did not dare and contented himself with urinating in the washbasin; then he put on his nightshirt and the slippers his mother lent him (his own were full of holes) and knocked. "Are you ready?" he asked. "Yes, yes, come in." Bergère had slipped a black dressing gown over sky blue pajamas. The room smelled of eau-de-cologne. "Only one bed?" Lucien asked. Bergère did not answer: he looked at Lucien with a stupor that ended in a great burst of laughter. "Look at that shirt!" he said, laughing, "what did you do with your nightcap? Oh no, that's really too funny. I wish you could see yourself." "For two years," Lucien said, angrily, "I've been asking my mother to buy me pajamas." Bergère came toward him. "That's all right. Take it off," he said in a voice to which there was no answer, "I'll give you one of mine. It'll be a little big but it'll be better than that." Lucien stayed rooted in the middle of the room, his eyes riveted on the red and green lozenges of the wallpaper. He would have preferred to go back into the bathroom but he was afraid to act like a fool and with a brisk motion tossed the shirt over his head. There was a moment of silence: Bergère looked at Lucien, smiling, and Lucien suddenly realized he was naked in the middle of the room wearing his mother's pom-pommed slippers. He looked at his hands—the big hands of Rimbaud—he wanted to clutch them to his stomach and cover that at least, but he pulled himself together and put them bravely behind his back. On the walls, between two rows of lozenges, there was a small violet square going back further and further. "My word," said Bergère, "he's as chaste as a virgin: look at yourself in the mirror, Lucien, "you're blushing as far as your chest. But you're still better like that than in a nightshirt." "Yes," Lucien said with effort, "but you never look good when you're naked. Quick, give me the pajamas." Bergère threw him silk pajamas that smelled of lavender and they went to the bed. There was a heavy silence: "I'm sick," Lucien said, "I want to puke." Bergère did not answer and Lucien smelled whiskey in his throat. "He's going to sleep with me," he thought. And the lozenges on the wallpaper began to spin while the stifling smell of eau-de-cologne gagged him. "I shouldn't have said I'd take the trip." He had no luck; twenty times, these last few days, he had almost discovered what Bergère wanted of him and each time, as if on purpose, something happened to turn away his thought. And now he was there, in this man's bed, waiting his good pleasure. I'll take my pillow and go and sleep in the bathroom. But he did not dare; he thought of Bergère's ironic look. He began to laugh, "I'm thinking about the whore a while ago," he said, "she must be scratching now." Bergère still not answer him; Lucien looked at him out of the corner of his eye: he was stretched out innocently on his back, his hands under his head. Then a violent fury seized Lucien, he raised himself on one elbow and asked him, "Well, what are you waiting for? You didn't bring me here to string beads!"

It was too late to regret his words: Bergère turned to him and studied him with an amused eye. "Look at that angel-faced little tart. Well, baby, I didn't make you say it: I'm the one you're counting on to disorder your little senses." He looked at him an instant longer, their faces almost touching, then he took Lucien in his arms and caressed his breast beneath the pajama shirt. It was not unpleasant, it tickled a little, only Bergère was frightening: He looked foolish and repeated with effort, "You aren't ashamed, little pig, you aren't ashamed, little pig!" like the phonograph records in a train station announcing the arrivals and departures. On the contrary, Bergère's hand was swift and light and seemed to be an entire person. It gently grazed Lucien's breast as a caress of warm water in a bath. Lucien wanted to catch this hand, tear it from him and twist it, but Bergère would have laughed: look at that virgin. The hand slid slowly along his belly, stopped a moment to untie the knot of the drawstring which held the trousers. He let him continue: he was heavy and soft as a wet sponge and he was terribly afraid. Bergère had thrown back the covers and put his head on Lucien's breast as though he were listening for a heartbeat. Lucien belched twice in a row and he was afraid of vomiting on the handsome, silver hair so full of dignity. "You're leaning on my stomach," he said. Bergère raised himself a little and passed his hand under Lucien's back; the other hand caressed no longer, it teased. "You have beautiful little buttocks," Bergère said suddenly. Lucien thought he was having a nightmare. "Do you like them?" he said cutely. But Bergère suddenly let him go and raised his head with a spiteful look. "Damned little bluffer," he said angrily, "wants to play Rimbaud and I've been playing with him for an hour and can't even excite him." Tears of rage came to Lucien's eyes and he pushed Bergère away with all his might. "It isn't my fault," he hissed, "you made me drink too much, I want to puke." "All right, go! Go!" Bergère said, "and take your time." Between his teeth he added, "Charming evening." Lucien pulled up his trousers, slipped on the black dressing gown and left. When he had closed the bathroom door he felt so alone and abandoned that he burst out sobbing. There were no handkerchiefs in the pocket of the dressing gown so he wiped his eyes and nose with toilet paper. In vain he pushed his fingers down his throat, he could not vomit. Then he dropped his trousers mechanically and sat down on the toilet, shivering. "The bastard," he thought, "the bastard." He was atrociously humiliated but he did not know whether he was ashamed for having submitted to Bergère's caresses or for not getting excited. The corridor on the other side of the door cracked and Lucien started at each sound but could not decide to go back into the room. "I have to go back," he thought, "I must, or else he'll laugh at me—with Berliac!" and he rose halfway, but as soon as he pictured the face of Bergère and his stupid look, and heard him saying, "You aren't ashamed, little pig?" he fell back on the seat in despair. After a while he was seized with violent diarrhea which soothed him a little: "It's going out by the back," he thought, "I like that better." In fact, he had no further desire to vomit. "He's going to hurt me," he thought suddenly and thought he was going to faint. Finally, he got so cold his teeth began to chatter: he thought he was going to be sick and stood up brusquely. Bergère watched him constrainedly when he went back; he was smoking a cigarette and his pajamas were open and showed his thin torso. Lucien slowly removed his slippers and dressing gown and slipped under the covers without a word. "All right?" asked Bergère. Lucien shrugged. "I'm cold." "Want me to warm you up?" "You can try," Lucien said. At that instant he felt himself crushed by an enormous weight. A warm, soft mouth, like a piece of raw beefsteak, was thrust against his own. Lucien understood nothing more, he no longer knew where he was and he was half smothering, but he was glad because he was warm. He thought of Mme. Besse who pressed her hand against his stomach and called him "my little doll" and Hebrard who called him "big beanpole" and the baths he took in the morning imagining that M. Bouffardier was going to come in and give him an enema and he told himself, "I'm his little doll!" Then Bergère shouted in triumph. "At last!" he said, "you've decided. All right," he added, breathing heavily, "we'll make something out of you." Lucien slipped out of his pajamas.

The next day they awoke at noon. The bellboy brought them breakfast in bed and Lucien thought he looked haughty. "He thinks I'm a fairy," he thought with a shudder of discomfort. Bergère was very nice, he dressed first and went and smoked a cigarette in the old market place while Lucien took his bath. "The thing is," he thought, rubbing himself carefully with a stiff brush, "that it's boring." Once the first moment of terror had passed and he realized that it did not hurt as much as he expected, he had sunk into dismal boredom. He kept hoping it would be over and he could sleep but Bergère had not left him a moment's peace before 4 in the morning. "I've got to finish my trig problem, anyhow," he told himself. And he forced himself not to think of his work any more. The day was long. Bergère told him about the life of Lautréamont, but Lucien did not pay much attention; Bergère annoyed him a little. That night they slept in Caudebec and naturally Bergère disturbed him for a good while, but, around one in the morning, Lucien told him sharply that he was sleepy and Bergère, without getting angry, let him be. They returned to Paris towards the end of the afternoon. All in all, Lucien was not displeased with himself.

His parents welcomed him with open arms: "I hope you at least said thank you to M. Bergère?" his mother asked. He stayed a while to chat with them about the Normandie countryside and went to bed early. He slept like an angel, but on awakening the next day he seemed to be shivering inside. He got up and studied his face for a long time in the mirror. "I'm a pederast," he told himself. And his spirits sank. "Get up, Lucien," his mother called through the door, "you go to school this morning." "Yes, mama," he answered docilely, but let himself drop back onto the bed and began to stare at his toes. "It isn't right, I didn't realize, I have no experience." A man had sucked those toes one after the other. Lucien violently turned his face away: "He knew. What he made me do has a name. It's called sleeping with a man and he knew it." It was funny—Lucien smiled bitterly—for whole days you could ask yourself: am I intelligent, am I stuck-up and you can never decide. And on top of that there were labels which got stuck on to you one fine morning and you had to carry them for the rest of your life: for instance, Lucien was tall and blond, he looked like his father, he was the only son and, since yesterday, he was a pederast. They'd say about him: "Fleurier, you know, the tall blond who loves men?" And people would answer, "Oh yes, the big fairy? Sure, I know who he is."

He dressed and went out but he did not have the heart to go to the lycée. He went down Avenue Lamballe as far as the Seine and followed the quais. The sky was pure, the streets smelled of green leaves, tar and English tobacco. A dreamed-of time to wear clean clothes on a well-washed body and new soul. The people had a moral look; Lucien alone felt suspicious and unusual in this springtime. "The fatal bent," he thought, "I started with an Oedipus complex, after that I became sadico-anal and now the payoff, I'm a pederast; where am I going to stop?" Evidently, his case was not yet very grave: he did not derive much pleasure from Bergère's caresses. "But suppose I get in the habit?" he thought with anguish. "I could never do without it, it'll be like morphine!" He would become a tarnished man, no one would have anything to do with him, his father's workers would laugh when he gave them orders. Lucien imagined his frightful destiny with complacency. He saw himself at 35, gaunt, painted, and already an old gentleman with a moustache and the Legion d'Honneur raising his cane with a terrible look: "Your presence here, sir, is an insult to my daughters." Then suddenly he hesitated and stopped playing: he had just remembered a phrase of Bergère's. At Caudebec during the night, Bergère had said, "So, tell me—are you beginning to get a taste for it?" What did he mean? Naturally, Lucien was not made of wood and after so much caressing . . . "But that doesn't prove anything," he said, worried. But they said that men like that were amazing when it came to spotting other people like them, almost a sixth sense. For a long while Lucien watched a policeman directing traffic at the *Pont d'Iéna*. "Could that policeman excite me?" He stared at the blue trousers of the agent and imagined muscular, hairy thighs.

"Does that do anything to me?" He left, very much comforted. "It's not too bad," he thought, "I can still escape. He took advantage of my disorder but I'm not *really* a pederast." He tried the experiment with every man who crossed his path and each time the result was negative. "Ouf!" he thought, "it was close!" It was a warning, nothing more. He must never start again because a bad habit is taken quickly and then he must absolutely cure himself of these complexes. He resolved to have himself psychoanalyzed by a specialist without telling his parents. Then he would find a mistress and become a man like the others.

Lucien was beginning to reassure himself when suddenly he thought of Bergère: even now, at this very moment Bergère was existing somewhere in Paris, delighted with himself and his head full of memories. "He knows how I'm made, he knows my mouth, he said: you have an odor I shall not forget; he'll go and brag to his friends and say 'I had him' as if I were a girl. Maybe even now he's telling about his nights to—Lucien's heart stopped beating—to Berliac! If he does that I'll kill him: Berliac hates me, he'll tell the whole class, and I'll be sunk, they won't even shake my hand. I'll say it isn't true." Lucien told himself wildly, I'll bring charges, I'll say he raped me!" Lucien hated Bergère with all his strength: without him, without this scandalous irremediable conscience, everything would have been all right, no one would have known and even Lucien himself would eventually have forgotten it. "If he would die suddenly! Dear God, I pray you make him die tonight without telling anybody. Dear God let this whole business be buried, you don't want me to be a pederast. But he's got me!" Lucien thought with rage. "I'll have to go back to him and do whatever he wants and tell him I like it or else I'm lost!" He took a few more steps, then added, as a measure of precaution, "Dear God, make Berliac die, too."

Lucien could not take it upon himself to return to Bergère's house. During the weeks that followed, he thought he met him at every step and, when he was working in his room, he jumped at the sound of a bell; at night he had fearful nightmares: Bergère was raping him in the middle of the Lycée Saint-Louis schoolyard, all the *pistons* were there watching and laughing. But Bergère made no attempt to see him again and gave no sign of life. "He only wanted my body," Lucien thought vexedly. Berliac had disappeared as well and Guigard, who sometimes went to the races with him on Sundays, told Lucien he had left Paris after a nervous breakdown. Lucien grew a little calmer: his trip to Rouen

119

affected him as an obscure, grotesque dream attached to nothing; he had almost forgotten the details, he kept only the impression of a dismal odor of flesh and eau-de-cologne and an intolerable weariness. M. Fleurier sometimes asked what had happened to his friend Bergère: "We'll have to invite him to Férolles to thank him." "He went to New York," Lucien finally answered. Sometimes he went boating on the Marne with Guigard and Guigard's sister taught him to dance. "I'm waking up," he thought, "I'm being reborn." But he still often felt something weighing on his back like a heavy burden: his complexes: he wondered if he should go to Vienna and see Freud: "I'll leave without any money, on foot if I have to, I'll tell him I haven't a cent but I'm a case." One hot afternoon in June, he met The Baboon, his old philosophy prof, on the Boulevard Saint-Michel. "Well, Fleurier," The Baboon said, "you're preparing for Centrale?" "Yes sir," Lucien said. "You should be able," The Baboon said, "to orient yourself toward a study of literature. You were good in philosophy—" "I haven't given it up," Lucien said, "I've done a lot of reading this year, Freud, for instance. By the way," he added, inspired, "I'd like to ask you, Monsieur, what do you think about psychoanalysis?" The Baboon began to laugh: "A fad," he said, "which will pass. The best part of Freud you will find already in Plato. For the rest," he added, in a voice that brooked no answer, "I'll tell you I don't have anything to do with that nonsense. You'd be better off reading Spinoza." Lucien felt himself delivered of an enormous weight and he returned home on foot, whistling. "It was a nightmare," he thought, "nothing more is left of it." The sun was hard and hot that day, but Lucien raised his eyes and gazed at it without blinking: it was the sun of the whole world and Lucien had the right to look it in the face; he was saved! "Nonsense," he thought, "it was nonsense! They tried to drive me crazy but they didn't get me." In fact he had never stopped resisting: Bergère had tripped him up in his reasoning, but Lucien had sensed, for instance, that the pederasty of Rimbaud was a stain, and when that little shrimp Berliac wanted to make him smoke hasheesh Lucien had dressed him down properly: "I risked losing myself," he thought, "but what protected me was my moral health!" That evening, at dinner, he looked at his father with sympathy. M. Fleurier had square shoulders and the slow heavy gestures of a peasant with something racial in them and his grey boss's eyes, metallic and cold. "I look like him," Lucien thought. He remembered that the Fleuriers, father and son, had been captains of industry for four generations: "Say what you want, the family exists!" And he thought proudly of the moral health of the Fleuriers.

Lucien did not present himself for the examinations at the Ecole Centrale that year and the Fleuriers left very shortly for Férolles. He was charmed to find the house again, the garden, the factory, the calm and poised little town. It was another world: he decided to get up early in the mornings and take long walks through the country. "I want," he told his father, "to fill my lungs with pure air and store up health for next year." He accompanied his mother to the Bouffardiers and the Besses and everyone thought he had become a big, well-poised and reasonable boy. Hebrard and Winckelmann, who were taking law courses in Paris, had come back to Férolles for a vacation. Lucien went out with them several times and they talked about the jokes they used to play on Abbé Jacquemart, their long bicycle trips and they sang the *Artilleur de Metz* in harmony. Lucien keenly appreciated the rough frankness and solidity of his old friends and he reproached himself for having neglected them. He confessed to Hebrard that he did not care much for Paris, but Hebrard could not understand it: his parents had entrusted him to an abbé and he was very much held in check; he was still dazzled by his visits to the Louvre and the evening he had spent at the Opera. Lucien was touched by his simplicity; he felt himself the elder brother of Hebrard and Winckelmann and he began to tell himself he did not regret having had such a tormented life: he had gained experience. He told them about Freud and psychoanalysis and amused himself by shocking them a little. They violently criticized the theory of complexes but their objections were naive and Lucien pointed it out to them, then he added that from a philosophical viewpoint it was easy to refute the errors of Freud. They admired him greatly but Lucien pretended not to notice it.

M. Fleurier explained the operation of the factory to Lucien. He took him on a visit through the central buildings and Lucien watched the workers at great length. "If I should die," M. Fleurier said, "you'd have to take command of the factory at a moment's notice." Lucien scolded him and said, "Don't talk like that, will you please, papa." But he was serious for several days in a row thinking of the responsibilities which would fall on him sooner or later. They had long talks about the duties of the boss and M. Fleurier showed him that ownership was not a right but a duty: "What are they trying to give us, with their class struggle," he said, "as though the interests of the bosses and the workers were just the opposite. Take my case, Lucien, I'm a little boss, what they call small fry. Well, I make a living for 100 workers and their families. If I do well, they're the first ones to profit. But if I have to close the plant, there they are in the street. *I don't have a right*," he said forcefully, "to do bad business. And that's what I call the solidarity of classes."

All went well for more than three weeks; he almost never thought of Bergère; he had forgiven him: he simply hoped never to see him again for the rest of his life. Sometimes, when he changed his shirt, he went to the mirror and looked at himself with astonishment: "A man has desired this body," he thought. He passed his hands slowly over his legs and thought: "A man was excited by these legs." He touched his back and regretted not being another person to be able to caress his own flesh like a piece of silk. Sometimes he missed his complexes: they had been solid, heavy, their enormous somber mass had balanced him. Now it was finished, Lucien no longer believed in it and he felt terribly unstable. Though it was not so unpleasant, it was rather a sort of very tolerable disenchantment, a little upsetting, which could, if necessary, pass for *ennui*. "I'm nothing," he thought, "but it's because nothing has soiled me. Berliac was soiled and caught. I can stand a little uncertainty: it's the price of purity."

During a walk, he sat down on a hillock and thought: "For six years I slept, and then one fine day I came out of my cocoon." He was animated and looked affably around the countryside. "I'm built for action," he thought. But in an instant his thought of glory faded. He whispered, "Let them wait a while and they'll see what I'm worth." He had spoken with force but the words rolled on his lips like empty shells. "What's the matter with me?" He did not want to recognize this odd inquietude, it had hurt him too much before. He thought, "It's this silence . . . this land. . . ." Not a living being, save crickets laboriously dragging their black and yellow bellies in the dust. Lucien hated crickets because they always looked half dead. On the other side of the road, a greyish stretch of land, crushed, creviced, ran as far as the river. No one saw Lucien, no one heard him; he sprang to his feet and felt that his movements would meet with no resistance, not even that of gravity. Now he stood beneath a curtain of grey clouds; it was as though he existed in a vacuum. "This silence . . ." he thought. It was more than silence, it was nothingness. The countryside was extraordinarily calm and soft about Lucien, inhuman: it seemed that it was making itself tiny and was holding its breath so as not to disturb him. "*Quand l'artilleur de Metz revint en garnison. . . .*" The sound died on his lips as a flame in a vacuum: Lucien was alone, without a shadow and without echo, in the midst of this too discreet nature which meant nothing. He shook himself and tried to recapture the thread of his thought. "I'm built for action. First, I can bounce back: I can do a lot of foolishness but it doesn't go far because I always spring back." He thought, "I have moral health." But he stopped, making a grimace of disgust, it seemed so absurd to him to speak of "moral health" on this white road crossed by dying insects. In rage, Lucien stepped on a cricket, under his sole he felt a little elastic ball and, when he raised his foot, the cricket was still alive: Lucien spat on it. "I'm perplexed, I'm perplexed. It's like last year." He began to think about Winckelmann who called him "the ace of aces," about M. Fleurier who treated him like a man, Mme. Besse who told him, "This is the big boy I used to call my little doll, I wouldn't dare say it now, he frightens me." But they were far, far away and it seemed the real Lucien was lost, that there was only a white and perplexed larva. "What am I?" Miles and miles of land, a flat, chapped soil, grassless, odorless, and then, suddenly springing straight from this grey crust, the beanpole, so unwonted that there was even no shadow behind it. "What am I?" The question had not changed since the past vacation, it was as if it waited for Lucien at the very spot he had left it; or, it wasn't a question, but a condition. Lucien shrugged his shoulders. "I'm too scrupulous," he thought, "I analyze myself too much."

The following days he forced himself to stop analyzing: he wanted to let himself be fascinated by things, lengthily he studied egg cups, napkin rings, trees, and store fronts; he flattered his mother very much when he asked her if she would like to show him her silver service; he thought he was looking at silver and behind the look throbbed a little living fog. In vain Lucien absorbed himself in conversation with M. Fleurier, this abundant, tenacious mist, whose opaque inconsistency falsely resembled light, slipped *behind* the attention he gave his father's words: this fog was himself. From time to time, annoyed, Lucien stopped listening, turned away, tried to catch the fog and look it in the face: he found only emptiness, the fog was still *behind*.

Germaine came in tears to Mme. Fleurier: her brother had

broncho-pneumonia. "My poor Germaine," Mme. Fleurier said, "and you always said how strong he was!" She gave her a month's vacation and, to replace her, brought in the daughter of one of the factory workers, little Berthe Mozelle who was seventeen. She was small, with blond plaits rolled about her head; she limped slightly. Since she came from Concarneau, Mme. Fleurier begged her to wear a lace coiffe, "That would be so much nicer." From the first days, each time she met Lucien, her wide blue eyes reflected a humble and passionate adoration and Lucien realized she worshipped him. He spoke to her familiarly and often asked her "Do you like it here?" In the hallways he amused himself making passes at her to see if they had an effect. But she touched him deeply and he drew a precious comfort from this love; he often thought with a sting of emotion of the image Berthe must make of him. "By the simple fact that I hardly look like the young workers she goes out with." On a pretext he took Winckel- mann into the pantry and Winckelmann thought she was well built: "You're a lucky dog," he concluded, "I'd look into it if I were you." But Lucien hesitated: she smelled of sweat and her black blouse was eaten away under the arms. One rainy day in September M. Fleurier drove into Paris and Lucien stayed in his room alone. He lay down on his bed and began to yawn. He seemed to be a cloud, capricious and fleeting, always the same, always something else, always diluting himself in the air. "I wonder why I exist?" He was there, he digested, he yawned, he heard the rain tapping on the windowpanes and the white fog was unravelling in his head: and then? His existence was a scandal and the responsibilities he would assume later would barely be enough to justify it. "After all, I didn't ask to be born," he said. And he pitied himself. He remembered his childhood anxieties, his long somnolences and they appeared to him in a new light: fundamentally, he had not stopped being embarrassed with his life, with this voluminous, useless gift, and he had car- ried it in his arms without knowing what to do with it or where to set it down. "I have spent my time regretting I was born." But he was too depressed to push his thoughts further; he rose, lit a cigarette and went down into the kitchen to ask Berthe to make some tea.

She did not see him enter. He touched her shoulder and she started violently. "Did I frighten you?" he asked. She looked at him fearfully, leaning both hands on the table and her breast heaved: after a moment she smiled and said, "It scared me, I didn't think anybody was there." Lucien returned her smile with indulgence and said, "It would be very nice if you'd make a little tea for me." "Right away, Monsieur Lucien," the girl answered and she went to the stove: Lucien's presence seemed to make her uncomfortable. Lucien remained on the doorstep, uncertain. "Well," he asked paternally, "do you like it here with us?" Berthe turned her back on him and filled a pan at the spigot. The sound of the water covered her answer. Lucien waited a moment and when she had set the pan on the gas range he continued, "Have you ever smoked?" "Sometimes," the girl answered, warily. He opened his pack of cigarettes and held it out to her. He was not too pleased: he felt he was compromising himself; he shouldn't make her smoke. "You want . . . me to smoke?" she asked, surprised. "Why not?" "Madame will scold me." Lucien had an unpleasant impression of complicity. He began to laugh and said, "We won't tell her." Berthe blushed, took a cigarette with the tips of her fingers and put it in her mouth. Should I offer to light it? That wouldn't be right. He said to her, "Well, aren't you going to light it?" She annoyed him; she stood there, her arms stiff, red and docile, her lips bunched around the cigarette like a thermometer stuck in her mouth. She finally took a sulphur match from the tin box, struck it, smoked a few puffs with her eyes half shut and said, "It's mild." Then she hurriedly took the cigarette from her mouth and clutched it awkwardly between her five fingers. "A born victim," Lucien thought. Yet, she thawed a little when he asked her if she liked her Brittany, she described the different sorts of Breton coiffes to him and even sang a song from Rosporden in a soft, off-key voice. Lucien teased her gently but she did not understand the joke and looked at him fearfully: at those times she looked like a rabbit. He was sitting on a stool and felt quite at ease: "Sit down," he told her. . . . "Oh no, Monsieur Lucien, not before Monseiur Lucien." He took her under the arms and drew her to his knees. "And like that?" he asked. She let herself go, murmuring, "On your knees!" with an air of ecstasy and reproach with a funny accent and Lucien thought wearily, "I'm getting too much involved, I shouldn't have gone so far." He was silent: she stayed on his knees, hot, quiet, but Lucien felt her heart beating. "She belongs to me," he thought, "I can do anything I want with her." He let her go, took the teapot and went back to his room: Berthe did not make a move to stop him. Before drinking his tea, Lucien washed his hands with his mother's scented soap because they smelled of armpits.

"Am I going to sleep with her?" In the following days Lucien was absorbed in this small problem; Berthe was always putting herself in his way, looking at him with the great sad eyes of a spaniel. Morality won out: Lucien realized he risked making her pregnant because he did not have enough experience (impossible to buy contraceptives in Férolles, he was too well known) and he would cause M. Fleurier much worry. He also told himself that later he would have less authority in the factory if one of the worker's daughters could brag he had slept with her. "I don't have the right to touch her." He avoided being alone with Berthe during the last days of September. "So," Winckelmann asked him, "What are you waiting for?" "I'm not going to bother," Lucien answered dryly, "I don't like ancillary love." Winckelmann, who heard the words "ancillary love" for the first time, gave a low whistle and was silent.

Lucien was very satisfied with himself; he had conducted himself like a *chic type* and that repaid many errors. "She was ripe for it," he told himself with a little regret, but on reconsidering it, he thought, "It's the same as though I had her: she offered herself and I didn't want her." And henceforth he no longer considered himself a virgin. These slight satisfactions occupied his mind for several days. Then they, too, melted into the fog. Returning to school in October, he felt as dismal as at the beginning of the previous year.

Berliac had not come back and no one had heard anything about him. Lucien noticed several unknown faces. His right-hand neighbor whose name was Lemordant had taken a year of special mathematics in Poitiers. He was even bigger than Lucien, and with his black moustache, already looked like a man. Lucien met his friends again without pleasure: they seemed childish to him and innocently boisterous: schoolboys. He still associated himself with their collective manifestations but with nonchalance, as was permitted him by his position of *carré*. Lemordant would have attracted him more, because he was mature; but, unlike Lucien, he did not seem to have acquired that maturity through multiple and painful experiences: he was an adult by birth. Lucien often contemplated with a full satisfaction that voluminous, pensive head, neckless, planted awry on the shoulders: it seemed impossible to get anything into it, neither through the ears, nor the tiny slanting eyes, pink and glassy: "man with convictions," Lucien thought with respect; and he wondered, not without jealousy, what that certitude could be that gave Lemordant such a full consciousness of self. "That's how I should be; a rock." He was even a little surprised that Lemordant should be accessible to mathematical reasoning; but M. Husson convinced him when he gave back the first papers: Lucien was seventh and Lemordant had been given a "5" and 78th place; all was in order. Lemordant gave no sign; he seemed to expect the worst. His tiny mouth, his heavy cheeks, yellow and smooth, were not made to express feelings: he was a Buddha. They saw him angry only once, the day Loewy bumped into him in the cloakroom. First, he gave a dozen sharp little growls, and blinked his eyes: "Back to Poland," he said at last, "to Poland you dirty kike and don't come crapping around here with us." He dominated Loewy with his whole form and his massive chest swayed on his long legs. He finished up by slapping him and little Loewy apologized: the affair ended there.

On Thursdays, Lucien went out with Guigard who took him dancing with his sister's girl friends. But Guigard finally confessed that these hops bored him. "I've got a girl," he confided, "a *première* in Plisnier's, Rue Royale. She has a friend who doesn't have anybody: you ought to come with us Saturday night." Lucien made a scene with his parents and got permission to go out every Saturday; they left the key under the mat for him. He met Guigard around nine o'clock in a bar on the Rue Saint-Honoré. "You wait and see," Guigard said, "Fanny is charming and what's nice about her is she really knows how to dress." "what about mine?" "I don't know her; I know she's an apprentice dressmaker and she's just come to Paris from Angoulème. By the way," he added, "don't pull any boners. My name's Pierre Daurat. You, because you're blond, I said you were part English, it's better. Your name's Lucien Bonnières." "But why?" asked Lucien, intrigued. "My boy," Guigard answered, "it's a rule. You can do what you like with these girls but never tell your name." "All right," Lucien said, "what do I do for a living?" "You can say you're a student, that's better, you understand, it flatters them and then you don't have to spend much money. Of course, we share the expenses; but let me pay this evening; I'm in the habit: I'll tell you what you owe me on Monday." Immediately Lucien thought Guigard was trying to get a rake-off. "God, how distrustful I've gotten!" he thought with amusement. Just then Fanny came in: a tall, thin brunette with long thighs and a heavily rouged face. Lucien found her intimidating. "Here's Bonnières I was telling you about," Guigard said. "Pleased to meet you,"

Fanny said with a myopic look. "This is my girl friend Maud."
Lucien saw an ageless little woman wearing a hat that looked like
an overturned flower pot. She was not rouged and appeared
greyish after the dazzling Fanny. Lucien was bitterly disappointed
but he saw she had a pretty mouth—and then there was no need
to be embarrassed with her. Guigard had taken care to pay for
the beers in advance so that he could profit from the commotion
of their arrival to push the two girls gaily toward the door without
allowing them the time for a drink. Lucien was grateful to him:
M. Fleurier only gave him 125 francs a week and out of this
money he had to pay carfare. The evening was amusing; they
went dancing in the Latin Quarter in a hot, pink little place with
dark corners and where a cocktail cost five francs. There were
many students with girls of the same type as Fanny but not as
good looking. Fanny was superb: she looked straight in the eyes
of a big man with a beard who smoked a pipe and said very
loudly, "I hate people who smoke pipes at dances." The man
turned crimson and put the lighted pipe back in his pocket. She
treated Guigard and Lucien with a certain condescension and
sometimes told them, "You're a couple of kids," with a gentle,
maternal air. Lucien felt full of ease and sweetness; he told Fanny
several amusing little things and smiled while telling them.
Finally, the smile never left his face and he was able to hit on a
refined tone of voice with touches of devil-may-care and tender
courtesy tinged with irony. But Fanny spoke little to him; she
took Guigard's chin and pulled his cheeks to make his mouth
stand out; when the lips were full and drooling a little, like fruit
swollen with juice or like snails, she licked them, saying, "Baby."
Lucien was horribly annoyed and thought Guigard was ridiculous: Guigard had rouge near his lips and fingermarks on his
cheeks. But the behavior of the other couples was even more
negligent: everyone kissed; from time to time the girl from the
checkroom passed among them with a little basket, throwing
streamers and multicolored balls shouting, "Olè, les enfants,
amusez-vous, Olè, olè!" and everybody laughed. At last Lucien
remembered the existence of Maud and he said to her, smiling,
"Look at those turtle doves. . . ." He pointed to Fanny and
Guigard and added, "nous autres, nobles vieillards. . . ." He did
not finish the phrase but smiled so drolly that Maud smiled too.
She removed her hat and Lucien saw with pleasure that she was
somewhat better than the other women in the dance hall; then
he asked her to dance and told her the jokes he played on his

professors the year of his baccalaureat. She danced well, her eyes were black and serious and she had an intelligent look. Lucien told her about Berthe and said he was full of remorse. "But," he added, "it was better for her." Maud thought the story about Berthe was poetic and sad, she asked how much Berthe earned from Lucien's parents. "It's not always funny," she added, "for a young girl to be in the family way." Guigard and Fanny paid no more attention to them, they caressed each other and Guigard's face was covered with moisture. From time to time Lucien repeated, "Look at those turtle doves, just look at them!" and he had his sentence ready, "They make me feel like doing it too." But he dared not say it and contented himself with smiling, then he pretended that he and Maud were old friends, disdainful of love and he called her "brother" and made as if to slap her on the back. Suddenly, Fanny turned her head and looked at them with surprise, "Well," she said, "first-graders, how're you doing? Why don't you kiss, you're dying to." Lucien took Maud in his arms; he was a little annoyed because Fanny was watching them: he wanted the kiss to be long and successful but he wondered how people breathed. Finally, it was not as difficult as he thought, it was enough to kiss on an angle, leaving the nostrils clear. He heard Guigard counting "one—two—three—four—" and he let go of Maud at 52. "Not bad for a beginning," Guigard said. "I can do better." Lucien looked at his wrist watch and counted: Guigard left Fanny's mouth at the 159th second. Lucien was furious and thought the contest was stupid. "I let go of Maud just to be safe," he thought, "but that's nothing, once you know how to breathe you can keep on forever." He proposed a second match and won. When it was all over, Maud looked at Lucien and said seriously, "You kiss well." Lucien blushed with pleasure. "At your service," he answered, bowing. Still he would rather have kissed Fanny. They parted around half past twelve because of the last metro. Lucien was joyful; he leaped and danced in the Rue Raynouard and thought, "It's in the bag." The corners of his mouth hurt because he had smiled so much.

He saw Maud every Thursday at six and on Saturday evening. She let herself be kissed but nothing more. Lucien complained to Guigard who reassured him, "Don't worry," Guigard said, "Fanny's sure she'll lay; but she's young and only had two boys; Fanny says for you to be very tender with her." "Tender?" Lucien said. "Get a load of that!" They both laughed and Guigard concluded, "That's what you've got to do." Lucien was very tender. He kissed Maud a lot and told her he loved her, but after a while it became a little monotonous and then he was not too proud of going out with her: he would have liked to give her advice on how she should dress, but she was full of prejudices and angered quickly. Between kisses, they were silent, gazing at each other and holding hands. "God knows what she's thinking with those strict eyes she has." Lucien still thought of the same thing: this small existence, sad and vague, which was his own, and told himself, "I wish I were Lemordant, there's a man who's found his place!" During those times he saw himself as though he were another person: sitting near a woman who loved him, his hand in hers, his lips still wet from kisses, refusing the humble happiness she offered him: alone. Then he clasped Maud's fingers tightly and tears came to his eyes: he would have liked to make her happy.

One morning in December, Lemordant came up to Lucien; he held a paper. "You want to sign?" he asked. "What is it?" "Because of the kikes at the Normale Sup; they sent the *Oeuvre* a petition against compulsory military training with 200 signatures. So we're protesting; we need a thousand names at least: we're going to get the *cyrards*, the *flottards*, the *agros*, the X's and the whole works." Lucien was flattered. "Is it going to be printed?" "Surely in *Action*. Maybe in *Echo de Paris* besides." Lucien wanted to sign on the spot but he thought it would not be wise. He took the paper and read it carefully. Lemordant added, "I hear you don't have anything to do with politics; that's your business. But you're French and you've got a right to have your say." When he heard "you've got a right to have your say," Lucien felt an inexplicable and rapid joy. He signed. The next day he bought *Action Française* but the proclamation was not there. It didn't appear until Thursday, Lucien found it on the second page under the headline: YOUTH OF FRANCE SCORES IN TEETH OF INTERNATIONAL JEWRY. His name was there, compressed, definitive, not far from Lemordant's, almost as strange as the names *Fleche* and *Flipot* which surrounded it; it looked unreal. "Lucien Fleurier," he thought, "a peasant name, a real French name." He read the whole series of names starting with F aloud and when it came to his turn he pronounced it as if he did not recognize it. Then he stuffed the newspaper in his pocket and went home happily.

A few days later he sought out Lemordant. "Are you active in politics?" he asked. "I'm in the League," Lemordant said, "Ever read *Action Française?*" "Not much," Lucien confessed. "Up to now it didn't interest me but I think I'm changing my mind." Lemordant looked at him without curiosity, with his impenetrable air. Lucien told him, in a few words, what Bergère had called his "disorder." "Where do you come from?" Lemordant asked. "Férolles. My father has a factory there." "How long did you stay there?" "Till second form." "I see," Lemordant said, "it's very simple, you're uprooted. Have you read Barrès?" "I read *Colette Baudoche.*" "Not that," Lemordant said impatiently, "I'll bring you the *Deracinés* this afternoon. That's your story. You'll find the cause and cure." The book was bound in green leather. On the first page was an *"ex libris* André Lemordant" in gothic letters. Lucien was surprised; he had never dreamed Lemordant could have a first name.

He began reading it with much distrust: it had been explained to him so many times: so many times had he been lent books with a "Read this, it fits you perfectly," Lucien thought with a sad smile that he was not someone who could be set down in so many pages. The Oedipus complex, the disorder: what childishness, and so far away! But, from the very first, he was captivated: in the first place, it was not psychology—Lucien had a bellyful of psychology—the young people Barrès described were not abstract individuals or declassed like Rimbaud or Verlaine, nor sick like the unemployed Viennese who had themselves psychoanalyzed by Freud. Barrès began by placing them in their milieu, in their family: they had been well brought up, in the provinces, in solid traditions. Lucien thought Sturel resembled himself. "It's true," he said, "I'm uprooted." He thought of the moral health of the Fleuriers, a health acquired only in the land, their physical strength (his grandfather used to twist a bronze sou between his fingers); he remembered with emotion the dawns in Férolles: he rose, tiptoed down the stairs so as not to wake his family, straddled his bicycle and the soft countryside of the Ile de France enveloped him in its discreet caresses. "I've always hated Paris," he thought with force. He also read the *Jardin de Bérénice* and, from time to time, stopped reading and began to ponder, his eyes vague; thus they were again offering him a character and a destiny, a means of escaping the inexhaustible gossip of his conscience, a method of defining and appreciating himself. And how much he preferred the unconscious, reeking of the soil, which Barrès gave him, to the filthy, lascivious images of Freud. To grasp it, Lucien had only to turn himself away from a sterile and dangerous contemplation of self: he must study the soil and subsoil of Férolles, he must decipher the sense of the rolling hills which descended as far as the Sernette, he must apply himself to human geography and history. Or, simply return to Férolles and live there: he would find it harmless and fertile at his feet, stretched across the countryside, mixed in the woods, the springs, and the grass like nourishing humus from which Lucien could at last draw the strength to become a leader. Lucien left these long dreams exalted, and sometimes felt as if he had found his road. Now he was silent close to Maud, his arm about her waist, the words, the scraps of sentences resounding in him: "renew tradition," "the earth and the dead"; deep, opaque words, inexhaustible. "How tempting it is," he thought. Yet he dared not believe it: he had already been disappointed too often. He opened up his fears to Lemordant: "It would be too good." "My boy," Lemordant answered, "you don't believe everything you want to right away: you need practice." He thought a little and said, "You ought to come with us." Lucien accepted with an open heart, but he insisted on keeping his liberty, "I'll come," he said, "but I won't be involved. I want to see and think about it."

Lucien was captivated by the camaraderies of the young *camelots*; they gave him a cordial, simple welcome and he immediately felt at ease in their midst. He soon knew Lemordant's "gang," about 20 students almost all of whom wore velvet berets. They held their meetings on the second floor of the Polder beerhall where they played bridge and billiards. Lucien often went there to meet them and soon he realized they had adopted him for he was always greeted with shouts of *"Voilà le plus beau!"* or "Our National Fleurier!" But it was their good humor which especially captured Lucien: nothing pedantic or austere; little talk of politics. They laughed and sang, that was all, they shouted or beat the tables in honor of the student youth. Lemordant himself smiled without dropping an authority which no one would have dared question. Lucien was more often silent, his look wandering over these boisterous, muscular young people. "This is strength," he thought. Little by little he discovered the true sense of youth in the midst of them: it was not in the affected grace Bergère appreciated; youth was the future of France. However, Lemordant's friends did not have the troubled charm of adolescence: they were adults and several wore beards. Looking closely he found an air of parenthood in all of them: they had finished with the wanderings and uncertainties of their age, they had nothing more to learn, they were made. In the beginning their lighthearted, ferocious jokes somewhat shocked Lucien: one might have thought them without conscience. When Rémy announced that Mme. Dubus, the wife of the radical leader, had her legs cut off by a truck, Lucien expected them to render a brief homage to their unfortunate adversary. But they all burst out laughing and slapped their legs saying: "The old carrion!" and "What a fine truck driver!" Lucien was a little taken back but suddenly he understood that this great, purifying laughter was a refusal: they had scented danger, they wanted no cowardly pity and they were firm. Lucien began to laugh too. Little by little their pranks appeared to him in their true light: there was only the shell of frivolity; at heart it was the affirmation of a right: their conviction was so deep, so religious, that it gave them the right to appear frivolous, to dismiss all that was not essential with a whim, a pirouette. Between the icy humor of Charles Maurras and the jokes of Desperreau, for instance (he carried in his pocket an old condom end which he called Blum's foreskin) there was only a difference of degree. In January the University announced a solemn meeting in the course of which the degree of *doctor honoris causa* was to be bestowed on two Swedish mineralogists. "You're going to see something good," Lemordant told Lucien, giving him an invitation card. The big amphitheatre was packed. When Lucien saw the President of the Republic and the Rector enter at the sound of the *Marseillaise,* his heart began to pound, he was afraid for his friends. Just then a few young people rose from their seats and began to shout. With sympathy Lucien recognized Rémy, red as a beet, struggling between two men who were pulling his coat, shouting, "France for the French!" But he was especially pleased to see an old gentleman, with the air of a precocious child, blowing a little horn. "How healthy it is," he thought. He keenly tasted this odd mixture of headstrong gravity and turbulence which gave the youngest an air of maturity and the oldest an impish air. Soon Lucien himself tried to joke. He had some success and when he said of Herriot, "There's no more God if he dies in his bed," he felt the birth of a sacred fury in him. Then he gritted his teeth and, for a moment, felt as convinced, as strict, powerful as Rémy or Desperreau. "Lemordant is right," he thought, "you need practice, it's all there." He also learned to avoid discussions: Guigard, who was only a republican, overwhelmed him with objections. Lucien listened to him politely but, after a while, shut up. Guigard was still talking, but

Lucien did not even look at him any more: he smoothed the fold in his trousers and amused himself by blowing smoke rings with his cigarette and looking at women. Nevertheless, he heard a few of Guigard's objections, but they quickly lost their weight and slipped off him, light and futile. Guigard finally was quiet, quite impressed. Lucien told his parents about his new friends and M. Fleurier asked him if he was going to be a *camelot*. Lucien hesitated and gravely said, "I'm tempted, I'm really tempted." "Lucien, I beg you, don't do it," his mother said, "they're very excitable and something bad can happen so quickly. Don't you see you can get in trouble or be put in prison? Besides, you're much too young to be mixed up in politics." Lucien answered her only with a firm smile and M. Fleurier intervened, "Let him alone, dear," he said gently, "let him follow his own ideas; he has to pass through it." From that day on it seemed to Lucien that his parents treated him with a certain consideration. Yet he did not decide; these few weeks had taught him much: by turn he considered the benevolent curiosity of his father, Mme. Fleurier's worries, the growing respect of Guigard, the insistence of Lemordant and the impatience of Rémy and, nodding his head, he told himself, "This is no small matter." He had a long conversation with Lemordant and Lemordant well understood his reasons and told him not to hurry. Lucien still was nostalgic: he had the impressions of being only a small gelatinous transparency trembling on the seat in a café and the boisterous agitation of the *camelots* seemed absured to him. But at other times he felt hard and heavy as a rock and he was almost happy.

He got along better and better with the whole gang. He sang them the *Noce à Rebecca* which Hébrard had taught him the previous vacation and everyone thought it was tremendously amusing. Lucien threw out several biting reflections about the Jews and spoke of Berliac who was so miserly: "I always asked myself: why is he so cheap, it isn't possible to be that cheap. Then one day I understood: he was one of the tribe." Everybody began to laugh and a sort of exaltation came over Lucien: he felt truly furious about the Jews and the memory of Berliac was deeply unpleasant to him. Lemordant looked him in the eyes and said, "You're a real one, you are." After that they often asked Lucien: "Fleurier, tell us a good one about the kikes." And Lucien told the Jewish jokes he learned from his father; all he had to do was begin, "Vun day Levy met Bloom . . ." to fill his friends with mirth. One day Rémy and Patenotre told how they had come across an Algerian Jew by the Seine and how they had almost frightened him to death by acting as if they were going to throw him in the water: "I said to myself," Rémy concluded, "what a shame it was Fleurier wasn't with us." "Maybe it was better he wasn't there," Desperreau interrupted, "he'd have chucked him in the water for good!" There was no one like Lucien for recognizing a Jew from the nose. When he went out with Guigard he nudged his elbow: "Don't turn around now: the little short one, behind us, he's one of them!" "For that," Guigard said, "you can really smell 'em out." Fanny could not stand the Jews either; all four of them went to Maud's room one Thursday and Lucien sang the *Noce à Rebecca*. Fanny could stand no more, she said, "Stop, stop, or I'll wet my pants." And when he had finished, she gave him an almost tender look. They played jokes on him in the Polder beerhall. There was always someone to say, negligently, "Fleurier who likes the Jews so much . . ." or "Leon Blum, the great friend of Fleurier . . ." and the others waited, in stitches, holding their breath, open mouthed. Lucien grew red and struck the table, shouting, "God damn . . . !" and they burst out laughing and said, "He bit! He bit! He didn't bite—he swallowed it!"

He often went to political meetings with them and heard Professor Claude and Maxime Real Del Sarte. His work suffered a little from these new obligations, but, since Lucien could not count on winning the Centrale scholarship anyhow, that year, M. Fleurier was indulgent. "After all," he told his wife, "Lucien must learn the job of being a man." After these meetings Lucien and his friends felt hot-headed and were given to playing tricks. Once about ten of them came across a little, olive skinned man who was crossing the Rue Saint-André-des-Arts, reading *Humanité*. They shoved him into a wall and Rémy ordered "Throw down that paper." The little man wanted to act up but Desperreau slipped behind him and grabbed him by the waist while Lemordant ripped the paper from his grasp with a powerful fist. It was very amusing. The little man, furious, kicked the air and shouted "Let go of me! Let go!" with an odd accent and Lemordant, quite calm, tore up the paper. But things were spoiled when Desperreau wanted to let the man go: he threw himself on Lemordant and would have struck him if Rémy hadn't landed a good punch behind his ear just in time. The man fell against the wall and looked at them all evilly, saying *"Sales Français!"* "Say that again," Marchesseau demanded coldly. Lucien realized there was going to be some dirty work: Marchesseau could not take a joke when it was a question of France. "*Sales Français!*" the dago said. He was slapped again and threw himself forward, his head lowered, "*Sales Français, sales bourgeois,* I hate you, I hope you croak, all of you, all of you!" and a flood of other filthy curses with a violence that Lucien never imagined possible. Then they lost patience and all had to step in and give him a good lesson. After a while they let him go and the man dropped against the wall: his breath was a whistle, one punch had closed his left eye and they were all around him, tired of striking him, waiting for him to fall. The man twisted his mouth and spat: "*Sales Francais, sales Français.*" There was a moment of hesitation and Lucien realized his friends were going to give it up. Then it was stronger than he was, he leaped forward and struck with all his might. He heard something crack and the little man looked at him with surprise and weakness. "*Sales . . .*" he muttered, but his puffed eye began to open on a red, sightless globe; he fell to his knees and said nothing more. "Get the hell out," Rémy hissed. They ran, stopping only at Place Saint-Michel: no one was following them. They straightened their ties and brushed each other off.

The evening passed without mention of the incident and the young men were especially nice to each other: they had abandoned the modest brutality which usually veiled their feelings. They spoke politely to each other and Lucien thought that for the first time they were acting as they acted with their families; but he was enervated: he was not used to fighting thugs in the middle of the street. He thought tenderly of Maud and Fanny.

He could not sleep. "I can't go on," he thought, "following them like an amateur. Everything has been weighted, I *must* join!" He felt grave and almost religious when he announced the good news to Lemordant. "It's decided," he said, "I'm with you." Lemordant slapped him on the shoulder and the gang celebrated the event by polishing off several bottles. They had recovered their gay and brutal tone and talked only about the incident of the night before. As they were about to leave, Marchesseau told Lucien simply, "You've got a terrific punch!" and Lucien answered, "He was a Jew."

The day after that he went to see Maud with a heavy malacca cane he had bought in a store on the Boulevard St. Michel. Maud understood immediately: she looked at the cane and said, "So you did it?" "I did it," Lucien smiled. Maud seemed flattered; personally, she favored the ideas of the Left, but she was broad-minded. "I think," she said, "there's good in all parties." In the course of the evening, she scratched his neck several times and called him "My little *camelot*." A little while after that, one Saturday night, Maud felt tired. "I think I'll go back," she said, "but you can come up with me if you're good: you can hold my hand and be real nice to your little Maud who's so tired, and you can tell her stories." Lucien was hardly enthusiastic: Maud's room depressed him with its careful poverty: it was like a maid's room. But it would have been criminal to let such an opportunity pass by. Hardly in the room, Maud threw herself on the bed, saying, "Whew! it feels so good!" Then she was silent, gazing into Lucien's eyes, and puckered her lips. He stretched himself out near her and she put her hand over his eyes, spreading her fingers and saying, "Peekaboo, I see you, you know I see you, Lucien!" He felt soft and heavy, she put her fingers in his mouth and he sucked them, then spoke to her tenderly, "Poor little Maud's sick, does little Maud have a pain?" and he caressed her whole body; she had closed her eyes and was smiling mysteriously. After a moment he raised her skirt and they made love; Lucien thought, "What a break!" When it was over Maud said, "Well, if I'd thought that!" She looked at Lucien with a tender reproach. "Naughty boy, I thought you were going to be good!" Lucien said he was as surprised as she was. "That's the way it happens," he said. She thought a little and then told him seriously, "I don't regret anything. Before maybe it was purer but it wasn't so complete."

In the métro, Lucien thought "I have a mistress." He was empty and tired, saturated with a smell of absinthe and fresh fish; he sat down, holding himself stiffly to avoid contact with his sweat-soaked shirt; he felt his body to be curdled milk. He repeated forcefully, "I have a mistress." But he felt frustrated: what he desired in Maud the night before was her narrow, closed face which seemed so unattainable, her slender silhouette, her look of dignity, her reputation for being a serious girl, her scorn of the masculine sex, all those things that made her a strange being, truly *someone else*, hard and definitive, always out of reach, with her clean little thoughts, her modesties, her silk stockings and crepe dresses, her permanent wave. And all this veneer had melted under his embrace, the flesh remained, he had stretched his lips toward an eyeless face, naked as a belly, he had possessed a great flower of moist flesh. Again he saw the blind beast throbbing in the sheets with rippling, hairy yawns and he thought: that was *us two.* They had made a single one, he could no longer distinguish his flesh from that of Maud; no one had ever given him that feeling of sickening intimacy, except possibly Riri, when Riri showed him his wee-wee behind a bush or when he had forgotten himself and stayed resting on his belly, bouncing up and down, his behind naked, while they dried out his pants. Lucien felt some comfort thinking about Guigard: tomorrow he would tell him: "I slept with Maud, she's a sweet little kid, old man, it's in her blood." But he was uncomfortable, and felt naked in the dusty heat of the metro, naked beneath a thin film of clothing, stiff and naked beside a priest, across from two mature women, like a great, soiled beanpole.

Guigard congratulated him vehemently. He was getting a little tired of Fanny. "She really has a rotten temper. Yesterday she gave me dirty looks all evening." They both agreed: there have to be women like that, because, after all, you couldn't stay chaste until you got married and then they weren't in love and they weren't sick but it would be a mistake to get attached to them. Guigard spoke of real girls with delicacy and Lucien asked him news of his sister. "She's fine," said Guigard. "She says you're a quitter. You know," he added, with a little abandon, "I'm not sorry I have a sister: you find out things you never could imagine." Lucien understood him perfectly. As a result they spoke often of girls and felt full of poetry and Guigard loved to recite the words of one of his uncles who had had much success with women: "Possibly I haven't always done the right thing in my dog's life, but there's one thing God will witness: I'd rather cut my hands off than touch a virgin." Sometimes they went to see Pierrette, Guigard's girl friend. Lucien liked Pierrette a lot, he talked to her like a big brother, teased her a little and was grateful to her because she had not cut her hair. He was completely absorbed in his political activities; every Sunday morning he went to sell *Action Française* in front of the church in Neuilly. For more than two hours, Lucien walked up and down, his face hard. The girls coming out of mass sometimes raised beautiful frank eyes toward him; then Lucien relaxed a little and felt pure and strong; he smiled at them. He explained to the gang that he respected women and he was glad to find in them the understanding he had hoped for. Besides, they almost all had sisters.

On the 17th of April, the Guigards gave a dance for Pierrette's 18th birthday and naturally Lucien was invited. He was already quite good friends with Pierrette, she called him her dancing partner and he suspected her of being a little bit in love with him. Mme. Guigard had brought in a caterer and the afternoon promised to be quite gay. Lucien danced with Pierrette several times, then went to see Guigard who was receiving his friends in the smoking room. "Hello," Guigard said, "I think you all know each other: Fleurier, Simon, Vanusse, Ledoux." While Guigard was naming his friends, Lucien saw a tall young man with red, curled hair, milky skin and hard black eyelashes, approaching them hesitantly and he was overcome with rage. "What's this fellow doing here," he wondered, "Guigard knows I can't stand Jews!" He spun on his heels and withdrew rapidly to avoid introduction. "Who is that Jew?" he asked Pierrette a moment later. "It's Weill, he's at the Hautes Etudes Commerciales; my brother met him in fencing class." "I hate Jews," Lucien said. Pierette gave a little laugh. "This one's a pretty good chap," she said. "Take me in to the buffet." Lucien drank a glass of champagne and only had time to set it down when he found himself nose to nose with Guigard and Weill. He glared at Guigard and turned his back, but Pierrette took his arm and Guigard approached him openly: "My friend Fleurier, my friend Weill," he said easily, "there, you're introduced." Weill put out his hand and Lucien felt miserable. Luckily, he suddenly remembered Desperreau: "Fleurier would have chucked the Jew in the water for good." He thrust his hands in his pockets, turned his back on Guigard and walked away. "I can never set foot in this house again," he thought, getting his coat. He felt a bitter pride. "That's what you call keeping your ideals; you can't live in society any more." Once in the street his pride melted and Lucien grew worried. "Guigard must be furious!" He shook his head and tried to tell himself with conviction, "He didn't have the right to invite a Jew if he invited me!" But his rage had left him; he saw the surprised face of Weill again with discomfort, his outstretched hand, and he felt he wanted a reconciliation: "Pierrette surely thinks I'm a heel. I should have shaken hands with him. After all, it didn't involve me in anything. Say hello to him and afterwards go right away: that's what I should have done." He wondered if he had time to go back to Guigard's. He would go up to Weill and say, "Excuse me, I wasn't feeling well." He would shake hands and say a few nice words. No. It was too late, his action was irreparable He thought with irritation, "Why did I need to show my opinions to people who can't understand them." He shrugged his shoulders nervously: it was a disaster. At that very instant Guigard and Pierrette were commenting on his behavior, Guigard was saying, "He's completely crazy!" Lucien clenched his fists. "Oh God," he thought, "how I hate them! God how I hate Jews!" and he tried to draw strength from the contemplation of this immense hatred. But it melted away under his look, in vain he thought of Leon Blum who got money from Germany and hated the French, he felt nothing more than a dismal indifference. Lucien was lucky to find Maud home. He told her he loved her and possessed her several times with a sort of rage. "It's all screwed up," he told himself, "I'll never be *anybody*." "No, no," Maud said, "stop that, my big darling, it's forbidden!" But at last she let herself go: Lucien wanted to kiss her everywhere. He felt childish and perverse; he wanted to cry.

At school, next morning, Lucien's heart tightened when he saw Guigard. Guigard looked sly and pretended not to see him. Lucien was so enraged that he could not take notes: "The bastard," he thought, "the bastard!" At the end of the class, Guigard came up to him, he was pale. "If he says a word," thought Lucien, "I'll knock his teeth in." They stayed side by side for an instant, each looking at the toes of their shoes. Finally, Guigard said in an injured voice, "Excuse me, old man, I shouldn't have done that to you." Lucien started and looked at him with distrust. But Guigard went on painfully, "I met him in the class, you see, so I thought . . . we fenced together and he invited me over to his place, but I understand, you know, I shouldn't have . . . I don't know how it happened, but when I wrote the invitations I didn't think for a second. . . ." Lucien still said nothing because the words would not come out, but he felt indulgent. Guigard, his head bowed, added, "Well, what a boner. . . ." "You big hunk of baloney!" Lucien said, slapping his shoulder, "of course I know you didn't do it on purpose." He said generously, "I was wrong, too. I acted like a heel. But what do you expect—it's stronger than I am. I can't stand them—it's physical. I feel as though they had scales on their hands. What did Pierrette say?" "She laughed like mad," Guigard said pitifully. "And the guy?" "He caught on. I said what I could, but he took off fifteen minutes later." Still humble, he added, "My parents say you were right and you couldn't have done otherwise because of your convictions." Lucien savored the word "convictions"; he wanted to hug Guigard: "It's nothing, old man," he told him; "It's nothing because we're still friends." He walked down the Boulevard Saint-Michel in a state of extraordinary exaltation: he seemed to be himself no longer.

He told himself, "It's funny, it isn't *me* any more. I don't recognize myself!" It was hot and pleasant; people strolled by, wearing the first astonished smile of springtime on their faces; Lucien thrust himself into this soft crowd like a steel wedge; he thought, "It's not me any more. Only yesterday I was a big, bloated bug like the crickets in Férolles." Now Lucien felt clean and sharp as a chronometer. He went into *La Source* and ordered a pernod. The gang didn't hang around the Source because the place swarmed with dagos; but dagos and Jews did not disturb Lucien that day. He felt unusual and threatening in the midst of these olive-tinted bodies which rustled like a field of oats in the wind; a monstrous clock leaning on the bar, shining red. He recognized with amusement a little Jew the J. P. had roughed up last semester in the Faculté de Droit corridors. The fat and pensive little monster had not kept the mark of the blows, he must have stayed laid up for a while and then regained his round shape; but there was a sort of obscene resignation in him.

He was happy for the time being: he yawned voluptuously; a ray of sunlight tickled his nostrils; he scratched his nose and smiled. Was it a smile? Or rather a little oscillation which had been born on the outside, somewhere in a corner of the place and which had come to die on his mouth? All the dagos were floating in dark, heavy water whose eddies jolted their flabby flesh, raised their arms, agitated their fingers and played a little with their lips. Poor bastards! Lucien almost pitied them. What did they come to France for? What sea currents had brought them and deposited them here? They could dress in clothes from tailors on the Boulevard Saint-Michel in vain; they were hardly more than jellyfish, Lucien thought, he was not a jellyfish, he did not belong to that humiliated race, he told himself, "I'm a diver." Then he suddenly forgot the Source and the dagos, he only saw a back, a wide back hunched with muscles going farther and farther away, losing itself, implacable, in the fog. He saw Guigard: Guigard was pale, he followed the back with his eyes and said to an invisible Pierrette, "Well, what a boner . . . !" Lucien was flooded with an almost intolerable joy: this powerful, solitary back was *his own!* And the scene happened yesterday! For an instant, at the cost of a violent effort, he was Guigard, he saw the humility of Guigard and felt himself deliciously terrified. "Let that be a lesson to them!" he thought. The scene changed: it was Pierrette's boudoir, it was happening in the future, Pierrette and Guigard were pointing out a name on the list of invitations.

Lucien was saying, "Oh no! Not that one! That would be fine for Lucien. Lucien can't stand Jews." Lucien studied himself once more; he thought, "I am Lucien! Somebody who can't stand Jews." He had often pronounced this sentence but today was unlike all other times. Not at all them. Of course, it was apparently a simple statement, as if someone had said, "Lucien doesn't like oysters," or, "Lucien likes to dance." But there was no mistaking it: love of dancing might be found in some little Jew who counted no more than a fly: all you had to do was look at that damned kike to know that his likes and dislikes clung to him like his odor, like the reflections of his skin, that they disappeared with him like the blinking of his heavy eyelids, like his sticky, voluptuous smiles. But Lucien's anti-semitism was of a different sort: unrelenting and pure, it stuck out of him like a steel blade menacing other breasts. "It's . . . sacred," he thought. He remembered his mother when he was little, sometimes speaking to him in a certain special tone of voice: "Papa is working in his office." This sentence seemed a sacramental formula to him which suddenly conferred a halo of religious obligations on him, such as not playing with his air gun and not shouting "Tararaboom!"; he walked down the hall on tiptoe as if he were in a cathedral. "Now it's my turn," he thought with satisfaction. Lowering their voices, they said, "Lucien doesn't like Jews," and people would feel paralyzed, their limbs transfixed by a swarm of aching little arrows. "Guigard and Pierrette," he said tenderly, "are children." They had been guilty but it sufficed for Lucien to show his teeth and they were filled with remorse, they had spoken in a low voice and walked on tiptoe.

Lucien felt full of self-respect for the second time. But this time he no longer needed the eyes of Guigard: he appeared respectable in his own eyes—in his own eyes which had finally pierced his envelope of flesh, of likes and dislikes, habits and humors. "Where I sought myself," he thought, "I could not find myself." In good faith he took a detailed counting of all he *was*. "But if I could only be what I am I wouldn't be worth any more than that little kike." What could one discover searching in this mucous intimacy if not the sorrow of flesh, the ignoble lie of equality and disorder? "First maxim," Lucien said, "not to try and see inside yourself; there is no mistake more dangerous." The real Lucien—he knew now—had to be sought in the eyes of others, in the frightened obedience of Pierrette and Guigard, the hopeful waiting of all those beings who grew and ripened for him, these young apprentice girls who would become *his* workers, people of Férolles, great and small, of whom he would one day be the master. Lucien was almost afraid, he felt almost too great for himself. So many people were waiting for him, at attention: and he was and always would be this immense waiting of others. "That's a leader," he thought. And he saw a hunched, muscular back re-appear, then, immediately afterwards, a cathedral. He was inside, walking on tiptoe beneath the sifted light that fell from the windows. "Only this time I am the cathedral!" He stared intently at his neighbor, a tall Cuban, brown and mild as a cigar. He must absolutely find words to express this extraordinary discovery. Quietly, cautiously, he raised his hand to his forehead, like a lighted candle, then drew into himself for an instant, thoughtful and holy, and the words came of themselves. "I HAVE RIGHTS!" Rights! Something like triangles and circles: it was so perfect that it didn't exist, you could trace thousands of circles with a compass in vain, you could never make a single circle. Generations of workers could even scrupulously obey the commands of Lucien, they would never exhaust his right to command, rights were beyond existence, like mathematical objects and religious dogma. And now Lucien was just that: an enormous bouquet of responsibilities and rights. He had believed that he existed by chance for a long time, but it was due to a lack of sufficient thought. His place in the sun was marked in Férolles long before his birth. They were *waiting* for him long before his father's marriage: if he had come into the world it was to occupy that place: "I exist," he thought, "because I have the right to exist." And, perhaps for the first time, he had a flashing, glorious vision of his destiny. Sooner or later he would go to the Centrale (it made no difference). Then he would drop Maud (she always wanted to sleep with him, it was tiresome; their confused flesh giving off an odor of scorched rabbit stew in the torrid heat of springtime. "And then, Maud belongs to everybody. Today me, tomorrow somebody else, none of it makes any sense"); he would go and live in Férolles. Somewhere in France there was a bright young girl like Pierrette, a country girl with eyes like flowers who would stay chaste for him: sometimes she tried to imagine her future master, this gentle and terrible man; but she could not. She was a virgin; in the most secret part of her body she recognized the right of Lucien alone to possess her. He would marry her, she would be *his* wife, the tenderest of his rights. When, in the evening, she would undress with slender, sacred gestures, it would be like a holocaust. He would take her in his arms with the approval of everyone, and tell her, "You belong to me!" What she would show him she would have the right to show to him alone and for him the act of love would be a voluptuous counting of his goods. His most tender right, his most intimate right: the right to be respected to the very flesh, obeyed to the very bed. "I'll marry young," he thought. He thought too that he would like to have many children; then he thought of his father's work; he was impatient to continue it and wondered if M. Fleurier was not going to die soon.

A clock struck noon; Lucien rose. The metamorphosis was complete: a graceful, uncertain adolescent had entered this café one hour earlier; now a man left, a leader among Frenchmen. Lucien took a few steps in the glorious light of a French morning. At the corner of Rue des Écoles and the Boulevard Saint-Michel he went towards a stationery shop and looked at himself in the mirror: he would have liked to find on his own face the impenetrable look he admired on Lemordant's. But the mirror only reflected a pretty, headstrong little face that was not yet terrible. "I'll grow a moustache," he decided.